Shoulders

Shoulders

A NOVEL BY

GEORGIA COTRELL

Firebrand
Books
Ithaca, New York

This book may not be reproduced in whole or in part, except in the
case of reviews, without permission from Firebrand Books, 141 The
Commons, Ithaca, New York 14850.

Book and cover design by Betsy Bayley
Cover photograph by Mimi Pfeil and Joslyn Baker
Typesetting by Bets Ltd.

Printed in the United States of America by McNaughton & Gunn

This publication is made possible, in part, with support from the Litera-
ture Panel, New York State Council on the Arts.

Library of Congress Cataloging-in-Publication Data

Cotrell, Georgia, 1949–
    Shoulders.

    I. Title.
PS3553.07645S5 1987   813'.54   87-7413
ISBN 0-932379-26-5
ISBN 0-932379-25-7 (pbk.)

to the women of Austin,
with a nod and a tip o' the hat to Machado de Assis

A Beginning

Miriam says, "Begin *sotto voce.*"

Just now in the bathroom she said that. I was sitting on the edge of the tub, washing her back, doodling tic-tac-toe with the lather, wondering how to begin this story.

I asked her, "Well, do you mean *whispering?* Like, 'Psst! Hey-you-bub,' or something?"

"No, no, I mean humbly, just start it off humbly. Somewhere between meek and modest. And quietly. It should be very still, very soothing at first." The soap slid out of my hand, plooped through the overlayer of bubbles, disappearing. Miriam probed around for it under the water, nabbed it, slipped it back into my hand with a scant sigh and a cluck. Lanky old seal, all tan and pink and gleaming in the suds.

So. All right then, humbly, quietly. Bathing the back of the woman I love.

Somnambula

It is 1962 and I am nine years old, standing wan and woozy in the choir loft of the dark, dank chapel of St. Christopher, then a proper saint in the eyes of the Church. I am attending Benediction, and I am sick with remorse and dread because I have sinned. My whole small life is a sin, and my whole unimaginable life to come.

All around me the other nine-year-old choristers break into Gregorian chant, *"O Salutaris Hostia."* On the altar below, the baby-faced priest in his white satin vestments vigorously swings the clicking brass censer to and fro, up and down, out and back, fanning around the incense blend of myrrh, bay, bergamot. The smoke is making me nauseated; it is dangerously close up in the loft. Now Sister Dolores raises her long white hands again. The other children begin:

> *Tantum ergo sacramentum veneremur cernui,*
> *Et antiquum documentum, novo cedat ritui,*
> *Praestet fides supplementum, sensuum defectui.*

I gaze blearily across the pungent smoke into the downcast ruby-black eyes of Christ crucified, above the altar. *I didn't know, I hadn't. . . it felt good, forgive, help, me,* staring and staring at the glass eyes, my own eyes glazing over, focusing out, until slowly, slow as dreams, Jesus raises His bloody eyelids to me, looks—at *me,* sorrowfully, the pain of the world—then closes them again. My legs become water. I lose consciousness.

Earlier that day I had asked my brother Artie, "What are *fairies?*" He had chortled maliciously in the smug way of big brothers and had told me, "Guys who do it with guys." And this had made me realize, with the full-body shock of a sudden and immense crack of thunder, what it was that had happened between my friend Monica and me, what it was that we had together committed only last week in the airy concave of briar canopy out behind her father's pasture. We were *fairies,* she and I. . . .

I was to forget all this, forget Christ's eyes, the fainting, even Monica, sweet little Monica herself. I would bury this shimmering and elliptical knowledge about myself in some uneasy shaft of my mind for another eight years.

Fishlips

It is now 1970 and I am being chauffeured home from the Our Lady of Sorrows junior-senior prom by my brother Artie. Tom Carter, my date and the somewhat older brother of my schoolmate Susan, has begun to inveigle his shockingly clammy hand over mine as we sit primly side by side, spines as upright as ladder-back chairs, in the back seat of my dad's '63 Mercury. Tom and I are talking and giggling, nervous. Up front, Artie is chain-smoking Marlboros and periodically ruffling his fingers through his shoulder-length hair. Artie has the radio turned up very loud to the Jefferson Airplane to drown us out, Tom and me. After a while Tom extracts his left arm from its humid wedge between us and gingerly sets it on the back seat behind me, letting it slowly slide, with the successive corners Artie is making in the Merc, to sift over my shoulders, the other equally shocking and clammy left hand falling to cup the shaft of my upper arm. In a painfully unassured motion, Tom reaches with his right hand and turns my face toward his, leans in solemn and serious for a kiss. Our lips meet. They are cold, dry, unalive. We hold the kiss for a small eternity; nothing happens. From deep down I feel a smile, blazon of the absurdity of holding this dead fish kiss, bubble its way to my lips.

Tom says, through the kiss, "Don't laugh, goddammit."

A Dream Waltz

It's ten months after Tom Carter's attempt at passion, and I am standing around after ballet class, sweaty and jejune in red wine tights, pulling idly at the ends of a towel draped around my neck and snapping spearmint gum. I am waiting for the ballet instructor, Rachel Carmichael, to herd off the rest of my classmates so I can speak with her alone. I do not know why it's necessary to speak with her alone. I am trying to come up with something to say to her, a line, two lines, anything, rehearsing an imaginary dialogue. Rachel Carmichael is the most interesting thing to happen at Our Lady of Sorrows since I've been there. I *like* Rachel Carmichael.

And there she stands, auburn-haired, Dresden pale, her slight, wiry dancer's body poised tight and firm as an exclamation point. I am stealing sidelong looks at her while she speaks with Yolanda Guerra, Celeste Cooper, Marta Cruz. Carmichael is gesturing point-counterpoint with her hands, the long, bony upturned fingers of her left coming together with the thumb, then fanning apart, gently plucking up at the air as though for pendant apricots, the right reaching up with the same finger-tip funnel as the left falls again, like chain pulleys in a grandfather clock. I am just out of earshot, not so much trying to imagine what it is she's describing with this clockwork motion as drinking in its grace, her sensuous execution of it. Now, still talking, she has closed those great green eyes, the wide full lips slowly shaping words I can't hear. Her shoulders are hunched dramatically; but then everything about Rachel Carmichael is dramatic. My friends and I cannot understand why the nuns hired her; she is so Bohemian, so vibrant, so unlike the other dried-up lay faculty there. Nor can we fathom why Carmichael herself has contracted with the Sisters, who no doubt pay her a very grim salary indeed. These then, I decide, are questions I shall pose to her, when we speak.

The last kid has begun to saunter away from Carmichael, out of the broiling Quonset hut. She spots me, smiles widely, dabs at her face and head with her towel, and sighs.

"Do you think the Sisters will ever air-condition this thing for me, Bobbie?" she asks. And this is precisely why I'm so intrigued by her: she seems to care what I think.

I snap my gum again, then turn away, grinning cynically. "Sure," I tell her, "they're gonna surprise you with it next week when the Pope gets married." She cocks her head at me sideways a little, laughing quietly (not that great a joke). "Wanna soda?" and she digs a coin purse out of her knapsack. Together we amble over to the vending machine. She plunks in coins, the cans slam out. What in hell am I gonna say.

"Miss Carmichael. . ." I begin.

"Call me Rachel, Bobbie." Hoof! A quick shrill thinning in my blood, a soft pounding, elation! And something else. What?

And because I am no less an asshole than anyone else at sixteen, I say, "O.K., Rachel Bobbie," and out of nowhere think to ask her about a bit of classwork choreography with which I profess to be having difficulty, a turn of hand and foot together, a curving sweep. She shows me how, again. Our conversation then strays to ballroom dance. It seems the nuns want her to teach it next year. By next year I will have graduated, I remind her, and add, just wistfully enough, that I'd always wanted to learn how to waltz.

"You don't know how to waltz!" she laughs, "and you a flaming roman-tic!" Rachel slugs back the last of her Coke, deftly tosses the can some fifteen feet into a garbage can next to the machine. "Come on. I'll give you a quick-ie lesson right now."

And there's the thinning-pounding again—this time striking my knees, zap-ping tissue, dissolving tendon. Rachel moves toward a gunmetal grey supply cabinet and unlocks it, flinging open the door with a magisterial sweep and sending up a wave of hollow steel reverberations throughout the vaulted roll of the Quonset. She rummages through her albums. "This oughta do it," she says, extracting one. I am standing stock-still, my breath shallow and tenu-ous, as Rachel with her back to me positions the record on the turntable and sets the ponderous tone arm down with care, not to the first cut presumably. She swivels back around to face me as the first few notes crackle out of the ancient P.A. system.

Rachel unfurls her arms wide toward me with the proud flare of an acrobat. I move toward her slowly—in memory now as though walking under water. She is smiling at me kindly, indulgently, seeing my shyness. "This is Khachatur-ian," she says to settle me. "Do you like it?"

I am standing less than a foot from her. The music is an opulent brocade of minor chords, a Russian-sounding refrain. I remember that at the time I was always reading nineteenth-century Russian novels. Before I can catch it, I hear myself saying, "Makes me think of Anna Karenina and Count Vronsky." And then I blush, blush absolutely, violently. Rachel the Bohemian laughs at me (what is she thinking!), and throwing her head all the way back like Garbo, gives me a quick sisterly hug and whispers, "Come on." Then she leads me by the hand out to the center of the floor.

"Now remember, don't look at your feet. Everybody makes that mistake trying to learn to waltz. Just look straight at me, right into my eyes. The rhythm is *one*-two-three, *one*-two-three, *one*-two-three, *one,* as we turn around." And as we do begin to revolve with the music, and I to step on her feet, I am too skittish to look her full in the face, much less directly into those incapacitating celadon-green eyes. I keep looking just beyond her head, at the hall swirling around us all too rapidly, at the north mirror wall especially, in which we dark blurry figures are darkly reflected. I become dizzy, lose my balance a little.

Rachel halts the lead abruptly, cups my jaw tight as a vise, peers into my face but centimeters away, her breath, her scent (spring moss, ginger, cloud banks) exhaling themselves over me, melting me. "If you don't look right at me, right *into my eyes,* you are not going to learn how to waltz. Besides, it cuts the dizziness. So look at me, O.K., Bobbie?"

"O.K." Cowed, I obey her, making a Herculean effort to compose my face as we continue, which I imagine is trembling as my whole body seems to tremble. Gazing full into her eyes I fight back a feeling of vertigo, try to concentrate on the rhythm, until, gradually, round by round, I relax, turning with her, spinning, the cadence falling to me as a great cape dropping to the shoulders, clinging about the legs.

"See? You're getting it, aren't you?" she smiles, and the room turns and turns, and I am losing myself, succumbing to the waltz, to Rachel's eyes. And in one split-second, ferret-quick glance, hardly lowering my eyes at all, I see one corner of her mouth curve in ever so slightly, a wisp of saliva seeping there, her tongue darting to catch it, her lips parting open. Back to her eyes. But there had been something to the mouth, in seeing her tongue, that made the whole lower half of me fall away. And now her eyes are different, strange: darker, fuller, more moist somehow, the light spinning behind them, in them, around us, as the music swells. I am suddenly aware of a huge, pervasive heat below my skin, and of a light chilling on top of it. Am I going to faint, is this fainting?

But the waltz ends and we stop, our arms falling away from each other, almost tentatively. The nicks in the record grooves click and hiss over the P.A. as we stand before each other, neither of us smiling. Rachel, in fact, looks unsettlingly grave and pallid, and I am out of breath, addled, and not knowing why. In another second she perceptibly snaps to and smiles at me, sets her hand gently, a little hesitantly, on my shoulder, then squeezes it.

"So. Now ya can waltz, Vronsky." She strides over to the bench where her kit rests, gathers it up. "Have a good weekend, kiddo," and she bounds out of the Quonset, whistling the waltz melody.

From that afternoon on and for weeks thereafter, Rachel Carmichael became the constant object of my daydreams and pre-sleep musings, asexual though they were, still.

Revelation...

Citronella: false citrus, sharp and stifling, indispensable balm at late May rains for safeguard against water-bred vermin, fleas and chiggers and ticks. With the deluge this year the mosquitoes' wingspreads could span quarters. "There's one behind your knee, Bobbie." I smack and of course miss it, the nasty, canny thing. Rachel smiles absent-mindedly. "Better put more citronella on," she says, and returns to her tending of the barbecue pit. She yells over her shoulder into the house, "Cam? Would you look under the sink and see if we have any punk left?"

I hear the small tinny voice from the kitchen window moon, "What?"

"Punk. Check under the sink, we're being devoured out here, babe!" The pit bellows up sweet clouds of hickory smoke, ribs drip and sizzle on the coals, white hot. To me Rachel mutters, "You'd think with all this smoke out here we'd be all right." She takes a full-throated swig from her beer, a Lone Star longneck, and wipes her forehead with the back of her palm. "Cam? When you can come out, another *cerveza, por favor?*"

From even further away the voice says, "What? I can't hear you."

"Never mind, Cam, thanks anyway, I'll get it...watch these for me, would you, Bobbie?"

I dutifully flip out of the hammock, young catlike, stretching and boastful, and take the prong from her. She turns on her heel, runs lightly up the kitchen steps. A fracas of metal and glass, of cans and bottles being shoved around rapidly and carelessly, resounds from inside the house. An icebox door slams thickly shut. Then silence, deep and protracted. I return lazily to the grill, scoot the fat slabs of beef around, piercing and lifting. All around me in Rachel's wild and ramshackle back yard, a rich evening breeze sifts through the scrub mesquite, cicadas slacken their whirring, crickets begin to sing to one another through the mauve light. A vintage lawn sprinkler (though there is scarcely a lawn, only scattered patches of soon-to-be-brown Bermuda plocked among the Johnson grass which alone thrives in the pink caliche) sisses out a thin tight stream, pivots, *chook-chook-chook-chook-chook*, then shudders fitfully in one position, to pivot and siss again the same slim stream at the next fixed angle.

I am at this frail and soothing moment, dear reader, happy without precedent. Not only have I been championed by my mentor of the dance and given entree to her life away from Our Lady of Sorrows, but I have also been accepted at the University for the following September and, after some ritualistic resistance from my parents, loath to relinquish me to the libertine life of an out-of-town college, I have finally been granted their doleful leave to slip the nest. Already I've undergone painful tremors with this twofold development: that in going off to school I would also be leaving Rachel behind—the first pang of leave-taking. But this was May; I had an entire summer ahead of me, and my pangs were, for the time being, deferrable.

The back porch screen door screaks open, then bams shut. Rachel pounds down the decrepit stair planks two at a time. "No punk, but these babies are almost ready anyway, aren't they?" She leans in close to solicit my opinion again, aah. She stands beside me, rhythmically shifting her weight from one hip to the other, stretching her dancer's legs and drinking her Lone Star. Years later as I recall this night it is Rachel's voice—the deep, rich quality of that voice—that floats back to me first, as sumptuous and seductive as jewels, as rubies and topaz made magically molten, the sultriness of it alive with the young evening, with young me, the blazing Texas summer coming on, the good times ahead.

Rachel forks the meat up onto a huge plum-rose platter, her strong sinewy wrists jiggling each rib free of the prong to slap down upon the plate. Again the back of her hand quickly brushes her brow, she sighs, and again smiles at me, whispering, "Head 'em up." Together we cross the yard and clunk noisily up the rickety back steps.

In the dining room Cam—Camille Hibbs of Amarillo, the handsome, drawling roommate of Rachel and a teacher of high school English, a blonde Kansas cornfield woman of whom I am totally and undisguisedly jealous—has set the table and is seated there already, coolly exhaling cigarette smoke from her nostrils, stubbing out the butt end. She smiles an auntly, somewhat condescending smile at me. My suspicion is that Cam dislikes puppy me and my now frequent visitations to her meticulously maintained home, for, as Rachel has confided to me (how I thrilled to her mundane confidences), Cam is a "stickler" for a clean and orderly domicile, and "company," as Cam often refers to me even in my presence, invariably leaves disarray in its wake.

After dinner Cam winds up sinuously from her chair like a spiralling sloth and stacks all three of our plates to take out to the kitchen. I clear the rest of the table as Cam begins to do the washing up alone, preferring to let the dishes drip-dry on the rack. Rachel disappears to her study. As is fast becoming customary, I am treated rather familially, often left to my own resources.

I retire to the front porch with a stack of Rachel's back-issue *Village Voice*s;

I, as millions of others, am smitten with some ideal of New York. Even with the yellow bug light on, the buffalo moths proliferate. Scads of June bugs plack and whirr against the screening. Turning a page I center on a joint feature story, the title "Theatre for Ideas: A Night of Lib & Let Lib" spanning the two articles. The one on the left is called "What Happened to Mozart's Sister?" while the other, more racily entitled, decides me on reading it: "Sexism—A Better Show Than Sex." The articles are write-ups of a "debate" on women's liberation that had taken place at New York's Town Hall on April 30, four weeks ago. The actors in the event were Germaine Greer, the famous Australian Amazon; several women I'd never heard of before (Jacqueline Ceballos, head of the National Organization of Women, and Diana Trilling— both of whose photographs adorn the twin articles, and a last, Jill Johnston); and, unbelievably, the infamous Norman Mailer who, more unbelievable still, had served as moderator for the thing. I am reading:

> Jill Johnston (author of *Marmalade Me*), *Village Voice* typeface assembler, Sapphic firebrand, classy phraseologist, tomboy-slim owner of—surprise!—a pert little-girl voice...

Sapphic firebrand. Sappho. Sapphic. I read on, numbing somewhere.

> Jill Johnston next, in the epitasis or middle of the action. "I'm a woman hence a lesbian," starts her evangel, "all women are lesbians except those who don't know it." And like that: a fine sermon of shockers capped by an effort to translate faith into praxis, that is, by onstage showbiz lovemaking between herself and two other handsome girls...

There is a chill, alien paralysis in my arms and legs, my stomach has collapsed. I scan on:

> ...Johnston...moments later rolls around the stage petting with two movement sisters (Robyn and S.K.) as with two Eddie Brackens, six legs of slapstick haunting you with their perverse innocence.

And yet again, this from the other article, which I have by now queasily skimmed to:

> They came up on stage and proceeded to caress and embrace one another and to roll on the floor in playful simulation of play.

By the time I read this paragraph, my pulse is way up, panic or something like it has begun to set in, the realization but moments away from me, its shadow burgeoning huge ahead. A woman making out on stage with two other women . . . suddenly I look up from the paper, a metallic noise off to my right distracting me. Through the open venetian blinds I see Rachel standing over her desk, her tortoiseshell hornrims balanced at the very tip of her nose as she leafs rapidly through a book. Ah God. Then I know. Then I remember (this all at once, knowing and remembering) the little girl Monica, the briar cave, our tiny fingers probing in, delighting one another.

I sit staring at Rachel, my pulse throbbing in my hands like a bird flapping wildly against the clasped hatch of a tin cage. That's why. That's why. Like a sleepwalker I pick up the stack of *Voices* and return them to their former place in the living room. I hear an automaton self calling out to Rachel and Cam, "Hey you guys, I gotta get goin', Artie's got a date and he wants the car." Without stopping their own doings, the two of them from separate rooms exclaim their Bye, Bobbie, See ya laters, and I turn and walk out their front door, letting it clatter-slam behind me. Outside in the warm night air my face is hot, tingling; I can't, won't think. My feet propel me down the sloping gravel drive to the street to the car, my fingers pry open the heavy metal door, my legs swing me inside behind the steering wheel. I sit there for an indeterminable amount of time, not thinking. Reaching into my jeans pocket for the keys, I discover them missing, remember they're lying on the living room coffee table back in the house. Mechanically, I walk back up the slope. The yellow porch light's been turned off, along with the living room lamp. Swift upon my departure, Cam's begun her battening down for the night.

As I cross the lawn to mount the front steps, a murky vision strikes my eyes from the other side of the great bay windows: two slender silhouetted figures stand holding each other in the bright frame of the kitchen door. One, fair-haired, reaches up to the taller darker one, combing her fingers through the other's hair. I see their faces, or what would logically be their faces if I could truly see them, come together, hold. A long time. A very long time. Their heads twist slightly, one one way, the other the other, now moiling faster, their arms clutching deep around each other, and hard.

I watch them break off the kiss. When they break from each other, I begin to walk slowly back down the hill and walk the long walk home, leaving both car and keys there. I don't care what Artie'll say.

Right Off the Bat, Fear and Desire _____

Most fortunately my folks had gone out for the evening. I had gotten home late and, miraculously avoiding Artie (who, I discovered the next morning, had called up Rachel and had had one of his buddies take him over to get the keys and the Merc), managed to filch some of Dad's Ballantine's scotch into a Kerr jar, watering down the fifth after the fact. I took the jar along with me on a short, still-stunned stroll up the silent indigo streets to a vacant hilltop lot overlooking the suburban development in which my family and I lived.

I do not remember clearly what I was thinking as I sat up there. Too many things, I was feeling too many things, looking down at all those yellow porch lights, contours of newly planted ash trees, moth swarms whirring in the violet haze of mercury streetlamps, and the grey glow issuing from row after row of obligatory picture windows—television screens tuned in to some Saturday night fare, Lawrence Welk, a movie.

I do remember that the scotch worked very quickly and very well. Now I knew, mute and shaking, I wasn't destined for the likes of the suburban landscape I saw below me, nor for community as I had come to know it—marriage, family, church, etc. But what in the hell would happen to me? What did I want?

I wanted a woman. That much I did know: I wanted one of my own.

But what would my friend Magda say? Would I tell her tomorrow? How could I not? And what-oh-what would my parents do if they found out? Good God! What if the nuns found out?

As it happened, Magda took the news quite well, cavalierly even, simply saying, "Maybe it's a phase"—she really did say that—"and if it isn't, you'll just have to be very careful, won't you?" It turned out not too many years later that Magda herself took a woman for a lover, although she did eventually marry a male, an attorney for the City of Ardmore, Oklahoma, where she now raises a family of three.

My parents also found out, several years later. The knowledge shocked and crushed them, and we have never reconciled on this aspect of my life. They don't ever talk about it with me, nor do they ever ask me any more if I plan to marry. In the interest of familial peace, reader dear, I'm going to leave them out of this story; they'd prefer that, I'm sure.

All through the night I gazed down at those houses, at the big Buicks and Oldsmobiles and Pontiacs swinging up the various street rows to their own look-alike driveways, the porch lights and the television sets switching off one by one. And every time I thought about Rachel and Camille kissing, a two-foot flame shot right up through the center of me, and every time I thought about telling my parents about myself, everything sank back down again with a hideous jolt. Mercifully, I fell asleep after a while and, some time before the sun came up, I snuck back into the house and in my own bed quietly lay my body down, scared, excited, and glum, all together at once.

Town Hall Nights _____

Late the following morning I learned that Rachel had called me earlier, around eight. I called her back. "Where in hell did you go, Bobbie," she said, evenly, slowly.

"I walked, Rachel, I went for a walk."

"What's wrong with you."

"I'm just tired."

A pause. "Why."

"It's nothing I can talk about right now. I'm O.K. Thanks for squaring it with Artie." She had coerced him into keeping his mouth shut about the whole thing.

"No sweat. Just call me later, O.K.?"

I did call her later, checked in with a fake report. I'm fine, I'm all right, I just have some stuff on my mind, college, you know, things.

For two weeks I kept away from Rachel, didn't telephone, didn't go over, nothing. I simply couldn't face her; I wouldn't know what to say to her or how to say it, whatever it would be. It wasn't really the case that I was still jealous. Nor, actually, was I depressed about my self-discovery. It never occurred to me to be depressed, because suddenly there was a world of pursuable pleasure lying in wait for me. I was a little scared still, but not paralyzingly so. What I was in fact was continuously hot, deep-down hungry for the first time in my life, and in those two weeks especially, and throughout the summer nights to come, I grew rapidly adept at the sweet craft of self-fondling, my fingers acquiring a greater and greater intelligence until one time shortly after midnight (I know because the glass sea clock downstairs struck twelve and with each chime the waves spreading through me rose and rose, lifting me, filling me, spilling out of me), I invented the orgasm. In this and in dozens of subsequent reinventions I fantasized about Rachel and Cam kissing, about Jill Johnston (I had no idea what she looked like so she took on Rachel's features) kissing Robyn or S.K., and the scenarios would shift and slide, and I would arrange and rearrange them constantly as I stroked faster or slower, speeding up or eking out the fantasied action, the building to The Kiss, to coincide with my own newfound rainbow climaxes.

In the various fantasy tracks I would choreograph, I, the camera, am downstage of the denim-clad Johnston-Carmichael as she stands at the lectern, softly speaking her mind. After a while, Mailer the Greying Heavy interrupts her gruffly: *Time,* he barks into the microphone; Johnston ignores him. Then he asks for a voice vote from the audience: Should she be allowed to continue, yay or nay? The times are ancient: the deep-registering male Romans bellow down to the arena, *Nay.* In the pandemonium, Robyn-Cam emerges from backstage, walking quickly for once with measured, careful strides, until she's just beside Johnston at the lectern. She reaches up slowly to Jill's shoulder. Johnston turns toward her, slips an arm around Robyn's lower back, pulls her to her. There are painfully bright lights, flashbulbs and arcs from the pit and the hall bursting all around them. Now everything's in slow motion, the camera men getting up and shifting angles, kneeling and shooting at a dreamlike pace. On my camera lens, in my frame of the two women, there is that Vaseline smear around its perimeter as in old close-ups of Loretta Young. Though there is in fact a great roar rising from the audience, it's been muted to a barely audible degree by the sound mixer—me. Now it's almost silent. Jill and Robyn continue their embrace, the willowy Johnston towering over the other woman. As she leans in for the kiss, time, the rolling film, stops. The director (also me) whispers, *Let's shoot it over. We're not ready over here yet* (ahh-ahh). *Let's swing the camera upstage, front and center. Take 2.* The audience soundtrack roars back up to full power, the flashbulbs pop and hiss, the speed of the film reverts to normal, and Johnston follows through, kissing Robyn long and hard, their arms entwining, Amazonian liana. Jill-Rachel breaks off the kiss, looking over Robyn-Cam's should to me, right at me, and says very quietly, *What's my motivation, coach. What'm I thinking?*

On some of my many Town Hall nights that summer, Jill and Robyn are reserved and staid, formal in their kiss. On others they reach absolute abandon with it, toppling to the floor as S.K. leaps from behind the curtains and begins to kiss and lick them both. And I would sometimes wonder, as I plied myself upon my damp cotton sheets night after boiling night, how could Johnston have borne that tumult of adrenalin rocketing through her veins?

Not Fishlips

Following those two weeks of nightly self-love and show-biz fantasy, I screwed up my courage to telephone Rachel again and ask her if I might come over some night, to which she replied, "Sure, I'll be around tonight, if you like."

Understandably, I was pretty damned nervous about seeing her. The bicycle ride over to her house was executed in remote control, but fortunately without mishap. She was watching television when I arrived, but switched it off promptly after letting me in. And Camille, dear Camille, was not there (thank-you/thank-you/thank-you), having left three days earlier for a family reunion in Amarillo. I was hot and flushed from the biking. In an unprecedented gesture Rachel offered me a beer, and, honored, I accepted. We sat together decorously on her couch, and after several minutes of uneasy, rote chatting, she paused, cleared her throat a little, then asked me point-blank: "So, what was really wrong with you the night you left the car here." Staying on target. Her eyes were solemn, dark, and there was a slim protruding edge of paranoia to her voice: she'd doubtless pieced it together—the keys left on the coffee table, their kissing, my return, etc. It was a milestone moment, and I didn't know what to say to her next, still. The silence in that room was an almighty, living thing. After a moment Rachel bailed me out, prompting: "You came back up to the house to get your keys, didn't you."

"Yes."

Slow, judicious: "And you saw us, didn't you."

Yes I saw you, yes, "Yes."

"Jesus," she muttered quietly, a wave of worry, guilt, and—what was it? pride?—traversing her face like cloud-shadow. She squirmed on the couch, resettling her legs underneath her. A few seconds passed, then she began the speech she'd probably been rehearsing for much of the entire two weeks: "Bobbie," (pained, careful), "I'm sorry you had to find out that way...."

It was my turn to do some bailing. "Rache," (I'd never called her that before, but Cam did), "it's O.K., it's O.K. You know I'll never tell any—"

She flicked her wrist, dismissive. "I'm not worried about that. You're a friend, I trust you. It's just that, well, I...I'm not sure I would have told you about us anyway, what with your leaving in September and all, but I just hadn't wanted you to find out like that."

From outside the droning of crickets filtered through the screens, alleviating the gravid quiet. The summer light had begun to fail, suffusing the room with a thick, almost palpable crimson gloss. My heart was taking irregular half-leaps up my thorax. Rachel was red and gold, my hands, my arms were red and gold, everything, everything. Very still, very.

This is it. "I . . . ," a pause, and the words went clean away.

Rachel turned to face me on the couch. "What. What is it?" she said softly, curious.

In a mercury-fast stream: "I wanted to thank you, I wanted to thank you because you made me understand, I think I'm, I think I'm—" Damn! It was *not* this hard telling Magda! What is it? All of a sudden, I couldn't look at Rachel, couldn't look her in the eye, just like when we'd waltzed.

Then, from whence I do not know, came a voice as old as Isis rumbling out of me, and slowly, with a surety that felt alien and powerful, I spoke. "Rachel, I know you're Cam's girlfriend, I know that. And you know I'm leaving in another two months. I don't want you to hold me, I don't need your solace, but I would like very much, if you'd let me just this once, to kiss you, and then I'm gonna clear outta here."

Rachel laughed, a disbelieving gasp. Now I could look at her. She was, predictably, dumbstruck. And oh, how beautiful she looked at that moment! A decade later, and I can still warm to the memory of that lovely incredulity. But just then, her smile became amused, wily. Sexed, is what it became. "Crawford, you are incredible," was all she said. And after several seconds, much lower, much softer, she sighed resignedly, "Come here."

A thousand alarms were going off everywhere, but I hoisted myself right over next to her on the couch. The room was quite dark now; we were iron-red, she and I, sienna. Rachel put her arm around my left shoulder against the back of the couch, and with her other reached for my right shoulder to hold me at bay a moment. "Just one, all right?"

"Right," I said, breathless, leaning in, but she pulled back, laughing a little. Ach, the shame of puppydom!

"Whoah, hold up, take it easy," (gently said). She herself leaned in toward me, taking my chin most tenderly between thumb and forefinger, guiding my face to hers. "Close your eyes," she whispered, smiling, so I closed them, then.

When her lips touched mine, when her lips touched mine, earthquakes, Vesuvian eruptions, supernovae. . . .

One of my hands darted out to circle her waist, the other to touch, stroke her neck, unendurably soft. She lifted up from the kiss momentarily, but kissed me quick on the nose and returned to my lips once more. Then her tongue, in an astonishing, utterly unexpected move, flitted across my lower lip and, drawing the breath right out of me, plunged in past my lips, through my teeth, to turn around and over and under my tongue, now its own entity, wetter, harder. There was our breathing, fast and deep; there was her skin, possessed of unimagined kinetics; there was—

Rachel broke away from me, out of breath now too, and pulled back, taking her arms away, leaning back on the couch. I could barely make out her features. She said, "I just thought we oughta make it count," and I could see the white of her teeth grinning through the half-dark.

Up and Out _____

Well, the staying power of that kiss counted indeed. It bore me up and through the remainder of that sweet nascent summer, through afternoons of swimming and naps in the back porch hammock and magazines and Monopoly and Delaney & Bonnie's "Motel Shot" album and matinees with Magda and twice-weekly or so junkets to Rachel's. We kept that kiss under great wraps, Rachel and I, and yet I often imagined that Cam knew about it somehow, because she was more intolerant of me than ever after that. I didn't much care, because Rachel and I still had a great time together.

When it came time to pack and leave for school in late August, Rache sent me a dozen long-stemmed yellow roses ("For your debut," she'd scribbled on the card), and the night before the night before I was to take the Greyhound on out, she and I and Cam and Magda ate fried chicken and potato salad and got maudlin and cried and hugged and laughed our asses off in the face of my rite of passage.

The morning I left, standing in the hall with my suitcases at my feet, I took one very long look into my room and knew it would never be the same, never feel the same again, at home.

I Arrive _____

Having kept watch of the ascending numbers of cross streets as the city bus followed its route north, I, Bobbie Crawford (née Barbara Jean but I'm gonna change that legally some day), city and campus maps tucked snug under my arm, deftly swung my Navy duffel up and over the Steinway-like legs of the damp and voluminous woman who had chosen to grace the seat beside me. I forwent pulling the cord, walked wobblingly up to the front of the bus, a-hemmed, and as politely as I could asked the bus driver to stop at the corner of 26th, thank you. The bus driver, Black and thin as scissors, continued to chew his gum at exactly the same pace, apparently expressionless behind a pair of aviator-style Ray-Ban sunglasses. But he stopped the bus smoothly, more smoothly, I thought, than he had done before. I disembarked lightly down the steps, with a heart-in-my-mouth leap to the pavement, just as the bus, pulling away, backfired a great carbon monoxide fart.

Even after the minimal air conditioning inside the bus, stepping out into such an August afternoon in Texas was a crushing assault: the barely perceptible chill my skin had managed to acquire dissolved in the fetid heat like a dream almost remembered at morning. A Marlboro man billboard with a digital read-out on top flashed 101. At the corner, on a hill that would in less opaque air provide a spectacular view of the town, I paused to squint up at the sky, an opalescent sheet of grey, a high-albedo mantle. I was considering of a moment that the fair-skinned and blonde like myself burn bad in weather like this, when a white Dodge pickup roared by and honked a series which, according to Magda's grandmother, meant "fuck you" in Mexico, although of course the old lady had merely said that it meant "the worst possible thing" and wouldn't elaborate under any circumstances. A worldly-wise girlfriend of Magda's had later supplied its interpretation. A fat red-faced cowboy with green Ray-Bans leaned out of the truck window on the shotgun side and bellowed, "Hey-hey-hey!" at me, just like Fred Flintstone. Without hesitating, I flipped the bird at the rear of the Dodge just as it disappeared around a corner, then shifted the duffel bag around on my back and began to walk as slowly as one ought to in such heat in the direction, according to my map, of Barton Hall, the women's dormitory in which I would take up residence this my first semester at college.

Like many a baby-boom baby I'd been inculcated with the notion that a college education was the pinnacle of all aspiration, the crown of human endeavor, the way, like I said, up and out. The trouble was that I didn't have the slightest idea what I expected to accomplish in college or thereafter. I'd put down "fine arts" on the application as my intended major, but although I could draw and paint passably well, I wasn't passionate about either, passion counting for a lot in my scheme of things, then as now. My grandmother (you I love, rest in love, old party girl) had long ago urged me to become a commercial artist, to Granma an apt profession for her doodling Bobbie, and to me this had seemed as good an idea as any; it just didn't matter all that damned much.

My Roommate—Really

But long before any of that, even before passing through the great bronze umbonate portals of Barton and giving myself up to the onslaught of registering and meeting and smiling, I first of all flung my duffel, then myself down upon it, onto the cool grass—ignoring the keep-off sign—in the shade of an enormous pecan tree fronting the dormitory lawn. It felt good, so good just to lie there and feel the sweat all over my body begin to cool a little, to relax, my musculature slowly untensing from the harrowing journey. As I closed my eyes, patches of scarlet/black/scarlet flashed beneath my eyelids. The wind had picked up a little, and the highest boughs of the old pecan had begun to creak overhead, the fearsome sun breaking through the cover. Relaxing, releasing, letting go the innumerable kinks and cricks a body retains, a smoothing out, a catharsis of the muscles. But alas I was thirsty too, and badly: the corners of my mouth were caked dry with saliva and dust. Just as I was readying myself to sit up, walk inside, find a Coke machine, I heard, "May we help *yew?*"

I did sit bolt upright then, turning to the direction of that Texas-flat voice. Two girls with excessively cultivated suntans and impeccable long blond hair, dressed in white tennis shorts and polo shirts, one navy, one red—Ignorance and Intolerance—were staring concentratedly at me. One of them even tapped a foot twice inside its oxblood penny loafer.

"Well, thank you, no. I was just getting ready to go inside and register." I got up, brushing grass and leaves from my butt.

"Oh." Intolerance grappled, the grappling evident in every niche of her overly bronzed face, for something else to say to this lawn-straddling interloper. Finally it was, "Well, O.K." And perfunctorily the two of them bounced off toward campus.

It was too darned hot to get ticked off. I bent over for the duffel and once more jerked it over my shoulder, then sauntered inside, first to find that Coca-Cola, then to stand on line at the dorm desk, my very first college queue, at last signing in and meeting my "buddy." My guide was a soft-spoken little woman with platinum hippy glasses, a Susan Entwistle, second-year math major. Susan didn't live in Barton but in McAllister, a smaller less rigid women's dorm, so she said, just down the street. After her brief rundown on tomorrow's schedule and a gracious departure, I found the elevator and headed up to my new room.

Once inside I sat down on one of the two single beds and checked it out—dreary, institutional green cinderblock walls, casement windows, overly effective air conditioning. I shivered. Having polished off the last of the tepid Coke, I pulled the light chenille bedspread up over myself and within minutes was felled by a wave of sleep.

A short time later I snapped into consciousness at the door's being slammed open. A gangly, lanky woman with close-cropped brown hair and mirror-lens Ray-Bans, unbelievably loaded down with five grey Samsonite suitcases in her gibbon arms, swung through the door, grunting, and began to hurl her bags one by one on the other bed. The last one hurled, she turned to me and said, "Hey." Hers was another Texas voice, this one deep, honeyed, at ease.

A return "hey" automatically sprang from my lips. The girl ("tomboy-slim"— where had I heard that?) perused the contents of her outsize leather shoulder bag and pulled out a black suede sunglasses case. Then, after throwing her shoulder bag down on top of the luggage, utterly unburdened, she slowly and evenly eased the stems of her shades off from behind her ears and, having folded them neatly and sheathed them in their case, tossed them lightly on the mattress. That done, she faced me, smiling a glorious, somewhat dopey smile. Her eyes were a rare translucent blue, the whites stung with red. Their piercingness made me think of the Fondas. Rounding out the all-American effect, her huge stooped shoulders suggested Jimmy Stewart, the green gingham western shirt she had on exaggerating their span even more.

She spoke. "They told me at the desk you were already here," and she grinned (an award-winning grin!) and extended her hand to me, swaying slightly as she leaned forward for the handshake. I stood and took her hand, which dwarfed mine. We both said our names at the same time, then laughed together at this. My God we were charming.

"Bobbie Crawford," I said.

"Jackie Taylor, and I need to *sit*," and so saying she flopped down on the edge of the bed I was on and commenced taking off her boots, a real nice pair of beige Noconas. Then she scooted back against the wall, pulling up her great legs and folding her arms over her knees, a long-limbed, folded-up mantis. She stared dejectedly at the mountain of suitcases on the other side of the room.

"I should unpack, but I am so goddam tired." Jackie Taylor took out a green bandana from her hip pocket and wiped her forehead. "Shew-whee. Incredible."

"Is there still that big line down there at the desk?" I ventured.

"Now, it's not so bad. My buddy didn't show, though. Guess I was too late. But they did give me a big envelope fulla shit for registration."

"Yeah, I got that too. When do you register?"

Jackie turned her face toward me. Its expression seemed to move in the direction of sizing me up, ending in some sort of approval.

"Thursday, I think. How 'bout you?"

"Tomorrow. But I've already got a pretty good idea of what I'm gonna have to take—life drawing, English, history, government, a Spanish poetry course."

"Yeah, that sounds familiar, except for the drawing and the Spanish," she replied. "Say. I am really thirsty. Does this place have any ice?"

"I think down the hall to your left." In her stocking feet (white crews), Jackie padded out the door and returned by and by with a small plastic bag of ice which she set in the bathroom sink. Crossing back to her luggage she fished around in a small overnight case for a coffee cup and recrossed the room in two giant steps to fill it with ice and tap water. Throwing her head back in a dramatic sweep she downed the ice water and refilled the cup with water three more times.

"Ah. Better." Drink in hand Jackie sat down beside me again. "Where you from, Bobbie?" In the conversation that ensued, she and I stuck to glib banter, manneredly facile talk: about family, pals, hometown stories, clothes, but not, as I considered the next day, about boys. After a while Jackie began to unpack and unearthed four salami and cheese sandwiches her mother had that morning made in Dallas; we ate two apiece. After another spell of chatter I pleaded sleepiness and, rooting down to the depths of my duffel, extricated a very long, soft, white cotton T-shirt, my favorite thing to sleep in. At this Jackie stood and jerkily popped the quasi-mother-of-pearl buttons of her western shirt apart. Barechested, she started clearing the suitcases off her bed. I gingerly undid my own white buttondown, took off my bra, slipped the T-shirt on, then ducked into the bathroom and brushed my teeth. Jackie stuck her head inside the bathroom, addressing my mirror image:

"Hey," she began, "you shower mornings or what."

"Mornings."

"Shit. Me too. Well hell, we'll work it out," and she withdrew from the mirror.

Little intimacies. They were awkward for me. It wasn't like being with my sister Laura, that was for sure. It was more like gym, of course, the tingling they-*see*-me when changing clothes in front of the other girls. For one, I was shy about my boobs, which I thought were too big. But as I looked up from my bed at Jackie, who was sitting up still shirtless reading a Leon Uris novel under a tensor light, I realized that here was something altogether beyond gym, sharing this tiny little room with another woman—and someone who evidently had none of the self-consciousness I was having. It would take some getting used to. I murmured a goodnight to my new roommate, and as soon as my head hit the pillow, I fell instantly asleep.

Two Dreams

Just before daybreak, when I usually awoke, I had two dreams, the first one about Rachel. True to form, her glasses were propped on top of her head, and she was soothingly explaining some point or other to me. After a while she stopped talking and began to stare fixedly, in the mesmerized, slow-motion logic of dreams, beyond me; she stood up and then virtually glided over to a far wall. We seemed to be in a basement. Abruptly, in a skip the dreaming eye didn't catch, she was perched on top of an old radiator; she was peering out the narrow window that ran just below the basement ceiling, her taut dancer's calves straining to raise her high enough to see out. Her face reflected an amber glow that illuminated from outside the window. Then Rachel turned her face away from this eerie radiance toward me and, sweetly, smiled an utterly reassuring smile.

In the second dream I was swimming and, most rare for me, I was watching myself in the dream as I swam—a backstroke, slow and easy, my body pulling effortlessly through butter-colored water. The power-surge was thrilling: I felt triumphant, splendid. Then, far away to shore somewhere, an unseen whistler struck up some unnameable, sorrowful tune; it echoed over the water and instantly strummed a reverberant center way inside of me, where something wistful and hard was, hurting deep within my shoulder at triangulate midpoint with chest, neck, and blade. I slowed down to hear it better, cutting in very gently over the water, my ball-and-socket joints turning, my arms slicing silently through the milk-yellow water. But by then the whistling had stopped.

At the Lake

When at last I did awake I still felt that buoyancy, that sadness for a second, but these were immediately usurped by first-waking's familiar slow thickness about the real head and limbs. I shuffled into the bathroom, showered, and once I had brushed my teeth began to feel a little more mobile; a new shirt and a clean pair of jeans helped, too. But just as I was slipping out the door, Jackie Taylor lurched up in bed. She scared me.

"You off?" she yawned, rubbing her eyes with big-knuckled fists.

"Yeah, I have to be at the gym by ten o'clock and I'm hungry."

"Listen, do you think you'll be through by two o'clock?"

"Oh sure, sooner than that, I hope."

"Well..." Jackie's voice trailed off as she scratched behind her head, groggy Mr. Smith on the Senate floor, "they tell me there's a fantastic lake just outside town. Think you might want to go for a swim later?"

I smiled, warmed by the coincidence. "Sure. Meet you here at two."

"See ya," she said, promptly rolling back over and pulling up the shee*

It was already in the mid-nineties as I began my wait on line, a v~ long line outside the gym. Like nearly everyone else in the lin~ to bring something along to read, an oversight I would t~ correct. At long last though, I was below the vaulte nasium where fall registration was sluggishly un~ emanated from the camber windows at the upperm I had fortunately been seated; the air seemed t~ But it was still suffocating. I felt mildly console~ been set for this hour instead of later, when dic come infernal. The university administratior along with one army surplus cot, for the anemic-looking female in a calico shirtw~ with a wet and skimpy white washclo~ ridden boy in a lime-green Banlon sh~ the cot, a thermometer in his mouth ingly sweatglandless nurse fanned notes on a clipboard.

The waiting, the pathos of the electric fans, the officious stamping of official computer cards for courses, the waiting again, the bill paying—all of it seemed interminable, in the clenching way hellishly boring moments have of seeming to teeter at the brink of space-time, as if this cattle stockyard of a gym had slipped the bounds of physics and had swept up miserable me along with it. But finally it was done; it was one-fifty. My madras shirt was drenched through, my head was soaking wet. I loaded a couple of dimes into a soda machine, irritably punched the plastic plate for an orange Nehi, and downed the entire canful in moments. I headed back for the dorm.

After a quick stop at the Wazoo Burger stand, Jackie and I were wheeling out north toward the lake in her robin's egg-blue Chevy pickup ("Momma was dead set against it at first, but I made her see it was the best thing for me," she explained matter-of-factly). Her truck radio was tuned in to a country music station having a Patsy Cline memorial ("My God I love that woman," Jackie muttered fervently). The first part of the road out was comprised of a strip of neon/plastic signs and their accompanying businesses, a full thirty or so blocks' worth of teeming commercial mistake: fast food joints, tire stores, shoe shops, plumbing outfitters; establishments for sports equipment, western wear, pets, plants, and insect extermination. But gradually the route became less urban-dense, giving way to open fields of high corn and rolling cedar-pocked hills, then to the sinuate mountain road of the lake country itself. Around one bend the lake folded out before us, a vast glittering citrine mirror deep-set within steep buff cliffs of limestone. A number of sailboats with primary multicolor sails flitted over the brilliant water. Scrub cedar and mesquite, oleander and crape myrtle, dotted the cliff rim. Around one more bend Jackie turned off the highway down a dirt road. "I think this's it," she whispered. We travelled down it bumping along for several minutes, finally meeting up with the water. Jackie brought the truck to a slow standstill, grav- crunching under the big tires. The two of us jumped down and selected nooth and shady spot beneath one of the taller cedars, then spread our down. Jackie at once began peeling off her cutoffs, and in moments king her way down the cliff-side in the burgundy tank suit she'd worn th.

in' in?" she yelled back over her shoulder, squinting into the sun

."

he water Jackie paused, mammoth hand on puerile hip, and She bent down to screen the water, then stuck in a ginger r bath!" she giggled, and arching her long and lissome tly in.

stroke through the water: she swam fast, easy, straight over on her back and inelegantly spouted lakewater out of her mouth. Some old habit kept me from jumping in right off, some infixed rein, probably of Catholic origin, that was always trying to squeeze up the utmost anticipation for even very small pleasures. But whatever nonsense it was I didn't heed it long. Within minutes I was working my way down the cliff and slipping into the lake. It was warm indeed, delicious. I stretched out into a backstroke, felt all over again that rush of dream-power I'd felt at dawn. But of course the longer I swam, the more my arms and lungs strained against the water's resistance. I slowed my pace down then, eventually coming to a stop and just floating. Cumulonimbus clouds filled the pale August sky overhead; a sweet breeze flickered over the shallow waves, earth-music. When I craned my neck out of the water a little, I saw that I'd swum a good hundred feet or so out onto the lake. Jackie was already back on shore climbing up the rocks. After floating peacefully a while longer, I swam back in and joined her underneath the cedar.

"Hey, terrific, huh," Jackie said quietly.

"Yeah, great."

Jackie gazed thoughtfully at me a moment, or seemed to behind the Ray-Bans, and in a small serious voice asked, "Hey Bobbie, you ever smoke grass?"

I laughed; yeah, I'd smoked it once before. My cousin Carol from Houston talked me into it, but it'd only made me sleepy.

Jackie poked around in her shoulder bag and pulled out a fat wheat-straw reefer and a Zippo lighter. Cupping her hands around the flame she lit up, snapped the Zippo shut with an imperious clip, and began sucking up the smoke. "Fantastic shit, here," she said, draughting up the words as she held the smoke down deep in her lungs, handing me the joint. I inhaled. The smoke clawed at my throat, ravaging, triggering a couple of light coughs.

"No, no, you've got to take a lot of air in with it, it's real strong."

"You're telling me," I managed to wheeze out, wiping tears from the corners of my eyes.

"Just take in a little, that's all it takes." So I tried again, again exhaling too quickly. "Bobbie, you're not holding it in," Jackie observed, disappointed. So she pantomimed the maneuver for me, deep-breathing through her mouth first, then curving her lips inward to a funnel. "Then all you do is put the reefer up to your lips and go." I tried with this new technique, and still failed. But just as I started to take in another hit, Jackie said, "Here," and reached over and gently punched me in the stomach. I doubled over, a cough exploding out of me. My pal jumped up and began hitting me on the back. "That's it, Ace, you got it," she chirped happily. "See, you weren't inhaling."

Still choking I gasped, "Yeah, I guess I wasn't inhaling." (Soft, wave, Marcel Marceau, bloodstream velvet, coral flow to the spine and skull. Xylophones. Oh Bobbie. Oh Cisco, Oh Pancho.)

"Fantastic shit," she said again. The two of us continued to pass the joint back and forth, getting to the high you get when you forget what you're talking about, try to remember, get lost, then crack up in torrents of apoplectic though usually groundless laughter. Later, neither of us would be able to recall what droll remark had caused us both to fall apart, rivulets of tears streaming down our little hyena faces. At one point I was staring with glazed saucer-eyes at Jackie's feet: they were a gargantuan trip—at least a ten, probably more, with long skinny brown toes and tiny little toenails.

"You really, you have *really* got big feet," I wondered out loud, then instantly blushed at my thoughtlessness. But she acknowledged this self-evidence blandly. "They have always held me in good stead," she said evenly, perhaps a stock response to comments about her feet. She added, "I do track. I'm on the team up here, as a matter of fact. Second string."

Just as she said this a jolting thunderclap cracked overhead—a speeding summer storm, the only climatic reprieve in Texas summers, was barreling down from the black north. Another skull-shattering crash blasted over the surface of the lake; then the wind picked up, cooler, lovely.

"I bet it'll blow over real quick," Jackie mused, rubbing her chin in the manner of rustic venerables, "but we better get the hell out from under this tree. Let's get below to that rock cliff down there." We both rallied and moved quickly down the cliff-face to a protuberant shelf of rock. But the rain, hard-breaking now, still lashed in underneath, so we scurried about and found four cypress branches and stuck them in the cream-colored mud, draping our towels over them and improvising a frail lean-to.

"Makes you feel like a refugee, don't it," Jackie chortled, snapping on a navy blue baseball cap and yanking up a couple of cans of Gatorade from the styrofoam cooler. She handed me one. Out on the lake several sailboats caught off guard by the storm were scuttling back to shore. One, a twenty-foot sloop with an orange and red sail, had attempted a starboard jibe and was capsized. For a long time we watched the sailors struggle to loosen the mainsheet and rotate the boat back into the wind. At last, however, they righted the craft and began to head back in.

We were sitting so close to one another, Jackie and I, that I, downwind, was able to catch drift, sweet intimate intelligence, of my new friend's scent: a hale and nubile fragrance, clean and young as new-mown grass in summer. I felt myself strong sitting with her, the two of us stoned water rats staring out over the lake, nestled under a dank jaw of Texas rock in the now subdued and subduing rain. Suddenly Jackie stood and scavenged around for several chunks of limestone, then skittishly began to build a small pyramid with them, a rock barrow. "Somebody'll probably knock it down tomorrow," she said, "but we'll know we were here, huh."

"If you say so, "I agreed lamely, tired now. With that inanity we collected our wet gear, and through a damson dusk breaking through the back of the storm, we headed into town.

The Obvious Question _____

I bet you're wondering, friend reader, and maybe even wondering if I was wondering, about my new roommate's sexual preference. Although of course I would not have then, over a decade ago, thought of it quite that way, in that much more recent phrase, *sexual preference.* I remember that I was taken with Jackie's lean and confident good looks, her easy carriage with those big shoulders, her eyes, the grin; but whether or not the question, *Would Jackie make love with another woman,* actually occurred to me right at first, I don't remember. She was a handsome kid, no doubt about it. A track star, a big ol' Texas girl, and for all the world quite probably a dyke. Although I'm equally sure the word *dyke* would not have crossed my mind then, either.

Far more to the point, I do not remember there being desire—not in me, and not from her. There was something missing for that, the chemicals, I guess. Those primeval hormones just did not go barrelling through our budding young bodies for each other, Jackie's and mine. *Nada.* No register.

But all this hardly matters, given what came to pass not two months later, just as speedily and forcefully as that lakeside summer storm.

At the Track

It was one of those cloudless, crystalline afternoons that make Texas a joy to live in during the autumn months: cool in the shadows, warm in the sun, a day for sitting at home in one's garden and listening to music, for drinking pots of tea and making a pretense of reading poetry.

But instead, I was at a university track meet for women, surrounded by many dozens of young females yelling themselves hoarse in the stands. I was there because Jackie was to figure in the last event of the afternoon, the women's 5000-meter finals. Despite the uproar all around me I was lulled by the soothing sunlight. I was drifting off and daydreaming, oblivious to the chasm about to open in my behalf.

For this reason, and because my attention, such as it was, was more or less attached to Jackie, I had paid no heed of the line-up announcements for the race. Would that, for the purposes of this chapter, I had been taking notice of the names and numbers of the runners, so as to begin by extolling the lean power of the winner's sinewed thighs poised at set, by giving you a crisp description of her fierce snap forward at the gun, by marvelling at her amazing strength and speed, lap after lap after lap. But I was on the moon. Too bad.

After the race was over, the spectators began spilling out onto the track, giddy throngs of chattering young women calling out to one another and patting winners and losers alike on the back. I sought out Taylor, who'd come in fourth. She was stretching out, warming down against the wall skirting the track. Dejected, downcast. "Twenty-two five. Shit. Thought I had third wrapped up." Evidently she'd clipped her pace too much during the first 1000 meters. "Lost it in the four minutes. Shit."

I was trying hard to console her when a very short, very chubby little woman with short straight blonde hair and fitfully bad skin edged through the crowd and came up behind Jackie to buckle her knees into Jackie's from the back. Taylor introduced this pudgy cutup as Joya Gardner, an assistant coach for the team. As we shook hands Joya nodded her head slowly at me, grinning and chewing gum the whole time. She too made an effort to buck Jackie up, finally announcing that Edie and Merle (whoever they were) were going to have this really great party that evening (something so insinuative in her voice)—*a really great party*—and would the two of us be interested in going. We both said we would, so Joya jotted down the address for us, adding, "Lissen, you guys gotta help me. Edie wants me to invite one really great mystery guest." Then to Jackie, elbowing her in the ribs, "Somebody great, Taylor. Somebody who walks right."

They both giggled at this, an inside joke, then Jackie looked over at me nervously. Seeing this, Joya said, thumbing her thumb at me, "Well, I haven't seen her walk yet, but I figure if she lives with *you*...," at which Jackie instantly cupped her huge fingers around the back of Joya's neck.

In a deadly sounding sing-song, Jackie said, "Shut up, Joya...."

"What's this 'walk' shit?" I asked.

Unsmiling and somber, Jackie replied, "Tell ya later, Ace."

So I dropped it. But Joya took up her case again. "You guys gotta help me. Who can I ask, Taylor?"

"Why don't you ask Moran? Tell 'em she's Pancho Villa's great-granddaughter or something." At this the two of them turned about and cast street-quick glances at a woman seated on a bench not six feet from where we stood: a copiously perspiring Chicana stretching out two of the hardest-looking legs I'd ever seen on a woman—a towel around her neck, a bottle of water clutched in her hand. I recognized her for the girl who'd just won the 5000-meter race. As I began to turn back toward Joya and Jackie, who themselves were in a huddle haggling over who was going to extend the invitation to Moran, I saw from the corner of my eye that this person, this Moran kid, was apparently eavesdropping on Jackie's and Joya's conversation. Her head was turned aside, but the one eye I could see was cocked demurely in our direction. And there was something in that coy, stolen look that moved me to the core, I almost wanted to cry, I didn't know what the hell it was.

Eventually Joya and Jackie moved over close to Moran, and I with them. It was Jackie who started up, at first talking over the race. I stood there, unable to shake the feeling I'd gotten from Moran's—her name was Alma, Alma Moran—sidelong peeking. And yet the more I stood there, at first trying not to gape at her too much, the more spellbound and gaping I became. Her hair, damp from the race, was long and full, a rich blue-black color, kept back from her face by a red terrycloth headband; her eyes, their expression fixed but placid, were black, enormous, with whacking great eyelashes that made the eyes sweetish and vulnerable and very pretty, really, very pretty; her wide, full-blooded lips were parted slightly, the corners of her mouth drawn, tired from her run; and her golden skin, beautiful! A saffron cream color, a Renaissance ocher, only lighter. In short, a lovely young woman, yet somehow serious-minded-looking, too—so much so that when she smiled at some mild witticism Joya made, suddenly uncovering nacre-white teeth, her eyes no longer impassive and doll-like but luminous, vital, alive to the moment, the metamorphosis was quite simply astonishing. I thought she was the most beautiful woman I had ever seen. I thought I heard her say, at one point, "Too fucking hot."

The Walk Shit

Jackie and I walked back to the dorm after the meet.

"All right," I said, "what was all that *walk* business about back there?"
Jackie, after a half-turn doubletake with her shoulders, replied, "It's this little game Joya plays."

A significant pause. Jackie said, "Joya thinks you can tell certain things about certain people, about women, by the way they walk."

Another pause, more significant still. Finally Jackie said, "Joya says, Joya thinks she can spot a, uh, lesbian in a crowd by the way she walks."

Hoo-ha. Finally. But I wasn't about to let Taylor off the hook. This was too rich. "A lesbian, huh? So. How does a lesbian walk, Jackie, according to Joya, that is."

Jackie stopped cold where she stood, her canvas shoulder bag slung back behind her arms, now akimbo. Oops, she was pissed. "Dammitohell, just like you and me, asshole!"

What if Jackie'd been wrong? I might have been straight; it was a dangerous moment. Obviously she'd wanted to confirm herself to me anyway, as I to her, but it was that extra, added step, that little splay of bravada—just like *you* and me, asshole—that made me stop walking at that very instant, turn back around to face her, and without a word move in close to her and hug her with all my might.

Λ Party _____

On the way back over to the dorm and for the rest of that late afternoon and early evening, Jackie and I told each other what there was to tell of our sex lives thus far. She had about as much to report as I did, having fallen in love with her best friend, who had freaked out but bad when Jackie'd come out to her, essentially abandoning Jackie and the friendship. Very sad. But soon enough we were cheering ourselves up with the prospect of the party we'd been asked to that evening. There was, Jackie said, a whole spate of women Joya knew who were either lesbians or bisexual, many of whom would doubtless be at this party tonight, since the hostesses, the aforementioned Edie and Merle, were themselves lovers.

Lovers. That may have been the first time I'd ever heard that word applied to two women. I liked it. I liked it a helluva lot. On hearing it spring from Jackie's lips, I thought suddenly of Moran, and, at the further thought of possibly seeing her at the party tonight, it felt as though my entire midsection dropped clean away from the rest of me, in one hot disequilibrate wave.

To Taylor I announced: "I'm gonna wear the suit," and, good girl, she gasped. Yes, the suit. This party was my first and foremost opportunity that fall to drag it out—my Edwardian-cut black German velvet drag, with trousers of course, that I'd had tailored down from a dress bequeathed me by my grandmother. Later on, with the air as dry as it was, it would be plenty cool enough outside to wear it. I loved that suit deeply: nothing bad ever happened to me in it.

There was no mistaking that the great sprawling two-story white house on the corner was where the party was: the Supremes were blasting out the windows and onto the porch at a dizzying decible level. As Jackie pulled the screen door open and we passed through, I spotted a three-by-five lavender index card stapled to the rusted screen:

THIS TEMPLE IS CONDEMNED.
KEEP OUT.
THIS MEANS YOU.
Isis & The Demimondes

There were several score people inside those spacious, high-ceilinged old rooms, mostly women, lining the walls and perched on the stairs. At the front hallway a couple of grey-bearded professorial types, almost twins, were trying to get a word in with a statuesque woman in her forties, dressed from head to toe in black, wearing a long skirt, earrings down to her collar bone, but she was talking ninety miles per hour nonstop and puffing wildly at her cigarette—something about Yeats' gyre. A Green Bay Packer of a guy with a handlebar moustache was gently tapping from behind the shoulder of a willow-tall young man who could have been the young Adlai Stevenson. About seven or eight women Taylor's and my age, athletic-looking, were standing about in one corner of the living room holding plastic beer cups and laughing intermittently with one of their company who was speaking in a falsetto and stabbing at the air with her forefinger. "Let's find the keg," Jackie hissed to me, so we went on back to the kitchen to seek it out. Back there we were met with the turning heads and stares of about a dozen or so women (are these lezbeens, en masse? surely the hair on the back of my neck was electrically alive), one of whose voices trailed heedlessly on, high and bitchy, above the others: "That boy's talents always seem to lie in helping rich and clever women just like Eloise get through major traumas. . . ."

I could have sworn several of the women in the kitchen were at this point almost leering at Jackie and me. At first this made me real uncomfortable; then I started to like it. There were a great many bottles of liquor out on the counter, exotica like Pernod and Campari, Dubonnet and Drambuie. Hunks of cheese, cheddar, Swiss, and blue, had been hacked out and lay on a breadboard with some flatbread and butter. A woman in Blackwatch tartan slacks was craning on a stepladder, trying to reach for something from the very top cabinet. In a far corner next to the icebox stood the lower half of a mannequin with a face painted on its sexless crotch. Beside this bizarre wonder a tiny, dark, aspirate-voiced little woman smoking a long Dutch clay pipe was hurling cubes out of the icemaker into the sink.

The woman on the ladder said to her quietly, in a soft Alabama drawl, "Baby be careful, you're gonna kill somebody doin' that." Then, spotting Taylor and me, she lit up all over in a stagey, campy shift to cordiality. "Beer's out on the back porch, darlings." Darlings. I grinned ear to ear, told her "thanks," and holding Taylor by the arm, shuffled obediently outside. Out there by the keg, two men too gorgeous to be heterosexual were having an argument ("No that is *not* what I told him, he's lying, I don't know why, I think we ought to discuss this later," this last said looking up at me, annoyed), and standing off to one side, half-sitting on the railing, was a big, burly good-natured-looking hippy with a red beard and wire-rimmed glasses, smiling knowingly or just drunkenly at Jackie and me as we came through the door. Taylor pulled us a couple of brews, and we headed back into the fray, passing again under the gauntlet of eyes in the kitchen. It was beginning to feel better and better. "Let's see if we can find Joya," Jackie whispered.

The elfin Joya was unearthed in a dimly lit back bedroom upstairs, smoking pot with two other women, neither of whom was Moran, alas. "Bobbie?" she rasped, holding the joint out to me. I took it, but as I looked up holding the hit Taylor winked at me, making me laugh and lose it. Joya and the two other women giggled. "Bobbie, Jackie, this is Katherine and this is Janet," and we shook hands all around, real Texans. "You guys seen Moran here yet," Joya asked, her eyes glittering.

"No, I haven't, is she here?" I replied, as blandly as I could.

"She was a few minutes ago. Hey! Have you met Edie and Merle?" No we had not. "Well, come on then," she said, and took the two of us by the elbows and guided us out into the hall. Over her shoulder, to the red-eyed Janet and Katherine, she said, "See you guys later."

Just as Joya was about to head us both back down the stairs, I saw in my periphery a flash of saffron skin and black hair disappear behind a closing door, the bathroom, presumably. "Uh, you guys go on ahead. I have to take a leak." Crafty.

I stood outside that door for what seemed a millenium, my heart pounding like six-guns, trying to compose myself. After a moment the door swung open. Sure enough, it was Alma.

"Hey," I said, and smiled my charmingest.

"Hey," she said, smiling back, a really nice smile too. "Jackie's roommate, right? Bobbie?"

"Yeah. Hey, I'm glad to see you. I was beginning to think I didn't know anybody here."

"Well, I've already done a tour around and I don't know anybody here at all except Joya."

I looked down at her beer cup, empty. "Lemme stop in here and then let's go get another one, want to?" After I'd relieved myself basically unnecessarily, we picked our way down the stairs, over and around the bodies nestled there. I felt as though I were dreaming, I was so excited I was almost nauseated. She was breathtaking, breathtaking! wearing all white, a cream color, really—a silk shirt with long full sleeves, hopsack trousers the same shade, sandals. As we moved across the living room, I could feel the pull of her back before me like a magnet. I wanted to pin the backs of her shoulders to my chest, stop them from gliding through the crowd like the falcon's wings— perfectly poised, untouched, airs above the ground—they reminded me of.

Then we were at the kitchen once more, and the eyes went to full alert the second Alma rounded the corner. The woman in the tartan slacks was on the telephone. "No, no I don't. Yes. Thank you. Hold on. . . ." She spotted Alma and me, and clapping her thin bony hand over the receiver, she said, "Don't go 'way, hold up. I've got some woman named Helen on the phone who wants me to sample somebody's 'soup product.' Jest a second, hold up," and she reached out and grabbed me by the forearm. Alma turned and grinned at me, looking down at the hand on my arm. "No, I really can't talk now. You've connected with a convention here. But you have yourself a nice evenin', darlin'. Best of luck to you." Click. "Jesus." She turned to us and beamed: "So! And how are you two and who are you two?" she asked sweetly, batting her eyelashes. From nowhere, Joya popped her head in among the three of us and made introductions. The tartan-woman was in fact Edie, and just as we were chatting with her, the little woman with the pipe came huffing up and leaned in on Edie's arm; this was Merle.

"Dearest," her voice was almost Irish-sounding, "we seem to be needing to tap the other keg. We must all be having a good time," this wickedly said, glancing quick from Alma to me and back at Edie.

"Baby why don't you just go get Georgie for that—he's made a career out of tapping kegs," and she turned back to face us again, sighing and martyred.

"Beloved that's just not possible at the moment because dear old Georgie is puking his guts out in the front yard. Or so I'm told."

Edie turned to Merle, face to face. "Oh dear. Merle, you want me to do it, am I right."

Merle leaned in to Edie's neck. I thought for a brief instant she was going to bite it. Her mouth was open, I could see the lips pull back over the teeth, but suddenly she just kissed the air beside Edie's neck and rolled her eyes, mock-urgent: "Come with me, baby. I gotta ask you something." And like a pair of squirrels the two of them scurried out busily through the back door.

"Well Alma," I said. "Maybe a drink instead of a beer?"

She asked for a gin and tonic. I poured us out two, two-finger-sized, light on the tonic. Handing her the glass I bent in close so the other satyrs wouldn't hear: "I think I know a place we could sit where we'd see everybody at this party sooner or later."

"Oh yeah?" she answered, pulling back, amused. "Lead on then." So we filed out of the kitchen, and I blazed the careful trail through the bodies back up the stairs to a bedroom, yes, but with the door open, a big brass bed inside, directly across the hall from the bathroom. Ta-da. Alma actually tittered, sat down on the bed. "See?" I said to her, forgivably proud of myself, "great view from here."

Of the following conversation, our first full-length, I recall principally that Alma mentioned two former boyfriends of hers, one who'd become a seminarian, the other a mime studying in Los Angeles. And at these singular facts, I managed to take a little heart. She herself was from the Valley, San Martín, somewhere between Hebbronville and Falfurrias. ("Where they make the butter?" I asked ingenuously. "Yes," she replied.)

After a time we wandered back downstairs to the coven in the kitchen. There, Merle was passionately or just heatedly discussing something or other with a most noticeably thin and beautiful boy, all angles, elbows and jaw, with jade-green Buddha eyes and a deep lustrously seductive voice. As Merle spoke with him, and just as Alma and I were passing by them, she reached out quick and grabbed Alma by the hand. Holding it midair she asked the boy, "Have you met this sumptuous creature yet, William? You are, after all, the two prettiest people at this goddam party." Alma smiled a little uncomfortably but graciously, and began easing her hand out of Merle's, taking Merle's hand between her own two and patting it lightly and sweetly, as one might shape dough, an eloquent, gentlewomanly gesture.

With a second round of drinks in hand, we eventually sauntered into the living room where there were—jolt and amazement—female/female and male/male couples dancing with one another to a slow dance, Roberta Flack. I couldn't look at Alma; I just bombed on through back to the kitchen, Alma following me. There were far fewer women there now. Edie was standing at the sink talking with a very chic older woman with oddly attractive turtlelike features. Edie was herself devouring a most juicy nectarine, a bit of which clung to her chin. She looked up at Alma and me and smirked blatantly; she looked pretty swacked. I was getting that way too, actually. I made an awkward about-face into Alma, whose eyes avoided mine. As we passed back through the living room I heard myself say, right out of the outright blue, leaning in over her shoulder, "You wouldn't wanna dance with me, would you Alma?" O horrors, who said that?

She swivelled round to face me, her eyes blacker, brighter, her expression at first nonplussed, unreadable, but then grinning, switching immediately to something a shade brassy, accepting the dare.

"Sure, why not."

Sure why not. O yà. Hurriedly, hurriedly I found a niche in the crowd and pivoted back to Alma. Christ, who'd lead? I was taller, I'd lead. I held my hands out to her, and she slipped hers into mine, moving in close to me. There is a power in such moments that words cannot wholly evoke.

And maybe they shouldn't anyway.

I was holding her as negligibly as I could, turning slow with the music. I kept trying to pretend, to diffuse the volatility, muffle the volcano rumbling in me, that this dancing was just like my all-girl high school, girls perforce dancing with girls, but then I'd open my eyes and see the other couples shuffling around Alma and me, and the slim pretense would sulfurize, shrivel away in the dark blue light of that smoky den of deviance. Those boys, those girls, they were just scandalizing the hell outta me, and if they were scandalizing me, surely Alma must be *escandalizada* too. So then I made some crack, I don't remember what. It broke the tension, we laughed, and in laughing I pulled her a little closer in to me, my head just beside hers, suddenly isolating the perfume she wore—Givenchy, *L'Interdit*.

Far, far sooner than I would rather it have, the song ended. Alma and I backed off self-consciously from one another. I could feel my face mirroring hers: sheepish, smiling, and, fundamentally (whew) still amicable, undistant.

We moved slowly out to the front porch then, outside to the dark, speaking not at all of the scene inside, of the men and the men and the women and women, but I could feel that our talk and laughter—we were giddy, nervous— had become charged, uneasy. Something. As of less than ten minutes ago there had materialized the incontrovertible fact of our being together at a gay party, of our having just danced a slow dance together at a gay party, of the obvious thing, the question I knew had to be flicking through Alma's mind: *You asked me to dance here—are you a dyke.* And mine: *You accepted, are you.* But I couldn't, something held me back, I couldn't ask that question just then, and it wasn't only because I was afraid to, either. The words held uppermost in my brain and overrode everything else, whatever the hell it was we were talking about out there on that porch, but to have given them voice would have been ill-timed and cloddish. To have given them voice would also have robbed me (us?) of the charm of not knowing, of suspecting strongly, of The Mystery of It All. And of course, charm be damned, if Alma wasn't a lesbi- an, I was covered.

After some time Alma stood up, a little unevenly I thought, and said she needed to get back to her dorm. I told her I'd walk with her, since my dorm was just beyond hers. I went to find Jackie to take my leave. Taylor scrutinized me, a multifaceted look on her face, of motherliness, envy, cunning. "Now just you watch yourself, Crawford, just you watch it." Jackie seemed a little loaded, too; I was glad we'd walked over.

When Alma and I reached the corner just before her dorm, she paused on the sidewalk to ease a pebble out of her sandal, leaning on my shoulder for support—even this taintless touch flaring, firing down my arm. Straightening up again, but leaving her hand where it was (*oh*), she said, "Bobbie, thanks. Thanks a lot. I really enjoyed it."

I did too, I said. But don't drop the ball, Crawford, think of something, dammit, don't freeze. Yet before I could find the words, Alma said brightly, comfortably: "Uh, lissen...let's go to the movies next week, ya wanna?"

Five Weeks Later

Her hand lies open on the pillow. She sleeps. The fingers, long and thin, are crisscrossed with tiny hairline cracks; the nails are clear and shiny, healthy, well-trimmed. A blood vessel in the soft fleshy mound of her palm, in the heel of her hand, twitches, and this is followed by another spasm in her index and middle fingers, like a trumpeter's fluttering a trill. Lying on my side in the single bed I incline my face over the hand, just inches above it, and smell again the smell I have for the first time smelled today. I can't help myself: my tongue flicks lightly down between those fingers, barely touching, barely pressing in between them. Thumb and ring finger, once, twice, lighter still. After a moment I risk looking down at her face and see her awake, gazing up sleepy-eyed at me. She sighs, yawns and smiles. Turns on her side toward me, half-propped on her elbow. With her left hand she reaches out to the side of my head, slips a curl behind my ear, etches the upper rim of cartilage with a finger. She is staring at, smiling at my mouth, glancing up into my eyes, then down at my lips again. Pulling the sheet out between us she brings her face in close to mine, her lips falling soft to mine and licking.

She whispers, kissing me, *Now.*

Whoah, Back Up...

My apologies, reader *mia.* I got antsy and had to skip on ahead to that part, to Alma's hand on the pillow. Doubtless you had a fair idea of what was going to happen anyway. Nonetheless, let me give you a quick recap of those five weeks.

We went to see not one but three movies during that time: two on campus and one out at a shopping mall to which we'd taken a city bus. *Closely Watched Trains, Juliet of the Spirits,* and at the mall *Murmur of the Heart.* Like me, Alma loved the movies. Within a year at the university she would change her major to radio, television, and film; within two she'd join the campus film committee, ordering French, Italian, British, Czech, Polish, and Japanese films to bring to Texas.

But from our very first movie date, for which Alma came swaggering out in long extravagant strides (how had I never noticed that walk before?) down her dorm steps to greet me, the quintessential and still unposed question came to be less and less, *perdóname,* query-like and more—gradually, in little gestures, in more sidelong glances and in bolder smiles—a matter of tacit and accepted fact. As it had been from the beginning on that front porch at that party, to have asked it, to have committed it to words instead of these slight shadings and oblique intimacies that kept building between us, would have broken the spell, fouled the brewing magic.

In short and in sum we knew damn well we were courting each other.

Then, on one blistering cold Texas blue-norther afternoon—a Monday, I think, I know we both cut class—I borrowed Taylor's truck and drove back out with Alma to the swimming hole Jackie'd taken me to in August. We took a walk away from the water's edge along a deer run of caliche winding through a low cedar wood. After strolling a few minutes, Alma suddenly broke into a dogtrot and pulled ahead of me, the back of her olive-drab suede jacket disappearing at the curve of the deer trail. I kept following the path, snuggling my ungloved hands deeper into my jeans pockets; the shriek of the wind was making me tear, my ears were ringing from it. For what seemed a rather long time I continued along the deer run, finally looking at my watch, Alma still nowhere in sight. Because it was too cold to stop walking, I kept on, quickening my pace; then it was a full ten minutes later and I started getting edgy.

Around a sharp steep turn in the path I came to a clearing, a high hyssop-covered field with lurking clumps of cactus and several sizeable granite boulders. A red-shouldered hawk took languid flight from the top of one of these as I ventured out into the open, the hyssop snapping and falling before me as I walked. The trail had disappeared. Where was she.

I was standing in the middle of the clearing, boulders on either side of me. Suddenly, coronary-sudden, I simultaneously heard a Hollywood-Apache whoop and felt arms and a body land from above me on my back, throwing me to the ground. Through the wind screaming and the pulse booming in my ears, I could hear Alma laughing, feel her poking me in the stomach, the ribs. Without hesitating an instant I rolled her off my back, swung my leg over her torso, and pinned her arms down hard.

"Oooooo," she laughed up at me, "I'm scared to death." Then, unsillying a little, "Don't be mad."

"You scared the shit outta me, Alma!"

"I'm sorry, Bobbie." She did not look sorry. "You seemed so cold and forlorn."

"It *is* cold and forlorn out here, goddammit!"

"Calm down, calm down now."

I continued to hold her wrists down, feeling the pulse in me slacken off, start to settle. She was grinning up at me, a little breathless, still pleased with herself, I could tell.

Then it hit me. I was looking at her, I was still nettled. And then the hunger, huge and caving, roared up the hollow of me, I could feel it pummeling out, unstoppable, I could feel it in my eyes, my mouth, the roots of my tongue.

And then Alma could see it. I saw it register in her eyes. For a second I thought to recover it again, I got flustered, maybe I blushed. I loosened my hold on her wrists but didn't let go.

Then, empathic, condoling, her eyes darkening and warm, she said softly, "Hey."

I said, "Hey," back, and we were smiling at each other then, dark smiles, rich ones, the bubbling heady wealth of longing long suppressed suddenly sprung, popped out, spuming over, and I began to lean down and in toward her face, slowly and slower still, the wind-stirred hyssop clicking all around us. Her eyes closed in on my lips, her lashes falling to, her lips parting a little as mine met them, their touch, their meeting scarcely a brush, slight, glancing, weightless. I pulled back up from her, releasing her wrists, letting my hands glide down the undersides of her arms, down the sides of her rib cage, resting at her waist.

And here it was. The moment I'd dreamed of night and day since I'd met her. And I had no idea whatsoever of what to say, what to do next. I was gazing down at her and she up at me, the third joint of an index finger loosely between her teeth, not gnawing it, just holding it there, the corners of her mouth, her eyes alive with, *yà*, amusement, her own hunger, yes, and with, *Now what.*

Shifting my weight a little I started to say "Alm—," when she lurched up abruptly, the flats of her hands slapping hard against my shoulders, knocking me back and over. Before I could get upright again she was straddled on top of me, had me pinned down tight.

"Ha!" she laughed, throwing her head back up at the slate sky and shaking her hair back behind her shoulders. "Gotcha," she gloated down at me. "*Jota.*"

"What's *jota* mean?"

Alma pressed her knees in snug around my ribs. "That's what you are. You're a *jota*. Dyke." She was grinning ear to ear at me, exuberant, queen of the mountain. And then she sobered a little; one of her eyebrows flexed and relaxed. She sucked her lower lip between her teeth, looking down at me, thinking godknowswhat. But she just sighed then, shook her hair back behind her again, and the top half of her body began leaning in and down to me. She was smiling now, and she came in close and kissed me, a kiss just like mine but wetter, sweeter, even more forbearant. Alma pulled back from me but didn't release her hold one bit: she honed down in to my face and kissed me again, firmer this time, then grazed her lips soft above my mouth, the side of my nose, down my cheek and to my lips once more. My tongue darted up light into one corner of her mouth. She drew back up quick, looking down at me with feigned contempt.

"Tongues too, huh? *Jota.*" But she dipped back down to me with another kiss, even harder, holding her lips to mine, her lips opening, taking my upper lip between them, her tongue pressing past my lips, inside, rolling over my tongue, around it, beneath it, fusing me, feeding me, hottening and slick in my mouth like freestone peaches in June sun.

We stayed out there in that field kissing and kissing for a great long time, I don't know how long, at least til the light began to fail and we were blue from the cold. When we drove back into town, Alma nestled in close to me in the truck, her head on my shoulder.

Not that night but probably the next we were in her dorm room and I kissed her and we started in kissing again. And we talked about the kissing and all of it and we loved the kissing. But we decided that we would just wait until we could move up to it, until it felt just right, for anything above and beyond the kissses. So for another two weeks or so we would meet at either her room or mine at times when the roomies were known to be away and kiss, a universe of kissing.

Then, finally, she showed up unexpectedly at my door early one morning.

Jackie was at class; I was still in bed. Having let her inside, I, still modest, popped back under the sheets since I was again wearing only the long white T-shirt. Alma sat down on my bed and we talked. She was uptight about two midterms and a paper, she was about to get her period, and then somehow the subject of her father's death came up. At fifty-one years of age her father had been gored to death by a bull in the Morans' own pasture.

Alma was fourteen when it happened. She and her younger brother and sister had all been away at school. Her mother had been out in the back yard hanging up clothes when she'd heard the crack of the top beam of fencing, the thud of hooves landing on the other side, the furious gallop. The creature had knocked down a wasps' nest and been multiply stung. Hector Moran, bearing two buckets of well water, was walking back to his barn when the bull saw him and charged. By the time Leticia Moran reached the bottom pasture fence, her husband was, unknown to her, already dead. She screamed and waved at the beast to pull it away from Moran, just escaping the bull's horns herself by shinnying up a mesquite. When the bull's rage had subsided and it had loped off across the field, she got down and ran to the house to call for an ambulance and load up her husband's shotgun. Back at the pasture she took aim and shot the animal once in its chest. It went down immediately, falling hard on its knees. She reloaded and stood within a few feet of the dying bull and fired the second round into its skull. By that time the ambulance had arrived. One of the men walked Señora Moran back up into the house and telephoned her sister Dora for her. When Dora arrived the men took away Moran's body. Dora had brought brandy; she was standing in the kitchen pouring out two glasses when Alma, Rosa, and Berto came home from school. Alma's mother had been sitting in the bedroom looking out the window and weeping, but when she heard the children at the front door she went out into the kitchen, dabbing her face dry. Her eyes were swollen with the crying, her nose and lips were ruddy and moist. Dora made her sister sit down. She put the glass into Leticia's hand, tenderly folding her fingers around it. Alma's mother didn't drink it. Alma had said, *Mama, what's happened.*

By the time Alma finished telling this story, her eyes had filled with tears. "Man, I'm sorry," she said. "I had no idea I was going to get into all of that."

I reached out to her shoulder and squeezed it faintly, at which she suddenly gave way to her tears, her hand darting up shakily to cover her eyes. I took that hand away, pulled her to me, and held her while she wept.

Don't, don't cry, Alma, I was saying over and over. I'm always demolished by other people's tears, and I started crying myself. Alma saw this and, despite herself, laughed. She said, You dope, and nubbed the pad of her thumb against the tip of my nose. I stretched over then for the box of Kleenex wedged in the headboard shelf. When I turned back to Alma she was looking at me in a way she never had before: I still can't rightly say what all was in her face, but it seemed like pride in me, somehow, and hunger, too. She whipped out one of the tissues and blew her nose, then slipped the sheet back from my legs and began gently rubbing the top of my thigh. We started in at our kissing again then, plaintive, fragile kisses at first, within mere moments building to the hotter, deeper ones. And she was stroking me too, running her fingers over my arms, my legs, my chest. After a while she drew back from me breathing hard, her mouth wet and full, and said, *I want to,* and started peeling off my T-shirt, and I began unbuttoning her, and we were both trembling like colts and she pulled the sheet back and got in with me.

She was so beautiful lying there it made me ache—that dark, rich, golden skin of hers on those frail white cotton sheets.

Sisters of the Spear

After a month, and the very first finals month at that, of disaccommodating poor Jackie (our signal was a rubber band slipped over the outside doorknob), and being ourselves on several occasions sickeningly panic-stricken by the unpredictable appearance of the dorm cleaning service ("You go into the bathroom"/"No, you go"/"But it's your room," etc.), and another month over the Christmas vacation of many, many long-distance telephone calls between San Martín and Notasonia, Alma and I decided we would live with one another. We would rent an apartment together upon our return for the spring semester.

So we did. An upstairs duplex in the south of town overlooking a park full of cedar trees. We didn't have a whole lotta money: our furniture consisted of two hulking armchairs and a wrought iron fifties floor lamp from the Salvation Army, plus a brand-new bed we'd bought together. On the grey, brutally cold and windy January day of the move, Jackie helped us load up into her pickup. After it was all upstairs and Jackie'd driven off, Alma and I took a hot soaking bath together, our first, phoned out for a pizza, and before it arrived made up the bed with great ceremony and inaugurated it.

Jesús, we were in love. Every silly damned thing we did together brought incalculable joy: shopping for groceries, walking in the park, going to movies and track meets, cooking and feasting on what we'd cooked. Writing term papers, adopting a kitten, growing tomatoes; even my sorrows (the kitten smooshed by our neighbor's station wagon, a tiff with Taylor, the emotional miasmas of menstruation) took on an often luxurious glow when Alma helped me dispel them.

I remember trudging up the duplex stairs one afternoon that spring, to hear Alma singing from within—I am not making this up—"*El Rancho Grande*":

> *Allá en el ranch grande*
> *allá donde vivia,*
> *habia una rancherita*
> *que alegre me decia,*
> *que alegre me decia...*

And I felt it possible, just for a moment, that my heart would burst apart from the happiness.

And there was another afternoon, that of my nineteenth birthday, when I came home to an empty house to find an immense mirror, easily six by six feet, positioned in its slim maple frame opposite our bed. In lipstick Alma had scrawled upon it, *Feliz cumpleaños, chica. Kissy-kissy, Love, Me.* When she got home from school later on we made love with the mirror people. At first we were giggling and self-conscious, then less so; then it became slightly voyeuristic, and at last virtually orgiastic. We must've climaxed each other three or four times that evening ["Three, only three," Alma contends]. We kept on and on until at one late point both of us began to feel almost queasy—hyperventilation and lack of food, I guess. So we sat up at the bottom of the bed and stared, just a little wanly, at our mirror selves: we were sisters of the spear, she and I, she as dark as I was fair, both of us young and strong, exultant in each other.

A Family Sketch

Her full name was Alma Caterina Violeta (the confirmation name she chose, an early clue—she said she'd seen it once, the name "Violeta," scribbled with chalk some eight or nine times all over a sidewalk in San Martín, and had decided upon it for herself right then and there) Moran, which many Anglos persist in pronouncing *More*-un. After Hector Moran's death, Alma's Aunt Dora, the family matriarch, put up a substantial amount of cash from her own savings to finance Alma's first year at the university. Alma's mother had also taken out a small loan in her eldest's behalf. Alma herself had worked for a year after high school at the five-and-dime in San Martín. The rest was procured from an athletic scholarship, then an academic one as well. For Alma, college meant being up and out of the Texas Valley, where the now totally matriarchal family Moran had dwelled ever since Alma's grandmother fled Mexico during the Revolution of 1916.

Her grandmother, Patricia Alma de Leon y Avila, escaped with her five very young children from the state of Morelos, stronghold of dark and fiery Mexicano blood, after Alma's grandfather, the village *taller,* the fix-it man, had been murdered by the elder of two Zapatista brothers; Alma's grandfather had accidentally overloaded a shell in the younger brother's six-shooter, and when the young revolutionary later fired his weapon, it had blown his hand apart.

Patricia somehow made it as far north as San Martín, where she became the cook for a local Anglo rancher who had taken pity on the proud young *morelense* and her brood of five: the baby, Leticia; Dora; Armando, who would die in a fuel pit explosion at Kelly Air Force Base; Rudolfo, Rudy, a victim of the meningitis epidemic of 1956; and Beatriz, who with Dora and then Leticia would years later run the family's café in San Martín.

One Saturday morning I was rummaging through our hall closet when I came across a gorgeous old hand-tooled leather case about as big as an attaché. Alma was putting on her socks in the bedroom. I asked her, "Mita, what's this?"

She looked at it and beamed. "Hand it here, I'll show you."

The case, Alma explained, had belonged to Elena Galvan, who had been

Tío Rudy's teenage girlfriend for the three years prior to his death. What the case contained was nothing more or less than Elena's scrapbook and memorabilia of her tenure as president of the Duncan Renaldo fan club, Duncan Renaldo having been the Mexicano actor who for five years, from 1951 to 1956, portrayed the Cisco Kid on television.

"The show started out each week with the announcer saying, 'Here's adventure, here's romance, here's O. Henry's famous Robin Hood of the old west, the Cisco Kid.' But you know, the character from the O. Henry story was white, and he shot Mexicans. Hardly a Robin Hood type."

There were numerous black-and-white autographed studio shots of Renaldo and of Leo Carillo, who played the Kid's sidekick Pancho; there were clippings of interviews with Renaldo at his ranch in Santa Barbara, *Rancho Mi Amigo;* there were stills of Renaldo from *Bridge of San Luis Rey* and *For Whom the Bell Tolls;* there were prints of Renaldo with John Wayne on the set of *The Fighting Seabees,* one of which had written on it, *"A Duncan—Vaya bien, Duke."* A small leather pouch held a silver belt buckle from the Kid's costume and the obligatory lock of hair, brittle-black and curly, *chino.*

"He was such a handsome man," Alma sighed, " 'such a *caballero,'* Dora always said." At the very bottom of the case, underneath a letter in green ink to Elena from Renaldo which began, *"Cara Elena, Soy tan feliz a...,"* the rest of it water or tear-stained and illegible, was a small faded Brownie snapshot of Dora and Elena together, dressed to the nines in high-fifties drag. They were walking down a city street arm in arm and smiling. On the back of the picture was this inscription: *"Con Elena, Laredo 1955."*

At the Track Again

Yet again I was sitting in the bleachers at the university stadium, for one of Alma's track meets, an intercollegiate biggie. I'd brought along a physical anthropology text since finals were a mere four weeks away. All of a sudden I was aware of a shadow over me, Jackie standing above me, huffing and puffing. She was in her white track silks, and they were drenched. I smiled up at her into the sun and beheld a most alarmingly blanched-out Taylor face.

"Come on down with me quick, Bobbie. Something's wrong with Alma." Adrenalin shot all through me, a liquid fire-and-ice implosion. I was on my feet, my pulse slamming against my skin, clambering after Taylor down the steep stadium steps, barrelling through the crowd. We shoved through spectators and competitors alike down along the track. A clump of women, several of them track team coaches, were standing over someone, Alma! sitting on the ground. There was a pool of vomit beside them, oh God. I put my hands around Joya's back, moved her roughly aside, and squatted down next to Alma. She was crying and shaking all over. I reached out to her, held her by her biceps, whispered, *Mita, what is it.* She looked up at me. There was horrific, unutterable terror in her face. *What is it, what is it,* I heard myself saying. Alma started to glance over her shoulder, then wordlessly blacked out. I and two others caught her before she fell over. One of the coaches bent down with smelling salts. Pushing one of the women aside at the knees, I looked back behind Alma: about thirty feet from us, tethered by four young men in cowboy outfits, was the university mascot, a longhorn steer. Something clicked. I stood up fast, pulling up Alma, who was beginning to come around, with me. "Joya," I snapped, "we've got to get her off the track, hurry." The two of us slipped her between us, her arms dangling puppetlike over our shoulders, and half-carried her off into the bowels of the stadium, to the elevator, and up into the team's locker room on the fifth floor.

Gradually, after a long slow rubdown from Joya, and me softly talking to her and stroking her head and her arms, Alma began to come back to herself. Her breathing settled, and eventually she got up and washed her mouth out.

At the sink she whistled low. "Man. Heavy *nanañares*"—a fantastically onomatopoeic word I'd heard her use before for "the jitters."

She couldn't talk about it yet, not even then. Much later on that evening over some chamomile tea and toast, she confirmed what I'd suspected at the track: that she was virulently phobic about cattle, and most especially bulls. A taurophobe, my beloved was.

Vamped _____

It is now early evening in January of 1973, and Alma and I have been living together for a year. She is sitting in the big rose corduroy armchair, the thick peanut-colored light of our kitschy old floor lamp bathing her as she reads and periodically slides the slipping frames of her glasses back up her nose. The gas-burning space heater flares dully in the corner, a bread pan of water atop it exuding limestone motes in the hard water steam. I am snuggled in another fatso armchair across from Alma, suffused by the same light, gazing up at her rather than reading my—what was it then, art history probably, who cares—textbook. I'm bored. I want to go over and sit in her lap and kiss her and get her all hot and make love, but she's got an exam tomorrow morning so I am having to squelch it. The phone rings (hooray) and it's Jackie, who wants to go over to Edie and Merle's, wants Alma and me to come with her. Alma says, "Baby, you go ahead and go," so I tell Taylor, "Sure, come on over."

By now Jackie and Alma and I have been at Edie and Merle's often, and I am entranced by both of them. Edie is Edie Vogel, thirty-two, a landscape architect. Merle Donnelly is twenty-seven, twenty-eight, and a sculptor whose current work, enormous room-straddling bronzes of intertwining female figures, has recently been accepted for a showing at a world-class gallery in London. Hell, I'm not just entranced by these women: to me they're gods. They're rich, or generally assumed to be so (I've been told that Edie's father, who irregularly sends huge amounts of money to Edie and her mother in cashiers' checks drawn on banks all over the world, may be a gangster). Edie and Merle are successful, attractive, witty, and brilliant, and to me at twenty years of age, they were the absolute exemplars of The Very Life. More and more I wanted to be near them, to be with them, to bask in their lightning-fast banter and razzle-dazzle. Since Merle has recently flown back from London, and the two of them want to go honky-tonking, I am on the verge of just that opportunity once more.

When Taylor and I walked on in to the big house, never locked, we rounded the corner into the living room and beheld Edie enthroned in their barber's chair. She startled us, sitting there like some Machiavellian prince, her short black curls gleaming, dangling around her face, her knees fanned far apart, her hands interlaced over her stomach. She wore a black turtleneck, black wool slacks, knife-thin black calf boots. But it's her expression that fired my double take: her eyes were far blacker than usual, shining, expectant, old, her slight smile not only wicked and carnal but omniscient. It's as though she were quite deliberately posing, waiting for us to walk in and see her there and be devastated. *You came to see me and this is what you got, you lucky babies.*

But what she really said was, "Hey kee-ids what's happnin'?" Merle was still showering, what could she fix us to drink. Edie's cocktails were established legend. From six o'clock on her Talavera-tiled bar would be replete with the juices of freshly squeezed lemon, lime, and orange, with twists and slices, with olives, onions, everything. Edie concocted our orders—I asked for a gimlet, I thought that was downtown then—as though she were performing some sacred ritual or sinister alchemy, stirring or shaking the drink in a clean-cut Scandanavian crystal pitcher, wiping up with crisp Irish linen, handing me the glass with a flourish as though it were an invitation to the dance. While we waited for Merle, Edie played us records, one of which was Ella's Gershwin. When "I've Got a Crush on You" came on, I was jabbering at Jackie and happened to look over at Edie behind the bar. She was fixing Merle a drink, Merle's ceremonial vodka martini, and she was staring at me while she stirred.

She was looking at me just as she had when Taylor and I came into the house, only direct, at me alone. It was grade-A carnivorous, that look, it sank me dead center. Then, still staring at me, she sang a little along with Ella: "...the world will pardon my mush/but I have got a crush, my baby, on you." My brain was short-circuiting, I think I started stuttering at Jackie. Just as Edie finished singing the line, Merle flounced into the room with all the sweep and brio of Zsa Zsa, just missing Edie's singing. Without missing a beat Edie glanced up at Merle, extended the drink to her, and said, unbelievably smooth, a buttery charm to her voice, "Your drinkie, beloved."

Throughout that evening, as we four flitted in and out of some two or three bars, Edie, at times when Merle's attention or Merle herself was away for even a little bit, would look at me and say something, some double-entendre, some sex-lexical double play, and blow me right out of the water again. For instance: she and I were talking about my recent attempts to tailor-make my own academic program at the university, to do a number of independent studies on my own—I had been encountering some frustrating bureaucratic resistance to these plans—and Edie, slipping her hand over mine on the table and patting it most maternally, really, honest! drawled, "Well you have just got to tell them precisely what it is you want." In looking at her then I could almost feel my pupils dilating, although I think I managed to maintain a stoneface, mumbling something back, sticking to the surface dialogue, "Yes, well, I have, but...." And another instance, at another bar, still later: I don't even remember what the topic of our conversation was, but Edie's line in it is forever branded in my brain. It was, "We're all just little animals anyway, aren't we?" Again I mustered my now seriously besieged sense of equilibrium and did not react to the line or the face. Damn, I was scared to. Scared of Edie and scared of Merle, as shaken as a fawn suddenly alert to a snapping twig, mulch-crunching footsteps, human scent.

At the end of the evening, while we were walking back to their car, a white 1955 Mercedes sedan they'd named Edith, Merle and Jackie were some distance ahead of Edie and me. Edie chose that moment to begin extolling her new office downtown in the warehouse district ("It's made me so happy, I'm so damn proud of it, it's so handsome," etc.), and asked me if I'd like to come visit it next week, drop by, have a look. . . .

Had I been listening for it, had I been capable of hearing it, I might've at that instant picked up on the thin serpentine hiss of blue-black ruin slithering before me, might've seen, felt, smelled the dissolution about to befall me. But I wasn't listening for it or anything else: I could only hear Edie's quicksilver patter luring me in. I was high, I was tempted, and, even if I had forseen them, I doubt I would've given a damn about the consequences.

So I said, "Yes, I'd love to see the new office." And she instantly pulled a tiny black appointment book from her back pocket, together with a tiny gold-nibbed fountain pen, flipped a few pages, and announced: "Thursday's good for me. How 'bout two-thirty?" I peered over her shoulder in the streetlamp light while she jotted this down: a small *B* on the two-thirty line.

The Assignation

Bundled up for the bike ride I'd taken downtown, trussed up in a couple of sweaters and a 60-40 parka, big as Baby Huey and feeling like Baby Huey, I was winding up the red metal hobnail steps to Edie's office. I was just feeling awkward, clunky; not guilty, apprehensive, mean or stupid. I'd say I felt like the playgirl of the western world mounting those stairs, but I was too cold to feel that just then. That came later, that feeling.

Edie pulled the door open, stood there, brandy in hand, looking me over head to toe, and said, "Jesus, the Huns have arrived! Why the hell didn't you take a cab? Come on in, ferchrissakes, warm up by the fire."

There was a wood-burning stove in one corner of the huge yellow pine-panelled room, the split top half of an old limestone warehouse, and, although Edie had had central air installed, the ceilings were so tremendously high, over twenty feet, that the place was about as toasty as a ski lodge. Edie was dressed to counter it in a navy blue commando-style oiled wool sweater and grey worsteds, a smoke-blue herringbone tweed scarf draped cavalierly around her neck. As I came in she had some old rock-'n-roll tape going full blast on her formidable sound system: Little Richard doing "Good Golly, Miss Molly," Chuck Berry's "C'est La Vie." She crossed the room and turned the volume down a little. After a few moments, the fire began to thaw my ass and legs, but I left my top layers on a bit longer nevertheless. Edie swung open a door in a high-tech stainless steel cupboard ("It's Italian, I got it last week, you like it?"), extracted a bottle of cognac, and splashed out a conspicuously generous dollop in a small snifter. "Here," she said, "you need it."

"So!" I said brightly, taking the glass and ostensibly ignoring the glimmer of the cat-and-mouse edge to that line, "this is where you make your millions."

"Oh baby," Edie sighed, strumming her fingers absent-mindedly along the line of her jaw, "landscape architects just do not make millions, not even in this state. And it is, after all, the dead of winter."

"And most especially inside this office, Edie. Christ, how can you stand it this cold?"

She turned smartly on her heel toward me, her dark eyes glittering with stagey pride: "Intestinal fortitude, my dear. Grit." (A pause here, a perfect one-count)—"Whether true or no." Just then, at the onset of Little Anthony's "I'm On the Outside Looking In," Edie suddenly snapped her fingers and excused herself, striding over to a white laterally-opening filing cabinet and pulling out a large, black leather-bound book. "Bobbie, I have just got to make this phone call," she said to me. "Why don't you go on up and check out the view from the roof? The staircase is back over there," and she flutter-pointed to a slim wrought iron staircase in a far corner.

I rezipped the parka, clanked heavily up the narrow helix, and gave a cursory look around up there. You could see the river, the mainstrip, most of downtown. Yeah, so what. Too goddam cold out here. I clanked back down. Edie was still on the phone, speaking so softly I couldn't overhear her—not a business call, then. I'd been quite purposefully diverted to the roof. I moved out of earshot and looked around the office some more. Her drafting table was surrounded by freestanding displays, models of gardens sealed with great plastic domes—tiny shrubs, tiny willows, tiny fountains, ponds, and bridges beneath them.

Looking not a little peevish, Edie put the receiver down and came over and stood beside me at the models. "Look at this one," she whispered, lightening up. "When Merle was in Britain she met this Arab who's buying a house in Houston. And my clever darling sweet-talked him into letting me, utter stranger, do his garden next October. These," she said, pointing, "are cypresses. They'll do just fine down there, as most of these will, provided Houston air doesn't kill 'em off eventually. Those are white Arabian maples, that's a persimmon, this is a line of mimosa, here, these are eucalyptus, palms, even a cedar of Lebanon. And over here we're gonna put in a coupla pecans. So he'll know he's in Texas."

Her long fingers traced the Plexiglas with visible tenderness, a thin gold chain on her wrist clipping the plastic as her hand hovered slowly over the various flora. And seeing that hand, following its soft careful movement over the model, noting its veins, the light freckles on its back, the why, no, the what of why I'd come there that afternoon became tangible, and human. It folded open and out before me with each consecutive motion of her hand, undulant and engulfing: I wanted her. God-dawg did I want Edie. But as I watched the hand, I knew I would do absolutely nothing, say nothing, to move the moment from here to there. Christ I was scared of her.

All of a sudden I realized Edie was silent, staring at me. She said, "What's wrong? You look like you're in the ozone."

I shrugged. "Oh. It's nothing. Nothing, really. I'm just a little groggy, that's all," I lied.

She was silent again. Then, "Bobbie."

"What. What?"

Edie stood back from me and folded her arms, smiling wry at darkling me. "Baby," she drawled, looking quick to the side of her shoulder and back at me. "Is this making you nervous."

O Jesus, here it comes, the fusillade. I was not ready. I was not ready for this. I cleared my throat and backed away from her, an abrupt, graceless movement, moving, almost bounding, over to a window in the west limestone wall. "Being here?" I was saying as I went, "What? I'm not nervous, Edie."

She actually clucked at me, laughed a little. "Sure you are. Sure you are! Look at you: you're halfway across the goddam room from me!" And she began to saunter over toward me, her arms still folded, the sauntering even and level right from her hips.

I giggled. This was right out of the soaps, and I was cast as the dumbshit ingenue. "Now Edie," I began, starting to crack up, but she was already smack dab in front of me.

She reached out to my waist, first with one hand, then with both, and pulled me slow to her. "Now Edie what," she said coolly, glancing up at the line of scalp, then to my eyes, then to my mouth.

I sighed, "Oh jeez damn." Scared or no, there was nothing to do but lean in and kiss her quick, draw back just as quick, like a pendulum. Edie smiled then, her whole face warming into the smile, a real sparkler, the little accordian wrinkles at her eyes spreading wide. From out of nowhere I heard myself delivering this line, this genuine tin-plate line: "How'm I doin' so far?" I said. (Where does this crap come from! How do I come up with this stuff!) But Edie threw her head back and laughed a great breathy ha! from down deep, so I guess she liked it, anyway.

"Great, just great," she said still smiling, gazing at me. Then she sighed, too. "Was *anybody* ever as young as you are Crawford," was what she said, and then she tch-ed, and she pulled me in close to her chest, and bent forward and kissed me, a sweet one, indulgent as an endlessly patient aunt to a wayward niece. But as her lips held mine, she began to slip her tongue past, just a little, to my lips, then to my teeth, then inside, delving underneath my tongue, pulling back out some to lick at the corner of my mouth, delve back in again. And as her tongue explored me she was wrapping her body tighter around mine, our breathing coming fast and deep; then she was kissing me all over my face, light, dandelion-soft baby kisses.

But suddenly, in the next instant, she was almost lifting me, sliding me backwards, away from the frame of the window, back to the wall, up against it, hard. The strength in her arms stunned me, the power of this maneuver sucked the breath right out of me. I was shaking all over as she kissed me again, our tongues furrowing in and out of each other, turning, roiling, soaking our mouths, our chins. She squeezed me fast up against that wall, pushing her body tight to mine, her hips swaying light, back and forth against mine. We stood there kissing and fondling, each kiss, each caress building higher on the one before it. Then Edie reached down between my legs, began rubbing me there on my jeans. My arms were draped over her shoulders;

I moved my hips to her hand, pinning it between us. She clutched me whole there then, then reached up to my belt, unbuckled it, unbuttoned, unzipped me, her fingers pulling back my pants, one long finger dipping down between the lips, spreading the labia, a honeypool now, apart, silver-wet and starving for that finger. When she touched me there I know I groaned, and she kept stroking me, up and down and slow, over and over and over, and kissing me, touching me swollen-thick, coating her hand with me as she stroked. At the verge she plunged her thumb up into me as far as she could, drew it almost out, drove it back in again. I was practically riding that thumb, skewered on it, the wave rising up deep in me, surging, spuming out, coming on her.

A Little Birdie

I am a little birdie, yes, a mute and humble sparrow, a fiction, a prop, and I am perched like a tiny nodding ghost on Alma Moran's shoulder, and it is almost daybreak.

She is pulling on her warm-up suit, her socks, slipping on her training flats, lacing them. Bobbie Crawford lies in bed still asleep. Alma slips noiselessly out of the bedroom to the kitchen and opens the icebox door, chugs a couple of swallows of orange juice from a quart jar, closes the door gently. Now she is in the living room, firing up the space heater with a kitchen match, settling herself down on the carpet to stretch her long lean legs. She counts, whispering: *One-thousand, two-thousand, three-thousand, four,* clasping the arch of one foot and bending her torso forward. Then she does her other leg, holding the other foot. She repeats the sequence ten times for each leg. She rises, rotates her neck full around several times, and descends again to stretch her quadriceps and the adductors of her inner thighs, lowering her hips first with one knee bent and one leg straight back, then switching, down on each leg twice for eight counts, three sets. She continues her warming and stretching for another five minutes, then eases out the front door, down the stairwell, out into the almost freezing February foredawn. My fellow birds, the real ones, are at their busiest, singing to one another and searching for seed. Alma walks for a few moments, looks at her watch, then breaks into a slow jog. Her running shoes hit the asphalt again and again, *ple-plut, ple-plut, ple-plut,* her breath billows out against the stinging air, the colorless half-light.

I know, I've been here all along and I know, that Bobbie has not told Alma about her now month-long affair with Edie Vogel.

Alma only knows that of late Bobbie's become a little distant, a little distracted, that their lovemaking, though sweet as ever, has tapered off to perhaps once a week, sometimes only once in two or even three. But Alma is philosophical: no one could expect that ardor such as theirs could prevail each and every time, with the same frequency as that of this, their first year together. These things come in waves, she had always heard—in peaks and valleys, in phase and out of phase, as with wave motion. Alma thinks, recalling a physics lecture of last week, *wave velocity = frequency x wavelength.* She fuddles through, trying to translate this statement of physical relationship to an analog for hers and Bobbie's lovemaking, but it's too early, she's not awake enough yet, never mind, *ple-plut, ple-plut, ple-plut.*

By now her breathing has begun to redouble, her legs have built to a long, fast stride for interval pacing, some speedwork to liven up the legs. As we pass along the winding southtown streets only a few signs of life are sparking: we hear a television news show droning from behind the front doors of two or three houses; a tall, blond crew-cut man toting a lunch pail and dressed in a safety-yellow thermal jumpsuit is climbing into his white Ford pickup; a very old, very short Mexican woman in an overcoat and slippers is slinging birdseed out for my compadres, bless her. Alma waves at her, the old lady waves, smiles back. Alma begins to whistle a chipper, perky little tune, the theme from *The Loneliness of the Long-Distance Runner,* a British film Alma ordered, which was shown on campus just the weekend before.

Alma is smiling, sleepy, on top of the world as the sun begins to crest the horizon and she turns back round to run the second half hour home.

And I, I, featherweight literary device, having never breathed (peeped, chirped) a word to Alma, lift up my wee wings and from her shoulder take flight toward an imaginary south.

A Letter, Ten Years Later _____

Dear Bobita,

The manuscript and your letter arrived safe and sound a week ago last Wednesday. Gloria and I both love it, though I'll have lots more to tell you about it when this first-of-the-semester smoke clears. I literally have three hundred and fifty students in my three classes. Who would have thought Latino film would be so hot, huh—though, cleverly, I don't pin it down to just that in the course description.

But I will make a photocopy of your baby for me to keep here and, promise, I'll send you back my scribblings on the other copy. [All, pardon, faithfully reproduced hereafter.] You know, it's better than you think.

Listen. I know you were in between the proverbial rock and hard place with having to let me in on your thing with Edie, even after all these years. But first of all, I want to thank you for not having told me way back then—things were hideous enough (as well you recall). But I'd known about Edie by the beginning of that next year anyway: Merle blurted it out one night when she was mean and low-down blotto, during that whole long time she and Edie were breaking up.

So. *No te preoccupes, chica.* It's all history now. Love to Mir and Sydney (how's the leg?),

Alma

P.S.: Gloria's lost a shitload of weight running with me. There's this babydyke at her office who won't leave her alone, now.

Hearts and Flowers

Reader, I just could not tell Alma. I didn't want to hurt her, I didn't want to lose her, but I sure didn't want to stop "seeing" Edie either (so quaint, that term). So I cheated on Alma. I was a cheater. And of course I felt guilty— the nuns had done their work well, though its applicability to my particular situation would inevitably gall them, and to no small degree.

Although at first there was something both ghastly tense and excruciating- ly pleasurable about having a *sub rosa* affair, after four weeks of duplicity my nerves had been worn gravely thin. I couldn't sleep; I felt as though I were going to blow apart at the seams all the time. Seriously overextended. I resolved to tell Alma I wanted to live alone. Mudhead that I was, I saw this as one means of facilitating the living of a double life. I didn't want to stop seeing Alma, but I wanted more independence, more time to myself. And that's what I told her.

Alma did not take it well. No, she took it agonizingly hard. She wept, and when she did it was as though some perfectly correct assassin had plunged and dragged a rusty sickle straight across and deep, deep through my loath- some, deserving chest. I wept too. *I do love you, baby, I do, I do.* And I real- ly did. I still do.

But I moved out on her, I did move out, some short time later, to a run- down, cabinlike, forties-built efficiency apartment near campus. And Alma helped me move. And we kept seeing one another, Alma and I, sometimes at my little cabin, sometimes at her new deluxe westside apartment. And I also continued to see Edie Vogel.

Then it was a gold-sublime afternoon in late March, and I'd been a cheater for almost two months. I was on my way to Edie's office that day, where we'd deadbolt the door, hook up the answering service, pull out the futon, drink the wine. Passing through downtown I happened to walk by a flower shop and saw in the window a canister full of fresh-cut violets. I bought a bunch for Edie, though they smelled oddly of floor wax . . . . .

I was standing outside Edie's office door, violets clutched to my chest, the picture of poignancy, and I could hear her talking from within. At first I thought the person she was speaking with was in there with her, but as I continued to stand there eavesdropping I recognized the cadence of her voice for a phone conversation. Edie was saying: "Right. No. It's not a matter of that." (A pause.) "No! Listen. . .that's just not fair, I can't. . .well dammit! O.K.!" (A longer pause.) "O.K., O.K. I don't know. Six maybe. What! When? Jesus, Merle!" (Jeeps damn, Merle—) "Why didn't you tell me? When? O.K., all right. Six then. I promise, all right? Sure, sure I do." (This last softly, tenderly.) "I will. Yes, I will." (A very long pause.) "Yes. I love you too, baby. See you at six. All right. Bye. Later."

It was obviously not a felicitous moment at which to have arrived. On the other hand, it was most uncomfy-making to be standing outside her office door with these goddam violets in my hand. I tapped the knocker as gently as I could.

After a few seconds Edie swung the door open. When she saw the violets she almost winced, a split-second wave of annoyance, I thought, but then she smiled at me, a tired resigned kind of smile, and she said, "Hey lover, come on in." I went on in. She closed the door behind me, leaned back up against it. I twirled the stems in my fingers, still holding the flowers close to me. Edie was looking at the violets, at me, and then she went into this dopey, affected embarrassment act: "Aw gee. . .gee whiz, Bobbie." Edie was always doing routines from Albee's *Who's Afraid of Virginia Woolf?* Only years later did I realize she had been doing one at just that moment: "You. . .you shouldna brung me dese, 'cause I. . .wull, 'cause you'se. . .awwwww hell. Gee. Here," she said, taking them from me, "let's dump these in some gin." She strode into her bathroom, emerging after a moment with the violets plocked in a Kerr jar full of water. She came over to me with them and kissed me, a hurried peck. There was whiskey on her breath; she'd been drinking already. Without stopping she crossed the room to her stereo, set the flowers down on top of the cassette housing, and slipped another of her rock-'n-roll tapes into the tape door. It began with a Barbara Lewis song I knew she loved, "Baby I'm Yours." But when she turned back around to me, she seemed a little squeamish. Edie said, looking at me, nodding, gesturing toward the futon-as-couch, "Come on over here sugar. Let's us sit down a minute."

Something, I felt then, was definitely up.

I went over and sat down beside her. She began rubbing the top of my thigh, a preoccupied, negligent sort of rubbing, the way one might absent-mindedly stroke the fur on a dog's spine. She began: "Bobbie. . .," and there followed a ninth-month pregnant pause during which I began to sense the throne-room trapdoor cocked below me, that vertiginous, pit-of-the-stomach prelude to shock, violence, death, or, in this instance, I almost knew already, Good-bye Charlie. And I was scrambling, then, to marshal all my feelings for Edie Vogel, to line 'em up, the little troopers, the rogues. What in hell were they! Where was I with this, with her? Well, there had never been any doubt—aw, some, some, a creditably human amount—but that Edie had merely been playing with me and I with her ("Baby I'm not leavin' Merle for you, you know that"; "I know that, I do know that, Edie—I'm bein' careful"), and that neither one of us loved the other in any profound and as yet enmeshing sense of the world. Not like Alma and me, anyway. She and I were enmeshed in a BIG way—boy howdy, were we ever. So, hell, I volunteered, "You want outta this, right, Edie?" I was so easy, so helpful, so calm.

Edie looked up at me then, with a slow, reptilian lift to her eyelids. "Yeah, yeah babe. That's exactly it. You hit it." She snatched a pack of Marlboros off the coffee table, lit one, shook out the match, then blew out the smoke in an edgy, jetfast stream.

I was wondering what to say to her next, whether to mention Merle, express my understanding, ask a question, the question, *Why,* when I realized I knew why. I knew damn well where I had always had to fit into Edie's life, and I knew too, felt, at that very instant, that this had been a dead end all along, she and I.

"See darlin'," Edie continued, looking at me with appropriately mournful eyes, "I know, I know what the flowers mean." And as she said this she reached out and took me by the hand. But when she did, when her fingers—soft, pitying, alive to me no more—touched mine, a legion of severed, screaming sensibilities recoiled from them, from her and from this unpremeditated, carbonsteel finality. Overload. The blood pounding, igniting in my ears.

I jumped to my feet saying, "I gotta get outta here, I gotta get outta here now."

Edie's face went all peevish again, irritable, impatient. I snatched up my backpack and, like a whirling dust devil, turned and was spun pell-mell out the door, down the stairs and out, out into the assault of sunlight, cars, people in the street.

And an Annotation _____

If she hadn't touched me, I've mused many a time since that afternoon so many years ago now, if despite her pity and indifference Edie had never reached out and actually touched me at that moment, if I had been spared that last tag of tenderness, that acrid keepsake to all our sweet afternoons together, it might all have been quite different: we might've laughed, cried, had a drink, made love one last time.

That's what I've mused anyway. But the craw-stuck fact of it all is that it was Edie who had called the shot, called it quits, and not me. And although what I was feeling as I blundered away from her office that day was not purely reducible to this, the chief component in that seething mix was my young, stupid, and insensate pride, which had for the first time in my life been fundamentally gouged.

When I told Taylor, my confidante and confessor, of Edie's kiss-off, she shrugged and said simply, sadly, "Welcome to the real world, toots."

Under the Carpet

Despite the demise of my affair with Edie Vogel, things were more than ever not right with Alma and me. I still loved her, loved to be with her, do stuff with her, sleep with her beside me, but the passion I had felt for her had become more and more intermittent, less and less spontaneous, and she could tell. She asked me about it, several times; I kept telling her that it was just something I was going through, that everybody went through, that things would be better, different, soon. At that point I still believed it.

So Alma and I went lurching on. One evening late that summer Jackie had a party in the big cheese-bo suburban house she'd rented with a track team bud, Mary Corrigan. Taylor had promised dancing, had cleared out the den and made tapes, and Alma was up for it. Alma was a genius dancer, held her shoulders high, hardly moved her hips at all, the kind of dancer who'll only dance to the song that really moves her, strums that deep chord in her, for her alone, like Zorba the Greek. After about a fifteen-minute go-round, we sat one out. Even with the a/c on it was hotter than beejeezus. I looked up to see Wendy Sherman, a crazy classmate of mine in an acting seminar Jackie and I'd taken the preceding semester, walking over to Alma and me arm in arm with a woman. Wendy introduced her, a Sandy Rosello, and the four of us sat down in the living room. After a while of trying to outshout Jackie's stereo, Wendy asked Alma to dance, and Alma accepted. In accord with some Byronic tradition I seemed to be attached to then (and to which I am now, after so very long, reattached), I had on one of my many black shirts, this one a western job with big red roses embroidered on the shoulders, front and back. I recall that Sandy admired it, at length, and that she also oohed and aahed over a diamond ring I was wearing, another grandmama heirloom. Me, I thought Sandy Rosello was one mightily attractive woman, blonde, big-shouldered, broad-backed—a swimmer, she told me later. I discovered that she'd grown up in Costa Rica, spoke impeccable Spanish. And that was about all the note I took of her, that night. She and Wendy tottered off from the party early.

Several weeks later I ran into Wendy at a coffee shop near campus. She sat down at my table and after some pleasantries and other catchings-up she said, "You remember that woman I was with at Jackie's party? Sandy?"

"Indeed I do," I said.

"Well, she's interested in you," Wendy replied. "Wants to call you, as a matter of fact."

"Oh," said I, "how about that."

"That's all you have to say, 'How about that?' "

"Well, it's very flattering, isn't it," I added.

"Look jerk," Sherman said blandly, "she asked me to get your telephone number next time I saw you."

And I thought, as I more or less automatically began pulling out pen and paper, oh what a tangled web we weave. Doña Juana striking again, the little shit.

Der Blau Engel

With Sandy Rosello I entered my Blue Angel phase. That is, I had realized very early on in our liaison that Sandy and I were about as irremediably mismatched as Emil Jannings and Marlene Dietrich in *Der Blau Engel,* although neither of us was total old man or total harlot but an interactive hodgepodge of each—you know, *reg*ular, like everybody. It was just that I was the one who knew it wasn't going to last. Yet I persisted in seeing her because (becausebecausebecause) Sandy Rosello was a magnificent lover: powerful, solicitous, insatiable, and, utterly unlike either Alma or Edie, very dominating, very male (what did I know) in her lovemaking. All right—she had a dildo. I'd never experienced that before.

I loved the dildo.

I loved the way she used it, moved it in me. When she made love to me with it I felt surrendered up to her, to the taut rhythmic force of her back and arms, to that all but animate latex rod—white and supple, about ten inches long, with a little cross-handle on it like a miniature halberd, a dagger, to keep one's hand from slipping. . . .

The Indictment

I was standing at the bathroom sink when I heard the front screen door banging, someone knocking. "Yo!" I yelled, "there in a minute." Grabbing a hand towel, I trooped out drying my face. Awash in the goldenrod bug light burning on the porch was Jackie.

"Hey Bobs," she drawled, "stand some company?"

"Course Ace, c'mon in." I unhooked the screen latch.

After pulling out a couple of Cokes for the two of us, I lolled into the living room and joined Jackie on the couch. "Goll-lee, I am tired," she said heavily. "Long week, too hot to live." She chatted a little then about her new part-time job in the library stacks: "Scare the crap outta you up there with all those miles and miles of books and not one soul, not another sound, nothing. And the lights up there make everything green, chartreuse. I get so weirded out up there late at night, I hyperventilate sometimes." Then she slapped me chummily on the leg, sighed, and said, "But hey. . .I got something real serious to talk with you 'bout, bubba."

"Oh yeah?"

"Yeah. I was over at Alma's last night. We had a long talk about you."

My heart sank. I still had not told Alma about Sandy Rosello either, though Jackie knew about it. It had been going on for about a week and a half, I was intending to talk with Alma, my conscience was murdering me day and night, and rightly so. I wasn't just going to tell her abut Sandy; I was also going to reframe things with us, with Alma and me, as I saw them. I'd already begun to encourage her to go out with, date other women. I even really hoped she would have an affair of her own. I wanted her to branch out, get free of me and my tyrannous little ways, or rather, the tyranny, as I saw it then, of Alma's own feelings for me, which I hadn't felt worthy of for months. And which I wasn't worthy of now, not one whit.

Taylor sighed again, then said, "Sheeit I don't know where in hell to begin." She looked at me sorrowfully, so sorrowfully it caught my breath up short. "Well," Jackie said, "I called her up and thank God I did." A pause, another sickeningly significant look at me. "She was drunk as a skunk, hon. I'd never known Alma to sound that drunk before, and it scared me. I could tell something was really wrong. I rang off, jumped in the truck, and drove over fast as I could. When I got there I kept ringing the doorbell, but she didn't answer, which really spooked me. The front door was open though, so I just walked on in. She was sitting out on her little balcony watching the sunset, half a bottle of Conmemorativo gone." Aaaah damn. Damn, damn, damn. A dangerous amount of tequila for most human beings, but surely nigh-near deadly for Alma. So it was no surprise when the next thing Jackie said was, "She threw up. For over an hour. I made her a pot of coffee, and she sobered up a little, and we talked." Taylor squirmed a little on the sofa, then cleared her throat. "Look Bobs," she said then, "I'm your friend. I love ya. What you do is your business, but I gotta tell you this anyway: You gotta let that woman go. It's time."

Hearing these words fall from Jackie's lips was like being indicted by a federal grand jury. *Let her go,* let her go. Let. Her. Go. It was right, it sounded right, it kept ringing in my skull like the lucid ping of lead crystal. Alma wasn't going to have a romance with another woman. She wasn't about to do that, as though somehow that would have been the catalyst that held us together, her and me. If she philandered, I could philander, and we'd both live together happily ever after. What a fuckhead I'd been, jiving myself all along, deluding myself about Alma, what she wanted with me, how she was. She loved me, she wanted to be married to me, faithful, constant, for*ever.*

Jackie said then, "You know Bobbie, she's started seeing a therapist." And that was a shot through the heart, boy, when Taylor let that one out. Alma hadn't told me. I'd had no idea at all.

"Because of me?"

"Yup." Jackie sipped her Coke, looked at me levelly. "And there's more."

"Christ, what."

"Yesterday morning before her nine o'clock she'd passed by that little bakery on Lamont and decided to stop in, pick up some *pan dulce,* and surprise you with it before you guys went off to class...."

Oh God. I knew what was coming then. I stood up, a dizzying rush, wrapped my arms around myself, started pacing. "Aw shit."

One of Jackie's eyebrows arched slightly. "You guessed it. The lot out front of your complex was full, so she'd parked the station wagon in the alley across the street."

Yesterday morning Sandy Rosello had been leaving my apartment at about eight o'clock. I had been standing in the door, seeing her off, the morning mists lifting slowly through the early sun. She had started to trudge down the stairs outside and had glanced back up at me in the doorway. Suddenly, she'd grinned, turned back around, and clambered back up the steps to me. She took me in her arms, tipping me back a little, and laid a big soft hot wet tonguey kiss on me.

And Mita had seen it all.

Jackie shifted her weight, crossed her long legs high above her knee. "She told me the whole bit, Bobbie, and she kept crying and crying and crying, and after a while we went on back into her room and lay down on her bed, and I held her while she cried some more, until finally she passed out."

Donde Te Quepa

With Taylor still there sipping at her Coke and staring, unstirring and dispassionate, I immediately picked up the phone to call Alma, to see if she'd talk to me at all. Something, anything. When she answered I said, "Alma, it's Bobbie," identifying myself like the stranger, *persona non grata*, I was, now.
Silence.
"Alma, I—"
"Bobbie, I don't want to talk with you now, not just now. Call me tomorrow." Click.

The following evening Alma opened her door to me and ushered me in with a curving sweep of her left arm like a matador's veronica. Her expression was impassive, glacial. The first thing I felt was the absolute inadmissibility of embracing her in hello, an impermeable barrier between us never there before, not even when we'd quarrelled, which of course we had. She flopped down in her armchair and tucked a leg up underneath herself. I sat down on the sofa opposite. I was looking down at my hands, clasped in front of me, my arms draped over my legs. The quiet in that room felt as infinite and lethal as that the detonation squad leader barely breathes through, dismantling doom. She was just staring at me. I began. "I know that saying I'm sorry isn't enough—"
"Damn straight, you fucker," she said, with bloodcurdling evenness.
"Alma, I hadn't wanted to tell you, I didn't want to hurt you," and I was thinking of Edie Vogel too then, not just Sandy, and feeling queasier by the second with deceit and apprehension. . . .
"How long have you been seeing her," Alma asked, her eyes sheer, expressionless.
"A little less than two weeks."
She closed her eyes for an instant, turned her face from me, looked out the sliding glass door to her balcony. "And were you ever going to tell me," she said then.
"Yes, yeah, a course, I was, I—ever since it started I knew I was going to have to—"

She turned back around to me, sharp. "You knew you were going to *have* to. Gee, that was mighty decent of you. Real honorable. Yessir."

"Look Alma—"

" 'Look' nothing, you little shit!" she shouted at me, whipping the one leg out from under her and flinging herself out of that chair, over to the glass door, her back to me. And she just stood there hugging herself, holding herself, rocking back and forth on her heels. I said nothing. From the arch of her shoulders, now softening, I could see she was trying to calm herself down. She turned back around to me. In a voice low and ragged with pain she said, "You took on the risk of hurting me, whether you told me or not, the first time you went to bed with her." Tears came to her eyes and she turned back again to the window. I was aching with wanting to go to her, hold her, soothe her, but there was nothing I could do. She would have flung me away from her like an insect.

"I know, Alma, I know that."

She wheeled back around to me, fierce, her arms still crossed. "Why! Why couldn't you have talked to me? You should have talked to me!"

"I tried, Mita, I tried. All those times I said you should go out, be with other people—"

"Oh yeah *that,* that talking to me," she said, the contempt in her voice catching her at the back of the throat. "If I started fucking somebody else, everything was going to be just hunky-goddam-dory, huh."

"Mita. Everything you're saying I've told myself before a—"

"Hundred times? A thousand? In less than two weeks? My but you've had a lot on your mind lately, haven't you."

"Alma this isn't going to—"

"Get us anywhere? What, the strain of just talking to me is too much for you now?"

"If you'd just let me get a word in, dammit!" I bellowed.

And so there we stood, all the way across the room from one another, shivering with the hurt, shattered apart and shattered. I sighed. "This isn't talking, Mita, we're not going to—"

"Look. Bobbie," she said, looking down at the floor, "I want this, I need this." Her shoulders slumped, she thrust her hands down deep into her jeans pockets, pivoted back around to the window again. Over her shoulder to me she said, very quietly, almost inaudibly, "Jackie told you I was seeing the therapist, didn't she?"

"Yeah. Yeah, she did."

A long silence then, punctuated from outside by the thick whirr of crickets in the pecan trees, the cooling September nightwind lifting and falling. Alma turned back to me, her face in virtual darkness in the dusk. "Would you see the therapist with me?" she asked simply.

There I was, poised at the brink of the pitch of the moment, holding the power, the capability, to turn our young lives back on a healing track, or, if not to healing, at least to an eventual grasping of the fact, with the therapist's help, that Alma Moran and Bobbie Crawford were just not going to be walking on together through this life.

But you know what? The next thing out of my mouth was, *No, Alma, I don't think I will.* And after all these years I still don't know why I said that then, at that moment. Was my back up? What was it? The easier part of the answer is that I didn't see the problem as our problem, as Alma's and mine—I thought *she* needed to work it out, get herself "free," though I still hoped she'd work all this crap out and stay with me. The harder part, the one that I had to learn to live with, was that I just didn't care for Alma the way I used to, that if she couldn't work it all out on my terms, I could in fact let her go. I would let her go.

"And if we stay together, you'll still keep seeing her?" Alma said sharply.

Yes, I told her quietly, I would.

She stood up quick then, her eyes burning black, red, a world of fury and pain in them, and strode over to her front door, hurling it open, holding it open for me. "You gotta get outta here now," she said low and dark under her breath. I raised myself up slowly from the sofa, racked from my throat down to the hollow of my stomach, and started to pass by her, out the door. But I stopped, began to reach out to her arm, saying, "Mita—"

She slapped my hand away from her savagely, almost hissing at me, "*Mete-telo donde te quepa*," then shoved me roughly out the door and slammed it shut, hard.

As I fumbled, dazed, down the apartment steps, I was trying to piece together what she'd just said to me. I didn't know what the verb *quepa* meant, but I had a pretty good idea. *Mete-telo donde* meant "put it where" and, sure enough, when I got home and looked it up, the radically changing verb *caber* meant "to fit." *Stick it where it fits.*

The Letter

If life did imitate art after all, and if certain dramatic formulae for endings applied unflinchingly in human events, then the finale to the last chapter might logically be either (a) girl loses girl, or (b) girl gets girl back. Neatly. Tidily. But as you, dear reader, are probably all too aware, nothing is ever quite so succinct in love. In Alma's and my case, life's blundering, haphazard nonpatterns beset us for days, weeks, months, and, mercifully, even years after she'd told me to stick it, that evening.

But just after that evening, the next day in fact, I telephoned Alma again, and again she hung up on me. This was followed by several more face-to-face confrontations, just as hurtful and ugly and unresolving, with more tears and more recriminations and more bluster. After maybe ten days Alma eventually settled it in her own mind that my relationship with Sandy Rosello was, by my definition of it anyway, principally sexual. She settled it in her own mind and, with the help of her therapist, Marian T. Love, PhD, no kidding, realized in another few weeks that she, Alma, just could not handle it at all, that she could not keep seeing me as she had, that she needed more and more time to think, to redefine. . .and with these crucial, self-sustaining feelings to guide her, my beloved wrote and sent me this letter:

Dear Bobbie,

There's this scene in some old forties movie, Howard Hawks I think: Thomas Mitchell or Walter Huston lies dying, John Wayne beside him. They're in the jungle, some airstrip there or something. The old man asks Wayne to get the other guys standing over him away from him, just to go on and let him die by himself, because he'd never done it before, dying, and he didn't want the other guys to see him fuck up if he fucked up.

That's kind of how it is with me, babe. I just don't want you to be around while I'm going through this. I need to do my little dying and being born again on my own.

So I'm getting out of here. I'm transferring to the

University of Colorado next spring. Joya's already done some talking with the track people up there and they're interested.

Please give me some time, a couple of weeks at least. I'll call you. *Con ciudado,*

Alma

Ghosts and Monsters _____

Throughout the remainder of that month and on into a gradually cooling October I was a sleepwalker, an eyeless grotto thing dividing my time among sweaty trysts with Sandy, school, and trying to earth over my feelings for Alma, which kept resurfacing with a noxious regularity I sought to subdue with equally regular dosings of tequila sunrises. I didn't think, I wasn't thinking. I was too busy being a monster.

Sandy, meanwhile, was beginning to show definite signs of encroaching domesticity, whipping up huge tasteless vats of mushy lentils (I abhor lentils) and baking innumerable loaves of thoroughly unpalatable dark-flour bread, which were so heavy that had they ever been thrown at a person's head would surely have inflicted concussion. So at intervals almost as regular as the tequila sunrises I would tell Sandy I wasn't the girl for her, that we really weren't made for each other, don't count on me, I'm not a keeper, etc., etc.—disclaimers and provisos to which Sandy would listen, and nod, and agree, and then continue lentilling and baking and calling and coming over, until one night she appeared at my door, quite out of the blue.

Sandy was a great one for "being in touch" with her feelings, which is exactly how she always described it, in that same psychological cant, and so she frequently indulged in bouts of anger, venting them recklessly and quickly on me, on her friends, on anybody in the line of fire. I, on the other hand, have never been inclined that way, particularly with respect to my rages. But that night, after I let Sandy in, she eventually succumbed to a tearful fist-pounding tantrum about where our relationship wasn't headed, about me, my coldness, my unconcern, and, though she didn't say this exactly, my not loving her. She was half on the floor and half on my bed, battering the mattress and crying, when something mean and desperate exploded in me, and I suddenly found myself roaring at her, I can never remember what, but in that roar shoving her away from me just as forcefully as I was able.

And you know? It worked. She heard that roar, the rumbling rancor of the grotto thing, she heard the truth of it where my words and disclaimers had never succeeded. She just stopped calling me after that, she just stopped. And it was only then, after shunting poor Sandy (the more loving than loved) away from poor monstrous me (the more loved than loving) so harshly, that Alma's ghost, for weeks ineffectually banished, began to make unbanishably recurrent visitations in my life.

I'd be walking to a morning class when all of a sudden I'd picture Alma at the movies, sitting as close to the screen as she could, right under it, shovelling popcorn down her throat, enraptured with the rolling film. Or I'd be standing at my kitchen sink filling a glass with water, and I'd remember this afternoon we'd spent in San Antonio at the McNay Art Institute, right after she'd bought the Ford, and we'd gone back out to the car and we'd gotten into the car and we'd just looked at each other and then kissed each other right there in the parking lot and had immediately driven back up the highway home like maniacs to rush up into our apartment, peel off our clothes, and make love. And there was a photograph a friend of ours had taken of Alma, of her standing by a mammoth clump of forsythia, one tendril of the yellow flowering shrub wrapped coyly around her. I couldn't bear to look at the picture. This was a ghost I could banish, so I hid it away from myself.

In the despotic silence of that tiny apartment of mine, in the blunt-instrument middle of the night I'd wake up, turn my body heavily to the amber light emanating from the bathroom, and remember: *She's gone, I'll never have her again, she's gone.* And together with these words, or scores more like them, came the palpable swash of agony in the hollow of my chest.

A Blueprint

Though doubtless you yourself have experienced it before, reader dear, whilst thinking of a recently lost love, allow me to—forgive me but I must—sketch the path of that pain, yours and mine, just a smidge more. It begins of course in the brain, a white sting at first, the mordant bite of anguish. Then it permeates, instantly, the chamber of the heart: a seeping, then a crushing surge full into the great dark cavity, the cold swell of sorrow's blood, the sickened sinking of auricle and ventricle under its leaden flow. To this I'd wake nightly, and it would greet me again upon first waking in the morning. Billie Holiday's "Good Morning, Heartache" ran through my mind far too often. Like a razor to glass the aching etched itself over my soul again and again, and more and more and more.

Quid Pro Quo _____

It was somewhere in early November when I decided I had to see Alma again. I had to have her back, or die of grief. I did not want to die of grief, so somehow I would woo her again, win her back, we'd pick back up where we'd left off. With this "plan" in mind I telephoned her late one afternoon. Her line was busy, stayed busy for a long time. Since the couple of weeks she'd mentioned in her letter and then some had already passed, I sensed it might be all right just to go on over to her apartment, drop in, sit down, have a chat. Pick back up where we'd left off. . . .

I bicycled over in a giddy frame of mind, hopeful, bright, sunny. It was a relatively warm day: bounding up the stairs to the second floor I could see that her front door was open, music, Mozart, wafting out from within.

I was almost in the door frame, about to knock, when I glanced back into the kitchen, and there at a slight angle saw—Jackie's back.

Jackie's back and Alma's arms around it.

Jackie's back and Alma's arms around it and Jackie tipping Alma back in an Errol Flynn embrace. The two of them exchanging an unmistakably big soft hot wet tonguey kiss.

I shrivelled away from the door frame, unseen, like an unguided wraith at the gate of hell.

Mississippi Getaway _____

I will spare you, friend reader, a recounting of the scenes with Alma and Jackie that followed my discovery of their romance; it'd only make me look worse than I do already. But although I was in no position whatsoever to bring up betrayal, I felt trenchantly betrayed. Bereft, disconsolate. However, after a three-day interlude in which I behaved like a compleat madwoman, a very good pass at Ophelia and Hamlet combined, walking about my apartment in a long white shirt, unwashed and bleary, snarling at the moon, drinking right out of the bottle, crying, breaking things, I telephoned Rachel Carmichael. The human psyche being what it is, namely, the most powerfully regenerative entity on earth, I had reached out to the one person who could help me bridge the gap, make it from here to there.

Rachel was an angel to me, gentling, assuaging, and dear. We talked for well over four hours, after which I was greatly settled down and able to sleep a reasonable night's sleep. Two days later she drove up to see me. By that time I had called up my champion Aunt Nora in Biloxi (always my favorite and I hers, dear old spinster Nora, though she never spun, dead now, so brave and alone for decades in that huge two-story place on old Breakers Road) and asked to stay with her for a "couple of weeks." Deft Nora asked no questions but acquiesed immediately, joyfully. Rachel of course tried to talk me out of dropping out of school, but in the end capitulated when I told her I would retake my dropped courses next spring, after my recuperation. She even loaned me a hundred bucks to make the trip, store my gear away. So one gallingly bright afternoon two weeks before Thanksgiving I took a Trailways bus to Biloxi, riding all through the night. After a brief stopover in the sleazy New Orleans bus station (though all bus stations are monuments to Sleaze, full of numbed and beleaguered-looking overnight travellers, their stark grey faces pinched tight with fatigue in the garish neon light), I reboarded the bus and continued on for the last few hour-of-the-wolf hours. A baby's intermittent crying pierced through my half-sleep, the long Spanish moss of Louisiana billowed and snaked in the water-standing cypresses along the highway. The bus finally pulled into the Biloxi station at 5:00 a.m., and there was Nora, smiling sleepily and blindly up into the Mylar-ed windows of the bus. It had been over six years since I'd seen her; she looked as strong and vital as ever, though her face was a little puffier, her paunch a little paunchier, her hair thinner, much more grey. When I was a kid Nora'd always remember my birthday, often sending me slotted birthday cards with dimes in them. She'd written me cheerful letters in a big, bold, beautiful longhand. As I got down out of the bus she hugged me very tenderly, still smelling sweetly of baby powder and lilac.

She pulled back from me, holding me by the shoulders for the once-over. "You look a little peaked, Bobbie honey," was all she said, then hugged me again, even more tenderly.

When we arrived at her house I didn't go to bed right away, nor did Nora overly exhort me to, but instead we sat out on her sleeper porch, rocking in her porch swing while she told me all about her winter garden and her cats: Theodore, Lawford, Patricia, and the white one with the black moustache—Adolph, of course. I drank a glass of icewater, and she drank tea, as we watched the sun come up together.

Most every morning I was in Biloxi, after Nora's gargantuan breakfasts—Kerr jars of figs and pots of hot chocolate and biscuits and cream gravy and wedges of Virginia ham—I'd borrow my aunt's clunky old blue and white Schwinn and ride down to the beach to walk along the brown roiling surf, gather seashells. Every evening I'd watch bad television and eat some specie of ice cream, very often butter pecan, with Nora, who knew full well something had deeply saddened me but never once asked what, nor did I volunteer to tell her. And every night in my great white empty bed, sorrow would break over me like the Gulf tide to the shore that day, only yellower, silent, ineludible.

But as the weeks churned along, my grief began to slowly diminish, hardly noticeable at first, as is often the case: you're in a hell-hole and then what had at first been inconceivable, being out of the hell-hole, becomes conceived in fact. This metamorphosis was aided by my increasing boredom with slow, sultry Biloxi, by loneliness, and by, at last, the gradual, sly return of (oh what the hell else) libidinal appetite. I hardly noticed this at first, either. But one afternoon I was in a bookstore downtown, leafing through some magazines, buying Nora a copy of Shakespeare's sonnets. I remember that I was looking outstandingly butch that day: faded boot-cut Wranglers, denim jacket, Justin boots, Ray-Bans dangling from the top buttonhole of my purple western shirt. Not obvious or anything. The walkway between the newsstand and the next row of paperbacks was quite narrow. Anyone standing widthwise along it, as I was, would obstruct the passage. Skimming through an issue of *The Atlantic*, wholly absorbed, I hadn't noticed that there was someone behind me. All of a sudden a pair of hands pressed me light about the shoulders, one hand pressing very slightly harder than the other on one shoulder in order to get me to move that shoulder lengthwise along the passage, parallel to it, and thereby clear the way. To say this touch was light is to miss the mark widely. There was something virtually personal about it—not Southern, in the way some Southerners have of limp, gratuitous gesturings, but intimate, just a second longer than it should, to its end, have taken. And without even turning around I knew that those hands were woman's hands. But her touch so rattled me that I went all shy, couldn't bring myself to look up at her as she passed by me, and only in my periphery did I see a dark figure, black cloak, black boots, long full black hair. By the time I snapped out of it and managed to look up for her, she was gone, out of the shop, a black form disappearing from my line of vision through the plateglass window, down the street and away.

O whoever you are, Mystery Woman of Biloxi, Mississippi, I thank you, thank you! Your touch reawakened me to life, to possibilities, to hope again! Simply: I began shortly after this incident to masturbate, at night or in the afternoon when Nora would nap. I'd fantasize about the woman in the bookstore, imagine seeing her again there, speaking with her, being asked home to her house for tea and poetry, you name it. Or maybe the fantasy was about some actress or other, Vanessa or Susannah York or Charlotte Rampling. In another week or so I even pilfered a cucumber out of Nora's icebox (of course washing it most fastidiously) and absconded with the thing up to my bed.

["Cheese-ass, Bobbie! You're not going to leave *this* in here are you? I'm worried about your boundaries!"—Alma's pop-psych analyzing at the bottom of this page of her manuscript.]

And, a-hem, yes, after maybe two or three cucumber nights, and one yellow squash, and altogether a sum total of about five weeks in drowsy Biloxi, I began to feel as though it were high time to go on back to Texas, and to the fray, once more. It was the week before Christmas. I placed another call to Rachel and, after taking a teary leave of dear Nora, rode the bus back.

Enter Cory & Gabe _____

After a warming Christmas respite in Notasonia with Rachel and old Cam, when I at last got back to the university I telephoned Wendy Sherman, who informed me that Jackie had pulled up roots and gone off to Boulder with Alma. I had been imagining something of the sort would happen, but there it was, incontrovertible, my very own Sisyphian rock. Sherman also said that the two of them were worried about me, that I should call Jackie's mother in Dallas for their new phone number and then call them. Call them. The couple, the pair, *la pareja*. During the bleak pause over the telephone line following this bit of news, Sherman cleared her throat, said, a little brusquely, embarrassed I guess, "Say, whaddaya doin' Friday? I got some friends I want you to meet." Wendy Sherman, Pro Liaison to Lesbians. I said, "Nothing, I'd love to meet them." I could surely keep pushing this mother-of-God rock back up the hill and just meet people, ferchrissakes. The Telephone Call to Colorado could wait, a bit.

Friday came, and for the first time ever I went to the home of Cory McIver and Gabe Simmons.

McIver, Jennifer Cora. Cory. Whose usual full name spoken very quick sounds like either a Southern Hemisphere spice root (*corimak-eye-ver*) or a South Seas atoll Marlon Brando hasn't bought yet (*cori-makai-ver*). And who, when Sherman introduced us that Friday evening, was just turning thirty and sitting on a huge enveloping forest green velvet couch. It may in fact have been for her birthday, or for Halloween, but somebody somewhere was having a party that evening, and Cory's face was masked with a pale but lustrously metallic ice-green grease paint, an inadvertent complement to the color of her couch.

She was sitting there, holding court among the half-dozen or so women present, some all doodied up, as Cory is wont to say, just like her, her own legs crossed high, ankle at the knee, one unbelievably long arm draped langorously along the back of the sofa. Her hair, she informed the group, was slicked back with Vaseline, which I later learned took her four days to get out altogether. The other women there, some plain vanilla still and some with greasepaint and glitter preapplied, with sherbet-colored scarves and plastic baubles around their necks and on their wrists, were listening to Cory and sipping Lite beer. I felt instantly at home and at ease.

McIver was expounding on the subject of balance in one's life: "That's all it is, is balance. It's good and bad, we're strong and weak, ying and yan."

"That's *yin* and *yang,* Cory," said one of the women, a Nancy somebody.

"Whatever." She went on unfazed. "You never get it to match perfectly, to have everything even out and all, but you keep trying, that's our job, you keep trying to hit that center point in yourself, equilibrium."

One of the women patted herself awake on the cheek and said droopily, stoned hippylike, "Hey man, you got any Equilibrium."

Just then I happened to look out the front window. It was one of those sweet oddities of Texas winters, a beautiful, warm, sunny day. Two little girls were riding by on a bicycle. One of them, about eight, was pumping the other one, maybe five and giggling like mad, on the handlebars. They both had on lavender polo shirts and cutoffs.

There will always be magic in this world, and there's just nothing you can do about it.

From somewhere far back in the house a big husky voice boomed, "Next!" and yet another grease-painted woman emerged from that direction. A small, thin blonde with bush baby eyes sprang to her feet, but before she could make it out of the room there appeared in the doorway from whence the big voice had come a great tall gorgeous freckled redhead grinning ear to ear.

"Hi!" she beamed, striding right over to me with her hand held out, "I'm Gabe."

"Bobbie Crawford," I said, taking her hand, very warm, dry, cozy in there, in its confines. Hers were eyes that gave you the feeling they could twinkle in the dark, hers the voice I'd heard, honey-strung, deep as the Grand Canyon.

Gabrielle Simmons. Gabe. Eventually I would learn that Gabe was the only girl-child born to her east Texas Baptist family, the baby. Her two older brothers had been named Michael and Raphael, so her parents stuck with the archangel trilogy and feminized Gabriel for their winking, bouncing baby girl. Gabriel—the saint of incarnation, the messenger, the seer. The source, the light, the voice. Just then she turned to the woman who'd stood up. "Hold up there, Kath. We got a new one here." Then back to me still grinning and then butting my shoulder with the pudgy ends of her fingertips, the handshape of a karate blow held gently back, "So how 'bout it, Bobbie Mae? You goin' to the party? Want your face done?"

I looked at Sherman. "I'm easy," she said, shrugging.

So I went on back to the bathroom with Gabe and surrendered myself up to this deliciously intimate transformation. About halfway through the job (I was peach and white and smoke green, Modigliani colors), Gabe went to the kitchen and got us two cold ones, and we laughed and chatted and found things out about each other, most of which I can't remember just now. Except that she was a painter, an artist; except that I know I felt wonderfully, miraculously alive and happy in that bathroom with that woman. Happier than I'd been in months.

This scene, the household full of women, the Lite beer, the grease paint, the crazy party we went to later—all of it would be reenacted scores of times in scores of different guises over the years I was to know Cory and Gabe.

And Life Just Goes On, Doesn't It _____

Well I went ahead and called Jackie's mom and then placed that call on through to Boulder.

There's really no need to linger over it now—three young people making a reasonably good show of civilized behavior via a telephonic device, my archipelago of tears after ringing off from them, certainly least of all my Bogey-Duke response to the whole wretched incident. This I made later in the evening with a commiserative Cory in the old darkwood-panelled Alamo Hotel bar downtown, the two of us sitting sipping very expensive Scotch steadily for several hours, me plocking in countless quarters in the bubble-lit Wurlitzer to hear Peggy Lee sing "Is That All There Is" over and over again. So. Yà basta.

Actually and mercifully the months that followed were not one great long premenstrual syndrome, but were instead rife with ennobling schoolwork, by-and-large clean living, and, most vital of all, gonza fun and pranks with Cory and Gabe and the girls.

Although I was working very hard at my art that semester, I could not finish most canvases I began, and new ideas in them, beginning well, ended badly. There was a series of women's portraits, not modelled for, with clever color contrasts, elaborately Matisse-like in design. Endless hours were spent on their settings, the print of the curtains, the carving of the chairs, on brimming vases of flowers beside them. But I couldn't complete the women's faces; at least a dozen of these labyrinthine attempts were as yet eyeless. After having looked at Gabe's work, impressive and impressively large canvases with great slashes of color, fat women with nice fat faces, a sparse Japanese quality to them, I'd asked her over one afternoon at teatime for a look at my own stuff.

The Gabe arrived late, smiling and breathless, fitted out in a black goose-down vest, Levis, and a big pair of buff suede roughouts, the late Texas winter having abruptly reverted to its dry, brute-cold self. Over a stout pot of Prince of Wales tea and several so-so scones I'd hazarded for the occasion, Gabe, chomping and hmmming, reviewed my paintings. I started to explain that they didn't have faces because I hadn't talked anyone into sitting for them yet when she interrupted me: "Naw. . .that's not it." Kind and placid, Gabe looked at me. I think she was trying not to smile. "Maybe you're just not ready for portraiture yet. Maybe it's not time for this." After slapping some lemon curd on another scone she snuggled into my Boston rocker and said simply, and it was blazingly simple and direct and obvious, and still she wasn't smiling, bless her, "Why don't you paint something else, Bobbie? Something you can finish." She glanced around her. "Just this room, maybe. Something close to you."

Something close to me. What? For the remainder of that semester I tried to find out what that could be. I painted things that moved and things that didn't—waterscapes, still lifes, flowers, my indomitable cat Ramón. But none of it clicked, none of it felt at all right. Over the drag-ass summer months before my easel, I began to feel more and more like a dabbling chimpanzee. Then, the following autumn, two momentous events took place: I took my very first computer science course and, in that class, I met Lover X. . . .

Enter X

Since, doubtless, prurient interest would override an explication of my burgeoning love affair with the computer, I will for the nonce stick to X's story. X was pre-med. Her attendance in Computer Science 101 was, like mine, part of a degree program requirement. At the beginning of the semester our teaching assistant had divvied up the class into study groups, and X was put into mine. After one especially long and frustrating evening at the lab, during which not one of the ten of us sitting before our CRT screens and gnashing our teeth was able to solve the exercise assignment, X asked me if I wanted to go out for coffee afterwards, "to think about this damn assignment some more," she said.

X was a little woman. I am very fond of little women. A British friend I'd met through Cory and Gabe, Ramona Kemp, my kitty's godmother, once theorized that all lesbians want to make love to a woman littler than they. While I conceded this, I also suggested it was probably equally true that all lesbians want to make love to an Amazon, as well as to someone exactly their own height. Nonetheless, X sure was itty-bitty, with a face like a freshly minted penny. She was energetic, optimistic, and infectiously joyful. And there was also, I noticed for the first time that evening, that giveaway gait of hers.

What can I tell you about X. Mostly, as I was to find out quite quickly, X was the marrying kind. Despite my knowing this as soon as I did, and despite my continuing aversion to a long-term coupling, I persisted in seeing X for over seven months. Why? Because X could make me laugh. Like nobody's business. She could jolt me smack out of the dreariest blues, to which I seemed more and more prone, in nearly always record time. She would tickle me or tell me jokes or sing lighthearted ditties most unobtrusively—"I'm Just Wild About Harry," "The Sunny Side of the Street," "Baby Face," or, best of all, Sousa marches, holding her nose. That was surefire for months, that one. X was a great silly girl, she was, a great kid. What else. Oh well—there was that peach thing too.

The Peach Thing _____

X's mightily flamboyant Fort Worth mama, Berte, an interior designer of inestimable *joie de vivre*—like her daughter—if not professional artistry, had returned after the new year from Italy, where she'd been on a buying junket. She'd also made a side trip to Sicily and there had purchased some unbelievably large fuzzy peaches, then green and big as softballs, and had just as unbelievably smuggled three dozen of them back in her new orchideous Gucci luggage. "Softer'n a baby's butt," Berte avowed, "and then that damn George (a young gay co-worker) stuck a goddam bumper sticker on one of 'em when I wudden lookin'. It said: I'VE BEEN TO GRACELAND: HAVE YOU? Took 'im an hour 'n a half to get it and the damn glue off, the jackass."

X returned to school that January with about half a dozen of these luscious wonders of the Latin world. Oh God were they ever sweet and fine! One night in bed X and I were devouring them like Tom Jones and Jenny. X had cut one in half and was snarfing the one half and holding the other, when all of a sudden she got this demonic look on her face and, chortling like a loon, took the uneaten half and smashed it and rubbed it all over my chest.

I was laughing but I said, "Aw, _____, I'm all sticky!" X didn't care. She just laughed at me quietly (she was always laughing at me), and then she leaned down to my chest and started lapping all the peach pulp up, beginning high at my throat, then down to my breastplate, and down between my breasts, over my stomach, slowly, myself barely breathing, she spreading the stickiness around with her tongue, continuing down to my thighs, down, and up again, and in, spreading that other stickiness there apart with her own sticky little fingers, nuzzling right up the middle of me, over and over, squaring on that sweet sycamine knot, that rubyflesh hub of the pointed arch, rosesheathed gate to heaven here, nubbing it hard and harder still, the wondrous heat shooting down my legs to the blessed soles of my feet. With my hands I was barely cradling her head between my thighs as we breathed together, currents and waves and all the colors of the spectrum flying and falling everywhere all over my body, licked wild alive and exasperated, my cries, hers, lost in this cliff-edge storm, finally bursting lavish down that milksweet efflorescence, flowing out and down to that softening sea, now becalmed as only this sea is—all tensions, hurts warmed away, soothed clear, utterly dispelled.

After a while I pulled her head, neck, shoulders up to me, laid her on my stomach like a newborn, where she, eyes closed, hair matted from peach and sweat and me, moved not at all, only breathed, breathing gently in the gentled sea with me. . . .

Exit X

Golden-haired Princess Ramona de Kemp, British philosopher-poet and Renaissance Woman, has also proffered this little gem, whilst inhaling deep from one of her Capstans cigarettes, always held in the continental manner, backwards and under, nestled between thumb and forefinger/middle: "The real reasons lovers break up very often lie in the tiniest bits of day-to-day minutiae: she won't put the cap back on the toothpaste tube, or she won't do the saucepans when she does the washing up, or she drops her undies on the bathroom floor and just leaves them there. Or perhaps it's the way she chews her food will end up driving you balmy. Little fings, tiny fings like that." And you know? I think old Ramona's on to something there.

I'm still never really sure what it was about X that first started driving me balmy, but something sure as shit did. Maybe it was that she was so consistently cheerful—though I don't mean to suggest she was pathologically chipper or anything. No, certainly X could and did fall apart. But X was a physiological "lark," that much was certain. Her metabolic rate allowed her to wake up every damned morning alert and sunny as all get-out, kiss me, hug me, then clamber out of bed and have made coffee and breakfast and read the paper clean through before I, slug, could even begin to roll out of our heaven-warm bed and hurl my comatose body in the shower, whereto she'd bring coffee for me and invariably wish me a far too hearty (and loud) "Hi!" first fucking thing. Decibel level has always counted for a lot with me.

Too, she still had a great many polyester clothes. And she still wore them.

Of music she liked Yes, and Bread, and America, none of whom I could ever distinguish from one another, and, anyway, to me they all paled pitifully in comparison with my own rock gods, the Stones. Decibel level has always counted a lot with me.

Last in the line of X's incompatibilities was her ancient dog Harvey. A very, very, very large white dog with chronic mange and two teeth, who always smelled like death, whom X kept inside year-round, except when she went out and then she'd take ol' Harve along with her, everywhere. And X had a subcompact, a wee faded-green fastback coupe, a Datsun. Had I loved her in some other, larger way (because I did love her), none of these things—

larkitude, polyester, music, nor Harvey himself—would have mattered in the least. No. It was me, it was her and me and who we were together that didn't work—wouldn't, couldn't, didn't. ["Yeah and she really wasn't the girl for you, Bibbie"—Moran's relentless scrawl in the margin.] The clock was winding down on X and me, and once again I, the more loved than loving, heard its deadly ticking first. By March of '75, after having planted scores of winter caveats in X's mind about my inappropriateness as her lover, I harvested my own mean little crop and succeeded in pushing her out of my life.

From mutual friends I later learned that following her graduation at the end of the semester, X had been accepted at medical school and had left to study in Guadalajara.

I never saw her again.

And a Little Crystal Gazing

For those among you, dear readers, who may be wondering when I'm going to get my comeuppance for all this bad karma and find myself the more loving than loved, stick around. It's coming. With a vengeance. As always it must. ["Too Catholic," scribbles Alma. "Change that."] All right: as it usually does. ["Better."]

Full Circle, Full Stop _____

Over the telephone I listened to Cory cackling, "So now you've broken up with her and you're coming back to us again, huh." Over the past seven months I'd been most neglectful of my friends, and Cory, *l'enfant terrible,* is never one to pass up a chance to razz one. She and Gabe and I were that morning making plans for the maiden voyage of their new dinghy, a twenty-foot, blue and yellow job Cory had ordered from France. "And I got a little surprise for ya over here, Bobs, so doubletime it, pronto," she added, old mysteriosa, and hung up.

Gabe answered the front door. "We're out back," she said, grinning in that way that could only mean my goat was about to be got.

"What's up, Gabe, what's goin' on." I jabbed her in the ribs.

To which she replied, "You'll see. Come on out back." And she winked.

I swung through the back porch door and there in the yard, standing tall next to the barbecue pit with tall McIver, was Jackie.

Walking over to them I felt like a six-year old being prodded out onto the stage for the Turkey Day pageant in a papier-mâché pumpkin suit, embarrassed, silly, pretty near pukey with dread. And Taylor looked like the overgrown kid in the corn costume being shuttled out from the other wing. Behind our Ray-Bans she and I were smiling sheepishly at each other. McIver took Gabe by the arm: "Let's us let these chirren have a word alone, Mother," she intoned, and slipped her arm up around Gabe's shoulder as the two of them strolled back up into the house.

When they were quite out of hearing range Jackie cleared her throat. She said, "I wanna hug you real bad, but I figger it might be a little easier for you to reciprocate on that if you knew something first."

"What, Jack."

"Alma left me, Bobbie."

Full Tilt Boogie

Jackie laughed, and then she started in crying.

"Aw, Jack," I whispered, and moved in to her and just held her while she held on to me.

"Hell, you are the *last* person whose shoulder I should be cryin' on."

I pulled her back from me, looking at her and holding her still, reached down for a tissue in my rugger-shorts pocket for her. "Naw. I'm the one." I laughed, chucked her under her chin. "Who else but me knows ex*act*ly how you're feeling, kiddo."

Then she laughed again, a good one this time, and hugged into me again and held there. At which point Cory reemerged from the kitchen and announced in her most imperious, step-it-up voice: "O.K. That's enough reunion now. Let's get this goddam show on the road."

"Fuck off Cory," we both said together, then me first, quick, "Jinx, you-owe-me-a-Coke," which got her laughing one more time. I nugeyed her light on the forearm. "See? You can still laugh. You, too, can join the March of, uh, Yucks, and win the fight against this crippling disease, the heartbreak of Heartbreak."

She bent her head over my shoulder. "You asshole, I love you."

"So what's not to love."

Commander Cory snapping orders: "Come ON! let us GO! Bobbie, get that rope off the garage wall, will ya?"

In another fifteen minutes we were out on the road trailing up to the lake. Cory had wanted to leave at one o'clock, Gabe at eleven; it was noon, straight up.

On the drive out Gabe was on a roll, wiggling around in her seat to me and Jackie in the back of their old VW van, laughing.

"Ooo, guess what?" she cooed. "Cory 'n me had a Tarot reading last week, and you know what? We both got the high priestess card."

"Pretty groovy, Gabe," Jackie drawled, fondling an ear. Me, I don't buy into that jazz much, myself.

"And we ran into that crazy Gin Black on our way out. You guys know her? You know that woman?"

We both shook our heads no. "Well, now she's a weird story, is that one," Gabe said. "Really. Just a little off kilter, she is."

"Gabe thinks she has this thing for her," Cory piped in.

"Well, she does, Cor, she does!" and she turned back around to us again. "I think she thought I was her mother or something, followed me around for a long time, just like a baby duck. I kinda felt sorry for her, you know? She's really a smart woman; she's just nuts, that's all."

"No shit she's nuts!" Cory squawked. "Gabe left her alone in our house one day, and when we got back she'd taken a Magic Marker to our den wall and scribbled all this shit all over it. I like ta died, 'fore I bit her head off."

"Oh, and she sure did, I can tell you," Gabe added. "Well anyway, I thought she was lonely and all so I introduced her to a couple of my friends, and she slept around with some of 'em, and then I heard a whole lot later she'd left town, went off and was living in Tunisia or something."

"Yeah and when we get back tonight we'll probably find twelve square feet of Gin Black graffiti in our bathroom. Woman's a menace. She oughta get help, but what can you do?"

"Oh, she's seen doctors, she's taken medicine, all of that." Gabe swivelled around to Jack and me again, saying sorrowfully, "Really, what can you do?"

"I don't know, Gabe. I don't know what you can do. Does she have any relatives here or anything?" I asked.

Gabe said, "Yeah, a sister. I called her sister once and told her she should think about calling their parents in Dayton. Gin had really been on a tear around then, crying all the time and everything, but it got back to Gin and boy! was she ever ugly about it. I dunno, I just don't know what you can do."

"Well, you can deadbolt your goddam doors, that's about it," Cory snapped.

"Oh Cory shutup," Gabe laughed, and hit her on the arm.

About thirty minutes later Cory was inching the van down a steep slope to the water's edge. As we neared the stretch of limestone and sand lining the lake Jackie was fumbling down within the bowels of her backpack. "I got a little sussie for you women down here," she proclaimed, and hoisted up a bottle of Jack Daniel's from the pack, "ta-da!"

"Uh-oh," all three of said in unison.

"Jinx, you-owe-me-three-Cokes."

After we'd pulled over and stopped, and while Cory and Gabe sweated out pumping up the dinghy, Jackie and I took a little stroll.

"So, Jackie," I began carefully. "If you don't want to talk about it now, that's O.K., but I sure would like to know what in hell happened."

She nudged her Ray-Bans farther up her nose, looked down at the sand as we walked. "I can talk about it. . . maybe not much, not too much, today." She looked at me. "Well, she met another woman, a course. Lawyer, Legal

Aid. Woman named Gloria Velasquez. Beautiful woman, really. Almost as pretty as Alma.

"And, well, Alma started spending more time at the library at night and we stopped making love and she kept looking prettier and prettier and then I got The Announcement."

I petted her back, put my arm around her shoulder as we continued to amble on a little further. We came up to a freestanding clump of mustain grape, a small arbor about fifteen feet in diameter. Walking around it we found an opening in the vines and we went inside, ducking our heads. The grapevines had grown up upon a now-dead pecan tree in the center of the arbor, a shady bower shrouded on all sides. Someone, the City probably, had sunk a tarred-over log bench in the middle of the arbor, spanning it.

It was wonderfully dark inside there, and almost instantly I remembered the briar canopy of my childhood and little Monica. Where was she now, I thought. Was she still alive in this world? Was she a grown-up lezbeen now, like me?

"Hey!" Taylor grinned, shattering my reverie. "Let's us make this our bar 'fore we set out, whaddaya think?"

"Well," I pondered, sticking my head outside and squinting over at Cory and Gabe, huffing and pumping away in their swimsuits, "they're gonna be at that a while, at least. Why not? Why don't you go get the ice and some of those tin cups Gabe's got in the back. I wanna sit here a minute," and contemplate little Monica some, and Alma, *mi alma*, too. . . .

Four full tin cups in hand, Jackie and I returned to Cory and Gabe at the dinghy to spell them pumping. Gabe stood back, untied the purple bandana from her neck to wipe the sweat from her face. Suddenly she went all still, reached out to my arm working the pump, and whispered, "Lissen! Stop a second, ho." A birdsong off somewhere in the cattails. "Didja hear that?" she said. We heard, we said, nodded, yupped. Gabe, doing the bird, chimed, "Pu-ching! birdie/birdie/birdie! A cardinal."

"Yeah, I thought that sounded familiar," Jackie murmured.

"Ooo, and that!" Gabe said then. We all listened up for this one, standing stock-still, the wind and the waves' song all around us. "That's an indigo bunting, hear it? It goes, 'Fire-fire, where-where, here-here.' "

"Hear, hear," Cory rejoined, extending her cup for a toast.

Jackie clacked her cup to Cory's. "Here's how," she said, and downed a big gulp.

Gabe started singing a song with a calypso beat, "Fire down Below" ("There's a fire down below/ down below in my heart"), then "Jamaica Farewell." All of us joined in, Cory working the pump again now.

"This's for shit!" she exploded, looking accusingly at Gabe. "What in hell's wrong with this damn thing!"

Well, forty-five minutes, half a bottle of bourbon, and several workshifts later, The Gabe finally figured out there were "hidden" valves to the dinghy nobody'd known about, and so none of our pumping had done jackshit. "Though it sure looked like it was getting bigger," Gabe mused. We were all having us one helluva time anyway, and once the valves got opened the dinghy blew up like six-guns. Within ten minutes we were out on the water, rowing to an island in the center of the lake. Once there, we promptly peeled off our suits, set our towels down, and prepared to sunbathe. Gabe was passing a bottle of sunscreen all around. "Be sure and put some on your boobies," she advised. "And don't you lie there with your legs open either."

Cory drawled, "The Sage of Crockett Island speaks."

"Is that the name of this island, Cory?" I asked.

"Naw, I just made that up."

"Let's name it!" cried Gabe. "Let's give it our own name."

"Isla Mujeres," suggested Jackie.

"Been done, Jack," Cory sniffed.

"I know that," Jackie sniffed back.

I proffered an even lamer one. "How 'bout Treasure Island."

"Well, we are all little treasures, aren't we?" Gabe smiled patronizingly, patting Cory's leg.

"Aren't we just," Cory droned. Then, craning her neck up from her towel and snapping her gimmie cap back, "Hey, we haven't even named the damn boat yet."

"How about 'The Easy Virtue'—the name Hepburn comes up with for that yacht model Cary Grant gives her in *The Philadelphia Story*?" This one was my idea.

"Well, there's a lotta that goin' around," laughed Cory, "but naw, that ain't it."

Finally we settled on The Mary (Cory's mother's name) Daniels (for obvious reasons) Kingston (from the calypso songs we'd been singing all afternoon). Cory stood up, walked over to the dinghy, and poured a little bourbon over the prow of the raft. "I dub thee the Queen Mary," she said, high-pitched and Cockneyfied.

Just then a speedboat rounded the far corner of the island. It was full of young males who, upon sighting us, started whooping and hollering and sitting on the boat horn. Cory just stood there in the altogether, unmoving and cool.

"Fuckheads," she muttered.

The men laughed and waved, sped on. "I hate those goddam boats," Gabe said.

Jackie held up the bottle of bourbon, by now a dead soldier. The sun was sinking fast and the wind was rising; it was getting cooler.

"Cory, we better get back before it gets too dark," Gabe warned.

"While we can still move, you mean," Jackie wheezed, standing up and tottering a little. So we gathered up our gear and piled back into the Mary Daniels Kingston for the jaunt back over the water. Gabe sat her still-naked self on the prow of the dinghy.

And me, I was just out-and-out loaded and leaning against Jack's leg as she and Cory kept sinking their oars into the choppy water. We were all laughing and singing more songs and badly sunburned anyway, though we didn't feel it yet, and I remember, gazing at the three of them, all tawny and gold in that rich dusk light, feeling more loved *and* loving than I'd ever felt before. And quite possibly, since.

Haloo/haloo/sin-a/sin-a/shunshunshun _____

By that summer, the summer of '75, I had made the politic switch from fine arts to computer science, averaging twenty course hours a semester and spending overlong evenings alone at Dobie Hall, where one of the many computer laboratories on campus was located. Nestled in a drafting chair before a CRT screen I was learning the intricacies of what was to eventually become my trade, programming. And that final year of studies seemed to just whiz by, from bleary September nights at the lab, click, to exhausted May mornings after term paper nights, click-click. The best thing about the year was what I was beginning to feel the world of work would be like, what goodness-of-fit work, and hard work at that, really was, the rigor of it, the sweet satisfaction of solving solvable problems, of deducing logical steps to a logical end. So that, what I could not close, resolve, or equate in love was for the time being compensated for, somewhat, by my devotion to computerdom, to this rational ordering of points on a plane, that grid of horizontal and vertical lines, to the finite series of x and y axes and their pleasingly apprehensible correlations.

The other great good of that year was my friendship with Ramona, my mainstay, my solace. Like myself Ramona was without a lover, so we were superb for each other, Ramona and I, that spring especially. I would meet her just off campus about two o'clock every day at the corner where she parked her cart and sold sandwiches, and the two of us would trek back over to the west campus mall. She would go into her lesbian-spotting routine, scoping them out, of course, by the way they walked. "There's one!" she'd screech. And you know, by 1976 there really did seem to be a great many more women in town with those telltale gaits for Ramona to screech at—I mean, big ol' Texas girls, Amazons from all over the state.

Despite this heartening trend, I felt jaded and closed off. Shoring up. I wasn't about to put my head on the block again, boy, much less somebody else's. She, whoever the hell She was, would have to waltz into my world like a surprise party, or not at all. I was burned, and burned out. Sure. Yeah. Well I was and I wasn't. Down, but not out. So, how untenable—to believe in love, to want it, but to forswear it. I was certainly not altogether reconciled to the

Beguine life, but I would not get off my butt. Something was bound to happen, something had to break down. Perhaps this dissonance reflected in my expression as I, longing but inert, observed the consecutive advent of japonica, redbud, and pear, the involuntary earth unfolding itself to the light and the rain, to iris, wisteria, primrose, and at last the older pecans, cautious veterans of late-spring freezes, leafing out. From my windows I would watch the magnolias, those creamy, seductive blooms, brown on the tree, fire ants and aphids settling within the hollow of their petals. Then, one evening, after Ramona and I had gotten our little hands on some mind-boggling greengold Afghan hash, I once again found myself mooning at those magnolias in the twilight, when this stoned vision of one great lone magnolia the size of Jupiter hit me. At first it seemed entrapped, unreachable, behind and in a phantom linear grid encompassing the entire universe, inset within legions of these powder blue north-south/east-west lines. But as the image of this astronomically vast flower loomed in my mind, I began to sense, in stronger and stronger waves of sensing, its absolute imperviousness to those lines and to everything else; that it was a dimension unto itself, eternally insoluble, omnipotent, massively alive....

Coryspeak _____

With her hand on my shoulder, her eyebrows rising and falling above those keen grey eyes for the appropriate emphases: "Bobbie Jean" (Cory's the only one who can call me that and get away with it), "when you stop looking for Her, that's when you'll find Her."

A Transition

Then it was June and I was a college graduate. I could not find work in town, and since I did not want to relocate or starve, I took on some pinch-hit work through Cory and Gabe's business contacts and became, that summer, a painter of houses.

A Single Sentence _____

Through June and July there passed a difficult time—of working broiling long days at devastatingly hard labor, of coming home alone and exhausted at night and trying to feel content and failing, of scorching days and sweaty nights laced over tight in frustration like a fugue.

And a Word from Chlöe

A three-year-old friend of mine, a honey-blonde named Chlöe, once told me that she felt *fwustwated*. Honest. No doubt her mother had used the word with pique, branding it permanently in the child's repertoire. Although it was fabulous to hear this word coming out of a baby, it also brought the larger reality of the thing home close: that from infancy on we feel thwarted and foiled in this oh-so intractable world. We begin early the lifelong battle for what we do not have, and cannot get.

The First Meeting

Under the anvil heat of that long grueling summer, the ambivalence that had marked my celibate, scholarly springtime was reforged and hammered out to another shape, and frustration is probably as good a word as any to describe what it had become. As Cory says, "Young blood do run hot." And besides that kind of frustration, painting houses was not exactly what I'd had in mind all those years in college. When I could, I continued to look for computer work, but for the time being none of my interviews were panning out.

How mysterious it is that when you reach the end of your rope, there is invariably another rope. I was about as bottomed out that summer as I'd been in Biloxi, when much the same kind of magic worked for me as it had there. Suddenly, soon, things would be altogether different, and by September I would be hard put to it to remember just how I'd felt all that long last school year or that summer, or even recall what I'd imagined the change in my life might be like before it actually came about.

And so it was on one blazing late July afternoon that I stood on my stepladder scraping the paint off a house I'd contracted for. Now scraping paint is ordinarily the worst part of this sort of work, but in the summer in Texas it's a hell-chore. My work clothes were soaked through with sweat; I was covered with paint flakes. Then, to my left, a window sash screaked up and out leaned a woman looking over and up at me into the sun, squinting, shielding her eyes.

She said, "Hi, how ya doin'."

Not a question I could give an honest answer to and be pleasant about it, so I just said, "Fine, fine."

"I'm the new owner," she said then. "Wanna take a break for a Coke in here?"

"Oh, hey. That'd be real nice, thanks." I climbed down slowly from the ladder, pocketing the scraper and wiping my forehead with the front of my T-shirt.

She opened the front screen door for me and asked if I wanted to wash up. The water had been on since Wednesday. Following her I clattered through the big empty house in my workboots. In the old hexagon-tiled blue and white bathroom a sweet cool chill settled over me as I splashed water on my face, head, and neck, drying myself with a bandana from my back pocket. Out in the kitchen again with her, she handed me a huge tumbler of Coke with ice, extending her other hand for a shake.

"Dana Pfeiffer," she said.

My First Impression of Her ⎯⎯⎯⎯⎯⎯⎯⎯⎯⎯⎯

Plain, mousey-housewifey, unsexed. She had been wearing an overly crisp-looking cotton shirtwaist and heels, her long wavy red hair pulled back in a bun. I did not then know that this was one of her many alternate disguises for the stonier members of the patriarchy with whom she had to deal regularly.

I really don't remember much else of that first meeting now, and she barely remembered it at all. We probably talked about the screen frames, as she later had me remix the green for them. Nothing, really. No register, business as usual. After a while she gathered up a bunch of papers and her keys and left.

The Second Meeting

Her check for my work on that house had been mailed promptly, but I was not to see her again for another month. That was when she called up my answering service, early September, leaving word that she had another job for me painting a rent house of hers on the southside. Would I meet her there for the estimate?

I was waiting for her on the front porch of this place when she drove up in a brown Audi with the windows rolled up—air-conditioned. Gathering up a briefcase from the back seat, Dana Pfeiffer emerged from her car. This time she was wearing a suit, this magnificently cut cream-colored linen suit with trousers, heart-clutchingly sharp. Suddenly, in that suit, she was a fascinating woman. And her hair, an incomparable auburn abundance, was down, now. I watched her stroll up the concrete walkway to the porch, smiling amiably as she went. And for the first time I did a take on her gait, a sauntering kind of half-swagger, her tan boots' metal taps clicking slowly on the concrete. How had I not noticed that walk before?

Pushing her sunglasses back to the top of her head (cheese, what a good-looking woman she was, *que zorra!*), she said quietly, "Christ, how can you work out in this heat?" I had been at my labors elsewhere that afternoon, so I looked like shit again, paint flecks all over my hair, covered in oil-sweat.

"Gatorade. And going to bed at eight o'clock."

She laughed, stuffed the briefcase under one arm, jangled her key ring around to the right one, and opened up the house. Slinging her jacket on the back of a solitary cane chair in the empty living room, she fished in the jacket's inner chest pocket, pulled out a silky handkerchief the same color as the suit, and carefully dabbed at her forehead and upper lip. "Go on ahead and take a look around, Bobbie," she said.

I made a quick tour of the rooms; they were in pretty good shape. In less than ten minutes' time I returned to the living room and gave her my estimate.

She whistled low through her teeth. "Jeez, that's terrific. You know," she dabbed her upper lip again, "I had a guy out here yesterday who quoted me a price twice that."

"Shit, don't mess with him again. My rates are competitive, but that's way too much for this job."

Dana looked at me and smiled big. She said, "I told him I knew a woman who could do this house for half his price. He hedged a little and came down a hundred bucks. I told him I'd check back with him, but I knew I'd give you the job anyway."

"Well, gee thanks, Dana," I told her. She stuck out her hand to me again and we shook on it.

Then, glancing quickly at her watch, she added, "Listen, do you think you could give me the outside estimate later?" And then she said, "You got your color chart with ya?"

"I do indeed," I said.

"Well, uh, you wanna go get something to drink, someplace cool, and help me pick out the exteriors? I think I wanna do something different with this house." She was picking up her coat jacket as she asked this, her back turned to me.

No, Crawford, you are not going to read anything into this. . .control, *chica*, control. . .this is just business, dammit. Well, all right, O.K. "Well, all right, O.K. Where to?"

"I know a place a couple blocks from here. Why doncha just follow me."

I followed her Audi in my pickup (Lucille, take a bow, this is your first intro—my '59 rebuilt white Chevy Apache), grinning like a kicker, listening to progressive country. On that short ride over the d.j. played Randy Newman's "A Lover's Prayer."

We turned some heads, she and I, walking into that cool, dark southtown dive: me, the epitome of blue-collar funk, and her in that impeccable suit. We sat down in a booth, ordered up some Lone Stars.

As she began leafing through the color chart, I asked her what she did for a living. She said she was a stockbroker.

"No shit," I said. That might explain the two rent houses, and her so young and all.

"No shit."

"Pretty successful at it, are you?" I asked.

"I do all right," she said. She was smiling and casual, digging into a bowl of peanuts on the table. She still had her shades on.

Talk about pins and needles. Only her manner and bearing cued me. She was just so relaxed and easy. I cleared my throat, "Well, me, I'm just trying to make ends meet this summer, painting houses. I'm really a computer programmer, but I can't find a job."

Dana looked up at me, or at least her face did behind the sunglasses. "No shit." She seemed genuinely taken aback. In fact, she finally took off the dark glasses and looked me in the eye.

Gah! It was a dangerous moment—I had not been in the least prepared for her eyes' effect. They were, trained on me, curious now, impressed, green, huge, sloe, and brilliant. They seemed monstrously intelligent, but *simpáticas*. Unendurable.

I swallowed quickly, heard myself saying "No shit" once again, and dammitohell, felt that ravaging fast-fire in the pit of my stomach. Oh God don't let me blush. I signalled the waiter and hurriedly ordered another beer; Dana declined. It took several seconds to harness the libidinous chaos I felt my face betrayed, before I could again look into those eyes. She was talking about her brokerage firm, where they were headed, their plans for buying computers. Said I was bound to find work real soon, there was lots of it around. The conversation went on and on like that as she continued flipping through the chart, though once I imagined that I saw a slight curve, that millimeter upward turn at one corner of her mouth which acknowledged the sexual weather—the Uh-huh, I see what's happening here, and I thank you but let's go on. Very smooth, very. Somebody in the joint played "Hot-Rod Lincoln" on the juke. All through the song I sat there across from her mesmerized by those eyes. I was talking, I know I was, and laughing too, and trying to keep it all reined in. And knowing damn well I wasn't. And then just not giving a damn that I wasn't.

After a while she decided on a color combo and announced that she had a six o'clock appointment. Dana stood up to take her leave, shaking my now dead-tuna cold hand once more. I said I'd do the outside estimate for her house that week, call it in to her answering service, arrange a time next week to get the key. She said, O.K., great, see ya later. Then she left.

I sat there, dazzled and free-floating, played "Hot-Rod Lincoln" three more times before I finally got outta there.

A Bidness Dyke _____

Through her answering service I was told she would leave the key at her office with her assistant, one Pat Eliot. So in I bopped in my paint-grubbies to the hallowed halls of Bache and Company one morning about nine o'clock to pick it up. After getting my bearings from the receptionist in the lobby, I wound my way through the dozens of desks in the immense neon-lit "hot" room, dozens of white males (and two women) with dozens of telephones on their desks, each and every one of them with one of those phones stuck in an ear, enormous noise. In a somewhat soundproofed cubby off to a far side of the tumult I found Eliot clicking furiously away at an adding machine, God knows how many feet of tape bunched up all over her desk. I knocked. She didn't even look up, said, "Be with ya in a minute," kept clicking away for a couple more seconds. She was a pinched-up, snooty-looking woman of maybe thirty, thirty-five, very short dark brown hair, a pair of square rimless glasses perched at the end of her nose. Like everybody else in the place she was dressed for bidness: a white buttondown oxford shirt, a navy blazer, beige skirt. She was chewing gum.

When she finally did look up at me, her whole face seemed to pin itself back, like a cat on the offense—an unbelievably blatant double take; slipping off her glasses, she literally looked me up and down from head to toe. Then, Pat Eliot grinned at me, a grin that purely and simply said, Have I got *your* number, dyke. Only slightly abashed, I felt myself returning something of the same smile to her; it seemed to fit her too.

"No doubt the painter," she said coolly.

"No doubt," I said back.

She reached down into her desk drawer, staring at me and holding that grin; she said, "Dana's told me a lot about you."

I felt a cool flash fire down my spine. Trying to roll off the line with as much of a Cary Grant inflection as I could muster, I answered, "I wonder what."

Eliot just smiled more broadly still, and then she actually batted her eyelashes at me—not so broad or vaudevillelike or anything, but just enough to establish the undercurrent of this encounter beyond the shadow of a doubt.

She said nothing, kept grinning, settled the key in my open hand as though it were the Hope diamond.

"You have a nice day now," she told me, and without taking her eyes off me, that shit-eating grin still on her face, she leaned forward over her desk, one hand propping up her jaw. "Dismissed," she said, sweetly.

Unanswered Prayers

In less than three weeks' time I had finished painting Dana Pfeiffer's second rent house inside and out, a fact I communicated once again to her answering service. The following day she called up mine and left word that I should come by her house that evening for the check, if that was convenient. But of course it was, and I was beside myself all day long, knocking off work midafternoon to go home, take a shower and a nappie, watch "Leave It to Beaver," and then shower again and slosh my entire person unstintingly with Givenchy. At the designated hour I drove Lucille into the driveway of Dana's swankola westside home fronting Lake Bowie.

She opened the door and said, "Hey. How you. Come on in," ushering me inside. And here she was her most radically transformed thus far, wearing a pair of greatly faded teeny-tiny cutoffs and a purple cotton tank top; her hair was plaited back in a big thick braid, a thin purple ribbon interwoven in the plaits. Please don't faint, Crawford. My stomach felt like that valley in Michoacan where swarms upon swarms of monarch butterflies migrate every year. With me following she walked—downright pugilistic, that walk of hers was, the hip-swung strut of a bantamweight—down the hallway and on through the living room. The living room (*Architectural Digest*, the Ritz East, *chez* Aga Khan!): ottomans and Kurds and burgundy hassocks and a Baldwin baby grand with eucalyptus sitting on top of it and everywhere, everywhere mirrors, bevelled and huge, reflecting in upon themselves from opposite walls, one pair angled to produce scores of Danas and Bobbies to the vanishing point as we passed before them and on out to her sundeck.

"Oh hey," I breathed, taking it all in, the lake glittering way beyond a line of cypress. "This's wonderful out here." There was a circular redwood cover about five feet in diameter at a far corner of the deck, a hot tub! "How does that work?" I went and squatted beside the hot-tub covering, running my fingers over the redwood—*yà*, a splinter. Will you puh-leese calm down, Bobbie....

"Take the cover off and punch that rubber button down. That one over there, the brown thing."

I took off the cover and jabbed the button. Nothing happened. I jabbed it again.

"You have to jab down hard, with your fingertips, right on top of it, hard from right above it," Dana said, sitting herself in a lawnchair and looking blankly at me.

So I jabbed it that way, and the thing came on with a big rumble, gushing jet streams of bubbles throughout the water. "A-ha!" I laughed over the din, and dipped my hand down in. It felt cool to the touch, perfect. Then I stood up and gazed down into the swirling, splashing eddy. It sure was hot out. What if she asked me if I wanted to get in there?

"Wanna take a dip?" she said, smiling a cipher smile at me from her chair.

Ogee. Hot tubs: why did the word ORGY keep flashing in my head big as the Bovril sign in Piccadilly? California, cocaine, the way-too-groovy. I guess she could sense my pandemonium, because she cleared her throat, smiled levelly again and said, "I've got a buncha tank suits hanging up over there, if you want one. But there's really nobody around, it's very private here." By now she was almost smirking at me. She was amused, my shyness amused her. Then she said, closing her eyes briefly and opening them again to me, very nice, "It's really a whole lot more pleasant without a suit."

Maybe I simpered. "Are you gonna get in?" *Please, answer my prayer.*

"Well, I might just dangle my legs over the side some. I've got an appointment in a little bit; I don't wanna get my hair wet."

An appointment. My heart sank. Then shit, no reason not to go on ahead, get on in this thing.

"You could go on back to the bathroom and grab yourself a towel, Bobbie."

So I did—I went back and undressed in the bathroom, I mean the Taj Mahal: green and cream and salmon-colored Mexican tile, a sunken tub and a shower stall too, brass spigots, a bidet. Holy Moly, this girl has got mon-*nay.* Surely not even stockbrokers make this kinda dough, but what did I know. Maybe I'd ask her something about it in a bit, I thought to myself as I primped in front of the wall-spanning mirror. I looked, I thought, pretty damn good: my skin was dark, tan and hard, my hair high-sunbleached from the summer-long barrage. Not bad for a white girl.

Back on the deck again I began easing myself shyly into the water, the towel wrapped around me, managing to drench a fair amount of it as I finally slipped in. The bubbles battered me from three different jets in the sides of the tub, like champagne blasting every square inch of me. I began melting away, dissolving into the bubbly sluice. Dana came and sat at the edge, slipping her legs into the water. It started getting easier and easier to talk with her, then, but I was still having trouble looking her in the eye. The Medusa Syndrome. But after a little while I began getting a grip on it, began looking at her for longer stretches of time—a feat I was able to accomplish only because I had submerged my face right up to my eyes, like an alligator; the semi-immersion gave me a semblance of control over my overall expression. And, of course, control was of the essence.

Dana asked me where I had applied for work, made some rather startling inside comments about a couple of those shops—I was quite surprised to learn just how much she did know about data processing—and suggested a few places I hadn't thought of before. As we spoke I found myself becoming more and more fascinated by her voice—soft, aspirate, faint and low, even slightly enfeebled, the kind of voice one might have when one first wakes up or after an act of love, warm, drowsy. I was trying to figure out a way to say something about my encounter with that Pat Eliot. . . .

"Pat mentioned she really enjoyed meeting you up at Bache," Dana said. But not a trace. Monotonic. Shielding her eyes with her fingers, she squinted at the sun setting into the lake. "So," looking at me and smiling again, but there was something admissive in that smile now, I knew there was, "what did you think of Eliot? Terrible bitch, but I love her madly, I'd do anything for her," she said, noblesse oblige, resting her chin on one knee drawn up close to her chest.

It was getting dark, I was floating, dreaming away. At least ten different responses to that question bubbled up to my hot-tubbed brain, but delivery, delivery was the key. I reshifted myself in the water. "She struck me—well she didn't strike me," this like Groucho, "—she im*press*ed me as being mighty competent, a real hard worker." Boiled-egg bland sentence Number 937. I was trying to match my expression to Dana's, eye for eye, grin for grin, but I don't think I was succeeding. Dumb delivery. Blew it.

"Oh she is," Dana confirmed, traceless again, "no doubt about it. You know, I had her job before I moved up to brokering. Took me two years to move up through the ranks."

"How old *are* you, anyway?" I asked. "I mean, excuse me, but you seem awfully well set up here," I said, nodding around to the deck and back toward the house.

"Well, I'm twenty-eight, but my Dad bought this house for me, and the other two rent places too, if that's what you mean. He's a lawyer, maritime law, Houston."

"You're from Houston?"

"Yup. Born and raised. Hate the goddam town," she said. Then, "Lissen, bubby, forgive me, but we've got to get you out of there. My appointment's in another half hour."

"Oh yeah, sure, thanks a lot, it's been fantastic." How'm I gonna get outta this thing?

"Here. Lemme give you a hand." Oh jeez, she's gonna pull me out. Tough it, Crawford. With her left hand she grabbed my left and with her right she clutched me just above my right elbow joint. With one foot up on the tub's interior bench and one coming up out of the water for the deck, I strained up and she pulled. Out of the lovely warm I felt weighted and thick.

"Ooof, it's cold out here," I said, shivering, folding my arms over my chest, but not before I saw Dana glance at my breasts—I saw her, saw that furtive look. I bent over quick and picked up the towel, wrapped the cold soggy thing around me.

"Uh, while you're changing I'll just go write out your check, O.K.?"

"Oh great, yeah, thanks a lot."

Just as I'd slipped my jeans and shirt back on, Dana returned. As she handed me her check, she said, a shade falteringly, "Listen, Crawford, how would you feel about letting me help you...help you find a job, I mean."

Concealing my delight, I scratched my head. "Why I'd feel just fine about that, Dana; what do you think I should do?"

"Well for one," she said, setting her hand on my shoulder, WHAH, "do you have any clothes? Business clothes, that is?"

"I've got a couple of things," I replied, "...a shirt and a blazer."

"Why don't you give me a call next week. You could come over and rummage through my stuff, pick out a suit or something. We're about the same size, aren't we? Is that O.K.? I don't want to offend you or anything but I can at least help with an interviewing outfit."

"Why yeah, sure, no, I'm not offended. I appreciate the offer, I really do."

"Well all right then," she sighed. "We'll get you all suited out next week." She started rocking on her heels, nervous.

Then she walked me out to the front door, stood in the door frame as I waved slightly over my shoulder back at her and climbed into Lucille. There was something there, something in her standing there, still rocking a little, holding herself, smiling distractedly now. Something between us. But— something for next week.

Suits and Suitors _____

The following week I reappeared at Dana's house the night before a big interview to try on her suits. And oh what suits they were! There was a three-piece navy gabardine, a gorgeous white linen, a grey-pinstripe worsted, an oatmeal-color shot-silk, with piping ("That's a Chanel," Dana mumbled, clicking the hangers along), and a crisp baby-blue seersucker, the one I finally settled on. As I stood modelling it in Dana's dresser mirror, she stood beside me, looking at my reflection too. "Oh yeah. That's the one. Definitely. Not too lording, but plenty snappy. Now, do you have any shoes to go with it?"

"Well, I have a pair I can wing it with for tomorrow, but I'll probably have to get some new ones to go with this baby."

"Pumps. I'm afraid pumps are what you need."

As it happened, pumps were not what I needed. Nor did her suit eventually get me a job. What I began to sense after several failed interviews in this suit of Dana's was that the interviewers seemed intimidated by the outfit. I got a number of "overqualified" assessments, which struck me as odd since I'd never had a job in computer programming before. Later on I was to figure out that the people who hire and fire in data processing shops are far more reassured by casual if not outright slovenly attire in a programmer, an affect born of their belief that programmers are cerebral loner types who could care less about such trifles as clothes. In fact, when I finally decided to go ahead and wear a khaki pants suit to one interview, it turned out to be the one that clicked and I got the job. A state job. I became a Computer Programmer I, a *bona fide* bureaucrat, for the then recent established *Lone Star Register,* an agency charged with the pathetically convoluted task of cataloguing all the umpteen-jillion Texas state agencies and publishing their current goings-on in a monthly periodical.

But back to Dana, that night.

As I say, we were standing there staring at one another in her mirror. "You know," she said, "there's something about your face, I don't know what it is. The moment I saw it I said to myself, 'There's somebody who's strong, and vulnerable, too.' Something in your eyes. Your eyes are almost snaky-looking, shrewd, but they're kind, too."

"Snaky-looking? How horrible."

["Horrible indeed. And so often so"—Alma sniping at the top of the page.]

Dana laughed, her arms folded over her stomach. "No, not so horrible, no. But now we've gotten this little job taken care of, how 'bout some sherry. You like sherry?"

"I like everything."

She gave me a straight look, I can tell you, back into that mirror, then. Well, a direct look. A split-second but precisely construable look. I know that look, I know it. She grinned (there it is again, there!) and flounced out of the room. I started peeling off the suit very carefully and not a little shakily, and skimmed back into my clothes. That look would be my safe-conduct; I would not forget it.

When I padded out barefoot into the living room, a silver tray with a crystal decanter and two wine glasses was sitting on top of the piano. Dana was seated at the keyboard.

"I taught myself this piece last week and I want to try it out on you."

She played a Brahms intermezzo, a beautiful thing, beautiful. Her face while she played was utterly calm, expressionless. Her white hands, the backs of them perfectly flat, flittered over the keys like the wave-bent tentacles of ghostly anemones. And all of a sudden I envisioned the little girl Dana, the six or seven-year-old red-haired child sitting primly at her piano, the metronome ticking steadily away, her child's face tight with concentration, purposefulness. Then, when the grown-up Dana had finished playing, she sat back on the bench and sighed.

"Gorgeous, huh."

"You are very good, Dana. Very. How long have you been playing? A long time, I bet."

"Since I was six." She smiled, gestured at the decanter. I poured us out two glasses, and we sat down with them on her couch. Dana began talking about her childhood. She told me, evenly and without emotion, that her mother had died in a car wreck when she, Dana, was four years old. On her way home from the dry cleaner's she had swerved into a telephone pole to avoid hitting a child who'd run out into the street. Her neck had been snapped, broken from behind by the cast-iron clothing bar she had strung across the back seat.

"Pretty bizarre, huh," she said grimly. "I have so few memories of her, really. A great many pictures, daddy's stories, but not much else." Then she went on to describe her father, got up and got a picture of him in fact. His name was Cy, a big man, white hair and a big full white moustache, blazing blue eyes, a little like Ward Bond. He looked wonderfully kind.

Looking at Cy's picture she said, "You know? You remind me a little of him, Bobbie. I'm not sure why. I guess because I trust you, maybe that's it."

That was totally unexpected. "Well, I'm glad you trust me, kiddo. I trust you, too." The question, to trust or not to trust her, had never crossed my mind. I just didn't know what else to say.

We continued talking about all manner of things: about her having studied history in school, her favorite professor there, about China, the Middle East, her travels (Europe, Africa, Australia), about chess (I didn't play, she'd played tournaments), gardening, God ("I'm with Bertrand Russell on that, I need more adequate proof," she said), Texas Democrats, depression, and music. The talk ebbed and flowed and spiralled and danced like midnight groves of wood sylphs, but not once did the subject of love, nor the objects of our love, arise. We were just sitting next to one another on that couch, sipping that amontillado at a steady clip. And Dana kept refilling my glass, until finally I blurted out, fairly well fuddled by then: "Dana, are you trying to get me drunk or something?"

She gave me that straight, I mean direct, look again. "No," she said softly, smiling, lowering her eyes. "I am not trying to get you drunk."

And a great deal more bashful than I had expected I would sound, I muttered, "Well, you know, you don't have to." I was looking down at the floor, down at her Persian rug, when I said this. And while I was looking down at the floor, Dana, at one swift stroke, swooped her head down before mine, kissed up at me, a buoyant mini-peck, right on the lips, then pulled back from me as abruptly as she'd zeroed in. Half-embarrassed and half acting embarrassed (her aggressiveness had stunned me momentarily), I looked back down at the carpet again and said, "Oh gee."

She laughed, said quickly under her breath, "Why 'oh gee'? What, what." I looked up at her. "You surprised me, that's all."

She smiled a cynical, oh-come-off-it smile. "Crawford," she said, "you are a treasure."

"I mean, I hadn't known, I wasn't sure. I like you a whole bunch but you scare the Dickens outta me." *A whole bunch, the Dickens.* Kee-rist, cornball-thick. . . .

"I scare *you*," she repeated slowly. "Huh. That's funny. You scare me, too." She paused, pulled her legs up underneath her on the couch. "You know," she said, "that's the first time I've ever kissed a woman."

I think my mouth must've fallen open. I watched her take another sip of sherry, flick her tongue to one corner of her mouth for a drop of it. When she looked back at me she was smiling again, radiant, regal. We stared at one another then for several seconds, rich, liquefying seconds, the barriers between us crumbling away like bits of old mosaic in a fountain. Finally, I said, "Well whaddaya think?"

Without hesitating an instant she answered, "I think you're too far away from me on this couch."

Dana and I kissed and kissed and kissed and kissed. At first her lips felt thin, her mouth small and dry. I wanted to kiss them until they were full and wet and soft, and after all this kissing they were, a little. Then I reached out to her breast, just setting my hand there. Dana took my hand away, breathed deep, pulled back from me. "You have a job interview tomorrow, bubby," and she arched an eyebrow in my behalf.

"Hah, ah, yessss," I said, rolling my eyes and slouching forward, dropping to the floor. I have this great fondness for falling down on the floor at certain moments, when the spirit moves me. Crestfallenness isn't always what spurs these little stunts of Keystone Koppia, either; sometimes I do it when I'm just really happy. In fact, I was at that instant both really happy and really crestfallen, and I just lay there, sighing, listening to Dana giggle, then feeling her toe poke me in the butt.

"Come on now, Bobbie. Go get your shoes."

A Sunday

Well I hadn't even gotten that new job I already told you about, much less started it, during that first week after Dana kissed me and sent me packing. I was still painting houses. All week long I would think about her, while I was taping and floating and spraying and tidying up. *The first time she'd ever kissed a woman.* What was I getting myself in for. I did wonder that. But it didn't stop my fantasies one whit. No, for the most part I just went around grinning like a loon, if loons can grin. Lunatics. That kind of loon. Already I had it bad. I just didn't know how bad, yet.

I had telephoned her answering service the afternoon following the interview to let her know how it had gone. Dropped the suit off at the dry cleaners. Thought about her mother. Thought about her motherlessness, what being motherless in this world meant. She didn't return my call, and that kind of rattled me.

That weekend I started a charcoal sketch of her, just kind of roughed it out. Thought I might ask her if she'd sit for me some time.

I called her service again midweek to see if she'd like to go have dinner with me. The following afternoon I came home and called up my service; Lorraine told me Dana'd suggested Sunday brunch. O.K. Sunday brunch, I relayed back. About ten o'clock that Sunday I called her house and got her tape machine: "Hi, this is Dana Pfeiffer. I'm not here right now, but...." I mumbled into the phone that I was home, was brunch still on.

An hour and a half later she called me. "I'll pick you up at noon," she said.

Shortly after that a for-Texas premature cold front moved through the city, bringing with it a spectacular thunderstorm and a chill, driving rain. I slipped on a sweater, unpacked from the previous winter—gack, mothballs—and delved into the far end of my closet for my trenchcoat. Sat down on my couch in the coat and listened to Andre Watts' recording of Chopin waltzes. Just sat there, waiting for her. Yup. I had it bad, all right.

She was late. Ten minutes, fifteen, twenty, twenty-five. An entire hour later the telephone rang—it was Dana. "Uh Bobbie, uh, sorry, m'sorry. I, uh, d'ya think we could do this another time, hmm?" She sounded as though she were almost asleep. Something was wrong, her voice was totally different from the one I'd heard an hour ago.

"What's wrong, Dana? You sound funny. Are you all right?"

She laughed, not a big one, not really amused, either. "Huh, yeah, yeah, I'm O.K., m'all right." There followed a long pause. I thought she was going to go on but she didn't.

"Dana?"

"What, what."

"Are you sure you're all right?"

"Oh yeah, sure. Sure." Another great long pause. Then she said, "Lissen. I got a buncha stuff over here for breakfast. Why don't we just fix over here."

"Sure," I said. "Do you need anything?"

Another ironic laugh. "Naw, naw." And another pause. "Just you, maybe."

A blood-hot wave in me downsurged midtorso, my pulse fluttered at my throat. A little breathless I managed to say, "I will be there in a flash. The proverbial blue streak."

Yet another pause. She was almost whispering. "Uh yeah, yeah, see ya soon." Click.

What in the hell was wrong with her?

On the drive over to her house, the wind and the rain and the lightning and thunder were horrific, but I always feel snug as a tick in ol' Lucille. I just turned on a C&W station and patted my hand on the steering wheel in counter-time to the windshield wipers, humming along with Tammy Wynette, still wondering why Dana'd sounded so damned funny.

Dana opened her door, and the way she looked knocked me for a loop: her hair was tousled and unbrushed, her eyes huge and glassy. She smiled wanly, "Come in, come in." I moved inside and took her by the arm, grasping it through the billowing sleeve of her white cossack shirt, unbuttoned halfway down her chest. She closed the door behind me, quick.

"All right, Dana. What is it. What's wrong with you."

She sighed, shrugged, removed my hand and patted me on my upper arm. "Come on back to the kitchen, we'll sit down, I'll tell you."

After wiping off my boots on the doormat I followed her on through the house, watching her walk, a kind of mincing, soft, overlight flow to her movements. She seemed drugged. Over her shoulder she said to me, "I'm a little stoned, Bobbie. Took a Valium."

"Good Lord," I said. "Not because of me."

She pivoted around to me, a little woozily, snorted, "Humph!" And there was that look again, the one that melts my feet. She said, "No, no, not because of you," and she moved in to me, encircling her arm around my waist, picking at the leather buttons on my coat. Dana leaned in to my face and kissed me, light and sweet. "Christ I'm glad you're here," she breathed.

Back in the kitchen she poured us out some coffee and we sat down next to the window at the table, the Sunday *New York Times* spread out all over it. The drapes were drawn. I said, "You want me to open these up?"

"Uh, no, no, just leave 'em, thanks." She cleared her throat, folded her arms over her stomach, crossed her legs. "There are probably less than five people in the world who know what I'm going to tell you now," she said. Good God, what's this? "It's just so goddamned humiliating." Dana lifted up the business section of the paper and slid out a pack of Marlboro Lights, lit one, her hands trembling slightly. "I have," she said, "uh, ceraunophobia." An inexplicably long pause here, she was biting a nail, staring off into space. I was waiting. "Tonitrophobia," she went on, "brontophobia, astraphobia. Whatever you want to call it." She looked at me. "I freak out bad during thunderstorms."

I just stared at her. She was puffing away on her cigarette. I think she was waiting for me to smile or something. But I looked down into my lap, back up at her again and said, "Uh, lissen. I've known someone (*I've known someone,* it echoed hollow as the wind whistling down a great basalt breach in the mountains) who had a phobia. I know how terrible they can be."

Her voice was high now, almost shrill: "Well it's such a little kid thing, being afraid of thunderstorms, it's such an embarrassing thing to have...but I saw someone once...I saw someone struck by lightning once."

"Jesus, Dana."

"When I was little my dad used to take me golfing; I liked to golf. We were on the terrace of the clubhouse, the storm had just broken, and all the golfers were scurrying back to shelter. And this one guy—"

"Look," I broke in quickly, "you don't have to tell me about it. It must have been hideous."

She looked at me levelly then. "More hideous," she said in a tone so over-dramatically chilling I almost smiled, but didn't, "than I hope you are capable of imagining."

Understandably neither one of us was particularly hungry then, so I steeped us some of her Earl Grey tea in a little white teapot and we just sat there in that closed-up kitchen and read the paper together for some time. By then the storm had abated, the thunder and lightning had moved south. Only the cold rain was falling soft, its patter on the outside lulling me, warming me. I felt totally at ease with Dana, with everything.

She looked up from the paper. "I can deal with just rain," she said.

But she still looked fairly haggard. "How about a back rub," I volunteered. "Iron all those neural wrinkles out."

She gazed at me, *that* look again. "Sure," she said, closing her eyes and opening them again (a seductive habit, that), "that'd be great."

Dana lay down shirtless on the big white bed, groaning as she hit the mattress. I slipped one knee over to one side of her, the other to the other, and sat down on her behind. I dropped out a little baby oil on my hands, rubbing them to warm it up. And I proceeded to give her a really long, good massage, kneading the flat white freckled flesh of her back over and over, shoulders to midback to lower, then starting again at the base of her skull with my thumb and four fingers pressing along her spinal column, all the way down. At first she would hum, groan, say, "Ah God," but after a while she was completely silent. It felt so sweet to be touching someone, to touch again, I didn't want to stop.

Finally, she mumbled, "I can't believe you're going on so long."

"I'm gonna stop pretty soon."

She arched her left shoulder back and up and began rolling over on her back. I lifted up from her and let her turn, sat down again on her legs. "Naw," she said, low. "That's enough. Wonderful. It was wonderful." She took my hand and squeezed it, held it. She was just staring at me, a little bleary, her face all smoothed out, relaxed now. "What am I gonna do about you," she said, tonelessly.

I laughed, short. "What do you think you're going to do," I said.

"Bobbie," she shook my fingers loosely in her hand, "I am not a lesbian. I've never made love to a woman before in my life."

Laudably deadpan I said, "Well, I assumed that since you said you'd never kissed a woman before that there was a rather good chance of that, too."

Dana smiled, sighed. I started stroking the inside of her arm; she hmmed a little. "Now men just do not understand that. That that, just having your arm rubbed, feels so good."

"I wouldn't know, Dana."

She smiled at me again. "No, you wouldn't, would you." She let me keep petting her, my fingers running as light as I could make them over and around and under her elbow, biceps, forearm. I was concentrating on the arm, intent on it, trying to think of nothing but her arm, and failing, thinking of how much I wanted to be naked with her, under her sheets, our bodies touching, close, wrapped around each other, a whole, warm and living. When I glanced up at her she was looking at me, her eyes were dark and full, soft. Then she whispered: *Kiss me.*

And I leaned down toward her; her eyes followed my lips as I moved. I barely grazed her lips, then skimmed to the side of her mouth, her cheek, her neck, her ear, a puff of air, back to her lips again. Pulling back, I slid off of her to her side; she turned over on her side to me, cupped my chin in her fingers, guided my mouth to hers, her lips open a little and wet. Then sideways, our lips perpendicular. She wrapped her arms full around me, pulled me in close to her, and kissed me hard, her tongue slipping past my lips, opening up my mouth, falling to on my tongue, rolling over it and under it. She drew back from me, her breath deep and low: "I don't know what the hell to do but I want to do it."

"You're doing it," I said, simply.

She unbuttoned my shirt, pulled it open, off my chest. Those long white trembling fingers, exquisitely alive, reached out to my breast, each finger, an infinitesimal point on the fingerpad, each finger in its turn exploring, imbuing a minuscule path of skin below it, touching, sounding, moving on, a quickening trail of neurons firing, singing in its wake.

"Ah God," she breathed, "God God God," and slipped the shirt from my shoulders, one side, the other, and off. And then we were silent, and still, holding one another, entwined, our faces close, as close as they could be and still focus, gazing, examining, warming in what we saw.

Silent, eloquent. Stroking and petting and kissing into being this wordless language of the senses, a syntax of caresses and heat, of blood and skin, and that mute unity beyond the skin alone—the ellipses of letting go, to gain; the gaining, only to let go again. So that when I touched her there finally, down there between her legs, my fingers mumming their fluent way past the sheaths of flesh up to that creamy pearl at their joining, all the combinative real words and turns of phrase and halting punctuation of the conveyable world spun off and into blank, interstellar space, powerless to translate in this realm we'd created, incapable in the face of its euphony and light, this unutterable joy.

She was shaking, arched and rigid with the trembling. I took her legs in my arms, feeling the sinews of her thighs flex hard, and began bending my head down over her, meaning to usurp my finger with my tongue there. But then I felt her hand on my shoulder, her fingers tightening. She whispered, "No, no don't; stop now. Please," and she started pulling me back up to her, beside her, holding me, her face flushed, a slight line of sweat glistening above her lip.

So we just lay there then, breathing soft together, not talking, not moving, and the grey late-afternoon light began slipping down greyer still around us in the room, one golden spear of sunlight piercing through a narrow edge of window shade, diffusing to a wider, softer strip of gold along a bottom corner of the bed.

And a Divulgence _____

Dana and I, after not seeing one another for a whole week following that Sunday (she'd had several business meetings, a pottery seminar, she was too wiped out—"That's one thing you'll learn very quickly about me," she'd said over the phone, "I don't do anything I don't want to do"), were the following Saturday evening driving downtown for dinner. Again it was raining, again it was cold. Behind the wheel she was telling me about her longest-lasting liaison—three years, a fellow named David. They had lived together in Houston, both students at Rice.

"I was crazy about him for the first six months," she explained, "but after that it was all downhill, a long, unbelievably long process of extrication. I'll never let that happen again, boy," she said, and gave me a quick, sparse look. Perhaps even as early as that moment she may have suspected me of harboring something very big indeed for us in my scheme of things, nothing less than the archetypal urge to marry (I was not in fact harboring it then, though I would, and with ferocious tenacity, soon). But I am quite sure now, and as sure as I can possibly be, that, at that moment and throughout her time with me, that something was far too big to fit within her own scheme of things, that to Dana marriage meant growing dull and insensate, letting the free-dancing self drop loose like a severed marionette dangling down dangerously far into the warm, connubial dark.

Dana, working the steering wheel just so, carefully pulled up the black kid gloves she was wearing. "I've had these babies for fourteen years," she said proudly. She reached out and switched on the defogger. "But Dave, Dave. He was in civil engineering. Always wore grey slacks and white short-sleeved shirts, always had this plastic flap of pens in his shirt pocket. A real stereotype. I don't know what it was about him for those first six months, but as soon as it wore off I could not believe what a boring goddam sonofabitch he was. We argued all the time. I think he'd bought into some little-girl image of me when we first fell in love, I don't know. But it was dead wrong and I couldn't get him to shake it. Three years, I tried." We turned a corner south onto Santana Avenue and skidded a little. "Damn," she hissed, and recovering, went on: "Anyway, the last year we were together he found Jesus. I mean, he really found Jesus. And then he got terminally boring. And that's when you should throw in the towel, right? Boring is death. So I left him," she said, and paused. "But not before he gave me his herpes." I'd been looking at her while she was talking and driving; at this her right eye rolled slightly in its socket toward me, then back quickly to the road.

This was 1976. I asked, "What's herpes?"

Alea Jacta Est _____

Yes, well back then nobody knew shit from Shinola about herpes. A cold sore was just a cold sore, the masses had never heard of Simplex I, much less Simplex II, and the paranoia that was to befall the sexually active of the western world about this virus was at that time nonexistent, unbegotten.

Except in Dana. Throughout the rest of our ride to the restaurant and over drinks before dinner, she proceeded to scare the living bejeezus out of me about the genital variety of herpes, which she did not have, and told me that the oral cold sore type, which she did have, could transfer to the genitalia and behave essentially the same as the dreaded II, and that, moreover, oral sex was usually how that happened. Again, she gave me that sparse look. I was rapidly descending to a morass of contradiction. Of course I was feeling sympathy for Dana, for her obvious sense of being a time bomb of contagion, and sexual contagion at that. I could see the torment she felt, though she was doing a very good job of hiding it—her shoulders straight and back, her back straight and up, while she chainsmoked and kept jouncing her neck a certain way so that her hair, down and full around her face, would swing back behind those shoulders, a kind of Rita Hayworth flair to this, a kind of Rita Hayworth tragedy to it, too. But I was also feeling, and trying to hide, a chillingly constrictive coil of panic for my own sweet flaming hide: had I already contracted it from her? If I continued to see her, wouldn't I get it sooner or later? But what about my feelings for her, my caring, my having it so bad already?

Before the antipasto arrived she had let me know, in a slim marvel of offhandedness, just how apprehensive sex of any sort made her, how guilty she had felt even with our lovemaking of the weekend before, how that Sunday afternoon might well have been a one-shot deal—how she wasn't sure how often we'd be able to have sex after that, if ever again.

If ever again. Over the fettucine, I despaired. I was totally dismayed, weirded out in the extreme. The rest of the dinner went by so uncomfortably that I was glad, as I'm sure Dana was, too, that it had been served as promptly as it had. Neither of us ordered dessert. When she later dropped me off at my apartment, we simply squeezed hands good-bye. Abject.

That week I telephoned the county medical referral service for a local specialist on herpes and was given the name of one Carol Oakley, MD, with whom I subsequently made an appointment for the following week. I had to find out more about this thing. Dana didn't call me that whole week long. And I didn't call her, either, though I could not stop thinking about her and about this maleficent blight that had befallen the rose of my future with her.

Carol Oakley, MD, however, put me to rights about the disease; she had been doing research on it for over three years. For forty-five minutes she answered every question I had about it, including the biggie: had I gotten it from Dana just kissing her? (I used Oakley's own lingo, "my partner," when I asked this.) Had I gotten it from my partner just by kissing? Without a cold sore present, no way, Oakley explained. And she explained a great many other things about herpes which were most reassuring and damned good to know. At the end of the session I couldn't see what in the heck Dana'd been so wigged out about, but then I didn't have herpes, myself. And if we were careful, I thought, if we avoided kissing and certain other intimacies—that's delicate, Crawford— when she had a cold sore (or when she felt the tremor of one coming on), there was just no reason to be uptight about it. That's how I saw it, anyway.

After the visit to Oakley, when I finally sat down with Dana at her house, I told her all about what I had learned. Although she said she was pleased, really, that I had gone to the trouble to check into it (though there was also a trace of resentment and hurt for my having checked into it, too; this she covered well, but I could see it nonetheless), at first she seemed, after my wrap-up, almost disappointed, as though her malaise had been diminished somehow, belittled, as though she had lost some sort of Medea-like valor. But after a while she agreed that she would go talk with Oakley herself. And she did. She was still very conscious of it anyway, even after her appointment with Oakley. It was a constant with her, something that had for so long been a source of shame and a thing to be hidden, that it was hard for her to let go of that entrenched wrongthink.

And now that she knew that I knew about it, and for other reasons I was still to learn of, she meted out her kisses to me like an exchange of *deutschemarks* at the bank—careful, correct, value for assigned value. And as to our lovemaking, weeks would pass before Dana allowed that to happen again. It was an awful time.

But then, a very great deal of all the time I was to spend with Dana turned out to be awful. Though by then, by the time she told me about the herpes and I realized how neurotic she was about it, my desire for her had become irreversible. My need for her—which by its own definition was wrongthink from the word go—had grown gargantuan, a leviathan, a juggernaut. The die was cast, the Fates had finally conspired on my behalf, and on with it I lurched.

A Sunday Drive _____

We took a drive, Dana and I, one windy Sunday afternoon the week before Thanksgiving, out to the LBJ State Park. It was that exhilarating kind of Texas late fall day that warms the skin and buoys the soul: crackling clear as a shot, the air of the great blue dome overhead dry, desiccant, the low-angled rays of the sun a tonic, sweet and healing. In an ancient hamper of Dana's we had packed up a glorious picnic lunch: peppered beef and Chinese radishes, a brie, a baguette, and an enormous thermos of hot peppermint tea. Dana was tired. She had been working very hard all that week, so I was given leave to drive the Audi. On the way out Highway 71 we spotted several deer bounding off up into the cedar hills and an armadillo scuttling beside the road, and, soaring high and plummeting fierce along the air shafts, a bird of prey neither of us could identify.

At the park we trekked in for about twenty minutes to seek the most remote enclave we could find, a live oak grove, and there we spread a blanket down and feasted and lay and moved the blanket out into the sun and sunned ourselves, torpid and dozy after the meal. Dana even fell asleep, and I watched her sleeping, the small thin veins around her eyes more protuberant than I'd ever seen them. How pale and nervous she looked, even in sleep, under that stark bath of sun. And how stubbornly confident I felt then that my love, my kisses, could lift that pallor from her, fill her out, satisfy her, eventually. Lately, she had given me hope to feel that. I was spending perhaps one or two evenings a week with her at her house, sleeping over, just sleeping in her bed with her; and we nearly always managed to share our Sundays together.

The week following this jaunt to the park we would make love again, for the second time. But once again I could not elicit her climax: again I stroked her and stroked her, and again she had reached that taut summit of frenzy that must be overtopped, her breathing cavernously deep and fast, but at the crucial moment she had pulled my hand away, lay back deep in her pillows, and whispered, *I can't, I can't*. And, as before, she had made no effort to reciprocate.

But for the moment I was still staring at her while she slept. I was lazy and full and content, my head propped up by my elbow as I lay. I had brought along a collected Shelley in the hopes of reading Dana some poems. I was mumbling over "Ode to the West Wind" and was at the line, "know/Thy voice, and suddenly grow gray with fear,/And tremble and despoil themselves: oh, hear!" when she awoke with a start and stared back at me with big glassy swollen eyes. "Christ," she muttered. "What a dream." I reached out to her hand and petted it with an index finger. "What." Dana yawned and stretched. "It was about you. You were an actor, behind stage, readying yourself to go on. And I was swinging," she laughed, "like a lemur from a rope pulley strung behind the curtain. I would swing in to you and kiss you and then swing away. Then I started showing off for you, pulling myself up higher on the tether, back and forth and back and forth, until you were quite out of reach."

"I wonder what your analyst will say about that one."

"She'll like the monkeyshines part a lot." Dana paused, slipped an errant strand of hair behind her ear, squinted at me in the strong white light. "For that matter, she likes you, does old Gittel."

"She does, huh."

"Yeah, she does. She thinks you're earthy or something. An anchor, a grounding force for me." Dana laughed, short. "But then I've always thought she was a dyke anyway."

I looked at her steadily. "And what do you think about me, Dana. What do you think about us."

She pursed her lips, amused, then jabbed on her sunglasses. "I think I never would have thought I could have this much fun with a girl. Excuse me," she laughed, "with a woman."

Fun. For all the things it had been and was yet to be, why had my time with Dana never seemed like much fun? We had had a lot of laughs, surely. She was not, I was not, a humorless drudge. But there was always that knot in her, that unrelenting, unyielding core to her, that I never felt I could affect. That in the final analysis I never did affect.

Then she said, "Come on. Let's walk this stuff back to the car."

That was a fairly good day, that Sunday, one of the best—probably the best time we ever did have together, Dana and me. Later on she drove us back on in through the dimming luster of the light, through gold to copper to cobalt and sulphur black. To our east I scanned the sky for the winter stars and constellations I knew: Orion, the hunter; the dense cluster of the Pleiades, Atlas's daughters gone to stars; a part of the $>$ of Taurus; and blue Betelgeuse, beetle juice; and yellow-red Vega. For the most part Dana and I were silent then, the engine humming strong in fifth. We were on the alert for deer; it was their time of year to be running. When the city lights began breaking through the hills, Dana reached out with her right hand to mine and squeezed it, saying hurriedly, "Listen, I'm kinda tired, Bobbie. I think I'll just drop you off at your place and go home and hit the hay." I had expected that, it was O.K. Everything was O.K., it would all work out. It would.

Eclipsed

Several weeks later, on a clear chill evening between Christmas and New Year's, Dana and I and Marty Harris, a lawyer pal of Dana's, were soaking in the hot tub, waiting for an eclipse of the moon. We were drinking espresso and popping Belgian chocolates and ticking off the minutes in the moonlight. Marty and Dana were having a spirited discussion about feminists in the work force, or, more precisely, feminists in the upper-socioeconomic status professions, or "professional women," that most regrettable phrase, and the nuances and travails of their interactions with businessmen. Me, I was just listening. This was a part of Dana's life she had never talked about before, and I was both intrigued and repelled by it. Theirs was the high-powered vernacular of the movers and shakers of this world, in thrall to the siren song of wealth and influence, and whether or not owing to my contemplative, step-by-step temperament, or some other aspect of self I had not as yet confronted, I felt deeply removed from the subject matter, despite my fascination with their deliberation of it.

Many weeks after this night Dana and I were driving along in her car, going somewhere, doing something, and she started talking about her goals. She wanted to be a major-league broker, and that would mean New York. Eventually she said: "I want power."

"Ah," I said, "for women, the women's movement."

Her neck arched slightly, slowly, her eyes narrowed in thought. She pulled her kid gloves up a little higher, tightened her grip on the steering wheel. "No...for me."

I didn't know what to say. I could understand wanting wisdom, for chrissakes, or simply money. But I knew nothing, felt nothing, about power and its acquisition. I had no use for it whatsoever. Recognition for work well done, yes, praise, hell yes, but what in heaven's name did *power* mean to Dana? Over whom, why? To what end? The expression "Power tends to corrupt and absolute power corrupts absolutely" slithered through my mind, a prickly rush of gooseflesh hackled along my spine—someone walking over my grave. I said nothing. The conversation moved on to something else.

But back to that evening with Marty. Dana had not disclosed the nature of our relationship to Harris, so before Marty arrived Dana had taken me aside and told me in so many words to put a lid on it. I was irritated, but I begrudgingly agreed. Certainly Dana's need for subterfuge with Marty, whom I knew to be one of her best friends, was at the heart of my feeling so distant that night. No doubt it also figured in my lack of enthusiasm when the earth's shadow finally did begin moving over the face of the moon. Again I slipped down alligatorlike into the bubbling water, only my eyes showing, my own shadow falling numb over me, closing me off to the present.

After a while I slinked out of the tub, thoroughly un-self-conscious now, and wrapping up in a big white terrycloth robe Dana had bought for me expressly for after-tub use, darted into the house for a stop in the loo. The phone rang, but before I could answer it, Dana had picked it up outside on her radio phone. Standing next to the phone niche, I happened to look down at the receiver and saw a column of numbers with names next to them—speed-calling, an AT&T service for those to whom we reach out and touch most often, a single digit per. At the top of the list was *service,* then *office,* then *Daddy, Gittel* (the analyst), *Farmer* (her MD), *bank, Merrill-Lynch,* and *Harris.*

It should have been as clear a sign as any that I was gravely deluded, but as I stood there staring at that receiver, despite my hurt at her not having told Marty about me, I began making a series of lopsided excuses for my name's not being on that list: she had her service, she usually called me at my office (I had the programmer job by now) from her office during the day, maybe she'd thought about adding my number here but hadn't had time, etc., etc.

After Marty had gone on home, oblivious, I told Dana that her nondisclosure had really upset me. But Dana was dismissive, huffy, just short of a snit, saying, "I just don't want my friends knowing my business, that's all, what's going on with me."

"But how can't you tell your friends, for God's sake? What kind of friends are they to you that they couldn't accept it? Or are you ashamed of what you're doing? Why don't you want them to know you're having a lesbian affair?"

She shot an icy look at me, then arched an eyebrow. "I am not a lesbian, Bobbie. I keep telling you that."

"Christ! What in hell are you talking about? What's been going on here, dammit! Are you out of your mind?"

"Look! Bobbie! I like you, I do, I enjoy spending time with you. You are. . .very dear to me." (I cringed.) "But you're making some assumptions here, darling, and you have got to realize that I am just not the answer to your prayers! I don't have any prayers," at this last she turned her face, sullen, away from me.

There ensued a very nasty scene indeed, the first of many harangues in the matter. Me trying to get Dana to admit her feelings for me (I knew she had feelings for me), her minimizing them, weasling, waffling.

After maybe less than half an hour of going around in what would soon become wretchedly well-worn circles, I stormed off in Lucille, pounding my fist hard on the steering wheel a good part of the way home.

I spent a bittersweet New Year's with Cory and Gabe and Ramona and a bunch of our friends. At one point during the evening, Cory and I, standing in the middle of the house with several score partygoers milling around us, had been talking about Pfeiffer. Cory just looked at me and put her hand on my shoulder as she always does, and then I just flat burst into tears, right there in front of everybody. She hugged me and then slipped out the bottle of champagne she'd had tucked under her armpit and refilled my glass. "Gonna be all right, Bobbie," she whispered. "You'll see."

It was over a month before Dana called me again, under the pretext that she had a computer program in mind she needed me to help her write and run on the new system at her office. After a little ceremonial hedging (I had not, as yet, lost all of my pride), I agreed to do it, because I knew she was trying to smooth it over with me, make amends, and that thrilled me. Terribly.

And so it was that we started up seeing one another again.

The Visitation

Throughout the by now six-months plus I had been seeing Dana, I had incessantly bent the ears of my closest friends about this conundrum of a relationship. Unfailingly patient and condoling were Jackie, Cory, Ramona, even Alma. Several months after Jackie had returned to Texas, I had written Alma a letter, and we had thereafter begun an at first spasmodic then eventually steady, caring correspondence. Then, that Christmas holiday past, she had gone back to San Martín to be with her family, and on her way back to Denver for her fourth semester of graduate school, she stopped through town overnight to visit with me. It had been almost three years since we had seen one another.

She looked more beautiful than ever: more womanly, more wise, more kind still. With a brand-new Pentax she had taken pictures of her family at Christmas, and these she set out on the kitchen table in neat little vertical columns. From another envelope in her satchel she pulled out prints of her and Gloria on a recent skiing trip in Aspen. Jackie had been quite right: Gloria was a real stunner—a big woman, tall, ivory-complected, her long thick black hair falling in wave after wave around her face, a Goya beauty, a Carmen. Her composure, her eyes, showed me a good woman, at peace with herself, a creature of joy, serenity, grace. They could have passed for sisters, Mita and Gloria: the two of them looked strong and sharp posing on the slopes, smiling big into the camera with their Ray-Bans, interspersed among some other women friends on a sundeck, laughing hard at a party in the ski condo they'd rented for that weekend. Unquestionably happy together, right for each other. I was relieved and grateful when at last Alma put the photographs back into their envelopes.

Following a cozy lasagna supper at home that evening, I told Alma that Dana was the only other woman in the world besides her worth having. Alma just looked at me impassively for several seconds, smoothly twirling the base of her glass on the tablecloth, then said slowly, "Bobbie, I don't know why, I really don't, but from what you've told me, I think she's using you."

The next day in the airport as I was seeing her off, she kissed me on the cheek and said, "Honey, there are some feelings that just never go away."

She was talking about us. I hugged her long and hard, right there in the terminal. After I'd returned to my apartment that sleeting forenoon, I lay down in my long black wool overcoat and boots on the bed where Alma had slept over with me, carefully platonic, and awkward, the night before, and I cried for a long time, I don't know how long, for a number of things, a host of things I save up crying for, while the space heater flared and sputtered, and the icy rain battered outside against the windowpanes, opaque with condensation. Despite Gloria, I knew what Alma had meant about those feelings never going away, and central among them for me that cold sorrowful day was—regret. A groundswell of it.

And More from the Dream Log ————————————

Over the spiralling course of that spring Dana made a number of trips up to New York on business. Although I fully expected that she might be negotiating for a job with Bache on Wall Street, for many weeks I could not bring myself to ask her about that, nor did she herself volunteer any specific information about it. That spring I had a great many vivid and telling dreams, a few of which were pretty silly, too. One, for instance, was about Liz Taylor. I dreamed that she was quite old and had reunited with Burton. For some reason Liz gave me a pair of ruby earrings; then, in another fleet frame of the dream, one of the rubies had somehow, in the nutso logic of dreaming, become embedded in Dana's earlobe, which had itself metamorphosized into a complex system of sheaths with skinfolds that had to be pulled back in order to dislodge the gemstone. The ruby kept slipping away from me, burrowing deeper into her ear, as though it were alive and moving. I never did retrieve it.

In another dream I was wading through something fluid all the way up to my chest, and pulling something by a rope, just like Bogey in *The African Queen.* In my periphery I noticed someone else, a woman, walking along beside me through the wet. It turned out to be Madge, the Palmolive saleswoman on TV. Nodding, she smiled a smile at me that was chillingly cynical, world-weary, and slightly accusatory. Still pulling the rope and whatever the weight was that was attached to it behind me, I wheezed, "Shit!" to which Madge replied, "Sure, you're wading in it," and as she said this, I looked down, and with a principally olfactory wave of revulsion, realized I was standing in sewage. I awoke instantly and felt perilously nauseated for a few moments, though I did go back to a further fitful sleep, eventually.

An Interloper Incident ————————————————

On a warm rainy mid-March Sunday morning, I was sharing Gabe's birthday brunch with her and Cory and Jackie and Ramona and Alice Bradford and Chuke Wheelock—mix-it-yourself omelettes and prosciutto and fresh-squeezed o.j., and for dessert, crêpes with almond cream, num-num. And great big glasses of cappuccino. Gabe, munching and humming, had begun to describe a harrowing event of several nights back.

"Cory wasn't here. She was out hooting around with Nancy Buchanan and Olive. I was getting ready to go to bed, the kids (Alf and Mary, the doggers) were inside. I was in bed and I switched off the lamp, and then I looked out the rear window. The drapes were pulled back, and—there was a man standing out there, a silhouette right up near the window, outlined in the moonlight." The brunchers gasped, there were whispers of "Jesus." Continuing, Gabe's voice was getting lower, deeper, almost a whisper; her eyes kept opening wide and then narrowing again. "I felt paralyzed, I wanted to yell, but my throat didn't work. But right off the bat he turned and ran across the yard, shinnying over the back fence. Of course by the time the cops got here, he was long gone."

With dramatized *sang-froid* Cory looked at me. "Everybody's nightmare, right?"

"Before the cops got here," Gabe went on, "I loaded up the .45 and just sat on the edge of the bathtub with the kids on either side of me. Shit *damn,* I wish I'd seen that face."

Lost in the Shithouse _____

There was a time when every brown Audi I saw clutched my heart to the very core, hoping it was Dana's, and Dana in it. It seemed as though everywhere I went I was met with giddying coincidence, random sightings of her all over town. I imagined I was psychic, that both of us were genuinely clairvoyant, that in line with some variant of simultaneity or synchronicity, waves of our molecular structure, infinitesimal subatomic particles, neutrino scouts! exuded from us in all directions, seeking one another out. From three stories up, out a window in a computer lab to which I had gone one day to pick up some printouts, I had seen her in the street, running slowly, badly, with a gawky, helpless-female kind of gait, her feet swinging out too far from the straight upright line of her body; she disappeared around a building next to a parking lot.

Another time I had been in the checkout line at the grocery store and looked out the storefront window to see her motoring down the road, that unbelievable mass of red hair hanging down full behind her, her chin held lightly up. Without seeing it, I pictured the expression that would accompany that upturned face, knew that she was feeling grand, in control, on a mission, graced, sprightly, expectant. Ah God and my heart beat faster, as it always does when she's that way; I hurried out to the sidewalk. But she had turned her car south, away from the direction of my house; she was not feeling splendid for my sake. And I felt jealous of whomever it was she was going to meet with her spirits up like that, and envy, envy of her herself, envy of the grace in her bearing, her well-being.

Deflated, I stood there on the pavement, grocery sack in my arms, a hack scene from a sitcom. She was not, I thought for the nth time, the woman for me: her life had defined, obtainable goals; she had the sense, though not infallible I knew, that she was powerfully in command of her life. And I was so mired in impossibilities, hers and mine, and mine. I only knew when I saw her all full of herself, loving herself, as she seemed to me in her car that day, I wanted her more than anything or anyone I'd ever wanted in my life. But more and more she was hiding that strength, her self-possession, from me, leaving me her mundane, operational self, her routine being, while

I still longed for that vitality of hers, so nurturant, so cherishable, that I had for months hung on and on for it, waiting for it, for her mood to rebound, shine on me, grow in me. I could not get at her and I would not get away.

I rode on home then, becoming angrier by the second with myself for being such a damned fool, a victim, for going on home alone as I did far too often those days and nights, periodically hoping the phone would ring, she'd want to see me, we could talk. But that day, as the cycle went, I was more my dominant self (though still feeling the waiting, still imagining she needed me). After I had unloaded the groceries, I gathered up my workout kit, prepared to go down to the gym and sweat this one out, immunize myself for the while against this enfeebling passion, this not quite requited love.

Not Fools

It was seven-fifteen in the morning when the phone rang. "Whatcha doin', B.J." The voice on the other end of the line was Cory's. She sounded terrible. "Just getting ready for work, Cory. What's up?"

A long, deep, agonized sigh, bursting in little spurts as it wound down. "Well...Gabe's in the hospital, Bobbie Jean."

Quickly, trying to level the panic in my throat, I said, "Oh Cor what happened."

Cory broke, she started crying. "Oh...I shot her, goddammitohell. The shotgun...I stumbled...." Cory and Gabe had been out hunting that weekend.

"Cory, Cor...take it easy, take it easy. Is Gabe...all right?"

"Oh...yeah, she's gonna be all right. It just hit her shoulder, she's gonna be all right. She's in St. Ann's right now, they'll let her out tomorrow."

"Cory. Cor, I'll be over in five minutes. You wait right there for me, O.K."

In a tiny, miserable little voice Cory said, "O.K., Bobbie, O.K. See ya in a bit." Click.

On two previous occasions, I had through Alma and Mrs. Moran arranged it so Cory and Gabe could go down to the Morans' ranch in San Martín and hunt. Both times before I had gone down there with them, not to hunt (I don't hunt), but to walk along with the two of them in the out-of-doors, observe, birdwatch. This weekend I had had to work. Gabe and Cory had driven down to hunt wild turkey, spring turkey, by themselves. I slipped into my clothes at breakneck speed, called my office, and drove carefully, rapidly, over to Cory's.

She had been crying; her face, her eyelids, were woefully swollen, she was sniffling, holding a Kleenex. Once inside the door I moved in to her immediately and put my arms around her, just held her, standing there.

"You're the first person I've told," Cory said finally, quietly. "I wanted to go over to the hospital again in another hour, I haven't slept, I wanted you with me."

"Come on sweetheart, let's sit down. Have you had any coffee?"

She nodded no, ran her fingers through the hair at top of her head.

"You want some? Let's make some. Come on back to the kitchen with me and tell me what happened."

"I feel like death warmed over," she moaned.

"Yeah well, and you don't look so hot either," I said.

As we walked back she laughed, a bitter, short little laugh, and blew her nose. "Well, shootin' your girlfriend will do that for ya."

I took her arm. "Come on, Cor, come on in here and sit down while I grind this shit up." I reached for the coffee beans in the icebox door.

Cory sat down heavily in one of the bar stools, moved her shoulders back and around, straightened her spine.

"Well...we had just seen a raft of the goddam things in a clearing about sixty feet or so ahead of us, and a course they zipped through the grass to the nearest brush line. Gabe was way closer to 'em than I was, pointed their path back to me and started moving toward the brush. I had seen three toms in with the hens and I pushed—pushed the safety back on the Browning." She stopped, and her hand flittered up to her brow. I went over and stood next to her, my hand on her shoulder. "I got so goddamned excited," she said, tears welling up again in her eyes. "We'd been hunting all damn day and hadn't seen turkey one." My hand pressed into her shoulder; I began rubbing her back. Cory looked down at the floor. "So I snapped the safety back. And, and...I wasn't running, I wasn't; I had just started to move quick toward that brush. I had the Browning, the butt of it, on my hip, barrel in the air. And I tripped. I—tripped." She started crying again. I put my arms around her shoulders and held her for a bit.

"Come on, Cory, come on now, it's O.K., Gabe's O.K., she's gonna be all right."

She straightened up again, went on. "It...went off as I was falling. I got up immediately, looked up ahead, Gabe had buckled, she was down. And I, ah God...."

"Take it easy, take it easy now."

"I set the gun down and ran, ran like crazy. She was conscious, stunned, just staring off, kinda, real white, white as a sheet, just sitting there, and the blood was splattering and spreading all over the back of her jacket."

Over the coffee, Cory continued telling the story. She had gotten Gabe back into the truck and had driven like hellfire over to Falfurrias to the clinic there. Gabe had taken an instant dislike to the doctor on duty, didn't trust him, so they asked if it would be O.K. to just clean and wrap the shoulder and drive back up to St. Ann's and have the shot removed up here. They had pulled into town around seven o'clock that night; the surgeon had operated on Gabe at nine-thirty. They gave Gabe Ampicillin and Darvon and sent Cory home around eleven.

Cory and I gathered up some pajama bottoms, a robe, Gabe's slippers, her make-up, a bottle of Shalimar, toothpaste, her toothbrush, a portable radio. She told me to get the book Gabe was reading out of her knapsack, which was thrown in a corner, along with Gabe's bra, plaid flannel shirt, and the bush jacket she'd had on when the accident happened. I unzipped the top flap of the knapsack and pulled out the book, *Even Cowgirls Get the Blues*. There were about a half-dozen holes shot in it; some of the shot was still embedded in the book.

I held it up to Cory. "Maybe we ought to buy her another copy, huh. Let's just stop at the drugstore and get her some magazines for now." I hurled the book back into the corner, picked up the rest of Gabe's blood-soaked things. "Cory, I'm just gonna set all this stuff in a sink of cold water, O.K.?"

Cory, sitting on the toilet, looked up and nodded wearily. "Thanks, yeah."

From the blinding illumination of the hospital corridor Cory and I filed through the open door to Gabe's room, awash in a shower of morning sunlight, an eastern exposure. Gabe was lying on her stomach, one arm dangling over the side of the bed. Her eyes were open. Gauze and tape were wrapped snug all over her right shoulder.

"Honey?" Cory asked softly. "Sweetheart, are you awake?"

On the bed Gabe's hand jostled a little, a frail half-wave. She cocked one eye up toward Cory, smiled wanly and said groggily, "Hi honey. Yeah, yeah, I'm awake. They already gave me breakfast. Oh hi, Bobbie," she said then, as I moved in to her periphery.

"Hey Gabe."

Cory pulled up a chair close to Gabe's bed, right in front of her. I sat down on the empty bed opposite.

"We brought you some stuff, girlfriend," Cory said quietly, and began taking the things out of the brown paper bag.

I thought my heart would break. There was something so painfully pitiful about Cory's pulling out those things, her hands shaking, and the pathetic, irritating rustle of the paper. She set the things up on the nightstand next to Gabe's bed. And Gabe. This big glorious tower of a woman, lying there so powerless and devitalized. Hurting. They both hurt. And I hurt for them. After Cory and I had been there for about an hour or so, a nurse brought in some more Darvon for Gabe. In about another twenty minutes she started getting groggy, needed to take a nap. Cory bent over her then and kissed her ever so tenderly, smoothed and petted her hair, backed off from the bed.

I squatted down beside Gabe right in front of her face. Through my teeth, in a Bogart accent, I said, "O.K., schweetheart: you be a good girl now, 'cos we're gonna spring ya tomarra."

Gabe, smiling, closed her eyes, opened them again. "You take care of this one, now, B.J. You get her home and make her take a nap."

"I'll take care of her, Gabe." I reached out and slipped a strand of hair behind her ear. I said: "Gabrielle, how can I have been in love with you all these years and borne it so—unobtrusively. The burden has been great."

Gabe flashed a grin at me, her eyes managing to twinkle through their drugged-over cast. She flicked her middle finger at my hand, resting on the top sheet. "Oh I dunno," she said still smiling softly. "I think it's been pretty—obtrusive."

Chuckling, I leaned in and kissed her lips as gently as I could. "We'll see ya later, gorgeous. Get some sleep."

Back at the house, Cory and I were once again out in the kitchen. She was pouring us a couple of brandies; I was standing at the sink, trying to scrub the bloodstains out of Gabe's clothes.

Cory sighed, nodding her head from side to side. "I feel worse'n fifteen fools."

I looked at her. "Fools don't know enough to feel bad, Cory." Turning off the cold water faucet, I thought of this too, and said it: "Chance has been very hostile to you just now, that's all."

She gazed at me dully. "Chance, huh."

"Sure. Chance."

For a long while we were both silent. Finally, Cory yawned, rubbed the back of her neck. "Speaking of chancy: you still seein' that woman?"

I turned back to the sink, continued scrubbing. "Less and less, actually." Peering out the window I added levelly, even devil-may-care, "I think she's going to move to New York."

"Hey, good! Great! Best goddam news I've heard all da—week." Cory had grown increasingly impatient with my Dana woes. I could feel her eyes on my back. She muttered, "Just let those things soak, Bobbie Jean. Best thing for 'em anyway." I rinsed my hands, dried them on a dishtowel. Cory went on, brightening still more, "Yeah, well I am very, very glad to hear that. Woman's been fucking you over for—how long now? Eight months? Am I right?"

I turned on my heel back toward her, folded my arms. "Yeah, well it hasn't all been shit, yunno."

Cory snorted, scoffed, "Ooo well, lessee, maybe 80 percent shit?" I stared down at the linoleum, not really wanting to continue the conversation in this particular vein.

She sighed again, a big loaded one. "You know what, Bobbie?" Her voice was rising. "You are just such a goddam Catholic, that's what you are! That's how you know how to suffer so damned much! And you know what else I think? I think you've been making yourself suffer with this woman on account of Alma, that's what I think."

I laughed, aghast. "What are you talking about! Whaddaya mean, 'on account of Alma'?"

Cory arched an eyebrow at me. "You know damn well what I mean. You've been feeling guilty about Alma Moran for years now, too goddam long. Enough's enough." She tched, stood up, moved toward me.

"Cory, that's ridiculous." It wasn't. She was right on, she had me dead to rights; I knew it the minute she said it. ["Ah Bobs. Still so Catholic. Was this really so? Well if therapy can channel my anger, maybe it can unload your guilt"—Dr. Moran, I love you.]

"Not ridiculous at all and you know it. You're always treating sex like it's some...religious experience or something. It's just fun, and, goddammit! it's funny too! It's too funny not to laugh at, despite all the other stuff that happens." She cupped my chin in her hand, pulled my face up to hers. "Look, I know it hurts; don't I know it. But you just gotta lighten up here, dammit."

There were tears in my eyes now. "But I love her, Cory. I've never loved anybody this much in my life."

Cory put her arms around me. "Well you just think you love her all that much, Bobbie Jean. It's just your feelings, is all. But this guilt business is gonna do you in. You gotta take it on the chin now, you gotta stop all this stupid...*pen*ance bullshit, wallowing in your own grief." She paused, squeezed my shoulder softly. "There's no glory in grief, yunno."

At this I began sobbing in earnest. Cory pulled me in close to her and held me while I cried.

After my weeping had died down some, Cory, staring up at the ceiling and swirling the brandy in her glass, said, "Well here it is, April the eighteenth, and there we are, a coupla royal fools seventeen days too late for our day of days." I looked up at her and sniffled. She reached for a bandana in her back pocket and handed it to me, saying, "Ya little jackass, I love ya."

Walpurgisnacht

I blew off work altogether that day, choosing to keep Cory company and fix a grand vat of chicken soup for her and for Gabe's return the day following. When at last I returned to my apartment, there was a note propped on top of the doorknob, wedged slightly into the doorjamb crack. Turning the key in the lock, I at once recognized the sprawling *Bobbie* on the envelope— Dana's handwriting. Stepping inside the door and flinging my windbreaker over the back of the couch, I examined the envelope: thick textured stationery in a thick cream color, with tiny, tiny multicolor squares flecked randomly all over it—mocha and apple green, vermillion, saffron, plum. And I considered, flopping down roughly on the couch and still staring at the envelope, that I might have expected such paper of her, that she doubtless always used such exquisite stuff—the stuff of notes, not letters—of hurried, stylish communication, breezy and minimal, straight to the point.

I sat there for some time on the couch, periodically slapping the envelope against the inside of my thigh, gazing out the window, coming back to the envelope again. It was a sucker's game, holding off opening it, but that envelope had a force to it, I could feel it, and I needed a moment or two to gear myself up for its message. Then I opened it and read, merely: *B.—Can you come over tonight about 7:30? Call me, Dana.*

That evening, as I pulled Lucille into Dana's driveway, I could see her just getting out of her Audi, reaching behind in the back seat for her briefcase. I walked up to her slowly, smiling. She smiled back, her face was taut and white; she looked exhausted, dreadful, dangerously brittle. Dana had been in New York for over five days, had been averaging at least two weekends up there out of every month for the past four months. I squeezed her arm. "Baby, you really look tired."

She sighed. "Yeah, yeah, I really am. Come on in, I'm dying to sit down."

Dana stood at the front door, squinting down at her keys in the half-light. After a second she pinched the top edge of one, shook the others off and down from the ring, slipped it into the lock and turned. Inside the hallway she set her attaché down on the marbletop stand, clicked open the hasps, and extracted a bottle of aspirin from one of the leather pouches inside.

I rubbed her upper arm lightly. "Headache?"

She turned, leaned in to me and kissed me, quick and light. "Life-ache. Aaa-ch. . . ." She took in a breath as though starting to say something else, then stopped, cut it off. "Lissen," she said then, "why don't you mix us up a pitcher of martinis. I think I'm gonna throw my body in the shower, see if that does any good."

Just a little later I was off in the kitchen, rummaging through the icebox for green olives, and I happened to see a stack of photographs on the counter. The lure of those pictures, to riffle through them, became instantly overpowering; I succumbed.

Most of the pictures were of Dana's house: front, back, the garden, the driveway, the deck, and the hot tub. There was one of Dana in there among them, and when I saw it, my heart sank, my throat constricted, my pulse started pounding in my temples. She was sitting out on the deck in what looked to be late afternoon light. But it was the expression in her eyes (she was staring right into the camera) that derailed me: there was in her face that unmistakable look, that old-time come-hithering, hunger, allure, just—sex. A look she hadn't expended on me in many, many weeks. And my mind started racing: who had taken these pictures? Who was that look for? How recently had they been taken? Why so many of the house? And the potential answers began flooding in, swamping me. I stared down at the snapshots with burgeoning despair. There was someone else in her life, someone else who was exciting her, making love to her, someone who'd taken my place. I was out of the picture, out of her life. At last. And I could think and feel "at last," and yet, gazing down at that photo, taking in the lust in those eyes, still feel my blood turn to fire-and-ice, a wild bellowing wellspring of desire—still. For her. Who no longer cared. For me.

But then I heard the bathroom door open down the hall. Quickly, I replaced the photographs exactly as they had been, grabbed up the jar of olives and the ice bucket, and headed out into the living room to the bar to finish the task at hand.

I was just stirring up the gin when Dana emerged from her bedroom wearing her rust-color silk *yukata,* a short-short kimono. She made a brief detour to the front hallway, came back out into the living room with a pack of cigarettes and her lighter. Looking like a movie star (I thought of Bacall, Hedy Lamarr, Veronica Lake), she was lighting one up, fairly sidling past that enormous mirror, and it occurred to me that she had never before looked as beautiful as she did right that minute. I clearly remember thinking that, just then: the small flame of the Zippo lighting up a glowing golden circle on her face as she held the cigarette to her lips; her hair, down, clinging full around her face; her hands white, her long fingers trembling slightly in the flickering light of the flame. Exhaling a big jet of smoke, she sat down cross-legged on the couch and pulled a large crystal ashtray toward her on the coffee table.

I handed her the drink.

She hummed, sipping, "Better days."

And here, cherished and inestimable reader, I must collapse the dialogue which in fact ensued, in large part because it would serve no reasonable purpose to reenact its meanness and stupidity, but also because the exact playbook of the Final Scene between Dana Pfeiffer and Bobbie Crawford began rattling itself off only after we had consumed most of the pitcher of martinis, and I simply cannot remember every nuance of our endscript. It was, for two women who were, sober, as articulate as Dana and I, sort of like the finale in grand opera when everybody is about to kill themselves off, and suddenly there is this total power blackout in the theatre. We just got drunk, that's all, and, given the circumstances, not such a bad idea—the gin helped shield us from the vitriol. Oh yes. It was a real stingeroo, all right.

First—no ifs, ands, or buts—came Dana's announcement that Bache had indeed offered her the job in New York, and that she was indeed going to take it. Probably move in another month. As she finished saying this, there was all of a sudden that feeling of the giant trap door below me again, waiting to spring open. I knew damned well Dana had no intention of asking me to come with her. And, in fact, the very next thing she said was, *Look, we both know things haven't been going real great for the two of us, and besides, I've met someone else up there. . . .*

Sproing, BLAP. My brain spun from the shock, advance clues and anesthesia notwithstanding, and a tiny, cylindrical core at the center of my midbrain (from whence affective disorder, da Blues, is/are thought to originate) began throbbing dully, more painfully by the second, pitchfork attuned to nothing save Dana's huge, stolid, incomprehensible indifference.

And another thing. Just before she told me about the other woman, and it was a woman (sorry, I'm still no good at putting this in an orderly sequence), just before that, just before it was almost out, I could sense it coming, that disclosure, see it smoking over her eyes, dilating the pupils, glittering lightly behind the irises. Before she'd ever said a word.

She called me cloying, spunkless. Said I had no ambition. Told me I lacked self-confidence, that she had no truck with crises of self-confidence. Told me she had too much self-respect to do that, berate herself. I hadn't been aware I was berating myself. And another javelinear exchange: "You don't love yourself." (D.) "That's the most vicious oversimplification I've ever heard—and, coming from you, downright pathetic." (B.)

Before I finally managed to hurl myself out of her house and drive off in a drunken nightmare of anguish, I remember asking her, quite quietly at one relatively fallow point during the *walpurgisnacht:* "The new girlfriend in New York. . .(and here a stage pause to break the hearts of millions), does she have—herpes?"

Dana said softly, evenly, "Why, yeah, as a matter of fact she does."

Not a Letter

In a well-intentioned effort to make a sort of separate peace with Dana, I sat down some two weeks after she had already left for New York and began writing her a letter. In a great sorrowful rage I later tore the thing up, but then reconsidered and saved the pieces; I have now reassembled it from its faded little envelope, carefully scotch-taping the bits together, thus being able to reproduce some of it here:

> Cara Binque (pronounced *Binkie*),
> What ho, hope you're getting settled. Down here, it's a
> splendid Sunday afternoon outside, just as ironic as the
> weather the day Jack Kennedy was shot. I should be out
> there in this weather, but time's been getting away from me
> lately and I feel a need to begin this letter right away, today,
> splendid weather notwithstanding.
> . . .there's the shiningness, the superstellar clarion streak of
> my passion for you—its sound, if it made one, would now be
> the Dopplered EEEEOHOHRRR of Darth Vadar's Imperial
> short-range fighter spaceship reeling out into the airless
> freezing black of space, the grating roar of a mechanical
> monster or a still voracious meteor contrailling its way out of
> this atmosphere, leaving behind pale me, quieter,
> holier. . .although like many comets, we who span the ages
> are scheduled to see it again someday; but for now it circles
> the nether ends of the galaxy, beyond Uranus it feels like,
> and all my frayed ganglia, echoing EEEEOHOHRRR them-
> selves, will eventually quieten down, resettle, smooth out. I'll
> begin to look a little older, a little more banal. Hegel had it
> right: "All things are in themselves contradictory, and it is
> this principle, more than any other, which expresses the
> truth. . . ."

Just as I was writing this, I heard a small *scritch-scritch* noise from out in the back yard and looked up out of my window to the big old pecan in the center of the lawn. At the base of the tree I had set a steer skull I'd found on a walk out in the country with Dana: a squirrel was gnawing on it, evidently sharpening its teeth. And seeing this slice of surreality, I felt a stab of pain that seemed to shatter behind my eyes in a burst of white light, settling and sifting down in me like radioactive air, right down to the marrow of my bones, bone-deep. I looked down at the letter I was writing and I realized: Dana would never answer it, that was all. It was really, really, really all over at last. And I looked up from the paper, across my bedroom to the huge maple-framed mirror Alma had given me years ago, and I stared back at myself. I smiled. It was a rather horrible smile, really, like the deadly end-of-the-road face Jeanne Moreau turns to Jim in *Jules et Jim* just before she drives their car off the bridge.

I did not, however, drive myself off a bridge. As my beloved Ramona said after Dana was not long gone, "No one dies of love in this day and age, old darling—too shame-making." Nor did I ever send Dana the letter, which was mostly unintelligible anyway. I finally considered that reminding her she had broken my heart (in the weeks after the break-up I remember standing out in my back yard in the moonlight and rasping a whisper at the moon, *You Broke My Heart)* would probably do nothing whatsoever to deflect her from her slash-and-burn trail through life.

Last Tag

As it happened I was, after that flash of white finality triggered by the skull-gnawing squirrel, far, far less macked out by the aftershocks than I had been throughout the acutal course of my affair with Dana Pfeiffer. Indeed I seemed to respond to life and living much as Jules, the cuckolded husband of *Jules et Jim,* was said to have done after Moreau's and Jim's deaths: his love for her had been so great, so immoderate, that his grief was rapidly overtaken by a sense of disencumbrance. In short, he felt tremendous relief. And so, with Dana gone and elsewhere involved (her lover's name was Amelia, poor soul), did I.

But it was not, of course, an utterly smooth transition. There were the usual waves of sorrow and loss, the worst ones always occurring in the dead middle of the night at 3:00 or 4:00 a.m. when I'd wake up and remember, *She's gone, it's over, she's gone* ("Ghosts and Monsters," reprise). Although her ghost did make an especially vivid appearance late one morning in my bedroom: I was making up my bed, tightening up the sheets, tucking in the bedspread, when all at once I was overcome by the vast emptiness of it, or rather, by how full the bed had felt when Dana had been in it. And with that feeling I suddenly remembered her lying there naked across it one afternoon, near the zenith, or what should have been the zenith, of our lovemaking, both of us sweating and breathless, my three fingers moving fast and hard in and out of her, the pinky snugged tight in her ass, and her moaning, moaning, *Fuck me, aw fuck me,* over and over again. . . .

A Single Life _____

The next three years were to go by slowly and uneventfully, abominably so. My life became a pallid blend of orderliness, a dilute mixture of days and nights and weeks and months accursed with an unshakable capricelessness. I went along ploddingly, unexpectant, my days a run of the commonplace, a colorless strand of hours, rising, working, tending errands, sleeping dreamless and alone.

Not that I had lost my sense of humor altogether, heavens to bets no. There were my good and stalwart buds to hang out with, Jackie, Ramona (though they both had new girlfriends by then, and getting together with them was more rare), Cory, Gabe, Sherman, Alice, Chuke, buncha other folks too. I wish you had time to meet all of them ["But this is a potboiler and you gotta stick to the basics, right? Signed, not stridently, Mita"—more Alma scrawlings from her copy of the manuscript.] Yes, I really do wish you could meet them, but this is a *romance,* a story of romantic love, and I've gotta stick to the basics, right? My friends know, they know I love them. They also know that many's the time I might not have made it, without their help. Well, I would've made it, but it would've been one whole helluva lot harder than it was anyway. So. Onward.

But, an unshakable capricelessness. I worked very hard at my job. Very hard indeed. Getting all those programs together that first year at the *Register* warn't easy; sniping errors warn't either. Many's the night I would work late, huddled over with tube work, untangling infinite loops and other snafus, debugging collisions, opening up the territory, juggling, juggling like nobody's business, crumpling up code sheet after code sheet and tossing them, with for the most part fair hook shots, into my garbage can, strategically located for my hooks an exact eight feet away. Most times I preferred working at night. At least at night the building manager would shut down the Muzak system. (I have it in my mind that there is one room in the myriad rooms of hell that holds a drove of the damned, condemned throughout infinity to listen to Hugo Winterhalter's rendition of "Nights in White Satin.")

I got so many headaches, that first year on my job. I remember a real beaut once, a lollapaloosa, my eyelids paper-thin and slow to raise and lower.

Codeine barely took the edge off it. It was close to sunset; I was cringing from the sunlight as it sheeted golden along the bronze venetian miniblinds on the southwest windows of my cubicle, although it was disturbingly beautiful, that light, and despite my pain I kept squinting at it for split seconds at a time. I had the feeling of something immensely powerful and protecting, a connection to something, some center of something somewhere, and it continued to feel like that to me for quite a while, even with the headache. I work with a hippie programmer guy named George, a revisionist Zen Buddhist who claims that programmers have "ties with the infinite"; but I hadn't heard George say that yet, that evening I had the headache. Maybe it's true. Or maybe headache, fatigue, existential malaise, and codeine can, at certain times of the year, combine to give one the feeling of connectedness to the infinite, or something like it.

After year one, my job stress abated quite a bit: I got better and faster at what I did, and arranging French leave—bureaucratic downtime—became easier. On occasion I got pretty bored with it all. Any job at which one can come in first thing in the morning and spend an hour and a half reading the newspaper holds a strong potential for imposing boredom on one sooner or later.

So the pall began settling over me, though I didn't realize it right off because my solitary routine was often very satisfying, in its own way. And I imagined, as mostly one does, that I was leading my life in the best way possible, although I know now that I was not, then, particularly happy. It was a regenerative, in-between time. No psyche-shattering lows, but then, no big flap of highs, either. From those times certain arid memories persist: of balancing myself on a soda chair in the dark as I stretched to change a light bulb; of one of a host of Sunday morning paper readings alone during which I had to listen several hours to a bluejay scream her rage and grief over the loss of a fledgling that Ramón my cat had earlier harried to death; of hunks of burnt angel food cake scattered beside the garbage bin of a neighborhood condominium. I would pad around the house in my sheepskin slippers, wash out lingerie on Sunday evenings, slip into bed (clean sheets! clean hair! clean me!) with a cup of cocoa. Read. One Saturday evening I got stoned all by myself and actually watched "Love Boat," and worse still actually found myself smiling at the ingratiating scenes. Worse, worse still, a few weeks later I caught myself watching it again and smiling again—I wasn't even stoned, that time. And then the late movie would come on. Lots of nights I'd stay up watching it and fall asleep before it concluded, wake up at two or three to the static hiss and screen glare of nontransmission, crawl into bed, and be nettled by the cold sheets for a while, unable to drop off to sleep again.

Every blessed thing in my life felt as though it could and should be deferred; nothing pressed at all. My work clothes stayed in last nights's pile, unrearranged. Dust settled where it would, until a nesting fit overcame me, usually once a month. One weekend day I was in fact dusting off my desk and happened to go through a box of old pictures. I selected two of them and set them out upright on the desk: one that my pal Rudy had taken the August before when I'd visited him in the Montrose, another that Jackie had snapped of Alma and me on the front porch of the Hotel Paradiso, our old home on Casper Street, six years ago. In Rudy's picture I'm standing in his den, with my Hawaiian shirt and blue nylon running shorts on. I am holding one of Rudy's cigarettes, gesturing in the manner of Tallulah and Bette, very grande dame, posed before a Whitman sampler-type embroidery framed upon the wall, a creation of Rudy's boyfriend Ted, which reads: "Who Isn't Glib Is Dead, Baby"—a Frank O'Hara-ism. So I was looking glib, the sly old thing at the party, the one with the broadest-based social intelligence, whose vivacity depends on social intelligence, the double-entendrist who waves farewell to all as she leaves the festivities, alone, in the midshank of the evening. I had put on some weight, last summer, and as I stood at my desk staring down at those pictures, I was even heavier than I had been that August.

In Jackie's picture I am considerably thinner and even cockier-looking, though uninformedly sly, a *tabula rasa* holding not a cigarette but a joint. I had apparently just taken a hit, and either Jackie or Sherman or somebody else off-camera had said something to make me laugh. I was choking back the laughter (my face muscles were contracting just that way, trying to hold the hit in, squelching the laugh). My other hand is loosely slipped inside Alma's belt. Mita is tense and frozen, younger than Thumper, probably stoned too.

They made an odd, unsettling juxtaposition, these two photographs. After a while I set them back into the shoebox marked PIX, and shoved the box back into the closet, high atop a shelf.

Night Spanner _____

My knockout next-door neighbor Lee was bounding up my front porch steps. Through the screen door she yelled inside to me that she and Nick (Nicky, La Nicolette, her lover) were going to the women's bar that evening—though Lee merely said *the* bar, I knew what bar she meant—and wanted to know if I'd like to go with them. Pushing my chair back from my desk, a wincing yawp over the old wood floor, I crossed the room and stood opposite Lee in the doorframe; she rocked gently on her heels as we spoke, a big woman, handsome, tall and dark, freckled and shy, soft-spoken, a little young, a little uncertain around her broad shoulders. I liked her very much, liked Nicky too. "Sure," I said, "why not." Lee nodded and said we'd leave around ten o'clock, bounded back down the stairs two at a time again. I watched her blankly as she strode across the yard whistling something improvised, her hands deep in her pockets, her long black hair falling loose in her down-turned face.

Returning to my desk I sighed, smiled at the sigh. Why not the bar, why not dancing and drinking? After all, it was Saturday night, and I hadn't been out for a while. And suddenly, out of nowhere, I envisioned myself picking up a heavy forged-steel spanner and with all my might hurling it skyward—sort of like the ape throwing the tapir bone up to the stars in *2001*. It was spring: why not throw the spanner into the night and watch it fall?

A Flashback-flashback

There was a time, I was musing as I ran my bathwater that April evening (in '79? '78? no, '79), when going to the bar excited a brittle sense of possibility, of expectation bordering on the manic. As I sank into the bubbles and set my rubber duckie adrift, I recalled, fondly, that lame-brain exhilaration and knotted-up stomach I used to feel on Saturday nights long ago, performing my matador's toilette—I thought I had those instincts then—getting all gussied up for the bar, for dancing, drinking, and flirting, for the very most part indeed (as I was then yet to learn) for flirting's sake alone. My own primping and preening rituals included playing old Stevie Wonder records while sipping on bourbon-and-water, debating which black clothes to wear (all my fave clothes were then, and would be again one day, black and purple, the very colors of witchery), posing like a juvenile stiletto in the full-length mirror, and luxuriating in the final douse with *L'Interdit,* applied precisely forty-five minutes before roadtime.

Bar-going, the Real Retrospect _____

In all those many, many Saturday nights of bourbons and black turtlenecks and God knows how many bottles of Givenchy, I never once took a woman home with me from the bar, nor was I taken home myself. I never asked anyone, and no one ever asked me.

Somnambula, Reprise _____

I was still soaking in the tub. From the part-way open window in my bathroom I looked up to see the crow moon just on the rise, and it was still light out—a sure sign of the inexorable slanting of the northern hemisphere back, back toward the sun, and...spring. Nothing I could do about it. Through no fault of my own, spring was really here. Across the yard I could hear young Lee warming up on her alto sax, tootling into an old Louis Armstrong song, "I Got a Right to Sing the Blues"; high notes, low notes filtered in bits and spurts through the window as I continued to play in the tub. I had recently bought a black Spanish bar soap called *La Toja*. Of late I had been getting sullen and irritable as I rinsed off pubic hairs from the big bars of Ivory; so to avoid that, to avoid being reminded that I had a pubis at all—things were that glum—I bought this black soap. But just then I happened to notice that, even though I couldn't see them, I could still feel the little curls stuck to the soap. Nothing I could do about it. I torpedoed the soap under the suds and slapped the tubwater (ploak!), creating a wave of bubbles that capsized one of the boats.

Who was that masked girl anyway, that black-turtlenecked hoodlum—so assured, no, so ruthless, un-ruthful, insensate? So stupid. And so damn sure of all the damned answers. No, not of the answers, just of the booga-booga sixth sense that was going to lead me to them. And now (just then) as I unstoppered the drain, I didn't feel the least bit sure of that sense. The magnetics felt awry, the needles spin, frantic. I felt my brow, my forehead, knitting down to a frown. I stepped out of the tub, towelled off, rubbed in baby oil all over, missing that one spot in the middle of my back, as always. Wiping off a small space in the steamy, unsilvering mirror, I squinted hard at myself. Things had really changed, boy. The fully adult version of that young smart-ass stared heavily back at me, and for a mini-instant, a wave of panic passed over the eyes like something shadowy and lethal snaking fast below water, of there being no answers other than the steady accumulation of little lines, crow's-feet, puffiness around the eyes, the lone line in that throat grown deeper than ever. Then, just as rapid as that shadow-look, an exorcistic smile broke from the mirror lips: reassuring, forgiving, loving, making my face—hey!—

suddenly real goddam good-looking again, worldly, a face with the proverbial story-to-tell.

It was a smile that made me think of one of my favorite screen smiles—Joel Grey's in *Cabaret,* cynical and sinister, glinting into the camera as the Hitler youth sang at the beer garden. And then I thought of Jack Nicholson in *Five Easy Pieces,* not smiling, staring at himself in the filling station men's room mirror, deciding to abandon Karen Black, waiting for him outside in the car. I said, out loud, to my reflection: "Being alone is better than being with someone who drives you crazy." And I thought but did not say: Being with someone who drives you crazy is sometimes preferable to being alone. Or, any port in a storm, any storm in a lull. And that sometimes evanescent, always untrackable sixth sense, whatever the hell it may be and though never dependable, is still the only homing device I have. This is not, I thought, an altogether bad face; its decency shows. *Who do you see in the mirror first thing in the morning, Dana had asked me once, and how do you feel about her? I don't know, Dana, I replied. Who do you see and how do you feel about her? That's a very personal question,* she'd said snippily, and changed the subject. Hell's bells, even Audrey Hepburn, the "inspiration," said Givenchy himself, for his *L'Interdit,* was once quoted as having said that there are mornings when she wakes up and sees this toad in her bathroom mirror—I mean, Audrey! I looked down into the sink and tightened the dripping faucet, then back up at the face. No, not altogether bad at all. I blew me a kiss, shuffled off naked into the kitchen, switched on the radio on top of the icebox to (ah magic) Little Anthony's "Goin' out of My Head":

> *I want you to want me*
> *I need you so badly,*
> *I can't think of anything but you . . .*

> *I must think of a way into your heart,*
> *There's no reason why*
> *my being shy*
> *should keep us apart. . . .*

I trotted into the bedroom to put on a T-shirt and jeans. Standing in the semidark of my room, I could hear the crickets begin to sing in the back yard, a sound that instantaneously soothes me, absolutely. Homing. Homing.

The Spanner Suspendu

In the yellow '59 Dodge pickup Lee had been so lovingly renovating for so long a time now, we three—big Lee driving, one arm propped on the open window ledge; Nicky, squirming and devilish, poking me in the ribs, kissing Lee's neck and rubbing her thigh and laughing; me fiddling with the radio tuner, sillying by the minute from Nick's high jinks—were hurtling across town through the rich spring night, the Gulf's nightwind reversal lifting deep draughts of mountain laurel and jasmine through the open windows of the cab. Lee had, artfully, blowtorched out two squares in the truck roof, welded the fittings for hatches, and inserted two clear plastic sliding bubble hoods, a t-top, a skyroof. That afternoon it had rained a little, so it was cooler out, the stars brighter.

As we sped along the streetlamps overhead cut arhythmic patches of mercury light over Nick's and Lee's faces and shoulders. Boy God were they ever a handsome pair, these two—handsome women, horsewomen. Lee, the *cavalière*, the swaggerer; Nicky the one with the horse sense and the jokes, curly and dark, dark like Lee but not quite as tall, the same straight back, square shoulders. Square shooters both. And they both had on bluejeans too, Lee in Levis (Lee has a Levi butt), Nick in Wranglers (a hiney for same), white sneaks, white cotton western shirts, painstakingly pressed. The moon, a peach opal now, was riding high over the river, and as I spotted it again I felt: this is probably as good as I'm gonna feel all night—in transit, these two pleasing young women, deep in love, now fallen silent beside me. I'm at peace; let it stop here.

Inner-city skyscrapers blocked the moon as we turned south toward the bar. Hitting the strip we saw that the town was turned out. Our town was on wheels, on foot, on dates, drunks and music everywhere this Saturday night—just another Saturday night,full of the illusions and delusions, the moment, the sense of time suspended. I thought again: let it stop, let it stop here, the spanner stock-still in the stratosphere.

Bar Thoughts

Spanner thoughts vanished as we parked and I looked up to see a very young woman, maybe eighteen or so, long brown hair, a babyface with superpale pink lipstick, tooling slowly down the street in front of the bar (its name, actually, is The Violet Crown) in a 1967 teal-blue Fleetwood convertible, low in the saddle, her young white fingers, covered with rings, draped easily over the steering wheel. She was chewing gum. She seemed so fresh, so uncomplicated. And I thought, she must've inherited that big old car, probably from some family matriarch. The Caddy and its Texas-girl driver turned the corner, disappeared. As Lee and Nick and I clambered out of the truck, the dull throb of disco music became audible, from a block and a half away. Briefly I considered this din's damage to eardrums—I mean, if you can hear it a block away—then blew it off. Because that's what you do when you go to a bar, you blow it the hell off, gear down to remote control.

Inside a radical dark assaulted the eyes. The rose-colored neon behind the stodgy gatewomen blinded us for an instant, like mule deer in the headlights. We fished for bills, forewent hand stamping. The management had recently done over the foyer in cheesy black-and-silver vinyl wall strips, uninspired contemporaneity. We pushed through heavy black-lacquered doors, through a second set of louvered saloon doors, into the dance hall. It was a warehouse once, this place—ceilings to the moon. Donna Summer thundered over us like Hoover Dam cracking, so loud she shuddered disconsolate in the torso, disrupting heartbeats. The three of us huddled at the long curved bar, our backs turned to the sea of women milling behind us. Four bartenders swished and poured in sleek self-conscious choreography. As one of them served up our drinks, I got nettled all over with that half-embarrassed, half-peacock switch to bar ethos, stage carnality.

With drinks in hand Nick and Lee immediately slipped off into the crowd, into the floating crush of Blacks chewing gum, of chain-smoking cowgirls, Chicanas butch y femme, intense or detached, wholesome freckle-faced teens in overalls and workboots. Burr cuts, high heels, kicker boots, eyeshadow. Punkers and preppies. The women in tweed blazers are lawyers. Good God how tough they all look! God, and so do I! And I felt proud, proud to be a daughter of Amazonas, a lezbeen and a Texan like all these young lezbeens and Texans, bravas from Dallas and Houston, Waco and Beaumont, El Paso, Corpus, Abilene, Midland. But as I stood at the bar I realized with a jolt that I was looking wistful, God forbid, totally unacceptable at the bar, and changed expressions to something more disinterested and rote. Ronda, one of the barbacks, caught my eye and, smiling most sweetly, wiggled her chubby little fingers at me. I smiled back at her—a good-hearted sensible woman, Ronda; drives a delivery truck by day.

And here we all were, we lesbians, simply following our social contract. I noticed again that none of these women ever look at one another for very long here, an obvious etiquette. Some of them were darting through the crowd, some small groups were standing loose together over there cattycorner to me; others had settled early at the tables skirting the dance floor, now packed with a thicket of dancers whirling and turning like one great shuddering beast. Pink and yellow lightwaves were splaying out from the glitterball's spin, washing over the dancers and lighting up here a head thrown back in laughter, there a swirling hand or huddled shoulders. The volume of the music made conversation with more than one other person arduous: you either bellowed or went outside. Up front, though, a clump of women were using sign language; one of them had evidently just told a joke, because they were all breaking out in deep hoarse guffaws. At the back of the hall were a brace of solemn, slim-hipped cowgirls in jeans and western shirts and boots, cigarettes drooping from their thin lips as they played pool fast and sharp. In one corner several couples of bored-looking women were lounging on Victorian wing-backed divans. I caught the scent of marijuana as two mountain women in matching plaid flannel shirts passed by me arm in arm.

Eventually, in dribs and drabs, five or six recognizable faces emerged from the dance floor, smiled at me or didn't, moved on. There for instance went Eve Cooper, on whom I had this major crush for maybe three weeks, who dated me once and never called again. It was all right. The crush faded of course. That was—three years ago. There was Nora Beck, with her new lover—Judy? Jamie?—who for years had made, for some reason I'd never understood, a career out of ignoring me each and every time she saw me. There was tiny Pam Gordon, fellow bureaucrat; Kathy Preece, who one night at a party took my breath away kissing me in the back yard, the kiss of a lifetime, I'd thought about it often; there was Aphra Williams, looking bored and hip as always, nodding her head back at me slightly as she saw me and slipping past quick, just touching my elbow; and, be still my heart, Anna Redding (Sherman fast on her heels), who I knew with failsafe certainty had always had the hots for me, as I for her, but in whose case circumstance of one sort or another—other girlfriends and timing, timing—had always intervened, keeping us narrowly apart; and last, Mary Reicher, with whom I had slept one nutso night out in the country, who I wish I could make love with again sometime, but not all the time. What a cauldron of stories, these! What melange, diversity, hodgepodge!

And seeing all these women, and all the other women in that bar that night, I recalled a remark of Gabe's, also here at the bar, one evening ages ago. We'd been standing close together, quietly watching everyone coming and going. "Sometimes I just don't know," she'd said sadly, shaking her head, "sometimes I just don't know what I think about women." I'm sure now that she'd meant women here, as we seem here, in this asphyxiating, hormone-charged dive, this endless smog of Camel Lights and Miller Lites, Marlboros, margaritas. And just as I had back then with Gabe, as I did most often in the bar, I wondered: What have these women learned? *What's my motivation, coach.*

Just then I noticed that a stunning girlchild, who must've presented a false i.d., long curly blonde ringlets and huge baby-blue Botticelli Venus eyes, *madre!* kept stealing carefully blank looks at me from across the far end of the bar, glancing up furtively from her beer. I raised my glass to her, *Salud.* She turned away and studied the dancers, then moved into the crowd. Oh that's rich. If her looking at me were mostly purposeless, then she has just removed herself from my misinterpretation; if not, then I, being older, should follow her, ask her to dance, ask her her sign, her major, any goddam thing at all. Ethos lesbos. But I was too inert, that night, to even make the effort. I stood my ground at the bar.

At the tables I saw a young Chicana couple, their arms intertwined, tossing back brandies; they leaned in to each other for a thick languorous kiss. And I, watching them, mildly inflamed, felt again that hateful stab of: isn't this sordid, this place, isn't it sleazy. (Calm down, Bobbie, calm down. . .they're just kissing because they can, here, because this is a lesbian bar, because they're safe here, kissing each other.) But I bet they won't go home and make love tonight, those two. They'll be too drunk or too tired, and there's always Sunday morning anyway.

Jostling me out of this revery, a woman easily six feet tall brushed by me close, turned and smiled a big silly smile at me. Another maverick. She hasn't really come here to pick anybody up. She's probably here with some bunch of friends; she'll probably go home to her bed alone too, like the other mavericks, like me. The jostling, the smiling, the looking, it's all just flirting, just soft bravada, lesbians playing with overture, with building up tension, a strong suit of ours.

Swirling the ice cubes in my drink, I noted that everyone here tonight looked eighteen—dewy, irresolute, swinging their small hips and laughing. Where are the older ones, dammit, the women who've learned that building love takes caution, and enormous luck; that love, once built, can vanish in the heat of summer, in the dead of winter or night or morning, simply like a door that was open, closing. They're probably home watching TV, washing out underwear, feeding their cats. Over my bourbon, I sulked. If they're there, then why was I here with the hip-swishers, raising my glass to disappearing children? Perhaps just for that, I thought then: to raise a glass, for gesture, for this form alone. Soft bravada—that in a woman's woman's world, even this, coming together in this noxious place, just coming here, showing up, dancing and drinking a little, is a gesture of love and bonding. Not so territorial as a touch, not the deep soft immersion of kisses, but a kind of love, tribal love, nonetheless. We have this bond. The Fates have been both generous and harsh with us. We have this bond.

Admirèd Miranda!

And then, just then, I saw Miranda—o Miranda Gray!—whose story I have, forgive me, neglected to tell you. Miranda! slouching up against an oak support beam to the side of the dance floor, Miranda gazing at the dancers, Miranda in a breathily soft-looking red shirt with a white tuber rose at the lapel. Miranda, how are you here? I stood at the bar grinning, watching her, still unseen by her, adrift in nostalgia, lightheaded with expectation. Let me tell you about that summer of Miranda's five years ago in a moment, beloved reader; right now I'm anxious to get over there and say hello.

I moved toward her, shouldering my way gently and confidently through this now greatly softened crowd. The closer I got, the more I could see that from her languid crunching of the ice in her drink, telltale habit, Miranda was quite in her cups. Her amber gaze, lingering tenderly over the dancers—cripes! those other-worldly eyes!—was brimming with thinly masked trouble; I wondered what. Then she turned and spotted me, her face instantly transforming, instantly releasing its sorrow. Fairly bubbling over, she hurriedly set her drink down on the stairs behind her and ran to me, slipped her arms stealthily around my neck, good fit still, and like a small child slowly kissed me on the cheek, a kiss of reprimand, and of absolution too. Then she pulled back, regarding me straight on for several seconds (yes, very looped), smiling happily. My arms, closing around her broad back, triggered memory: of Miranda and me riding horses in a maize field that summer, angling through the stalks, the horses skittish from our own skittish vigilance for snakes. In the saddle that August-white afternoon, I had leaned over to Miranda, laughing beside me, put my arm gaucholike around the small of her back, and kissed her, a salty deep crazy-hard kiss.

Miranda Gray and I had met that June through Cory, whom she was staying with en route to Los Angeles to begin work making the costumes for a film—a union daughter, her entree to the industry had been assured by her mother, a Hollywood *couturier* of the '40s and '50s. Miranda had just waded through a divorce from her husband, a young zoologist on the tenure track in Connecticut, a cold man, she had said, a cold marriage. So there we were, me still healing from Alma, she, even though she had filed, from Carl. We had reached out to one another like two drowning women, comforting each other as often only strangers can. Our need to dispel anguish and reassemble the substance of our lives was great, so immediately apprehensible in the other, that we exempted ourselves from the old code, acknowledging that neither was equipped for anything else than what we had, such as it was, to give each other then, for right then, nestling happily, unmindfully together in the hot short starless nights. It was a decent, sweet reciprocity, and throughout our summerlong foraging for our selves, we were together content. But enough: I must return to the Miranda of the here and now ["or the there and then"— says Alma].

"How in the hell have you been!" Miranda was yelling now, holding me by the shoulders. "We tried to call you tonight," and she pointed out McIver and Gabe on the dance floor, who had themselves spotted Miranda and me standing together and were shouting something over the racket to us, motioning us out to dance, smirking like the co-conspirators they are, twirling and vanishing into the dancer ocean. Miranda and I had written for a year or so after that summer, had called one another on occasion, and had then allowed Cory to transmit random bits of information about our goings on for us. But right now, she just took both my hands in hers, squeezing them lightly, her own fingers as intelligent as I now remembered they had been.

"I was working at home, I unplugged the phone," I explained. "You look fabulous, wonderful." And she did, better than ever, her thick black hair long and layered, her small round satyr's body shed of some of the pounds she'd put on after the divorce. Those cat's-eye ginger eyes of hers, though now grown older and looking a little weary tonight, still held the same light fire, the same needlelike glee they'd had back then. "Are you still in L.A.?" I was shouting at her.

She was, and was in between films (Miranda always calls them *features;* no one in the business, she told me, refers to them as *movies*) for a couple of weeks. She was just in town for the weekend. As we tried to talk over the roar, I began to feel slightly ill at ease and, weasling out of her hands, slipped my arm around her waist, an old friend's pose, but she quickly pulled me back to face her, resettling her arms around my neck, weaving a little and laughing, holding on. She leaned in for my mouth, grinning at me, kissed me on the nose instead, laughed again. I was embarrassed; my memories were crowding me.

"Miranda love, what are you drinking?" I asked, though I could smell the tequila on her breath.

"Mar-gar-ee-tas," she said, overrolling the *r*'s and tamping out the *t* like a too-full teakettle at the boil, "ha! What about you, chunkie, your usual bourbon and bourbons?"

"Correct."

"Let's go get us another drinkie, baby Bobbie." I didn't need another one and I knew she didn't either, but I followed her anyway as she pulled me by the hand back up to the front bar. She positively glided through that crowd, her hips and shoulders an ode to balance and grace. Suddenly she turned around and laughed at me again, that brave-new-world laugh of hers that effervesces from the core of her out through those magnificent fiery eyes, a whole language of mirth and pain and compassion, and, as she swivelled back and led on with me still in tow, I knew I was in for it.

What I Was In For

After we had darted back through the body-sea, maneuvering with our drinks to the oak post once more, Miranda took my drink from me and set it and hers down on a for-now unpeopled table, moved herself in close to me, pressing her forehead slowly but tipsily against mine, and said something I didn't hear. My lips began an odyssey across her cheek, over her hair to her ear, whispered: I didn't catch that. Her eyes closed as I read her lips: *Never mind; dance with me.* I didn't want to dance either, but I felt dutiful, so again I trailed behind her out to the dance floor. It was a slow dance, some sultry country and western number, maybe Tanya Tucker. As we danced, turning and shuffling, Miranda kept pushing me back from her and taking me in, beaming like a parent at her child's recital. Her hands and her back were warm and moist; when she'd pull me in close to her, I could pick up her scent, a sweet pungence like orange peel, pale woodsmoke.

And I began thinking again of that horseback kiss, the sibilant whirr of cicadas all around us as we drew our horses up, stopping to revel in the sight of each other in this cowgirl dream. . . . The horses stamp their hooves and splutter foam, jangling their bits. The stirrup leather winces under me as I lift myself and press my horse's ribs with my left leg, leaning to Miranda on my right. Her mare joggles into mine, jouncing me out of reach. Miranda laughed then, too (she was always laughing at me, I remembered). I snatched her saddlehorn with my left hand, steadying and balancing myself, and with my right arm took hold of her around the waist, hoisting myself over to her, ah Cisco! She had thrown her head back for my kiss with unendurable drama, had closed her darkening-fire eyes only as I neared her face, exhaled deep as my tongue dove down into her mouth, leaning back with me in the kiss as our horses shimmied away, breaking it off.

What I Was In For, Further Elucidated _____

Here I was at this bar, unexpectedly in the company of the real Miranda Gray, dancing in a kind of misplaced rapture, fixated on that spectacular kiss of five summers past. I could not dissociate myself from its memory: when the here-and-present Miranda would look at me, I would tune out to her ghost in the shimmering heat of that hill-country maize field. In short, her ghost seemed to be winning out, eclipsing the flushed and unsteady woman with whom I was dancing. Our past together had been perfect, or at least whole, an intact shadow play, and yet here we were in an imperfect present, tottering about in each other's arms like a pair of malconjugated verbs.

Nonetheless, the Spanner ————————————————

As Tanya or Dolly trailed off and the four-four thump of disco started up again, Miranda and I lolled away from the floor, her arm slung heavily over my shoulders, mine uneasily over hers. After we'd flopped down on one of the divans, a big dour-looking woman in rimless glasses came and cleared away empty glasses from the end tables, retreated to the back bar. Miranda and I were trying to chat about things, about her work and mine, her travels. Then I ventured a question about Gretchen. "Are you still with her?" No she was not, and from the expression in her face as she answered, I knew instantly what the trouble was I'd seen in her eyes earlier. Transcending the roar of the bass was impossible, though, so after the last round Miranda suggested we go gather up Cory and Gabe and return to their house, where she was of course staying over. I found Nick and Lee shooting pool in the back and took my leave of them. Lee pushed a whopping cannon of a joint into my hand and kissed me archly on the cheek.

Cory sat docile and blowzy in the front seat while Gabe, more sober, drove their new great white Blazer. Miranda and I were sitting, cozily now, very close together in the back as we rode along, she rubbing the top of my thigh affectionately, very dear, me periodically squeezing her left shoulder. We were all nattering like prom night kids as the cooling night sped by; our talk, our banter and laughs, both in the van and later on in Cory's kitchen over coffee and coffee-flavor Häagen Dazs, went by in a blithering late-night whirl. Only after Cory had made a mock-stately excuse for herself and Gabe, backing off from Miranda and me at the kitchen counter with Draculian formality, did Mir (I really did call Miranda *Mir* every once in a while) and I find ourselves confronted outright with what had been at the back of our loopy thoughts since leaving the bar: that unless I pulled a Doris Day, either at Miranda's behest or my own, and cabbed it home or slept on the sofa, it sure did look as though she and I were going to be sleeping in the same bed that night. And although we were both still well-anesthetized, we were a little uncomfy about that possibility, and were showing it—I mean, five years. . . . Finally Miranda just took my hand and said, "Come on baby, I'm tired," and we went on back to the back bedroom and skinned out of our clothes, she on one side of the bed and me on the other, slipped ourselves in between the sheets, and with the bed lamp still on smiled blearily at one another from our pillows.

"This is somethin', huh," Miranda laughed, rubbing her nose.

"Somethin'," I laughed too ["Scintillating repartee, Bobs. . .Um-wha, Me"— Moran striking again]. We kissed then, Miranda and I, a hazy thick insentient kiss, only a semblance of ardor (we were so tired, it was so late, we'd had so much to drink), and we kissed again, and the radio was on, and the lamp burned still, and I was retracing lines on Miranda's shoulder that five years prior I had traced with new-world awe, and I looked up and realized, with a wave of both sorrow and relief, that she had passed out.

A Morning After

The first thing I became conscious of the next morning was the home-sweet-home smell of bacon wafting throughout the house, with Cory in the kitchen being Mom, very quiet out there; the second thing was that my head felt as though it had had a very large goosedown pillow jammed inside of it. I lumbered out of bed. Miranda slept on, naked and crumpled in the mostly middle of the mattress. I put on my T-shirt and jeans and skulked off to the kitchen. Cory stood at the stove, nudging the bacon about in the pan with a fork. With big doleful eyes she looked at me, wordlessly handed me a cup, and pointed over her shoulder at the coffee pot atop the hotplate.

In a hushed monotone she said, "Good morning."

"And a good-good morning to you," I said, with the same deliberately grave expression. "And thank you, God," I said gazing out the back window, "for another beautiful day." I poured the coffee, added milk; it became a dead greyish color. "Gabe still asleep?"

"Went to buy a paper." A pause, the sizzling of the bacon the only noise in the kitchen. "Bobbie Jean, when you can focus those baby-blues of yours, would you squeeze up those oranges over there for us?"

"Sure I can, Cory, but wouldn't you rather I cut 'em up first?"

Cory gave me a slow withering look. "Oh we're feeling chipper this morning, are we."

"No, darling Cory, chipper is the very last thing we are feeling this morning."

She arched an eyebrow at me and asked, unsmiling, "Did we not get enough beauty rest last night, 'baby Bobbie'?"

I shot her the withering glance. "That, Cory Mae, is none of your goddamned business." McIver: Born to Snoop.

Cor looked at me levelly. "Passed out, didja?" and she cackled one of her big ha's! as she turned back around to her stovetop.

"Oh leave me alone, Cory." To hell with it.

There was a small mirror just beside the kitchen back door: I went over and surveyed the damage. "Jesus," I whispered. "Well, looks aren't everything."

Behind me I heard Cory turn, and in a voice that jarred me with its decibel level she snapped, "They sure as shit are!"

At that moment I heard the front door slam and Gabe striding through the living and dining rooms to make an appearance at the kitchen entryway. She was grinning from ear to ear in her Ray-Bans, from Cory to me and back. She said softly, still grinning, "So how we doin', you two."

Cory said, "Well I haven't killed her yet," and then, shooting me a sharp look, "but I might if she doesn't get honking with those goddam oranges."

"Oh all right, cheese-*us*," and I got them down from their hanging steel basket and began washing them in the sink. Gabe sat down heavily on one of the bar stools at the counter and started reading the paper. As I was slapping my hands dry on my jeans, I felt something small and lumpy in my back pocket and reached back to pull out a torn half of a joint, the reefer Lee had given me in the bar last night, all shreddy now. "If you guys have some rolling papers, this," I held up the half-joint, "might become extremely important after a while."

Returning her attention to the bacon again, Cory muttered, "Gabe does."

Just then Miranda rounded the corner and stood in the doorframe like a tousled gnome instantaneously transported from her safe, leaf-and-twig gnome's burrow to the very middle of New York's Lexington Avenue at rush hour. "Ouch," she barely squeaked, her eyes still closed.

Gabe, cracking up, got off her stool and went over to Miranda, put her arms around her. "Good morning to you," she sang gently, "good morning to you, good morning Miranda, and I love you too."

Miranda, murmuring deep into Gabe's chest, said, "Were there any survivors?"

Gabe laughed, hugged Miranda some more. "No honey, I don't think so." When Miranda pulled back from Gabe, Cory went through the same routine with her, handing Miranda the empty cup and pointing to the coffee.

"Well, the cornsensus seems to be we all had us a Big Time last night," Cory intoned. Miranda looked at me then, and this shadow of apology winced across her face. I couldn't help it, I laughed too, and I went over and slipped in front of Gabe and hugged Miranda myself.

Miranda groaned, giggled. "Happy anniversary, chippie."

I kissed her ear, put my arm around her shoulder. "Come here Mir, this coffee pot's singing to you too." Together we shuffled over to the counter. Just then Gabe, who had reseated herself at the counter and was reading the newspaper again, gasped. "Oh God," she said, as though someone had punched her in the head.

Cory looked up quickly, said rapidly, urgently, "What is it baby."

Gabe looked up from the paper to Cory. Her face was white, there were tears in her eyes. "Cor. It's Gin Black...she—she hung herself in Baylor Park yesterday morning."

"Good God," Cory whispered low.

Robust Response _____

I had never met Gin Black, and although Cory's and Gabe's connection to her had been tenuous and difficult at best, a suicide does not fail to sound the primeval dissonance soundable within us all, deep down at our darkest heart, where the death of hope lies always in wait. So at Gabe's suggestion the four of us had a wake for Gin: Cory, Gabe, and Miranda dressed themselves all up in white—in almost virgin painter's pants, a buttondown oxford-cloth, an Izod, and an Irish cotton sweater. Then we drove me by home so I could don something else of the sort, and we headed on out north to the lake, to Cuero Cove, passing by the old county cemetery on the way. On an Indian bedspread we sat out in the sunlight, benign and soothing that afternoon, listening to the water lap the shore, smoking a reconstructed version of Lee's joint, letting Cory recite from T. S. Eliot's "Ash-Wednesday." We ended the ceremony by singing along with Gabe as she strummed her guitar, Karla Bonoff's "Home" song.

Shortly later the balmy windblown drive back into town helped us all begin to feel hale and chipper again, as though the moist warm air buffeting us in the Blazer were dusting off the gravity of the day. We stopped off at the Safeway and bought us the fixings for a barbecue, shishkabob, New Zealand spring lamb, which Cory prepared and grilled perfectly, and which we all scarfed down like curs and Huns. Miranda's flight back to L.A. was due to leave midevening, so directly after supper we helped her pack her gear and drove her out to the airport. At the Continental gate we all hugged Miranda long and hard, got a little teary out there, caused a few eyebrows to raise merely indulging ourselves in the kind of scene humans indulge themselves in at airports, but we didn't pay them any mind, those eyebrows. Well, Cory sneered at one little redneck guy and he sort of ricocheted away from us. Miranda and I kissed one another on the lips, sweet and light but not as sad as all that, really, and whispered, bye. Cory and Gabe and I stood in the terminal and waved to her and blew her kisses as she disappeared around a corner of the skyway. And I thought: there's another door opening up and closing on you again, Crawford; and I wondered if it would ever reopen for us, for Miranda and me. Probably not. Strolls down Memory Lane are so short. But

I would always care, I still do care, and I always want to know what's going on with her, and Miranda the same about me. As it happens I know she's got another girlfriend out there in California these days—an Amazonian ex-trucker named Katy Kelly who owns a pizza place halfway between Venice and Santa Monica. They've been together three years now already, old-timers.

That evening in 1979, however, after bidding Miranda farewell at the airport, I climbed the stairs to my duplex utterly exhausted, melancholy and quiet but self-possessed, quite solidly, my self unto myself, my own woman, and damned glad of it.

The next evening, a Monday, I came across a pair of Miranda's earrings that I'd been holding on to for lo those five long years; I'd thought of them at least once during the day before out at the lake, but had subsequently forgotten about them again. Then something somewhere in my mind clicked with a click to beat the band. I was all of a sudden almost aware of something. . .and without really mapping it out in my thoughts first, I went to my linen closet and pulled out a pair of old ragged towels, one of which had been Alma's and another X's. Then I knew what it was: I would gather up all the leftover objects of my former loves that were still in my possession—those towels, an old pair of Dana's jeans, a bandana of Sandy's, and, of course, Miranda's earrings. I searched them out and set them all together in a small cardboard box. It occurred to me that I might go out to the back yard with them and have a bonfire, but Gin's wake the day before had fulfilled as much of a need as I had for ritual, so I simply put the box out with the garbage that night to be picked up the following morning. Perhaps that seems callous, reader dear, but at the time I know I considered it an utter necessity.

Settling in for the evening, I watched a late-night episode of "Star Trek," the one in which Flint, the genius who had been Brahms and DaVinci and Solomon and Alexander and Merlin and some other-galactic whirlwinds, had created "the perfect woman," an android who ultimately dies of love because she cannot decide between Captain Kirk and Flint (Mr. Spock actually says, "The agonies of love destroyed her"). As The Enterprise is warping out and away from Flint's ruined world, Spock does a Vulcan mind-meld on the sleeping Kirk, and with as much of a sorrowful look as Spock can muster, whispers into Kirk's ear, "Forget. . . ."

Then I clicked off the TV and decided I'd read in bed for a while: I was reading the *Chuang T'zu* for the first time then, and after a while came across the passage wherein Confucius and a disciple are discussing The Way—The Tao—and the student finally says that he can "drive out perception and intellect" and "forget everything," to which an admiring Confucius replies that he will then henceforth follow the student as *his* disciple.

I remember being not a little struck by the coincidence of these two tales popping up just after I'd routed out all my exes' old things. *Forget:* an android "destroyed" by love and Spock's subliminal exhortation to Kirk to forget her, coupled with that gonzo affirmation of the Tao's power, that, with a little teeth-gritting and breath-holding, one could succeed, even if only for a moment, in forgetting absolutely everything, in erasing one's tape entirely.

Are you wondering, dearest reader, if I were thinking that by chucking out the physical remnants of my former loves I could forget my loves themselves? No, I assure you, I was not, and yet the feeling I had as I drifted off into a rich glorious sleep that night was one of immense strength and a kind of, gosh, happy-go-lucky fearlessness, of calm and loneliness and power, the serene self-regard of hermits and certain vagabonds. I could live without a woman. I still wanted one, but by God I sure as hell could live my life and be happy, mostly, without one.

The next morning, a Tuesday, I was toddling off to work, and something magical happened—well, I recall that I set quite a great bit of store by it at the time, anyway. My new Toyota bureaucratmobile had run out of gas that morning, and I was trudging grumpily back up the road with gas can in hand to fetch the fuel, when suddenly there was this blinding ray of light! It wasn't like St. Paul or anything so flashy as all that. I mean, I didn't fall off a horse, drop to my knees, hear voices, that shit. No there was just this searing beam of sunlight that I could not shake from my line of vision as I walked east; I would turn my head this way and that, and still the beam followed my right eye unswervingly. It was having the optical effects you might expect: as I looked down at the sidewalk or away and out to the houses I was passing alongside as I walked, there were black and purple splatches striking my right retina, geometrical floaters. I just couldn't shake off the beam, no way, no how. It stayed with me the entire way to the filling station, twelve blocks. And I clearly remember thinking, clearly: this is happening because I stumbled across The Answer last night. Because Autonomy is The Way, The Tao. Because living loveless and alone is How It's Gotta Be. And although I cannot say I felt jubilant in any way whatsoever about this revelation, I felt its rightness as I never had before, down to my tootsies, where all those right-thinking nerve endings live.

So then and there I resolved to stop looking for Her. I told myself I would tuck my libido under my right arm (like Señor Wences's head-in-the-box, S'awright? S'awright). Yup, that's what I told myself: I said it's going to be all right. And I believed myself.

And some time after this quasi-mystical event I began to discover, at first to counter, though not consciously of course, the rigors of celibacy, and later on for the sheer health it brought me, The Wonderful World of Physical Fitness. ["Oh caca Bobs! This isn't going to be another one of these boring paeans to the joys of cardiovasculature, is it? *Rocky IX? Flashdance Rehashed?. . .* A.M."—Alma had here tried to obliterate this little outburst of hers, bits and shreds of gum eraser still adhering to the page, but I rubbed over it with a pencil and held it up to the light.] I became a jogger. Not a runner, I was too slow for that; just a little trotting about the neighborhood, half a mile at the onset, then a whole mile, then two, then four, three mornings a week, switching to evenings later that autumn when it began to cool down some.

Often, to get myself through an uneasy run, I'd fantasize about this virtual giantess I'd known in Notasonia, Carla Butterfield, Rachel's next-door neighbor, a legal secretary and a single parent with a beautiful little (then) four-year-old boy named Harry. Carla was six-foot-two; Carla was also a potent dazzler of the first order of dazzlement. In the fantasy Carla was the star of a Broadway play about Wonder Woman. She opened the show dressed in the standard blue and red satin Wonder Woman skivvies, the headband, the lace-up boots; she strode right out on stage in a single hot-pink spotlight, stood there dead silent, her hand on her hip, glaring at the audience. Then she pulled out a cigarette from a diminutive gold case, together with a big gold lighter, lit the cigarette, clicked the lighter shut, and as, dragonlike, she exhaled smoke through her teeth, she laughed a great invincible HA! right out at the audience. Carla got me through many a sluggish run that way, she did.

At about the same time I took to jogging, I also began to go to the gym again, now to lift weights. I had never had much in the way of upper-body muscles before, and it was thrilling to grow them, like tomatoes or squashes, day by every-other-day, with lateral and triceps extensions, reverse curls, bench presses, front press work, work, work. By the end of that summer I could deadlift one hundred pounds. After my workouts I'd feel like Popeye in the old cartoons, Popeye postspinach fix, my biceps and shoulders all puffed up like overinflated tires. I began to notice that many of the simple ordinary things I'd always done had become a veritable breeze now, a real thrill: I could, for instance, with one taut jut of my fingers slam up heavy sash windows that before had always stuck, always been a two-handed job. Pushing open pneumatically hinged doors was another fave snap. I could see my shoulders in my periphery, little deltoid mounds never there before, and just having them compelled me to keep them straight and back and up. In short, my posture grew more erect, graceful, and, I'll admit it proudly, proud. One evening that fall I was over at Cory's and Gabe's with Ramona. We were moving furniture around, resituating it for the winter: the couch was going to sit east-west instead of north-south, and as Gabe and I lifted the couch together, I saw her gaze fix on my biceps. She exclaimed, no, she positively lit up: "Bobbie! You've been working on your arms!" I beamed back at her, nodding yes, struck a muscle-woman's sideways pose, biceps flexed, turning my wrist.

The couch was now directly below one of Gabe's new colossal paintings: a montage of several punk characters darting about here and there, lots of movement, New Wave purple and orange hair, wraparound shades, sailor-stripe shirts, high-top sneakers, tough tough tough. And sometime after Gabe had begun her punk period, perhaps within another four months or so, I realized that a lot of us who knew and loved Cory and Gabe had begun to look like Gabe's paintings: we were getting the haircuts, we were wearing the clothes, we were punking out the wazoo here deep in the hearta, and it was a dark rich regenesis, a whole new rock'n roll era for all of us, though for me it would very soon become a new era for another, vastly more cogent reason than the merely vogue, or life imitating art, or Devo and the B-52s.

Enter, Cogent Reason _____

Throughout the end of that year I was working wrackingly long hard hours on a new program my co-worker George and I were developing, as many as twelve and fourteen hours a day, six and seven days a week, even over the holidays. At home my laundry overflowed its wicker hamper, the dust flocks once again nestled and multiplied at the parquet corners. I'd get home at ten-thirty and drink a glass of milk while setting out cereal for the aged Ramón, by then ravenous and huffy; pathetically mindless I'd watch him eat his kitty food, his crunching and the refrigerator's hum the only sounds in the apartment. My little shoulder mounds I'd worked so hard to grow that year were gradually deflating. One early January morning when the alarm clock buzzed, at the very moment I gained consciousness, a shock of fatigue swept over me and I started crying, went on crying for fully half an hour. Later on that day or a couple of days later I found a flier in my in-box about a two-day computer fair to be held on the UCLA campus later that month, one of the first such expositions of its kind, I recall now. My supervisor, the demanding and compassionate Esther DeBeque, had stapled a note to it, *Wanna go? Our treat.* She knew I'd been killing myself for five weeks solid: this was her idea of a perk. Perhaps the grey around my eyes had prompted this magnanimity, who could say, but it was very sweet indeed to have my hard work recognized and rewarded. I scribbled a reply to her, *Yes, and thanks.*

The Sapphire Hotel's young desk clerks, model Californian towheads, were demonstrating the stuff of their job training, smiling placidly but attentively at the woman opposite them at the desk. They were sorry but it didn't appear as though Mrs. Messger had a reservation and no rooms would be available until after one o'clock. Mrs. Messger sighed. Evenly and quickly, but not irritably, she began, "First of all, my darlings, I am not a *Mrs.*, and it's *Metz*ger. Perhaps we'd best have a look at how it might have been spelled into your computer—should be M-e-t-z-g-e-r."

British. With a great deal of Yank overlay, saying, for instance, *zee* not *zed.* From the lobby couch where I sat I peered over the edge of my copy of the *L.A. Weekly* at her. As the boy clerk about-faced to the CRT screen, Metzger pushed back ash-blonde hornrims and resettled a brown paper bag she was clutching to her chest. She looked idly about her as she unbelted, unbuttoned her trenchcoat. She was medium tall but slight, rangy, almost gawky, gangly even as she merely stood there, shifting her weight from one leg to another, not so much a tic of impatience as simply stretching, taking the pressure off. She looked to be in her mid- to late-thirties. The color of her straight shoulder-length hair, the exact same shade as her glasses, made me think of the sand at Padre Island, and under the scrutiny of the desk's fluorescents, I could see that there was lots of grey streaked through it. She seemed far too tanned for a blonde, the tanning had hardened her skin, her face and throat were scored by long deep lines, especially at the side of her mouth and at her eyes. Under the trenchcoat she wore a beige turtleneck and dark brown herringbone trousers; she had on a pair of Clarks Treks.

And the thought brushed over me, like warm wind lifting the fronds of a palm: that's a very attractive woman, over there.

Then, at that very instant, she caught me staring at her (ooch), but she smiled a bland, indifferent sort of smile at me, which I, carefully commiserative, returned as her glance dropped away, slow and blank as falling stars. But there had been something to that slowness, something unexpected in those eyes, though the glare on her hornrims had obscured it. Was it wit? No, yes, humor, and something else—recognition? *Ist sie lesbisch?* Did she spot me for one? Below the hollow of my stomach a doejump, the bloodswash burn following instantly, ebbing instantly. I cleared my throat self-consciously and shifted my duffel bag from one side of my legs to the other.

Having resolved the matter of her misassigned room, the British woman tucked her paper bag under her arm and, declining the girl clerk's offer to summon a porter, stooped and hefted two well-worn, well-crafted medium-size light-brown leather suitcases. Like two ginger pup pointers, the clerklets gestured her down the hall toward the elevator. "Thanks a bunch," she told them absently, and turning to catch me staring at her again, damn! (but she smiled at me again, charmingly, and nodded too), she strolled off in that direction.

The following morning I was wandering happily, coffee in hand, around the exposition hall, perusing the exhibits and taking stock of one in particular at Wang's, when I saw a woman sitting in a metal folding chair—that British-er! She was reading something most intently. The coincidence of it (actually, the companies sponsoring the show had suggested the Sapphire as one of five nearby hotels), of seeing this woman again, pleased me greatly, as did something about her studiousness at just that moment: she was arched sharply over a clipboard balanced on top of her legs, her face maybe six inches or so from the notepaper. There was something childlike about her being all doubled over like that, overly dramatic, slightly silly, even; she seemed oblivious to everything going on around her. Feeling that, what the heck, the Fates had tipped their hand in this, I resolved to go over and speak with her. (Lines, lines, which one?) "Excuse me...," I began.

Startled, she peered up at me over her glasses. "Pardon?"

The Texan in me took charge, stuck my hand out and at the same time drawled, "Sorry to interrupt you. My name's Bobbie Crawford, I was in the hotel lobby yesterday when you were registering." She conceded this bravada, smiling somewhat misgivingly, blinking, would she remember me? Her hand, huge and warm, enveloped mine, the ponderous fingers so soft and yielding as to seem boneless.

"Oh! Yes! You were, weren't you." (Thank you merciful Fates—) "Miriam Metzger; how'jadoo."

Now what. I surveyed the hall thoughtfully, or rather, struck a thoughtful pose, then turned back to her again. "Well. So. What do you think of all this?" (Awful, dammitohell!)

Pushing her glasses back, she emitted a small contemplative hum. "Well, I suppose—" she was saying, then all of a sudden broke off, her eyes glazing over, something overtaking her thoughts. "Please excuse me just a moment, won't you," uttered monotonically, vacantly. Rapid-fire, she began scribbling a mathematical equation full across the page (those are nice plain nails on those big brown fingers, plain as a nun's), then held up the pad, examining it at almost arm's length, quickly reaching up to scratch her shoulder, then slowly twirling her mechanical pencil across her lips and teeth. There were lots of equations spewed across that page, along with several smeared and unsmeared lead frottages of pennies, nickels, and dimes dotted within the left margin. As long seconds ticked by and she continued to sit there equationing, I felt discomfort needling up my spine much as it does in those first moments of alert before one has absolutely established, before the shriek, before whipping back the bedclothes, that the strange brushing under one's sheets is beyond doubt an insect. Awkward, Crawford, say something, get—and then in the next instant, while she continued to algebraize, I went calm all over, she was going on so crazily long with her ciphering, I became vanilla pudding, guileless, quite all right as I was simply standing there waiting for her to finish.

She coughed, slapped the pencil down on the board, and looked back up at me, beaming sheepishly, a smile to thank me for my indulgence, a very nice smile indeed. Up close I could see there was a slight gap between her two front teeth. Still smiling at me she blinked a few times, pushed the glasses back up the bridge of her nose. "Sorry. Something that's been on my mind for ages; can't get it right at all." Her voice had a low thick raspishness to it, like a smoker's, a voice both brittle-tough and tottery at the same time—it cracked hard at the tips of words, fell soft and breathy in the middle of them, glossy, honey-and-ice. As she spoke, heat, that heat again, jeez *damn,* shot fast all the way down my legs to my feet. She lurched over to the left of the chair and retrieved a large canvas satchel, stuck the pencil behind her ear, slipped the notepad under her arm, then stood up to face me again. She was all hearty and smiling, fidgety, full of good British bustle and affability. "Now. Hmmm. *This,*" she said, casting a glance around the hall. "Actually, based on my first go-round this morning, I rather suspect most of this won't be much use to me for a while yet. Money, you know."

I nodded at the notepad under her arm. "That was algebra, wasn't it? Are you an analyst, or what." (Hiya honey what's your sign what's your major—puke damn! Why does it always sound like this!)

"Well not a computer analyst, no," she said slowly. "Mathematician." She matter-of-factly punctuated this statement by sticking her chin out and curving her lips a little wider, a diminutive of the motion men make when they tie their ties or shave their throats. "I teach at the University of New Mexico—trigonometry, calculus." She smiled and sniffed modestly, looked quickly past my shoulder, then back down at me. "How 'bout you then? You an analyst, programmer, what."

"Programmer. I think my boss let me come because she was guilty about overworking me so much lately."

"Hmmph." She laughed politely and ran her fingers through her hair, sweeping the thick straight locks up from her face, a gesture of distracted genius, Chopin hulked over his piano letting George serve him tea; it was also just slightly provocative this movement, and I glanced away to avoid her seeing anything provoked in my expression. "Sort of a—what do they call them? Perk? Is that right?"

"Just so."

"Good word that: perk you up, keep you going."

Ist Sie Lesbisch? (cont.) _____

Forgive me, hallowed reader, for interrupting young Professor Metzger from her semantic reverie here (a perhaps not unusual preoccupation among non-native speakers), but recounting Miriam's and my next scene in its entirety would be odiously humdrum of me indeed. Our dialogue, as I recall, was the kind of vapid mindless patter utter strangers in an utterly strange city might be expected to exchange. The principal developments, however, were these: (1) that, after strolling about together for an hour or so looking at the exhibits and taking in the demos, we utter strangers in an utterly strange city eventually decided to go off and find an early lunch somewhere; (2) that throughout the time we spent together neither one of us betrayed the least intimation, not by omission or commission, tones or a-tones, of our sexuality; although she did inform me (3) that she had a dinner engagement that evening with a UCLA colleague named Hervé something-or-other. There were, nevertheless, a couple of particulars of this first day of ours together which registered as nebulous fluctuations in my seismology of Miriam's sexual stripe; that is, some gave me hope, and some did not.

Did I, so swift on the heels of my resolve to autonomy, want hope, reader mia? Well there's this funny thing about libidos, I found out: they just don't go away, try what you will. And this British Amazon had certainly prodded mine out of dormancy, that much was sure. I felt like I was playing the old game again, I felt alive again and I didn't care what happened or didn't happen; I liked her, it was pleasant, just being with her. I liked her.

But back to those particulars. One of the first things I was taking into account about her that morning was her outfit. The clothes she'd been wearing when I saw her at the hotel desk were things which any travelling British woman might wear, Europeans being as a rule so sensible when it comes to clothing. But that morning in the exposition hall Miriam had on this kind of khaki spacesuit thing, very futuristic looking, pretty butch actually, but also high fashion, a get-up a *Vogue* model or hybrid-vigorous rock star would wear. Tan-color kid boots, too, Italian. Something altogether spare and sharp about her.

A second particular had to do with her response to some disparaging remark I'd made about Los Angeles: she, bending over to poke me in the ribs conspiratorially, said, "Coo, isn't it *aw*ful! How do they live here, all these people? It's so bloody huge, teeming doesn't begin to describe it," the salient point here being her having elbowed my rib cage—that tactical just-us-girls mannerism so much more characteristic of straight women than lesbians.

A third item presented itself when Miriam and I first stepped out of the exposition hall into the cool, bright, gusty Los Angeles forenoon. Overhead the sun sifted through the high eucalyptus, their leaves plashing and whorling. We had to raise our voices to hear each other over the wind, fingercomb hair from our faces every few moments. To avoid the inevitable cafeteria fare on campus we headed out, Miriam slowly striding, me quick-marching to keep up, toward Westwood Boulevard to find a coffee shop. She stopped momentarily to fish something out of her canvas satchel. The something, I perceived, and my throat clenched at the sight of them, was a pair of Ray-Ban sunglasses.

I don't know, but short of wearing a purple shirt with a denim jacket and a pair of rough-outs, I doubt that there's a more automatic tip-off, lesbian to lesbian, than a pair of aviator-style Ray-Ban sunglasses.

The steadiness I was having to muster must have figured in my following thought, which was that Miriam would own a pair of Ray-Bans because Ray-Bans are so well-made, durability being a quality I imagined the aforementioned sensibility of Europeans would demand. Peevishly I remembered that I had left my own Ray-Bans in the hotel room.

But in the final analysis there really wasn't anything irrefutable, or I allowed myself nothing, to go on with regard to my initial instinct at the hotel desk about this woman. I remember that the hamburger joint we stopped in to was painfully overilluminated and that Miriam kept her sunglasses on throughout, a slightly disconcerting though spellbinding incidental. I think we talked shop, Hewlett-Packard holograms, dot matrices, interference waves, but I can't be sure now. Much later, after a second tour of the hall and several more demonstrations, we parted company back at the hotel and said we'd meet each other at the desk by nine-thirty for the second day of computer carnival. I shuffled up to my room to settle in for the evening, clicked on the television, cable! Channel 45 had Monty Woolley and Bette Davis, *The Man Who Came to Dinner.* Shortly later I ordered a room service bacon-lettuce-and tomato sandwich which was both the most expensive and delicious I'd ever had in my life. I watched Davis pace smoothly through her lines. A few weeks earlier I'd seen her on Carson's show, a seventy-year-old queen in leopard skin. She was reminiscing then that at thirty she had envied Hepburn's beauty, that no one else in Hollywood was like Hepburn, but that she, Davis, had some time ago reexamined several of her own films of the era and had said to herself, hey, not bad. But then, anyone who's seen *The Bride Came C.O.D.* could tell you that: not bad at all, Bette.

And Then, a Miracle

Pring
puh-ring, telephone, eyes, red light

I plunged over groggily to grab the receiver, stretched still further to swivel my watchface about on the nightstand: ten twenty-five, the set still on, a sportscaster rattling off the day's scores. I blurred into the phone, "'lo."

A split-second pause on the other end of the line. "Oh I say I'm terribly sorry, have I awakened you? This's Miriam."

Rally, blood, brain, show-biz: "Oh-no, no, I was just watching the news," and I snapped the receiver out toward the blaring screen and in a flash back to my ear to catch her saying:

". . .wondering if you'd be up for having a nightcap with me down here in this bar."

"Where, what, the hotel bar?"

"Oh, yes, sorry, right."

Stall, jammies, don't tell her, she'll think you're socked in for the night, granma. "Uh, yeah, sure, that'd be nice but, uh, lissen, Miriam. . .I need to finish up some paperwork here first, but I'll see you down there in say, fifteen minutes, s'that O.K.?"

"Sure Bobbie. See you in a bit."

"O.K. See you in a few."

Among my friends it's well known that I'm an excruciatingly slow slowpoke, the five-toed sloth of central Texas, Ramona calls me. Sherman once divulged that in extending invitations to me she often told me to come forty-five minutes earlier than everyone else to make sure I'd be there on time. After ringing off with Miriam that night in L.A., however, I moved with the smooth, sure alacrity of a young eland thundering through savannah grass. I leapt from the bed, snapped off the set, and bounded into the bathroom, each movement a marvel of fluidity and economy. Flipping on the cold faucet I filled the sink, mugged in the mirror (it is good, sometimes, to cross the eyes), and cupped the water up to my face in several semicircular sweeps, more guardedly to my eyes, still tellingly sleep-swollen despite the torrent of adrenalin pounding through me. I glanced down at the bottle of *L'Interdit* out on the sinktop counter: should I splash that on too? No, not enough time for it to settle down—"She smells best who smells not at all." I deliberately gave myself a sobering look (now calm down, goddammit, just cool it), but I kept grinning anyway: it was just so rich, this out-of-town hotel and a demi-Colossa of Rhodes, the conventioneer's conventional fantasy; it would be fun no matter what happened. And it was sweet to be feeling all this again, after such a long stretch. At the closet my clothes seemed alive, flying from their hangers to sheathe my arms and legs in record time. Last thing, socks and loafers (sit down, continue to breathe), a frenzied combing, my grey cord Eisenhower swooping to my back like harrier wings at the strike. Reaching for the doorknob I glanced down at my watch: ten thirty-three. Astonishing. Gleeful as a ninny I rode the elevator up and down a couple of times to round out the fifteen minutes. I couldn't stop grinning.

As with most bars it took my eyes a few seconds to adjust to the dark. It was a pleasant enough place, plush, comfortable feeling, with a Hindu kind of decor, golds and blues, latticework and a piano man, probably not Hindu, curly black hair, handlebar moustache, tinkling away cocktail tunes at the back; and last, at a table below a reasonable mural of the Taj Mahal, young Professor Metzger wiggling those big fingers at me, tossing her head back to get her hair out of her face, no glasses! As gracefully as I could I weasled through the tables toward her.

"Hey that was fast," she said, shifting her glass and its napkin over, clearing a space for me at the table.

"Just going over a program I've been knocking out back home at the shop," I lied, pulling a Persian blue chair closer in. "So. How was your dinner?"

Great God, what eyes!

Miriam's Eyes _____

You should know first that, although I had both looked at and been looked upon by Miriam Metzger throughout that same day, she had at all times been wearing either her glasses or those Ray-Bans. This said, I would have you, dear reader, remember that dangerous moment described earlier when Dana first took off her sunglasses to look me full in the face, the danger at that instant having consisted of whether I would fail to mask my self and betray what I could not yet afford to betray. At the present, however, upon first locking in to Miriam's eyes as I pulled up that chair, I really can't say one way or another exactly what my face betrayed. Probably everything, who knows. I think I was in shock. Or a trance.

To merely say that her eyes were blue would be like saying the Grand Canyon is big, Shakespeare wrote well, Einstein was smart. There was this ozone clarity, a quicksilver glitter to those irises, the brilliant dapple-play of sunlight on Caribbean water. But the eyes were also sloe-shaped and heavy-lidded, thick, full, with striate lines at the sides, which twenty-four hours ago had no doubt accounted for my impression of her as a woman of wit and which now, face to face, made her appear endlessly benevolent. So that there were these two counterpoints to them, Miriam's eyes: there was the warm fleshy languor of their shape, the eyelids, the sidefolds, and there was their messianic semiliquid color—they were of both bed and sky, sacred and profane, human and unknown. Beholding them at that moment I felt as though I were standing at the edge of the world, as though for an instant it were true that the world had an edge to it, that Columbus's doomsayers had somehow been right after all and in another second I would slip over the silent dreamscape vortex into ether and falling light.

And there was something else.

I wasn't afraid of them, I wasn't afraid to look right into those eyes of hers, and wonder.

And Wonder and Miracle Unfold _____

Dinner with the colleague, Miriam reported, had been "splendid," Hervé having taken her to a "terribly dear" French restaurant for coq au vin, at mention of which, coq au vin, I thought I saw a sly upward twinge at the corner of her mouth, "—and this absolute packet of wine," she was saying. "I hope I don't start blithering. Just didn't feel quite like popping right off to bed yet, you know? I was so glad you were still up—" (hoo-WAH she's just reached out and quick as a kingfisher flickered her middle and ring fingers over my hand and as quickly darted away) "—I do so loathe business trips, don't you? So tiresome."

Good grief, I do believe the woman's swacko! Definitely talkier, brighter color to her cheeks, a bit of perspiration dotting her upper lip. And I kept seeing or thinking I saw the same roguish curve at the corner of her mouth I'd noted at "coq au vin." The waiter's attention was direly needed.

I ordered a cognac, she ordered a cognac. Then she sighed, a biggie, as the waiter, another young California blond—God, do they all have skin like that?—bounced off with our order. She shifted her shoulders, resettled herself in her chair, fairly exploding this: "Damn! I've been under so much fucking stress lately, you know? Can't wait to get back home and start slowing down some."

"Yo, I know what you mean," I clucked. "And the pity of it is, when you're all the way under the gun, that's when you drop that new diet and exercise program you'd just started." Miriam laughed mildly at that; the waiter came back with our drinks.

She reached for hers, held it out to me. "I haven't the slightest idea what you're talking about. Cheers."

"Cheers," I rejoined. What a peach.

"So," she said, suddenly smiling most disarmingly, "what exercise program have you dropped lately?" She sat back in her chair and took me in, something distinctly professorial about that take, I thought. I mentioned the running, the weight lifting. "Cripes that's superb, Bobbie, that's superb, very good indeed. I don't do as much really. Garden. Bicycle, walk. Stretch. Old cat. But I suppose I'm not all that terribly out of shape for an old broad, nonetheless. . .it's just that, well, have you ever noticed, whilst engaged in some sports activity, working up a sweat, you'll have the idea—or even while you're in the midst of something else, not a sport, say, washing your face or something, and you'll think, Cor! I really do have good skin! Or: that's not bad for a thirty-six-year-old body—well of course you're not thirty-six, but you know what I mean. . .anyway, you'll say to yourself, I bet it's because of how I eat and sleep and exercise and all, you know, self-congratulatory. . .have you ever noticed, sometimes, that just sports, no matter what, are never enough to get you by? I mean, keeping fit's vital for the organism and all that, but if the organism can't. . .you know, give affection, touch, meet those other needs, you know (Good God, what's she saying! What's my face doing! Is the mask up?)—have you ever noticed that sports is just never enough?"

High-YA. Oh hell, just play it out, act dumb here, Bobs. . .this can't be happening; besides, she's obviously had a lot to drink. So for good grace, I kept it even-keeled. "Oh God yes, affection, of course; but I don't have anybody just now—lots of fantasies when I jog. A cat." True, that's all true enough. Now what?

She smiled vacantly at me, or rather, with what I sensed was a kind of stage-vacancy. It was a smile in which I took some heart, another soft clue to safe-conduct. But just then the piano man began playing "Just One of Those Things," and Miriam started in talking about Cole Porter, Gerald and Sarah Murphy, the Lost Generation, eventually winding back to ask me, no kidding, what kind of music I liked (hiya honey what's your sign what's your major), and I told her, everything but Hugo Winterhalter. She laughed brightly at that, she did, good for her! Then she asked me if I liked opera, and I told her I did (I do); and here she launched into her great love of it, I mean, the woman was holding forth! on Beverly Sills, Bing and the Met, *bel canto,* Marilyn Horne, the future of opera in America. The more she talked about opera, the more transfigured she became. She was, I could tell, genuinely passionate about it, and it was thrilling—well I was thrilled but then as I say I'm fond of opera—just to listen to her rhapsodize, wax more and more eloquent, an English spring garden of words on Verdi and Verdi duets, on La Scala, baritones ("They're always much younger than you think, actually"), what made Callas great. She was beginning to start in on the Santa Fe Opera, whose proximity to Albuquerque had been a deciding factor in her acceptance of the University of New Mexico appointment, when I made a motion to the waiter for a second round. Miriam's hand darted out instantly and lay lightly on my forearm, a gesture for interruption, oh what—

"I say," she began and glanced down for one count, moistened her lips, then looked up at me again (nice timing, there)—and her eyelids seemed faintly, faintly heavier in the return, or so I thought, said, "I've plocked out a ton of money on that meal tonight. . .listen, I've an absolutely untouched bottle of really excellent Calvados up in my room, and some opera tapes as well. What say we go crack it open, listen to music, and I'll tell you all about the Santa Fe, if you like."

Chaos, ice-and-fire, grip, Crawford! But before I could utter a word from my barely opened mouth (or was it gaping), her hand on my arm tightened slightly, she interjected, didn't let me answer: "What floor are you on? I'm on fourteen—we could pop over to yours, if you'd rather," removing the hand carefully, "or is it too late. Are you ready to turn in? Or what."

Or what. I couldn't possibly look directly at her just then, no way. Why? Because I was going berserk, that's why, masking myself was completely out of the question, *and now was not the time.* Inspecting my lap, I went into my Jimmy Stewart routine: "Uh, well, I, uh—" and then risked darting a glance at her. She seemed to have frozen her face in a photograph of expectation, yet the picture had something slightly wrong with it, something masklike too—only the eyes seemed alive, different, perhaps a bit darker, was that it? Timing, Bobbie, say something! "Sure—hell, yes! (Pure Texan, Jimmy Stewart becomes Strother Martin; this was not a smooth transition.) I haven't had a good Calvados, well, any Calvados, in, what? seven, eight years?" (not too thick, dope, put the trowel *down*).

She smiled, sat back (there was that goddam ghost of a smirk again, the sly turn, unmistakable now! wasn't it?). "Right then. We'll just settle up here and we're off." So we paid our tab, and Miriam grabbed up a claret-colored velvet jacket from the chair next to her. As she swung it round to slip it on it brushed my face, almost knocked over my empty snifter. It was startlingly soft, that velvet, like the cool sleek coat of a living thing. I stood up, pushed the chair back with my knees, my basic will to disbelief mightily jeopardized. We walked, I sleepwalked, out of the bar, past the lobby, to the elevator. Miriam pressed the up button, the great hand with its single round-cut ruby lingering momentarily, the fingers drumming lightly over the controls.

As we moved into the vacant elevator Miriam again pressed the button, for fourteen. Quickly she said, "Oh, s'that all right? My room O.K.?" The elevator door shushed closed. I was staring at the button panel and she was looking at me, I could feel her looking at me, and I knew I was going to have to look at her. . . .

And Then, and Then:

Well I was convincing, I thought. I looked at her right off the bat with that down-home face on, said, "Sure, fine." Smiling ingenuously, the sweet old neutered doggums.

That's what I said, that's how I said it. I said, sure, fine, looking right at her. And she was looking at me, my sensing of that was dead-on. She was looking at me, and I said, sure, fine, and she kept looking at me. Folding her arms she stepped back in the elevator, leaned up against the wall, cocked her head sideways a little, still looking at me. Masks still up. Elevator ascending. Silence.

Five seconds, ten. The darkened eyes behind the masks alive and dead, there and not there.

And then, the tiny curve to one corner of her mouth, the sly crook to one corner, really, then to the other. Then a softening smile spreading from the moist midcleft of her lips. Then broader still, her eyes joining in, crinkling up. Then a great-big goddam grin, with teeth. She sputtered out a half-laugh, throwing her head forward a little, breaking off the staring match. Then looking back at me again quickly, she reached up and combed her fingers through her hair, sweeping it up and out of her face, smiling hugely now, leaning back once more against the elevator wall. Her eyes were cobalt, flame.

Then, still grinning, her arms folded over again, she said: *You're a lesbian, aren't you.*

(HOO. *HAH.* Camp it, Crawford, you don't know absolutely yet, go slow, whoah.) I folded my arms too, swishing my shoulders as I stepped back (snappy move, that), started up a fake stammer that became real, "Uh, whuh, why, uh, yes, that's true. I am." Pause. "I am a lesbian. Yes." Another pause, smiling, blushing, dammit! my eyes blinking like strobes, shooting around her line of vision, not settling on her throughout this comic strip performance, this deft, I considered in sum, intermingling of charm and neurosis. And then they did. Settle on her. Still staring and grinning, she unfolded her arms, leaned slowly up from the elevator wall. And then she started moving toward me, still slow. And I started melting, everywhere. She was right in front of me now, close, closer, her face, her breath, just above mine. With her hands she reached out and cupped my face, gazed down into my eyes for several infinity-straddling seconds. Just gazed, her face a sea of solace, warm, merry.

"What in bloody hell are you so frightened of," she said, soft and low. The elevator door shushed open. She glanced up fast, not taking her hands from my face, to see if there were anyone standing there. There wasn't, I looked too. Back to me, over me, safe, home, she homed in for a superlight kiss, a baby peck, reached out and held the elevator door from closing, said, "Come on then," and I could feel everything, every soft muscle in my body, dissolving, sluicing out. Miriam took me by the hand, led me out into the hallway. I felt like I was five; no, I didn't. We heard voices around the corner coming up, let go our hands, smirking at each other as a waiter with a tray full of smoke-grey cellophane-covered things passed us blankly in the corridor. She began fumbling in a claret pocket for the keys jangling there. Room 1479. Turned the key in the lock, the heavy *kee-lunk* of thick steel, good Yankee engineering, and pushed the door open with splayed-wide fingers.

"After you." (*Aahfta yew.*)

"No, after *you.*" Oh great, the Marx Sisters. She shot me a look of mock-contempt, harrumphed, glided through into the room, and I after her, and I after her.

Amazonas

Fee-yump

But no onomatopoeia could replicate the sweet resonance of that cork being pulled from that bottle by that woman standing there that night, two long blonde strips of hair falling forward over her face. She carelessly splashed out two large glasses full of the golden apple brandy, slipped a cassette tape into a big Sony recorder, and crossed the room with glasses in hand to where I sat on the edge of the bed, at the edge of my seat. Set the glasses down on the nightstand. Sat herself down, right next to me.

The tape started rolling; instantly I recognized Beverly Sills. Staring off into space Miriam said quietly, "This's from *The Ballad of Baby Doe,* the last aria. She hits this note, the last note of the song—unbelievable how long she holds it, that note." The song, Sills' voice, were unignorable, perfect, exquisite. Miriam and I were still just sitting there on the bed, at the tippy edge of the mattress. We were both, for the moment, wholly attentive to that voice, that lovely music. "Here it is, here's the note," Miriam was saying, and for an instant, honest, I thought I would cry, hearing Sills put the song to rest so beautifully. After it was over, for another while longer I couldn't quite look at Miriam. The next piece on the tape was from *Traviata,* Sills as Violetta. "This's all Bubbles, this side of the tape," Miriam said then, crossing her legs. She turned to me, and I to her, then. Ever so cautious she reached over to me and pulled a strand of hair away from my face, her fingers lingering at my temple a few seconds; then she let her hand slide slowly down my neck, an index finger tracing a line down the great long muscle there, at the bottom all her fingers fanning out upon my shoulder. Her hand followed the right angle of the shoulder to my upper arm, the fingers sworling briefly there, down my forearm, running smoothly down the cord wales to my hand, over the back of my hand, sifting through my fingers, our fingers intertwining, molten gold. And we just kept sitting there, holding hands, looking at one another. "Something the matter," she said softly. "You're terrifically quiet."

I am always quiet at this, always. "There's nothing the matter." I leaned over closer to her, my face right before her face, whispered, "I'm just a little stunned, that's all."

Right back, her eyes warm and glittering, this, totally deadpan: "Not paralyzed, I trust."

Well that got a laugh out of me, it did, and it broke the ice, freed the tension. I smiled and said, "No, no, I don't think so," and I leaned in to those thin smiling lips, barely kissing them, backing off to take her in. She opened her eyes slowly as I pulled back.

She said, "You haven't tasted the brandy yet."

"Oh yeah the Calvados," and I stretched and picked up the glasses, gave her hers, held mine out.

"Here's to—what, to Bubbles?"

"Yeah, Bubbles," she smiled. "Salud-ooh, ooh, wait, no well, yes, your health and Sills of course, but especially: here's to Wolfgang, it's his birthday today."

"Oh all right, good idea, I like that. To Mozart." Clenk, thick cheap glass. Going down, warm, smooth, sweet. Where have I felt this before, all of this, this woman, the room, the brandy, before, must've been—naw, I dunno, never mind.

Then, rising, Miriam said, "He died when he was thirty-five, you know," and she excused herself to go take out her contacts, pulled something out of a suitcase first, and took it in the bathroom with her, closing the door behind her. Listening to the running water I wondered if I should take off my clothes and get into the bed—naah, leave 'em on. Well, take the jacket off. Then again: where have I felt this before, this—what was it, dammit! Was I sad? Why! But would this always seem a little silly and sad now?

A few minutes later Miriam emerged from the bathroom, blazer slung over her shoulder, the black silk shirt still on, unbuttoned low; she had on some sort of black cotton tank top underneath. Draping the coat over the back of a chair, she came and sat down again on the bed, not quite as close to me, and began pulling off her boots.

I jumped up to help. "Great boots," I said, and slung one leg over hers, turning my backside to her, tugging at the last, cupping the heel, "gorgeous, so soft—are they kid?"

"French calf." (*Cahlf.*) I glanced over my shoulder at her: she was looking at me and smiling, disbelieving.

"This's how they do it in Texas, taking off boots." Now who made that crap up, where'd that b.s. come from?

"Really." She was looking at me, then to my ass in front of her, then back at me; without taking her eyes from mine, without changing expression at all, she reached up and began stroking my inner thigh. The lower half of my body cratered again, the cartilage in my knees numbed out. There, that one's off. I didn't wait for the second one. I turned around and put my arms around her shoulders, standing over her, holding her, looking into her eyes. Then I kissed her, kissed the eyes closed, as light as I possibly could, softer still then to her upper lip, over her cheek, the side of her nose; to her lips once more then, firmer now, warm, our breathing rising; then curving my tongue through, parting her lips, to her teeth. Her mouth folded open to me as my tongue delved in, drawing up a low muted moan from deep down inside her like treacle boiled up from a cauldron. Ah God and that drove me wild, that did, and with my arms I tipped her back down on the bed and kissed her again, my tongue burrowing past her lips, lolling wet and thick around her tongue, over it and under it and out and licking soft at her lips, and back in again as I turned over with her on the bed; she was on top of me now and kissing me hard back, then burying her face in my neck, lapping flames with her tongue at the crook there and over my throat, murmuring up to my ear, taking the lobe in her teeth and sucking it, slipping her tongue lightly past and into my ear, softly, barely, exploding a sheath of heat out and off my skin all over my body. I reached up, fumbling for her shirt buttons; she started fumbling back for mine. Laughing—she was growling at my buttons—we finally peeled them both off. Trembling and breathless I was starting to pull up her tank top, yanking it out from under her belt, when suddenly she stopped me, stayed my hand.

"Wait baby," she said quickly, quick and low, and lay back down beside me on the bed, looking at me, oh so serious that look, holding me, still breathing heavily, but less and less so, slowing down. Then she smiled at me, and there was so much information in that smile—apprehension, valiance, at least those things—that I simply waited for her to say what it was she was going to say. Did she just want us to slow down some? I know some people like to keep their clothes on as long as possible, but—

She was still holding me, the complicated smile still there. Miriam looked down for a moment, cleared her throat, then said, "I need to keep that on, that vest."

"This?" I said, fingering the tank top.

"Yeah. The singlet." She was staring at my forehead, the smile was fading. "Ummm...I...had a...." She looked into my eyes again, then back to my forehead. "Two years ago I—"

"Come on, it's O.K., out with it," I said, slipping a strand of hair behind her ear.

"I had a mastectomy two years ago, Bobbie."

Another Transition

The very word itself chilled, sent a shock-flash down my spine, and of course I immediately wanted to look—though I succeeded in controlling myself—at Miriam's chest; any discrepancy between left and right there had obviously never struck me in the slightest. I remember that I was making perhaps the biggest effort of my life thus far to have my face look precisely as it had before, when I'd said, come on, out with it—and I mean, nary a glimmer of change: the selfsame shade of concern, the same receptivity, the exact same stamp of anticipation. But inside I was scrambling like crazy trying to think of what to say to her, although every line kept washing out, too maudlin, too glib, too callous, too much. Finally I was reaching a point of no return, still struggling to maintain the freeze in my facial muscles and realizing that if I didn't say or do something within the next three seconds, I would surely hurt her one way or another. So I sighed deep and just leaned in close to her and kissed her, a very sweet one, I think, very, very soft on the lips. Drew back a bit, still in her arms.

Miriam pulled a face, wry, inquisitive. "So. Whadja think," she said, licking along the inside of her upper lip, squinting at me a little, a shade of a smile beginning in her eyes, at the corner of her mouth.

This time I had a ready answer. Leaning in to kiss her again, I said quietly, easily, just before my lips pressed to hers, "Well. . .I think you should leave the singlet on for a bit."

The Shortest Chapter in the Book _____

We both had reservations out of Los Angeles for the following afternoon, a Sunday.

We changed them. To Monday.

Nope, Sorry, Take It Back, Shorter Still _____

Then we changed them to Tuesday, late.

Three Days That Shook the World _____

Surely, *chère liseuse,* I have regaled us with enough recountings of acts of love (zee Golden Moments of mah life) that to depict here the doings, if you will, of Miriam's and my three days and nights in that hotel room could only serve to diminish me in your eyes. Tut-tut, say you? Then I must again affirm, gentle reader, that this is after all a story of romantic love, replete with the beleaguerings that that implies these days, and what in fact took place in Room 1479 is anything but reducible to a mere play-by-play recap of the days' physical events.

See, the main thing was, we were falling in love.

It can happen like that, it really can, I'm here to tell you. I'd always heard it could, and lo and behold, it really did. Later on, oh, much much later, Miriam would tell me that at first she'd been attracted to my wholesome, she said, apple pie American good looks. She said, well, you were very well-scrubbed, weren't you. What else. She thought me cherubic; I liked that one, a whole lot. Oh, and lest we forget, Mir really was thirty-six when we met, ergo, ten years my senior, and ever so will be, nyah-nyah. Even today Cory still ribs her about cradle robbing, babydyke gibes.

And one more thing: Miriam had not, that Saturday night in 1979, made love to anyone in over two years.

For those three days it was like. . .the circus clown car over the trap door, clown after clown after laugh after laugh, spewing out in absurd numbers from the Morris Minor in the center ring.

I think we went out for supper Monday evening. The rest of the time room service did for us. We imagined we were providing a little spicier-than-usual gossip for the kitchen staff.

As for me, I was a goner's goner, in piteous, unholy thrall to Miriam Metzger: the way she laughed (we were laughing like idiots), running the gamut from deep belly laughs to uncontrollable giggling, I mean, unto involuntary weeping giggling. And I enjoyed, ah *yà* so much, the way she moved; I remember that as a primary point of my attraction to her. She shrugged her shoulders a great deal, and very broad bony shoulders they are too, and walked, walks, very lankily, almost cocky, but there's always something just slightly out of alignment about it—disjointed, almost—a hang-tough kind of saunter, purposeful but also a shade graceless, at times. Not all the time.

The fact that she had fought and won her battle with cancer only added to her glory for me, of course. Naturally, somewhere in the midst of those three days she unraveled the story of The Lump, the horror that is chemotherapy, the final coming to grips with the surgery, the surgery itself, and "living with less," as she dryly put it. But despite these terrors and agonies, to me still mostly unimaginable, Miriam said that she now felt surer of herself than she ever had before, that her life, the ways in which she responded to living, had changed so vastly much for the better, that she was "thoroughly, thoroughly" optimistic about her future. And there was something so true-sounding in her as she said this, true in the sense of certain quality steel or highly calibrated pendulums, that I believed her the instant she said it, believed absolutely that she was cured. And it is now four years later, and I still believe it, although once, last year at a party, I overheard Mir tell Gabe, "Well if they didn't get it all, I'll have far surpassed even the longest opera death, won't I."

The mastectomy itself had been a partial, the cancerous tissue having lodged just under her right armpit in the lymph nodes there; then it spread to a portion of her right breast, the far right of it, toward the top. Although she kept her singlet on those entire three days in L.A., at one point she stretched the cotton taut over the place in order to show me, pulling the singlet from just below the armpit and from the midpoint at her right nipple; and I could see then the hollowing in her flesh, the contour of a big, big chunk of her, "lasered away," as she glibly said then and still does. And then, she started cheerily rattling off the story of the laser's invention and ruby crystals and Charles Townes and Arthur Shawlow and their students at Columbia, including Gordon Gould, whose claim to the invention almost twenty years later fooled no one. When she was explaining the coherent light of lasers to me, Miriam became hushed, almost reverent; she said that prior to the surgery she'd used the mental image of a laser beam as a meditational object, a kind of visual mantra. She'd picked out, after scores of referrals and her own far-flung research, a young wizard surgeon at Sloan-Kettering in New York; she'd left Sydney with her grandmother in Washington—

Oh. Sydney. Sydney is Miriam's daughter.

How did I first hear about Syd. Oh, of course, Sunday morning. When Miriam and I were first deciding to play hooky from the world, the first order of business, she announced, was tending to Syd. She gave me a glowingly proud look: "That's my girlchild, Bobbie, muh wee bairn, eight years old." Miriam lunged over the side of the bed and hoisted her satchel up from the carpet, extracted her wallet, and began flipping through the plastic-sheathed credit cards for a snapshot, handed it to me out and open: a little dark-haired girl, dark eyes, sweet luminous pools of dark, a very serious-looking little girl, a lovely little girl.

Where did this child come from. How did this child—

"Uh, Syd's dad went dotty when she was about one year old, Alzheimer's disease, presenility—Christ that's another great lot of soap in my massively soaplike life." She ran her fingers through her hair, straightened up, stretching her spine. "His mum and sister and I committed him in '72, to a place in Phoenix out near where the sister lives." I handed her back the wallet. I remember thinking then, I wonder if I'll ever hear all of that story.

Mir sighed, slipped the wallet back into the satchel. "Yeah, well, and the hits just keep rollin," she said tonelessly, and then she casually slid her hand along the top of my thigh, reached over me for the phone. While she was waiting for the operator to clear the call, she scrambled up over me and resettled on the edge of the bed. She put her hand over the mouthpiece, leaned over and kissed me and whispered, "Keep yer fingers crossed."

She stood up then, nestling the transmitter between her shoulder and her right ear, and said brightly, "Hello Anna? *Està* Miriam. *¡Como estas! ¡Bueno, bueno! Oye* Anna: do you think you would be able to stay with Sydney again tonight, one more night? I might not be back until tomorrow. Really? You can? (Thank you merciful Fates, thanks girls!) Will you please call your mother and make sure it's all right with her, Anna? Thanks, thank you love. If I don't hear from you here at the hotel before three o'clock this afternoon, I'll assume you can stay over with Syd tonight, O.K.? Any problems today? No? Good, marvelous. What's on for today? Oh? Great! Well have fun, luv. Oh, and you can let Syd stay up and watch TV until ten, O.K.? Thanks. Now is Syd around, Anna? Oh she is? Could I speak with her then? And thank you again, Anna, *muchas graçias,* anh? (A pause.) Ullo, luv. Whatcha doin. (Another pause.) O.K., well you be sure they get lots of water first. Where you gonna ride then? That's O.K., that's O.K., just don't go out to the highway. Listen to Anna. Lissen luv: Mum's been held up out here in Los Angeles (Miriam pronounced it *Ann-je-lees,* shifted her hip weight from right to left) another day. Aaaaaaw, Sydney. . .now Syd, you know flippin well you're gonna have a fabulous time one more free night with Anna, aren't you? Telly 'til ten, deal? O.K. I'll be back home tomorrow. I don't know when yet. I'll call you both later on this evening, O.K.?"

They continued to chat, mum and daughter, a while longer, then eventually Miriam rang off. I watched her sit back down beside the nightstand, watched her set the phone slowly and carefully back down onto its cradle. She lifted her face to me and smiled drowsily. "They're going out on Thello and Lulu, our horses." She and I talked then, for a little while longer still, about Sydney, about their ranch house in Corrales, about horses, breaking off after a time to call our respective airlines and rearrange our flights back for Monday evening. It was noon by the clock; we'd been making love most of the night. After Mir'd slipped back into bed with me, we couldn't decide if we were more hungry than sleepy or vice-versa. As we were having this vital discussion we started up fondling one another again, then we kissed a little, soft and worn out as old rag dolls, and it was so rich, so soothing to be so exhausted and still touch and be touched, and we were both droning on about things, about ourselves, and asking each other questions, back and forth, and back and forth, and still trying to decide about brunch, and finally we just drifted off to sleep.

Then it had become Tuesday afternoon. The telephone exchange with Anna and Sydney had been repeated midafternoon Monday. Miriam had already missed one class. Neither of us could think of any other ploys to prolong heaven just a little further: we had to go back to our separate lives.

Still naked (well, Mir was wearing the singlet, but we only put on robes for room service) we were siting up on the bed and holding one another, our legs crisscrossed around us, a lovemaking position we had already tried at least once in past three days, though we weren't making love just then but talking about, for the first time, our future. Or we were just looking at one another, and the feelings were there, I don't remember. And I don't know if that was when the following dialogue took place or not, but it might as well have been:

Bobbie: "Do you really think we'll see one another again."

Miriam: "I'd say. . . ," and her voice trailed off, "there's more than a strong probability."

Bobbie: "When, do you think."

Miriam: "Oh soon. I think soon, don't you. I'll come to Texas. You'll come out to Albuquerque. Something."

A pause. "I don't think this's just a fluke, do you?" I asked. It didn't feel like a fluke, but then what did I know any more.

She laughed, or rather, huffed lightly through her nostrils and hugged me close. "Yunno, I just don't know how much I trust me-self any more about romance, but I do, I do have this rather particular feeling about you. . . I guess we'll just see, won't we." Kissing me on the cheek she said, "You do want to see me again, don't you?"

"Yes," I said. "I really do."

"Then," she said, "you really will."

Although I liked the answer it sounded a tad pat, and reminiscent too. "Is that from a movie, that line?"

Lightening it up, she turned silly on me: "Cor, yunno, I dunno! Sounds like it, dunnit! Never mind then, eh," and she started humming "We'll Meet Again," smiling at me with this Charles Boyer, WWI flying-ace smile (*Weep not, chérie*), and then she leaned in close to me and licked my nose.

Airport: I

We were standing amid the Boschian anthill that is LAX, the industry's abbreviation for the L.A. International Airport, scores of human beings darting past us, hovering around us, bumbling along with their luggage—grannies hugging stiff-backed grandchildren adieu, entire families kissing one another, singles bustling fast at the outer edges of it all. Overhead the P.A. flight announcements were, typically, mostly inaudible. But we already knew my flight was leaving first, and we were positioned just beside the corridor leading to Gate 10 and my Continental DC-10. Miriam had to go find a bathroom and trundled off across the nucleus of the masses. I leaned up against the wall adjacent to the corridor, my back pressed flat against it, one foot planted flat on the wall too, standing on one leg like a flamingo, for all the world quite Dietrich-like, I thought, but for my bluejeans and denim jacket and new sky-blue Nikes. Some time later Miriam came striding back across the very middle of the crowd again, twisting her way around the bodies, staring at me as she came with this devilishly wicked grin. She approached, passing into the shadow of an overhanging ledge just above me. My plane would start boarding any minute.

She reshifted her shoulder bag, moved her neck from side to side, getting out a crick. Looked me up and down, from head to toe, at the way I was standing there, and grinned at me, more a leer than a grin, really; in a soft German accent she said quietly, just under her breath, "Hey sailor—buy a girl a chtrink?" I lowered my leg immediately and stood there next to her on both feet.

She glanced down at her watch. "Well, then," she said then. "Well."

In her voice and in her eyes was her touch, the food of her scent, the coating of her cries and the sheeting that had been her tongue lapping slowly in the well of my palm, and at my wrist, all over me and me over her as well, and above all her lithe body against mine, the press of her to me. I could not believe that all this had happened. I could not believe that it was ending.

"I shall telephone you soon, you know," she said.

I was just looking at her, thinking, if I do not find something glib to fire off in the next five seconds, there is imminent danger of welling tears, when suddenly, so suddenly it made my heart skip, she slung her shoulder bag around in back of her, moved in close to me, slipped her right arm around my waist, her left arm back around below my right shoulder blade, and both turning me and dipping me over backward, tilted me all the way back from my waist, in front of God and everybody, and held me there a split second, a face full of camp irritation on her, then hissed right into my face, "Aaaaw cheer up, ferchrissakes!" and kissed me, hard, on the lips. I started to giggle, and she leaned me back up then, still holding her lips to mine, incredible strength in those arms! still wound about me, and she pushed me light up against the wall and kept kissing me and put her tongue in me and rolled it around in there for who knows how long, pressing her body close to mine. For an instant I thought I could faint. Finally, she pulled back.

Grinning ear to ear she whispered, *"Épater les bourgeois!"*

Breathless and blushing I breathed back, seeing in my periphery and beyond Miriam a few people standing stock-still staring at us, "What's that mean."

"To shock the bourgeoisie!" and winked. Then in a loud, rich, polished Royal Shakespeare voice she said, backing off from me in careful backward steps, "And may God bless you *and* the missions, Sister Ursula! Farewell!" and she grinned at me one last time, rehoisted her shoulder bag, cocked her thumb up at me RAF-like, and whispered "Bye!" at me so low I lip-read it. In the next second she had turned around and was walking off into the crowd.

Airport: II

For the month of February 1979, my telephone long-distance bill was an appalling $143.19. All to Albuquerque.

Miriam's was $127.03. She had called Boston, once.

We would talk until our ears started hurting from holding the phone up to them, or until Syd had to go to bed, whichever came first. Usually Syd.

But by the third week of February, a little eternity, I had finagled an entire Friday and half a Thursday off from my job, and since Miriam only had class on Tuesdays and Thursdays, we, *voila!* had us a three-day weekend. I hopped a midafternoon Texas International flight that Thursday, landing at the Albuquerque airport just after three o'clock. Scanning the mexicano-style lobby for Miriam, my excitement was at dangerously high levels. I remember that it was fiercely cold, cold and dry and bright in Albuquerque, just as it had been in Texas when I'd left, and yet I was sweating in that lobby, sweating and just faintly nauseated, a very volatile state of expectancy. Where is she, dammit. And then I saw her. She spotted me at about the same time, I think; her grin seemed to coincide with mine, anyway. There were the Ray-Bans (I had mine on too), and she was wearing a big ochre suede and sheepskin rancher coat. Jeans, boots. She teaches like that? Mir was chewing gum and leaning up against the wall, posing, I noticed then, with one foot on the wall just like I had in L.A. Cute, cute.

I began shouldering my way across the stream of the two dozen or so other disembarking passengers, finally made it over to her. I was beaming, brimming, standing there a second with the beam still on, not quite knowing whether to embrace her or not; after all she did teach in this town. Then she moved in toward me, putting her arms around my shoulders, and murmured, "Oh hell luv, we can hug, yunno—nuffing so damned incautious about that, here." My face just fit next to her neck, and there again was that scent, her scent, citric, iris, woody. Just Miriam, that's all. But it thrilled me so much at that moment that I shuddered outright. With one arm still draped over my shoulders she turned me around gently, asking, "'s that yer only bag, then," to which I replied, "Yup," and with that we headed wordlessly out toward the front of the airport, Miriam's arm gradually slipping away from me and coming to rest briefly at her side; then she dipped her hand down into her pocket, fished out car keys. And now we had lumbered our way out into the chill New Mexico sunlight, and the wind was up, brrrr. Mir moved in close to me as we walked, smiling and gazing over at me, our upper arms touching as we went along.

"Over here," she nodded, and we veered off beyond a line of cars and over a few rows. "That's me bus, the Volks." A red and white one. "A '73," she said. "A hundred thousand miles on it—think we'll make it home?" She slid the side door back, took my suitcase from me and set it on one of the back seats. After stepping nimbly up into the van Miriam turned to me, bending over from the waist to look into my face as I stood out on the asphalt. "Uh, dooo—do come in," and held out a hand to me. The touch of her hand to mine threw a line like current all the way up the inside of my arm. Miriam pulled me up into the bus. I was in front of her, just in front of the little passageway separating the two front seats. *"Aprés toi,"* she said, motioning me forward. So I did go first and of course you do have to bend all the way over in a van, so of course Miriam took instant advantage of my not entirely unself-conscious presenting and goosed me, sliding her fingers, her middle finger pressing hardest, right up the cleft of me, from the front of my jeans all the way up and back. I jumped, hit my head. "Oooo, cor, God, sorry," she said laughing, rubbing my ass and patting my bumped head at the same time.

The Road to Corrales

Driving away from the airport up University, at the junction of Yale Boulevard, Miriam pointed off to the right: "You can see the Sandias Mountains back there, see?" and there they were, great long black slabs really something like slices of watermelon, their crests covered over with a cap-line of snow. "And straight up there, further up University here, is me school," and she gestured up the road at it with her wrist and fingers as though shooing chickens, "my place of employ. Syd's and my source of income. Sustenance. Madness." We turned left at the intersection toward Interstate 25. Mir shoved a tape in, one that had been partly pulled out but still rested in the deck, the Stones' *Between the Buttons* album. Shifting up to fourth, Mir glanced over at me quickly as we took the access, nodded down at the speaker: "My heroes, these guys. Really. Nobody remembers how bloody squeaky clean the world was before them. Great nasty brutes, they were back then. Trailblazers. Nowadays everybody's nasty."

She started talking then about a concert of theirs in Washington in 1965, shortly after she'd first come to the U.S. She'd only seen them on television in Britain (Miriam had lived right down the road from Milton's house in Chalfont St. Giles, Bucks.). She and Roland (o stow it! there's already so much to tell! Roland, I had learned, was the name of Syd's Dad, Miriam's ex, another story, later, later) had taken the train down from Boston for the D.C. event (they were both then first-year doctoral students at BU); also to meet Roland's mother, whose house in Georgetown . . . (a diplomat's widow, Roland's dad— dammit, never mind!). Anyway, the Stones: "I just could not get over Jagger," Miriam was saying. "Well who could, but I mean, this guy was lewdness incarnate. The tiniest fastest hips in the Western Hemisphere. Yunno, at one point in that concert he actually slung his dick around the microphone stand, kind of flapped his balls around the mike thingie . . . I could not believe my eyes." Just then we swung off 25 west to 40, the Coronado Freeway. After we'd cleared the ramp Miriam gave me this mildly derisive, taunting sort of a look, or what seemed to be derision behind those damned Ray-Bans, pursed her lips just slightly, lemony lips. She smiled oversweet at me, "But then you wouldn't give much of a shit about that, would you."

I smiled affably enough back at her, shook my head, "Nope, not me." A four-second pause, still smiling at her. "And unless I hallucinated Los Angeles three weeks ago, neither would you."

From behind the Ray-Bans she just smiled at me, said nothing, her line of vision leading back and forth from the highway to me. And I remember, perfectly clearly, that at that moment the Stones' song "Complicated" came rolling off the tape. Miriam leaned over far to me and stroked the inside of my left thigh. "Christ it's good to have you here," and leaned back.

All right I said, "And it's good to be had here," just like Groucho and we both chuckled at that, but with the bus droning on in fourth and the highway placking along below us, while the Stones' bass overrode the din and the late-day sun straight ahead of us kept bursting crown-points on the windshield, I thought: God yes it's good to be here. Ho, yes.

Scratching her nose lightly, Mir nodded her head left over her shoulder: "And that's Old Town over there, only you can't see it from the freeway. I'll get Anna to stay with Syd tomorrow or Saturday and we'll go have supper down there. Blue torts. Not like Texas."

After we'd crossed over the wide smooth stretch of the mocha Rio Grande, we took the Coors exit and travelled north along Coors past the University of Albuquerque, past the Alameda airport, until Coors became Corrales, winding and snaking through the yucca-pocked ranchlands, past juniper, past piñon pine. We'd been driving for about thirty minutes when Miriam announced, "We're almost there," and turned off the high road onto a dirt trail leading down behind a clump of fir trees; a brace of birds took wing from behind them. "Juncos," Miriam pointed out after them, and she pulled the van over, grinding to a halt.

"Where are we?" I asked.

"I dunno," Miriam said, and unbuckled her seat belt. She got up and scooted around the gearshift, nudged me over in my seat with her hip. Slipped her arms around my waist. "Probably trespassin," and she leaned in and kissed me, her tongue just parting her lips, semi-wet. "Ullo," she said.

"Ullo."

"See, I figgered we'd have to be decorous and all with Syd and it would be hours and hours before I'd get you off to bed, and so I just wanted to get your lips ready for later, later on. Besides. I couldn't wait." And she leaned in again and kissed me, a big deep wet-hot long one that set the soles of my feet on fire. Then she got up, very abruptly, sat herself back down in the driver's seat, and said, "We'd best stop there, luv, before I can't."

Well, I just unbuckled my own damned seat belt then, jumped up quick and scooted her over with my hip. I kissed her back just the same, only I held it a lot longer and slipped my hand inside her jacket as well, cupped my hand around her breast, the left one, and stroked it a bit, rolled the nipple between thumb and forefinger a while longer, still kissing her. She pulled back from me, out of breath some, her lips, smiling, parted open; and I said, "Well we'd best stop there, before I can't," and sat back down in my seat. *"Touché,"* she said, and, turning the ignition, "whew."

Entrez, Syd-nay

Miriam was telling me that her ranch house in Corrales stood on twenty acres of land, "not particularly arable," she said, but green enough to raise a couple of horses anyway. We turned off the highway and down another dirt road, bouncing along for maybe a mile or so, crossing over one cattle guard to another small road, bouncing along it for a while, eventually slowing down as we approached a fuchsia mailbox with *1887* painted on it in very large lime green numbers. Mir eased the bus up to the box and pulled her mail out. "Christ, all bills, puke," she said, flinging the envelopes up on the dash. As she turned the van left across another cattle guard she said, "I was nuts about the place before I ever knew its box number; then I was sure it was right for me'n Syd—an omen, sort of. Eighteen-eighty-seven's the year of the Michelson-Morley experiment. . . ." She glanced over at me to see if that needed explaining. It sounded familiar, but I'd forgotten what it was. "The guys who established the speed of light," she said. Oh yeah.

I could see her place off in the distance then, a low sprawling adobe house with a rooftop of imbricate terra-cotta tiling, a plume of woodsmoke spiralling up from the chimney—oh goody, a fireplace. As we drove on in toward the house, a huge Dreamsicle-color dog, mostly Lab, Disney ears as big as flour tortillas, came trotting out from behind the house into the yard wagging and barking, its massive mechanical-bank jaw falling open almost forgetfully, disjunctively, *Ouruff* (pause), *rowf,* a Perry Como of a dog, cordial but nobody's toady. Mir was calling out to it as we pulled up, "Hey Mocks, assa girl," and as she, Mocks (the dog's name is Moxie, so it's Mox, really), as Moxie clambered forward, Mir set the brake, leaned out the window, and began making kissy noises at the dog—"Gi' us a kiss, come on, kiss-kiss" (Christ, people and their animals). Then she harked back to me and said, "She's a perfect sweetie, yunno—never fear," and we gathered up our things, mail and bags and decorum (I'll admit it, I was nervous about what was coming up, meeting the kid), and trudged across the yard up the porch step to the surprisingly low front doorframe, maybe less than five feet. "Watch yer head," Miriam said as she leaned in under it, going first. God, what a wonderful room.

Slim pine planks perhaps a couple of inches across formed the ceiling, a high one, certainly lots higher than that front door, a good twelve feet at least, and were spanned by thick umber support beams maybe a foot wide. There were little Bavarian-like latch windows, high up: it was late afternoon now and the light was beginning to fail anyway, but the room would surely have been dark regardless. The fire was in fact confined to a woodstove; nuts, no fireplace. Navajo rugs covered the floor and parts of the walls; the furniture was old-timey, Zane-Grey sturdy—a pair of couches, two easy chairs, all with yellow pine arms and legs, burgundy or viridian leather. Homemade book-shelves with hundreds of books on them ran all along the walls, all the way round the room. Brrr-brrr: it was damned chilly in there. Miriam dumped all of her stuff down on a round oak table at one end of the room, went over and lobbed a couple of log splits into the stove. Then she crossed back over to the front door and hit a light switch, throwing on a line of soft track light-ing on two sides of the room—much better, a nice pinky glow on it all now. She turned around and smiled at me. "It's quite old, yunno," she said. "I really don't know how old, precisely. Probably at least 1850s, from what I've been able to piece together. Some poor bloke supposedly did himself in here, sometime back in the forties." She stood looking around the room, hands on her hips, then began peeling off her coat. "Yeah well, I do get kind of weird vibes here, sometimes, particularly when I've smoked some pot. I got me hands on some peyote once and thought I saw him sort of shimmying past the doorway in the next room (I could hear a television blaring beyond the door, where she pointed), but you know how those heavy-duty variety drugs are—you can scare yeh'self shitless if you don't mind what you're about." She looked down at my suitcase, which I'd set down just beside me. "Well let's go stow that, then we'll meet the nipper," and she took me by the arm, just under my forearm, and guided me off toward one end of the room, toward the door at the other end, the one without the TV blaring from it. Into a hall-way. More books, stacked to the ceiling. "And here we have the kitchen," she said in a Julia Child falsetto, nodding to it on our right; all I had a chance to see was the floor, nice wide terra-cotta tiles, a white enamel and tin gin-gerbread cupboard, copper pots hung from a chain-suspended wagon wheel. "And here we have the, if you'll pardon the expression, master bedroom and bath," (*bahth*), and she steered me through the door, nabbed my suitcase, lifting it whole from me and dropping it on the bed, turned around and closed the door. Threw her arms around my neck. "Just once more," she said low, smiling into my eyes. "Syd's watching her tunes now anyway."

"Tunes?"

Miriam rolled her eyes, tched. "Christ. Being a mum's destroyed what's left of me brain. I mean cartoons: four to five's Bugs Bunny." She kissed me once, twice, then she said, "One more," and laid this humdinger on me, another foot-scorcher, knee-buckler. She pulled back slowly from me, a salivary wisp clinging an instant to our lips which broke as I gasped, a little huff of aching. Still in my arms she smiled at me: "God I do love to get you all hot and worked up. *Power*."

"Ah yes," I said, "but this's a dyarchy, don't forget," and I reached down between her legs and clutched her there—and it seemed from the pit of her stomach she exhaled, Oah, low, low—and I rubbed her there a little longer, kissing her, but then she squirmed away from my hand, laughing.

"Oh cripes, I must make the obvious pun," she said then: "You mean a dyke-archy, of course," and we both groaned the automatic pun-groan, and she kissed me again, lightly, and hugged me. Then she gave me this fake-solemn look: "Time to face the young music, luv."

"Lead on," said I.

We rounded the door into the TV-blaring room. Sydney was on the floor with her back to us, cross-legged in front of Daffy Duck; a teenage Chicana in a rocking chair beside her, a book open on her lap. Both of them were in bluejeans and several top layers of longjohns and flannel shirts and thick heavy-knit cardigans, Anna's navy, Syd's bright red. Another woodstove burning in the corner. More Navajo rugs all about. Kid books. An army of stuffed animals atop a yellow cord bedspread on a maple trundle bed. "Hey, you lot," Miriam said as they both turned around and smiled at us, though Sydney (there she is, look at that face) only for an instant, turning back to the screen, then back to us again, getting up slowly, a perfectly executed cue that she'd rather be watching her 'toons. Anna, a little sleepy-looking, a lovely girl, almond eyes, cheekbones, full lips the color of apple wine, and a long single blue-black braid of hair behind her, tiny wisps falling forward around her face, started rocking, still smiling. Syd walked over to us slowly (red Keds!), in careful, mincing little-girl steps; Mir squatted down and Sydney moved in close to her, falling into Mir's arms and hugging her around the neck. "Ooof," Miriam wheezed, slipping her arms all the way around Syd's back, "How're you then, sweetest."

"Fine, fine."

"Syd, this's Bobbie, as well you know." Mir stood up then, holding on to Sydney's hand. Syd turned and extended her left hand out to me, not the one she shook hands with normally, I could tell; she sort of clutched at my hand—something fairly Hollywoody about that, but delightful in a kiddo. She actually squeezed my hand then, quite softly, but a squeeze nonetheless, then let her hand drop—*very* Hollywoody.

"How'jadoo," she said evenly. Lord, will you look at those eyes.

"Nice ta meet ya, Sydney," I said warmly.

She lay her head in close to Miriam, just at Mir's rib cage. Smiling. She giggled, looked up at her mother, who was still gazing down at her with this mountain of maternal pride, then back at me: "I've heard a lot about you," she said—this, with an actual raising of an eyebrow!

Mir looked at me then. "She has, yunno, no lie." Turning to Anna, Miriam said, "Anna, this's Bobbie Crawford: Bobbie, Anna Maria Alejandra de Escobedo y Quinones...soon to be plain old Mrs. Spaulding, if she doesn't watch out." Anna tittered, said, "Hi," as we shook hands gently.

"Miriam," Anna said then, and her voice was soft and young and soothing, "I've got this big history exam tomorrow—do you think you could give me a ride home pretty soon after Syd's cartoons?"

"Oh sure, love, sure, absolutely."

Sydney, though still smiling during all this, started squirming. To Miriam she said, "Do you think we could talk later? Mom...."

"Oh sorry Syd. I neglected to prepare Bobbie for the importance of your 'toons."

To me, Sydney said, "If you'll forgive me," and she reached out and squeezed my arm this time, then brushed by me, gliding beyond me, back toward Sylvester and Tweety—a Scarlett O'Hara kind of move, *noblesse oblige,* and I almost burst out laughing but managed to stifle it at the last second—didn't want to mock the kid's act. "Of course," I said, not smiling with great effort, "of course. Later."

"Come along, Bobbie," Miriam said, grinning, "Let's us go slop some marinade on the steaks...Her Grace simply cannot be disturbed at this time."

A Morning in Bed

After Syd's 'toons were over, we all of us ran Anna back home, and a little later we had supper, some melt-in-your-mouth sirloin ("I'm not gonna do any real cookin while you're here," Miriam said, snatching baked potatoes from the oven. "Don't want to waste a minute of lark time," and she gave me this absolute scapegrace of a look). We eventually managed to settle Sydney down for sleep at a most gratifyingly early hour (the kid was a shade loopy from a glass of wine she'd had with dinner—"I'm a wine enthusiast, you know," she'd told me dead-serious at the table), and then, still later:

"Miriam."

"Yes love."

"Miriam, I have some grim, ungodly news. I started my period last night."

"Oh."

"Yeah."

"Well . . .we'll just have to be careful, won't we, towels, you know, and I've got some coconut oil." She slipped her arms about my neck, her hands cradling the back of my head, and kissed my ear.

"But. Uh—I'm allergic to coconut oil."

"Ooo cor! How'dja find that out? Ha!" Then, soothingly, "Poor little imp! Bet it was miserable."

"Quite."

"How 'bout sesame then."

The next morning we were awakened by a tiny tap-tapping at Mir's bedroom door—tiny, but persistent. Mir looked over at me, smiled, winced. Said huskily, "D'ja mind, luv—she always comes in, weekends," to which I, mostly lackadaisical, shrugged, as Miriam called out, "Come in, sweetie," and in she trudged, still in her white flannel jammies (with feet!) with the yellow bears, her little Royal Stewart Tartan wool robe, and moccasins too. Lugging the *Oxford English Dictionary,* itself virtually half her size. Huffing with it, smiling, mischief up. Looking from Miriam to me and back.

"What's this, then," Miriam said smiling, sitting part-way up in bed, pulling her singlet, a brown one this time, down. Me, I propped myself up on one elbow, pulling the sheet up over my chest.

Holding the Mona Lisa smile, Syd said nothing, set the tome down on Mir's side of the bed, set herself down in front of it alongside her mother, began leafing slowly through it, twirling the magnifying glass in her other hand—rather saucily, I'd say. Humming. I was not a little astonished to realize that the song was "Don't Cry For Me, Argentina." In the next instant, as she continued leafing through the dictionary, she began to sing it, but in a Peter Lorre accent. At this I really did burst out laughing, and Mir said, pleased, "Oh she's always doin' that, doin' Peter Lorre. She loves Peter Lorre, doncha Syd?"

Syd, not really looking up, just hummed an affirmative, kept on riffling through the *OED*. Then at one page she all of a sudden stopped, proclaimed, "A-ha! Here it is!" and fixed the glass on a corner of the page, her tongue curved up and over her upper lip in a fury of concentration as she read a little bit first to herself, then slowly out loud to us:

"Dike!" she announced grandly, and looked up at Miriam and beamed, and Mir poked her in the ribs, saying something like, "Fawww, Sydney!"

"Dike—" Syd continued, sobering, "and it's spelled d-y-k-e, too. Number one: 'an excavation narrow in pro. . .proportion to its. . .length, a long and narrow hollow dug out of the ground.' " All this rather falteringly. She looked up at the two of us with an angelical smile.

"Very clever, Syd," Mir said softly, smiling, squeezing Sydney's knee. "What else?"

"Uh. . .number two: uh, Mom, would you read it please? It's so hard to see." And she turned the book around to Mir, handed her the glass.

Miriam peered down with the lens, read, grinned. "Lots of what you'd expect," she said to me, and to Sydney: "Lots of references to dams and things, construction, water." Then scanning down the column, she laughed out loud: "Ha! 'A beavers' dam'!"

Sydney was laughing with us, not, I felt, informedly. "Beavers!" she chirped happily.

Then Mir said, "And this, from mining" (to Syd: "Working in coal mines, gold mines, mining—you know, like Yosemite Sam")—'A fissure in a stratum, filled up with deposited or in*tru*sive rock; a *fault*.' " Mir looked over at me, tched. Skimming down still further, she said, "Hey lissen to this. Number ten: '. . .as in *dike-hopper*. . .a person or animal (e.g., an ox or sheep)' "—to which I bleated a baby "b-a-a-a-h-h," getting another giggle outta Syd—" 'that leaps over fences; *fig.*, a transgressor of the laws of morality. . . .' D'ya suppose that's where it came from, then?" she asked me.

"Cows? God I hope not."

Syd was pulling at Miriam's arm: "So where's the lesbian part, Mom? Read that part."

"It's not in this one, Sydney," Miriam said, serious now. "Besides, it doesn't matter. Like we talked about, darling: only mediocre minds are going to call me" (and she looked over at me, then back to Syd) " 'n Bobbie. . .and Sukie and Mary and Jill—that name."

"And Phyllis," Sydney said.

"And Phyllis," said Miriam.

"'n Tina," Syd said, screwing up her nose.

"And Tina," Miriam sighed.

Syd whined, "But I wanted to see it, I wanted to read it."

"Go try the *American Heritage* one, sweetie," Miriam said, petting Syd's leg. "And while you're at it, I want you to look up a word for me, Syd—I want you to look up *precocity,* too."

"Pruh. . .pruh-ca—what?"

"Precocity, precocity: p-r-e-. . .c-o-c-i-t-y." They rehearsed this a few times. Syd looked down at the *OED*. "That'd be in the other one, the *P* to *Z*s."

Mir said, "Well go get it, then. Where's your intellectual curiosity, Sydney? Oh, and will you do mummy a favor? Will you just plug in that coffee machine for me? Did you get your juice yet?"

"Yes, yes," Syd said, a little grumpily, and then Mir, setting the *OED* to the other side of her, reached out and pulled Syd up to her, enfolding her, cradling her; and for an instant the love of those arms stunned me, tore at something deep down in the middle of me. Miriam whispered into Sydney's ear, "We're fixin waffles, chippo," which sent a, for all practical purposes, visible ripple of delight throughout Syd, who very promptly then bustled herself out of Miriam's embrace, nabbed up the dictionary, and huffed out of the room, humming "Don't Cry For Me" once more.

Another Family Sketch _____

Well, while Miriam's out in the kitchen doing up our waffles ("with walnuts in 'em, to mitigate the carbos"), and Syd's off in her room donning her dungarees—presumedly, it's real quiet in there—and being allowed to decide how the three of us are to spend the day, either horseback riding or kite flying, and I, at Mir's request, am in the process of setting out on the turntable a Berlin Philharmonic recording of Strauss waltzes for our morning music (once, on the Texaco opera show's intermission, Miriam had heard four out of five music critics respond—in answer to the question, "What music do you reach for when you're depressed?"—*Strauss waltzes,* after which she had without the least delay gone out and purchased this selfsame record), let us recap, gentle reader, a few of the many highlights of Miriam's life Before Me.

How to begin, since surely the essential question—where to begin—could only rest with the mysterious Roland Metzger. (Oh yes, Miriam kept his name. Her own name had been Colson, which during Watergate and the terrible times of Roland's descent into an untimely dotage held no irresistible allure for her; she'd never liked the coupling of the m and n endings of her first and last names anyway, and was moreover, she said, rather fond of her married name's alliteration.) But Roland. Here. Here's his photograph. A pale, thin, dark-haired young man with an Adam's apple, staring off from a mountainside verandah (*Rol at Mt. Mansfield in Vermont, '68*—Mir's scrawl on the back); coal-black eyes, almost painfully ethereal-looking, a slightly displaced, damaged air about him—intelligent, neurotic, an intellectual young Ray Bolger.

How, how on earth had it all happened, I'd asked her.

When they first met, she explained, they were both basically androgynous, neither of them had figured out their sexualities—or so Miriam had thought. That is, Miriam herself had never had sex with a woman before, although Roland, as it happened, had in fact slept with several men. The bleak truth of the matter was that Roland, who during the Dark Ages of the middle sixties was as repressed as the next gay, both lived with and subsequently married Miriam without ever telling her this most pertinent of facts—in the pathetic hope that his love for her would somehow iron him out ("And he did love me, yunno," Miriam said, quietly). However, Rol continued to sleep with men, whilst living with and later on being married to Miriam, and yet did not tell Miriam. Then, quite on her own, Mir discovered her own true sexuality with, as she said, chucking me under the chin, an older woman, one of her professors at Boston. Roland found a love letter of this Renée's that Mir had left in a dresser drawer, "probably quite purposefully," she allowed, and when Roland confronted her with it ("again, all quite purposefully, at long last"), the following conversation ensued:

Miriam: "Well. . .you've slept with women before. . .do you blame me?"

Roland: "No. . .no, of course not. . .do you, would you blame me, for. . . sleeping with men?"

To me Miriam said, "It was right out of *Cabaret,* only *Cabaret* hadn't been done yet."

During the course of her affair with Renée, Miriam had, as can happen under such circumstances, become much more loving and affectionate toward Roland: it was then that she became pregnant. And having become pregnant, she suddenly began battling her own natural feelings about Renée and about women generally, and decided, in part to iron herself out (o woe, the Dark Ages), and in part because she really, really did want a little girl, to go ahead and have the baby. (Because she was as bonkers as she was those days, she refused to believe that Syd would be anything but a girl—Syd's name having originated with a mutual pipedream of Rol's and Mir's, to run off to Australia and live at the edge of the world's last new frontier.) "Crazy, crazy days those were— panicked, deranged," Miriam was saying, shaking her head sadly, "and it only got far, far worse (what with Syd's infancy and Rol's burgeoning infantilism and the eventual decision to commit him, to shunt him and the total and absolute day-to-day responsibility for him, out of her life)". . .and then it got better again" (with her second and third lovers, the aforementioned Tina and Phyllis, respectively)". . .and then it got mordantly, edge-city bad again" (the cancer)". . .and then it got all right, quite all right, again" (post-surgery, and eventually, me).

We were sitting on the floor of the van, Mir and I, just at the open door, our legs dangling out and over the side; we were watching Syd work the kite, a nice big pink-and-yellow-checkered box job. Out there in the cold dry high-wind I'd gotten it airborne for her and then let her take over—*there* being somewhere east of an area between Alameda and Bernalillo, way out in the desert; we were way out in the middle of nowhere, at some point on a grid of dirt roads cross-cutting the sands. All of us were bundled up like the infantry, and Miriam and I were warming our hands around great whacking cups of tea. As Mir was pouring from an industrial-size thermos, she suddenly mused: "Tina was British too, yunno, from Exeter. . .and I've often thought the main thing about me that attracted her was the fact that I knew how to make a proper cuppa char." She then continued to pick up the infinite thread of her life for me, and was describing, following those bad old days of panic and derangement, her return to loving women ("—inevitable," she said, "simply due to the fact I hadn't gone altogether mad").

I had so many questions. Gazing out at Syd, standing prim and still in the cold sunshine, one was: "Mir, what's it like, having a baby."

She hummed, or umm-ed, sipping at her tea. "I always think of that line of Fanny Brice's, after she'd had hers—she said, 'Well, it's kinda like pushin' a piano through a transom.' "

I laughed, said, "Well in my imaginings I replay a M*A*S*H segment I saw once, where Colonel Potter was helping deliver a baby, and he says something like, 'Once a baby's shoulders have cleared the vaginal opening'— doctor/TV language, you understand—'then the whole body slips out.' "

"Yeah, that's about it, all right, that's what happened. But until those bleedin little shoulders pop through, cripes!"

Just then the kite took a nose dive and Syd started running out fast to recover, pulling in slack. "Go Syd!" Miriam cheered, and in another instant the kite was in an upshaft, stable again. Sydney turned around and smiled big, cocked her thumb at us in the same A/O.K. British way of her mum's at the L.A. airport. "Little fart," Miriam said gently under her breath, "my little googol."

"When's lunch?" Syd yelled from out there, squinting back at us into the sun.

"Whenever ya like," Mir shouted back. And to me, "She's developed her mum's passion for food, I'm afraid. You hungry, love?" she asked me. Stealthily stealing a begloved hand back behind her, I gave her left bun a through-longjohns-and wool-trousers tame, barely perceptible tweak, affirming that I was indeed quite surprisingly famished again. After Syd had gotten the kite safely down, we whipped out the picnic basket, set out a green Guatemalan tablecloth on the floor of the van, out of the wind, and began to devour chicken salad sandwiches and superhot *potage parmentier* ("much pissy-er than mere potato soup") and oatmeal-raisin cookies for afters, all of it splendid, all of it assiduously Mir-prepped by one stage or another the weekend before, and all topped off by more tea.

Seemingly engrossed in polishing off her present cookie and simultaneously selecting her next, Sydney said absently, or in a manner absent-sounding, "We've been to Britain twice before, to visit Gram 'n Harvey."

"Harvey being my mother's third husband," Miriam smiled, sipping.

"And we're gonna go again this summer," Syd added, nodding with authority.

"But we might just take us a holiday to Texas first, Syd, what say."

Ah and here was yet another milestone moment, friend reader, in our three lives together: let us freeze the action for but a few seconds and study it closely. To begin with, this was Miriam's first truly substantive mention of coming to Texas—Chicken Little-like, I kept expecting paradise to come shattering down around me. Furthermore, she had included Sydney in her plans for the junket. . .surely a sign of no small import. Was I hopeful, did I rejoice, was my heart soaring sky-goddamned-high? Well—yes and no. You see, I was, on the other hand, sitting there with bated breath waiting to hear what little Sydney was going to say to this. Not that Syd's approval was the *sine qua non* of things (Miriam had, besides, already told me that morning that Syd had informed her she thought I was funny, witty), but bated breath nonetheless. One of my first intros into the tyrannies of children.

She, the little tyrant, was picking a raisin out of her—"How many's that, Syd?" "Six"—sixth cookie, and she lifted her eyes to me with the perfect *sang-froid* of a neurosurgeon lifting a scalpel. This was in fact, I would come to learn in ensuing months and years, a quite practiced face, an expression of hauteur and composure absolute. She did it so very well, so chillingly well. Her timing, too, was perfecto; she was milking this instant for all it was worth. Then she said to me, kind of overperkily, "You gotta ranch?"

Mir and I both smiled and Miriam said, "Not everybody in Texas has a ranch, Syd."

Irritably Sydney said, "I know that, I know that. I was just askin." A few seconds later she asked, "Well, have ya got any horses then?"

"Nope, no horses either, Sydney. A cat. Lotsa friends, lots of women I'd like you to meet."

"Lesbians?" she asked then, brightening.

(Saved!) "Mostly," I said offhandedly, "yes."

"I was thinking we might go spring break, Syd," said Miriam. And to me, "That's in another three weeks—how about it?"

At the Copehart Tavern _____

Following an abundant family-style sit-down barbecue supper at the Cope-hart Inn (the sign out on Highway 21 read WELCOME TO COPEHART, TEXAS: POP. ~~27~~ 42 . . ."Christ, boomin," Miriam muttered), the bunch of us (Me, Mir, Syd, Cory, Gabe, Jackie, Ramona and her new girlfriend Judith, Sherman, Chuke and her new girlfriend—who had been Jackie's old girlfriend—Beth, and Rachel and Cam, who'd driven up from Notasonia) were sauntering through the town, rounding the street corner down to the tavern for a couple of games of pool. As we scuffed along in the middle of the road, the sun had almost set: a rose dusklight hung thick in the warm spring air, diffused from a haze low in the west, the sun's rays there fanning out and closing in upon themselves in concentric diamonds like a Oaxacan God's-eye, in butter-colored lines like lozenges. A gen-u-ine tumbleweed, no, three of them, tumbled across the street in front of us. Mir and I had fallen back a little from the others; Sydney was padding along up ahead between Cory and Gabe, holding hands with both of them and being periodically lifted whole off the ground, giggling wildly with every sweep. "Look at 'er, she's ecstatic with those two," Mir said, cuddling into me as we walked.

"Must've been watchin' her mum last night in the kitchen with Gabe," said I, baitingly. No kidding—the chemistry between Miriam and Gabe was so immediate and intense that both Cory and I had today already been making nervous snipes about it.

"No, Syd's gone crackers over *Cory,*" Mir laughed, leaning in closer to me and squeezing my arm, "—another *enfant terrible,* like you," she taunted. "God you know, I just can't get over all of them, these Texas women," she said, gazing after my friends as they traipsed along before us. "They're so big, and confident; so vital. Damn, I love the way they walk!" I could see her eyes following Sherman and Chuke, who were ambling off by themselves, peeking into a tack store window. "They walk like Margaret Mead! . . .or Mar-jorie Main . . . Madalyn Murray—crusty! Crusty as all get-out."

We were clumping up the old front stoop of the town beerhall; Cory was holding the screen door open for everybody as we filed in. Inside, the juke, an old Wurlitzer with bubble lights, was throbbing out Hank Williams' "Honky

Tonkin'." Once fully within the place I felt as though I really had stepped into a time warp; it was ancient, probably built as long ago as the 1870s. There were mustard-colored beaded-wood slats still on the walls, a hammered-tin ceiling maybe as much as twenty feet high, and ceiling fans that had to have been there at least fifty years, still whupping around overhead. A five-ball milkglass candelabra covered with cobwebs swathed the hall with the barest of light. A pair of cowboys—one with a long blond ponytail hanging down his back, the other with shoulder-length brown hair and a big bushy beard, the two of them in jeans and T-shirts and boots—were standing up at a ma-hogany bar with garlands carved into it. An iron woodstove, not burning, sat in the very middle of the hall; a shuffleboard ran along one wall. Just below the candelabra there was a table full of geezers, four of them, all seated in the middle right next to the woodstove: they were playing dominoes, and they looked up at all of us as we came in, smiled, nodded. Some four or five little girls aged six to ten were darting about the place in strapless halter tops and flipflops, one with a Hall & Oates T-shirt and Dr. Scholl's walking sandals, the eldest; Sydney's attention immediately riveted on them. McIver comman-deered the pool table, and Chuke took up the challenge. A number of bleep-ing, blooping video games stood at the far end of the hall; no one was playing them. After chatting with the grizzled old barkeep for a while, Gabe, grin-ning happily, walked back to all of us at the pool table with two pitchers of beer in hand. "Great place, huh," she says, and to me, nodding, "Why don-cha get us some cups, Bobbie Mae."

This then was Miriam's introduction to Texas, to a little of my world, and to my friends. And she was, I could tell, greatly pleased by it. Somewhat later on that evening, she and Cory and Gabe and I made a series of gonzo plans for a lesbian retirement home out by the lake—we'd call it Lago Lesbo—each of us picking out a job for ourselves at the home: I wanted to be the resident poet, Cory would be the rec sports coordinator, Gabe the musical therapist, and Miriam, after mulling it over a bit, said, "I should like to be The Masseuse." And we could open up an IRA for it, Cory said, and so on, and so forth. . . .

What else. Cory and Syd danced together. Well, they were two-stepping, and Cor found it easier to let Syd stand on her, on Cory's boots, move her around that way. They danced to Jerry Lee's "Thirty-nine and Holding" and Bob Wills' "San Antonio Rose."

Gabe came over and stood with us as we watched Cory take the table again, a great long run with one big beaut of a bank shot—everybody ya-hooed and applauded. On the sly Gabe said to us, "Will you look at her—she's had twice the beer I have and she's still shooting good."

Sydney was off playing with the little girls in a far corner of the dance floor. As I came out of the bathroom, I saw her over there standing above two of them playing jacks. Passing by the table of geezers on my way back to Mir and Gabe, I heard one of the old fellas saying most lovingly to three of the little girls, whom he'd gathered up close to him, "You girls are *all right*."

Miriam & Bobbie Long-Distance ⸻⸻⸻⸻⸻⸻

"—but that's when the honeymoon's over."

There followed a discomfiting silence at the other end of the line. Miriam, with a rare, thin slice of uncertainty in her voice, asked, "What do you mean by that. What do you mean, 'when the honeymoon's over'?"

There had already been, in the two trips I'd already made to Albuquerque and the one Mir and Syd had made to Texas, a handful of jokes about "when the novelty wore off," when she and I would become bored with one another, lapse into customariness, turn on the television set and really watch TV. At this particular instant, however, I was not suggesting that our passion would eventually die; I didn't know then nor do I know now if passion's demise is always inevitable. Clearing my throat then I told her, and I hadn't even rehearsed it, I was so proud of myself: "I mean that I suspect there really will come a time when I'll see you and not be overcome *each and every time* by this. . .hungering, this. . .that makes me want to tear your clothes off, throw you to the floor, and fall to on you with my tongue and my fingers and moan for your moans until the shuddering seizes you, and, it's done."

More silence at the other end. By and by a much smaller voice: "Oh. That."

Two Who Love

The press to cohabit did not of course assert itself all at once, although the actuality of our continuing on together may, I suppose, have been assured from the very first by the miraculously felicitous blending and counterbalancing of qualities in us that each of us recognized to one degree or another ("You're good for me"; "You are too"), and that each desired, and sought to learn about, and nurture, and grow with. Let us say, *Kismet,* and why not. So that, given several more trips back and forth from Albuquerque to Texas and vice-versa, and given several hundreds of dollars of long-distance bills, were you, gentle reader, to have overheard us saying such tellingly intensified things to each other as, "Isn't it obvious how bad off I am about you," and "Baby I just wish I knew what was gonna happen," you would not, I am sure, have been in the least surprised. Besides, there's page one of all this, isn't there.

But, sure, we missed one another like the blue blazes, and the partings just grew more agonizingly intolerable each and every time—and, just, well, *wrong* somehow, too. Magnify my nascent tearfulness at the airport in Los Angeles to the fifth power, and you will have arrived at an approximation of my dejection by Cinco de Mayo in Albuquerque, when the prospect of leaving Miriam again and flying back to Texas the following day seemed more than my spirit could bear. I wept. I wept as she held me in her arms, and then she wept too, trying to get me to stop that weeping, and she told me on the phone the Monday night after that that Sydney had wept as well, when my plane had taken off. Oh yes. Syd was getting all caught up in this too. Besides her easy affection for me (I really could get her to giggling, she was starting to crawl all over me, stuff like that—aw, we liked each other a whole lot, right off the bat), she was also increasingly gung ho about Cory, so much so that when Mir elected to leave her behind in Albuquerque one time on one of the Texas shuttles, Syd flew into a purple rage, then lapsed into an inconsolable crying jag so heart-rending and prolonged that Miriam eventually recanted and told her she could come along, saying, "But next time, you cannot do this, Sydney," not knowing then herself whether there would in fact be a next time or not. Oh, we were a mess all right, all of us.

(But of course Syd's falling in love with Cory only added to the already highly stacked deck. We had all seen a little girl come unglued with delight one evening when Cory asked Syd to go with her to the rodeo the following day—no mum, no Bobbie, no Gabe even. . .you should've seen the outfit: the tiniest cutest pair of Noconas I've ever laid eyes on, baby blue, and baby-blue corduroy jeans too, a little white western shirt, and a brand-new straw Cory helped her rough up a bit to look lived in.)

There was, of course, the preponderant question of our jobs. It wasn't that I felt so entrenched in mine; on the contrary. It was simply more the case that Miriam was feeling particularly despondent about hers. Oh she loved the teaching, the fifty minutes part in the classroom with the students and getting ideas across and watching the lights go on inside the heads, behind those eyes; she didn't just love that part—that's why she'd been doing it this long. She once said, "All right, I've got this rather good, no, it's superb, superb—superbly mercurial intelligence, a reasonable beauty, and a quite sizable talent for what I do, which is teach." But she had grown, bit by bit and month by month, ever more discontent with all the other crapola of academe, principally, the majority of her colleagues, the deadening administrative work, the ubiquitous axe of publish-or-perish. "Don't quit yer job, Bobs," she'd said in late April, "doan come out here. I dunno if I'm gonna stick with it here or not; I bin thinkin about chucking it in, here." But there was no resolution made then that time, either, of our two locations.

And there were other dimensions, other concerns. There were the fears, the qualms: "I, I doan think too many women could, can stand up to my spirit," Mir was saying as we walked around her ranch property one afternoon in May. "It scares them off, they. . ." (the implied context was the incomprehensible Phyllis, who seemed to have quit her just when the going got toughest, that is, six months after Mir was told she had cancer and was undergoing chemotherapy), at which I pointedly leaned my face down in front of hers (which had been gravely downcast as we walked along), and both crossed my eyes and stuck my tongue out at her. And she cracked up, laughing this enormous Hah! that burst right out of her, effervesced from those eyes. She grabbed me around the waist and tackled me, hard, tumbling me right down upon a soft bed of pine needles, rolling and tumbling and laughing with me and calling me a little shit. And then we made love out there all afternoon, out there below those pine tree branches lifting and sighing in the soft warm wind.

And at another time, me, my fears and qualms: "I don't know what makes them work any more, relationships. I can't promise you forever or anything—who could, in any honesty. I can't, and I know, with Sydney, all this is different, for you."

To which Miriam promptly, unhesitatingly replied, "Well. . .but do you think you could manage it for, say, two years? I think Syd would do very nicely with two years, if it should come to that."

"You mean. . .you want a two-year contract?"

"Yeah. Well not in writing or anything, don't be a dope. But just basically try and have things go as smoothly as possible for that time, and if by then things haven't panned out, sort through it again, then."

A somewhat bizarre proposal, but one of the first clear-cut instances of the burgeoning incontrovertibility of it all, nonetheless. Because of course in the final analysis we would have come together and lived together no matter what, simply because we were, and are still, two who love, and when you know it's right, you just *know.* Nothing quite else will do; anything else is out of the question.

In the ongoing unfolding there was also this, not unimportantly (reader, take heed) from Miriam: "It always goes in waves, passion—boredom, strength, weakness, cowardice, courage. The main thing is just to try and concentrate, try and settle down, try and bear in some part of your fore-mind that when things are their stinkiest, they're bound to improve. That when the wave's down in a trough, the crest's just coming up. And that *interference is always a part of wave motion*" (italics mine, reader *mia*). Here she looked at me most seriously, kissed me tenderly on the lips, said, "And if we choose to live together and love one another, there will always be the possibility that one of the two of us at one time or another will be attracted to someone else and want to make love to that someone else, and, well, I, for one, could quite probably act on that attraction, even at the risk of hurting you, or losing you. Bobbie, love, this isn't a condition of my love for you—it isn't a qualifier, a subclause; I love you now and I want to keep loving you. . .but Other People (capitals mine, too) and the dangers they bring are inseparable from any state of loving, in any dyad."

And I, in response to this, quietly told her that I accepted that in loving her I could hurt or be hurt in return, that. . .I agreed with her: this is the responsibility one shoulders when one loves. . . .

What I hadn't known was that while I was in Texas, Miriam had been having my local newspaper delivered to her out there in Corrales, and that she was daily scanning the classifieds for a job here. Then, one weeknight in early June, she telephoned to say she had arranged for a job interview here, with a soon-to-be-operational "artificial intelligence research corporation," a computer think-tank of the first order that had already begun building its headquarters out by the lake.

Friend, she got the job.

Now there was no getting around it. I flew out to Albuquerque the next weekend and we held one another that night and wept again and told each other we would always be gentle with one another and we were both actually trembling. . .and that, it seems, was how Miriam and I married one another—

trembling and weeping and promising to try and not hurt one another too much. Modern Romance. But then we blew our noses and cheered up a bit, went out to the kitchen hand in hand and Mir popped open a bottle of Dom Perignon while I put on a recording of the Jupiter Symphony, and we raised tulip glasses to one another, and sitting on the couch Miriam put her arms around me and said something like, we'll be brilliant as Mozart, lovey, endless improvisations, countless variations on a theme, the universe in octaves and numbers. . . .

And so it really began, our life together, although as I say it may also have really begun weeks and months earlier, when the Fates, those master puppeteers, had angled their fingers just so in California, thereby realigning the Metzger and Crawford strings, for Texas.

Our Family Album _____

The events of that summer took place with the frenzying, whirring rapidity of a motor-driven single-lens reflex.

Miriam was obligated to teach throughout June and the first week of July; her job with the think-tank was not due to begin until September. For the duration of that nutso summer she spent every other weekend in Texas house hunting with me, the other weekends back in Corrales, packing up her belongings and showing the ranch to potential buyers. The horses had to be sold and Syd's anguish over that unhappy unavoidability had to be contended with, though her foreknowledge of living in the same town with Cory did help assuage things quite a bit. By the end of June Miriam decided that it would be best to stash Syd in a safe spot during the replanting, so she flew with her up to Washington to leave her with Roland's mother until we could get situated. The trip to Britain and Mir's own mother was of course deferred for the nonce. Mir sold her VW van and bought a VW beetle. The ranch was finally sold by the end of July; by the first week in August we had still not found a home here, so Mir had the movers come and drive her stuff to Texas, where it was put into storage. She moved in, for the time being, with me in my duplex.

Oh, to hell with all these dreary details, reader-*amie!* For eventually, eventually, things really did work out for us, we did find us a nice big old rambling place right here off Baylor Park, we all got settled back down together, we began our journey together as a family, in earnest.

No, instead, let's scan over the quieter moments of that summer, the summer of '79, and over the two summers following it as well, as though they were all one great conglomerate inferno, one overarching sheath of white light and white flies, of loquats and lantana, trumpet vine and jasmine, oleander, honeysuckle—and the cool smooth limbs, smooth as arms, of white crape myrtle. There, out in our back yard, perched on a sheltering magnolia branch, a cardinal still singing during a violent, midday-darkening thunderstorm, in August? September? And here, here am I, with the fond patience of the native, little by little instructing Mir and Syd in the sweet craft of Texas-summer survivalism: the joys of late-afternoon movies; of dark, dank, icy-cold bars, and of beers (and for Sydney, of Barq's root beer); of Dr. Bronner's peppermint soap, bracingly cool to the skin; of Jean Naté *Après-Bain* kept in the icebox; of tall glass pitchers of homemade lemonade, and of iced Red Zinger tea in thermos jugs for afternoons at Bowie Springs, whose cool undercurrents chill the epidermis instantly, and whose towering cottonwoods soothe the soul with their whispering, pattering leafsong, slowly strummed by the soft hot wind. Here—here are the three of us picking mustain grapes along a farm road out beyond Enchanted Rock, Mir stopping to stand in their vaulting viny shade and interlace the grape leaves with their woody vines for garlands, Roman wreaths for our heads.

Here, standing in the hallway, Miriam switching on the kitchen light and gasping, running for a sandal, slapping a flying behemoth of a roach down to the floor into crunchy oblivion with her own warrior yell, *"Écrasez l'infame!"* ("Crush the infamous thing!"); my own cry being, "No one escapes!"

Here again, during one of those Augusts, are all three of us, together with Cory and Gabe and Alma and Gloria, back down at the Morans' ranch. We are taking a midmorning walk over to the creek and are dressed in attire indispensable to such Texas countryside strolls in summer: in boots ("Syd, now you stick with me down by that water," Cory is warning, "snakes get thirsty too"), and long pants to guard against poison ivy and sumac, and western straws and panamas to fend off the broiling sun and ticks dropping from mesquite.

And here once more am I, rounding the corner into our kitchen early one Saturday or Sunday morning in late June, about to get the coffee going, when JESUS CHRIST A BAT! resting stock-still in the middle of the floor. Oh. No. It's not a bat, it's a bird—and the instant I realize this, it takes wing, frightening me so badly it feels as though my heart will leap from my throat. But with the help of My Women, we manage to get the bird—it's a purple martin—out through the dining room, into the living room and out the screen door. A while later, after Miriam and I have compounded our adrenalin with caffeine, we deduce that the chimney flue had been left open, hence our visitor; and a few days later we secondarily deduce that this martin or one of its *compadres* (or rather, *commadres*) has fashioned a nest in the flue, because from it we can hear the chicks peeping in alarm whenever one of us opens the front door. Quite late one evening during the martins' term of residence, Mir comes home from an overlong day at the office, and I, as is my wont, am in our bed, reading a novel, cozily prone, perhaps just as you are now, dear reader. In she tiptoes and softly says to me, "Oh come 'ere, Bobs, it's so sweet," and we both go back out to the living room, and I hear the little chicks cheeping their alarums, but because it's so late they've been woken up, and their tiny, tiny cries are so dear and actually sleepy-sounding. . . .

More skipping on through this photo log, skimming through the other seasons of those first two years for other family-life high spots. All right, here—

right up front, Polaroids of the party Mir and I gave that first autumn, on the heels of the numero-uno coolsnap of the fall, for all the friends to meet Mir and Syd. Before our guests arrived, while Miriam showered, I had dressed all in white, in white flannels and a cambric peasant shirt, and had thereafter trucked off into the kitchen to put the sangria parts all together. Some time later Miriam bopped into the scullery to help me; she was wearing a white cotton v-neck and white ducks. When we saw one another we both froze a second, giving each other the once over, then we both started giggling, and Mir began humming Mendelssohn's wedding march and came in close to me and waltzed me around a bit, laughing and tch-ing. She said, "Oh lovely, this cannot be—I shall change."

And I said, "No I'll change," but then we both got busy doing other things in different parts of the house, tapping the keg out in the back yard, prodding Sydney along in her always laborious toilette, party-proofing with ashtrays out in the living room.

Eventually I got through squashing up the guacamole and headed back to our bedroom to change, slipping into an old black buttondown shirt and black twill jeans. Popping back into the kitchen then, I spotted Miriam standing at the counter, slicing up Jarlsberg: she had gone and put on a black satin western shirt and black cords. We both cracked up all over again. Then she said, "You wait right here!" and while she went off and changed a second time, I busied myself with the task of easing the block of ice down into the punchbowl. In a few minutes Mir returned, this time in a purple silk blouse and purple-and-white-striped seersucker slacks.

"*Now* are we dressed," she said, grinning, and just as these words were springing from her lips, Syd bounced into the kitchen in her purple cotton velour shirt and her new black denims. Miriam looked at me solemnly and said, "Blimey. It's genetic."

After everyone had danced their butts off and all the beer was gone and the cops had shown up at the front door to get us to turn the Stones down, Mir and I, with glasses of milk in hand, trundled off to bed. She began telling me how Gabe had taken her aside at one point during the evening ("I noticed," I said; "I noticed you noticed," Mir replied) and had, subtly nodding at this or that woman passing by, described who was going with whom at present, and, moreover, who *had* gone with whom, in times gone by. "I was aghast," Miriam laughed. "The incest in this town is absolutely amazing—how the devil do you all manage to be so civilized about it?"

And not on the next Sunday but on an October morning much like it, following a hot date out on the town with Metzger to celebrate her—thirty-eighth? thirty-eighth birthday, carousing 'til the proverbial wee hours at the Crown (though her birthday-in-fact wasn't until that Tuesday), Mir and I were way under the covers, beginning to gain a fairly fuzzy Sunday morning consciousness.

"Miriam," I mumbled into my pillow.

Silence.

"Mir."

"Nunnnhf."

"What ho, Queen of the Night." A groan. "Miriam. Love. What do you want for your birthday."

She rolls over in the bed, humming a short hmm. Yawns, wide. Blinks her eyes open at me. Smiles a little bit, sleepy, sleepy. "Uh...umm, uh. I think I would like to have...twelve naked women...sing me, 'Younger Than Springtime.' "

"Would you settle for one naked woman?"

"Do you know the lyrics?"

Or, on yet another Sunday forenoon in bed as we drank stout coffee and read the newspaper, I happened to ask her about the dime-sized emerald ink-spot which, Before Me, had evidently stained forever the epicenter of the wonderfully worn-soft cantaloupe-color cotton sheets whereon we lay. Snapping the newspaper aside at a rough quarterfold and peering over her glasses at the splotch, Mir frowned, then explained, brightly, that that little green stain was "Bloody Proof, capital *B*, capital *P*," that a former and formerly indiscreet student of hers (she really said *treach*erous, the first syllable cracking mock bitter, her light spittle lightly rolled yet contained between tip of tongue and palate), who had but one night only lain voluptuously coiled and damp upon these very sheets, was irrefutably the half-human, egg-born girlchild of a gargantuan gila monster, legend in those there parts back out Corrales way. "Her charm," Miriam continued drily, "had, let's say, a certain exhaustibility." Laying the paper down altogether she went on: "Ali—her name was Ali, she'd actually changed it to that—always carried a complete change of clothes and a toothbrush about in her backpack."

"Provident," I reflected.

"In a matter of days or weeks, however, I discovered that she was in sum possessed of something less than the vacuity of a newt. Oh God, so young, so young. But then with old bags like me, they're all young."

"Young bags," I murmured, sucking her earlobe, "and all their young baggage."

"They—I mean, we're not talking legions, you understand—"

"Oh! Understood, o-my-love."

She poked me in the stomach. "Ga-arn," she growled.

"Anyway, the younger ones—but not you Bobbette, oddly enough (and I poked her back)—they always seemed to come to me expecting answers, that because I was older, they figured I must've found some way of staying happy. Well, I've found better ways, yes, but none of 'em works all the time."

I was lying on the bed (Miriam calls our kingsize empire Love Field) with the side of my head flat against the mattress; I could hear her voice echoing in the box springs. But then I realized that my face might approach laceration in another instant, due to a number of vicious cracked-rye toast crumbs in the bed, artifacts of our breakfast. So I arose. Mir was in the act of flumping up her pillows. "Let's smoke a joint," she said. "I shall roll."

This done, we sat cross-legged on the bed and got high and later Mir said, gazing fondly at the ceiling, "Ah, mari-juana—drug of the old."

"Really feeling it today, aren't you, old darling." She tch-ed, rolled her eyes, ran her fingers through her hair. "Well cheer up," I ventured, "if you keep smoking pot long enough, it'll fuck your memory up so bad you won't be able to remember whether you're old or not." Miriam then took this opportunity to bash me over the head with one of her pillows. But with a lightning-fast celerity, the playfulness in her dissolved, her face sobered, hard. All of a sudden she just went away from me. I reached out to her hand and stroked it; she looked up to me, her eyes heavy for an instant longer, then lightened up, softening again. "I repeat," I said gently, "really feeling it, aren't you."

At this her expression dropped its solemnity, and she said, fairly purring from the back of her throat, "And a few other things besides. I'm not dead yet, thank you very much," and reached over to stroke my thigh. And. Well anyway. Then a not out-of-the-ordinary activity for a Sunday a-bed ensued. . . .

Back to the album: Syd's and my Hour of Happiness Haberdasheries. But perhaps I should discuss another development first. You see, within a very short time after Miriam had moved herself lock, stock, and barrel to Texas, I, at her request, had shuffled out some of my old canvases from the closet: the faceless portraits I'd begun in college, some somewhat more recent still lifes, some landscape sketches, and a really very good portrait of Cory (which Syd thereafter begged to be allowed to hang in her room).

Miriam said, with discernible emotion, "But my darling, you are an artist; you must take this up again!"

And perhaps a year, a year and a half after that afternoon, we both agreed—I, with no small amount of trepidation—that I should, for the time being anyway, quit my job and devote myself to painting. Oh, we talked about all manner of things when this first came up, the potential pitfalls of this plan of action: we were both worried that I would eventually feel housewifey or something—get stuck with the cleaning up, tending to Syd's and Mir's everyday needs; and we worried that Miriam's being the primary source of income for a while (though I did have some savings, and I cashed in on my pension fund from the Great State of Texas) would do injury to our homelife balance. But we agreed that, if resentment or petulance should arise and prevail as a result of the new arrangement, then I could bloody well go and get a new job. An experiment, it was. A new direction. Everybody needs one now and then.

So I quit my job. And I made the spare bedroom over into a studio, and I sat at my easel for an average of five hours a day. And I got very good.

I had a show. I even sold a few. My full-time artist's life lasted a little over a year, and then I decided to let it go again for a while—I felt painted out, actually—and went back to making regular bucks at programming. But all that's jumping far too far ahead. Back to the Hour of Happiness Haberdasheries, which took place throughout my stint as artist in residence.

Syd would get home from school at three-thirty or so; Mir, on a normal day, at about five-thirty. Syd and I had been larking about in her room with pots of day-glo paints, à la Haight-Ashbury '68. We began with orange and lime-green stripes on our faces, and we just got carried away, painting all over ourselves, until finally we decided we could take off our clothes so we could paint everywhere, like the "Laugh-In" go-go dancers (of course Syd didn't know what a "Laugh-In" go-go dancer was, so I told her). And when Miriam came through the front door, we leapt out from behind the couch, two all-nude, supervivid fluorescences.

It got to be a sort of continuing art event. We all loved it. Syd and I loved the art, loved surprising Miriam, and Mir loved the art and loved the being surprised. I guess we've gotten out of doing it of late, Sydney's gotten *sooo ma-tchoor,* you know; but probably we did the haberdasheries at least a dozen or so times. Unfortunately we screwed up in the beginning and neglected to photograph the early ones, but eventually we got systematic. Here, for instance, is one of Syd and me covered in tube balloons, all over our arms and legs and trunks—devilishly tricky trying to get them all tied on tight and hanging down just as we wanted them. And here's another one, with strips of multicolor construction paper glued all over us—well, all over some old thereafter disposed-of shirts and jeans. Ah, this one may well have been *la pièce de résistance:* Syd 'n me dressed up in low-tone drag. We had to go some to pull this one off. I had a tailor make us both some skin-tight satin skirts, split all the way up to our waists almost, Syd's blue, mine red. Platinum glamor wigs, for glamor. Black fishnet tanktops and black bras...you know, they don't make black bras for persons of negative breast, as Syd was then (she's getting them now, she's so relieved), so we had to buy a trainer job and dye it—in other words, hooker outfits. Syd had a couple of lines of French she'd rehearsed, one of which I believe was, "Surprise! (*Soor-preeze!*) Évidence de la vie!" Miriam almost wet her pants at this one, she was doubled up on the couch, she was crying, she was laughing so hard.

But onward through the album (flip/flip/flip). What's this? Our freezer? Oh yeah. One night during hurricane season it had begun hailing quite late; Syd had stood out on the back porch and watched it pelt down. With decreasing nonchalance Miriam kept calling out to her from our bedroom, Come to bed, Sydney, and finally Syd had trotted off into her room, softly closing her door behind her after bidding us goodnight. But in the morning I opened the freezer door and found a pile of malted milkball-size hailstones neatly stacked into a six-inch-high pyramid, and when I saw it, saw that oh-so carefully constructed little mound, carefully crafted by those deft baby bird-of-prey hands, the tears welled up, my heart wrenched. My love of Sydney Metzger at that moment swelled in me as it never had before: such a bright little girl, so dark and bright and full of life and devilment. My little devilfish.

And this, not a photograph but a postcard of Renoir's "The Boating Party," on loan from the Phillips as part of a travelling exhibit of impressionist paintings that opened at the University's art gallery the spring of '81. Gazing at the painting on the wall, I suddenly realized that Metzger had on a primary-color striped boatneck pullover, just like one a man in the painting was wearing. And the light in the gallery that afternoon was so beautifully muted—soft, dark, Hogarth-like; and Miriam looked so damned handsome, standing there rocking back and forth on her heels, her glasses perched at the tip of her nose as she scrutinized the painting. After a while she said, "You know, ol' Renoir was supposed to have painted some of his canvases, portions of some of 'em anyway, with his cock." She was smiling slightly as she said this, still examining the painting. Then, moving in close behind me, she whispered low over my shoulder into my ear, "And what does this particular canvas do for you, o-my-love."

Folding my arms and carefully brushing back up against her I said, under my breath, "Well, Renoir's methods notwithstanding, it does whet my appetite for—dancing."

She was still behind me, still hovering over my shoulder. "Wanna go home and dance," she said then.

I do not wish to portray my life with Miriam as an incessant stream of domestic bliss—an expression that seems inherently contradictory anyway. Hell yes, there were squabbles! We squabble still. Who among us, I should like to know, does not. So here for the record is one such unhappy moment.

Over a feast of Miriam's *sushi* one midsummer evening (we'd packed Syd off to a slumber party), the *sake* had begun to catch up with me and the pontification to roll on out. The subject was, I believe, evolution. "Although the female primate's instinct to have *some*thing up her vagina is still evolutionally vigorous," Crawford the Dryasdust was droning, "there are so damn many things other than peepees—" (at which Miriam harrumped) "—women can use, all sorts of things, nowadays. Take the cucumber, for an old instance, an excellent vegetable, only organic of course." No response from the now, I observed dully, trancelike Metzger, who was staring at me as though watching a television commercial; with the green tea she'd grown deadly quiet, her knuckles loosely burrowed under her cheekbones. I paused, bleary, and cleared my throat. "Ideas can fuck you too," I hazarded.

Miriam visibly bristled back to attention. "Yeah, right up the ol' slew—aw stuff it, B., I doan feel like it tonight." Stunned and blushing I turned my head quickly away, but her silky hand darted out across the table to my forearm to featherstroke, appease; although when I faced about to her, her head was averted sideways and she was staring off blankly into the hallway. "I didn't mean that," she whispered. "I meant, I know ideas fuck you, everything fucks you, can fuck you, I mean." I was foggy but not that foggy: she wasn't there, she'd sent an emissary to apologize, she wasn't even there. In her periphery she had to have sensed my gaze upon her. Hello? Anyone home? No? No. Broken connection. And just then, Brook Benton came on the radio; the song was "Hotel Happiness."

This being, as I must say yet again, reader *mia,* a story of romance, let us not dwell overlong on Metzgerian moodiness, nor for that matter on Crawfordic crabbiness, except perhaps for the highly creative aspect of Miriam's and my quarreling and our Making Up Afterwards. For Miriam Metzger is a gifted infighter, a flak-artist supreme, Discordia's own daughter, in a corner. After but a few months of living with her I discovered that she apparently utilizes arguing in much the same way as I do crying, that is, to rid herself of a plethora of tensions and knots and what-have-yous. I usually know we've begun to approach the downswing of a tiff when she starts hurling insults at me. One of the first times she did this she hissed, "You soulless little guttersnipe!" at me, which, for a second, sent me reeling, and then I noticed, I sensed, that she was waiting, waiting for a retort. Adrenalin pounding, I glowered at her, almost getting the drift of what was up. After a second or two I managed to say, "You're an unconscionable crud, you know that?" at which I could see she was perceptibly pleased. Her eyes brightened, a glint of a smile played at a corner of her mouth, she relaxed, a little.

"Better that than a poltroon, and a thwackhead," she replied, etc., etc., and leading up to, sometimes, laughing with one another, and many times, the Making Up Afterwards, to wit, lovemaking. Mir has so many epithets at her command that, I must confess, I every once in a while make up advance lists of barbed words and phrases with which to parry. One of my best, I think, was, "You are a fishhead and a mamba snake and I consign you to a lifetime of constipation and hemorrhoids." Drove her crazy; she loved it. Sometimes, though, I can really dredge them up, think on my feet: once she called me a fricatrice, and without all that much of a pause, I called her a cockatrice. Another time she yelled "Stinkhorn!" at me, and I came back quite handily, I think, with "Ragwort!"

Some of our spats, alas, have tended to ride overly roughshod; on occasion, "blood" has been drawn. But such is Married Life. Miriam once called me a deplorable smarminess, and it stung me so badly that I retaliated with "you humorless bourgeois shithead," which immediately brought tears to her eyes. And even worse than that was when I called her an abjection, and she, evidently not feeling the incipient Making Up Afterwards, called me a boring little drudge.

Oh God, and that was the killer, that was—to be boring to her. I just burst into tears; I couldn't deal with it, not one iota. And she came over to me and put her arms around me and said, "Aw dammitohell, of course you don't bore me, darling, you're dicey as all get out, Bobbie—I didn't mean that at all, forgive me, please." And *then* we had the Making Up Afterwards.

Just one more vignette, *chère liseuse,* and perhaps just one more after that as well, so, two more then, two more glimpses of domesticity before we move on from this zigzagging trail through our first two years together, to a new chapter. The first, for which fortunately I have no photograph, is of myself, sitting at my easel or taking a shower or listening to Gladys Knight, and the thought returning to mind that I have on order and am awaiting receipt of a dildo that I have ordered from San Francisco, the Kora Collection, about to be delivered to me, any day now, by the United Parcel Service. I sit at the edge of our bed and rub my toes, and I think about the dildo, and I realize that I am waiting on its arrival as one would a lover. . . .

The evening of the day the dildo finally arrived, it so happened that Miriam came home, her hands at her lower back, and groaned, "Cripes, am I ever stumped up!"—which is her way of saying that she's begun her period.

And this, this last bit of sketching that, again, was never photographed, but no matter: of Mir and Syd and me out shopping and errand-running on a humid, warm, fetid Saturday in February ("murderous weather," Miriam calls it), of the three of us singing old Supremes songs in the Volks (Miriam's voice, in song, loses its accent, she sounds like a real yank) in an effort to cheer ourselves up, though Sydney, now almost eleven, later falls silent and sullen in the back seat because Miriam has informed her that she will not buy her something or other. There are little packages, paper bags, coffee, cheeses, on the back seat with her (nibbling at a bit of Stilton, Syd makes a noise of disgust—*Peh!* I think it was—and then in a monotone, after she has gingerly spit the piece of cheese out into a torn-off bit of cellophane, *Yuck, pitooey*), the workers spending the week's wages (well Miriam's—I hadn't started back to work yet then).

In another attempt to brighten things up I suggest we stop for Chinese food for lunch. While waiting for our repast, we all of us cannot help but overhear the two couples at the next table talking. One of the men is saying, "You know, I'm not jealous of Shirley, not at all."

And the woman, presumably Shirley herself, adding, "And I'm not jealous of Bob," and then the other two, the other couple, chiming in to say that they weren't jealous of each other either, and the word *jealous* seeming to reverberate from all four of them almost simultaneously, seeming to float above them at their table like a small man-made cloud.

Syd leans in close to Mir and me and whispers, "Jesus. What's with them."

Richard _____

A little less than a month after that jangly shopping spree, I was tramping down our hallway with two sacks of groceries in my arms, and as I passed by the old phone cranny I could hear Miriam's voice coming from the kitchen.

"—cooo yes and I've got Sutherland's *Lucia,* we could listen to the mad scene, or the sextet first, then the mad scene," at which point the blender suddenly began to whiz. When I rounded the corner there was someone—I know I thought for just an instant, I remember this distinctly: that's a very tall woman, there—with (their) back to me, but the back turned as Miriam turned, smiling, toward me, and I saw a beautiful, beautiful young Black man. When our eyes met (what eyes, a sweet, yes! shy and sweet conflux of Nubia and Asia somewhere out far above the Arabian Sea—a son of the Arabian Nights, of Sudan or Ethiopia—almond-shaped, something feline there, and, I'd been right, most certainly female too, his long lashes so dark and thick that for a split second I suspected mascara), I was so taken aback, *so awe-struck,* that I felt myself blushing. I looked down, smiling, looked up again quick as Miriam said, " 'lo luv! Gimme one o' those," taking one of the bags from my arms "Bobbie, this's Richard, I work with Richard, or just down the hall from him—Richard Royce; Richard, the infamous Ms. Crawford, a/k/a Bobbie." I set the sack down on the counter and extended my hand to him, but there was something about him— something so young-godlike, the full-force beauty, the eyes, the skin the color of topaz and as lucid and hard as gemstone, the soft ringlets of hair coiling over his brow and down upon his neck, a single silver earring, a half-quarter sliver of Egyptian moon—that my hand slowed down, seemed to slow down to slow motion as it met his. I found myself letting him take my hand and just taking his and our fingers pressing together, our two thumbs setting upon rather than squeezing the fingers, and he said, in a voice so high and soft and gentle, I instantly thought, *Hoo, nelly-ola:* "Nice ta meetcha, Bobbie."

"Nice ta meetcha, Richard."

Richard had just begun to work at the company, and Mir said she'd only taken notice of him that morning in the data processing shop because he'd been humming˙the "Libiamo" from *Traviata* as she'd passed him by (ah yes, to joy, drink, love, pleasure) and promptly struck up a conversation with him about opera. Richard was going to join Stan Barnes' company next season ("a lovely tenor, Bobbie, wait'll you hear it," Mir'd said), Richard would take intensive Italian in the summer, and so on and so forth. And we spent a whole evening, that evening, sipping Miriam's Ramos gin fizzes and talking, and listening to opera records and finally sending out for pizza when Sydney deigned to grace us with her presence after reputedly studying with little Sara down the street. And I noticed that Syd did the same take on Richard that I had; I could actually see her blushing a little—and Sydney never blushes. Watching Syd react to Richard, and she really and truly seemed to be weaving her little wiles for him, I realized that both Miriam and I had been behaving in much the same way: more subdued, certainly, infinitely more subtle of course, but it was as though we were both trying to outcharm each other. Richard had our attention absolute, one hundred percent. At one point early in the evening I had taken Miriam aside in the kitchen and whispered, "This guy's gay, right? No question, right?"

And Miriam replied, "Yunno, I doan know yet fer sure. I really only met him just today. But he's gotta be, right?" And so neither of us knew, that night. And Miriam seemed to be undertaking a very delicate, gradual series of disclosures about us with Richard (from which I took my cue), little bits and pieces here and there, nothing monumental, but definitely nothing out-and-out overt, either.

For a short time, a couple of visits, it went on like that, with Richard coming over and our not really *tell*ing him about us, and Miriam saying, "Well, he'll come out to us when he wants to." But one evening Mir got Richard off to a bar by herself. And she just asked him, pointblank: "Richard, do you like boys?"

Richard said, smiling, "Do you mean, do I sleep with boys?"

"Yeah, do you sleep with boys."

He just kept smiling at her, "a wholly unreadable grin," Miriam called it, and then he said, nodding, smiling, shaking his head slowly, "No Miriam, I don't sleep with boys."

"Do you plan to?" Metzger asked, (without skipping a beat, I'm sure).

He laughed again, a soft gosh-shucks kind of chuckle (Mir said) that didn't give away a thing. "I don't know," he replied softly, and just as he said this (she said), he reached over across the table and, as gently as one can, squeezed her hand.

"So he's straight?" I asked, straight to the point, so to speak.

"You know, the next question I wanted to ask him was, 'Are you a virgin then,' because it seemed so fantastic, that he would have ever slept with a woman."

"So did you?"

"Naw—you can't ask someone if they're a virgin, even if they are. It's rude."

"So did you ask him if he liked *girls*, ferchrissakes?" I was losing patience. Miriam grinned this cat-cum-canary grin.

"Well dammit!" Indeed, I had now lost patience.

"He said he's liked a few girls, yeah."

I was exasperated. "So you didn't pin him down? How can that be? What is he anyway!"

"He's the most beautiful boy in the Western Hemisphere, and the dearest, and he sings like a goddam nightingale. And I got the very distinct impression he didn't think my knowing who he slept with was any of my goddam business."

That was round one.

Round two came a week later, when Miriam decided the time had definitely come to make our story, our love, crystal clear to young Richard.

"As if," I said, "there could be any doubt in his mind."

She said, "I want to tell him myself, alone."

"No problem," I said.

He had listened very attentively, very respectfully, while Miriam explained that she and I were lovers. He had repeated, very slow, smiling shyly, "Bobbie's your lover?"

"In the biblical sense and all that, yeah, you bet," Mir replied.

And he had laughed a little at that, and he smiled at her, very nicely, and he took both her hands in his, and he squeezed them, and he kissed her on the cheek. "I kinda thought maybe that might be," was all he said.

And that was round two.

Round three lasted for a couple of months, on into early summer, with Richard coming over once or twice a week, and Miriam playing him her opera records and talking opera and *libretti,* all her pants roles she'd learned so well, *Der Rosenkavalier* and *La Clemenza di Tito* and *Julius Caesar,* and he was so keen to learn everything and so gentle and manneredly, so princely, Richard was, with all three of us. . . .

Round four. Ah, round four. Where I tell on Mir. I cannot help but do it, she knows that, she's said, she's said, *I know that.*

All right then, round four. Wherein circumstances were such that I, returning prematurely from a seminar in Houston, came into the house from the back screen door, stopped and got a glass of water from the tap, looked at the bills on the sideboard, took a whiz, not flushing, and scuffed down the hallway to our bedroom, from whence music, solo cello, Bach, was wafting. I opened the door.

And there was Richard, and there was Miriam: Mir sitting under the sheet (with some sort of costume on?), at that instant a look of shock and sorrow splaying across her face; and Richard, most definitely costumed, in a white eighteenth-century billow-sleeved blouse and a white satin waistcoat and breeches, white stockings, now backing abruptly away from the bed—quickly, quickly wiping the back of his hand across his lower face.

I stand there a few seconds, I think, looking slowly back and forth, at both of them. And I see anguish settling in heavily over them, in their eyes and at their mouths, and my heart is beating deep and violent as a kettledrum.

Miriam is muttering, "Oh Jesus God," and she has propped her forehead up with the heels of her palms, her elbows resting on her knees, still halfway under the sheets. She shakes her head slowly from side to side: "Ah God damn," she says.

Richard squats to the floor, his back sliding down along and resting flat against our closet door, a huge breath going out of him. He no longer looks at me, but stares out across the room and out the window.

After a while, how long I know not, I can hear myself saying, and my voice sounds as though it's coming from a 16-millimeter camera amp in the next room, "Uh...uh. I...excuse me. I don't know what to say."

I close the door behind me, and I start walking down the hallway again, back to the kitchen, back out the screen door, and off across the back yard.

I go out and stand with my tomato plants, back out behind the garage. None of them died, this year. Over four feet already, looky there.

And here, o friend, my inestimable friend, I must give us pause. (A moment's silence, please.)

Thank you. I thank you.

Not: Erosdynamics _____

I had at one time intended to call this particular chapter Erosdynamics and offer you, beloved reader, a working, or mostly working, equation of some sort or another for love. A little something, I'd thought, derived perhaps from Newton's Third Law of Motion (to every action force there is an equal and opposite reaction force), or, say, the Second Law of Thermodynamics, as it might apply to human beings (where, in energy outflow, there is a resultant loss of some of the energy, and the loss is quantified as heat, and—well, that all systems tend toward disorder, and entropy), but I eventually realized I didn't know nearly enough about that stuff to put forth anything real solid for you about love.

And besides I began to think more and more about how things, the things of the physical world, have been since Einstein, the nonmechanical, un-Newtonian universe and all that. Stuff like time flowing backward and negative mass and eerienesses such as quarks and quasars, and just in general how unpredictable things have gotten. And I ended up feeling like that's how love is, love's that way too: a wild card, a rogue elephant, a masterstroke (I had smoked some pot prior to this reverie, a not unhelpful agent in any contemplation of twentieth-century physics)—and at any rate, nothing I or any other yahoo stoned or unstoned could ever put into a bleeding equation, ferchrissakes.

So this chapter is not called Erosdynamics.

But I can, I can, just tell you what happened to us, to Miriam and me, after Richard; I can try and give you an idea of that, at least.

What Happened Next

For forbearance' sake I shall sidestep the brunt of harangue and double talk that followed my discovery of Richard and Miriam in our bedroom, though of course some stepping into it is simply inescapable. The fact was, I learned, that that incident had apparently been the first, and as it subsequently turned out, only, interlude between them. A lucky thing, in a way, that I bumbled into the boudoir just then: the bludgeoning drama of their being found out, *in flagrante delicto* right off the bat, seemed to head off at the pass whatever romance might have ensued between them. Lucky, lucky.

But I will say that Miriam said to me, "I just wanted him," and "I know I've hurt you when there was nothing for you to get hurt about, and that's not it. *I still want you.* If things haven't been hot for us lately (and in fact, they had not), "it's not because I don't still want you. I want you right now actually, but I know that's wretched of me. I'm sorry, I'm sorry. . . ."

And she said she was ashamed, she said something about *"nostalgie de la boue"* (to which I shouted, "Oh what the fuck does that mean!" and she replied, "Homesick for the gutter"), and she said something like I'd been so marvelous all along that she had to do something awful so I could keep being marvelous, and I called that "Bullshit," which it was. She was scrambling, scrambling; I was wounded, and I was dangerous.

But, well, it just never entirely slipped my mind that Richard—well, Richard just never felt like a genuine threat to me. Had I come upon Miriam in the embrace of a young woman, or in some other unmisconstruable scenario, with a woman, I should not have felt the same.

And Miriam said, "You might've left me if I'd betrayed you with a woman just now, and I didn't want you to leave me, but I had to betray you, just now. . . ."

And I, eloquent as ever, replied, "Bullshit," again. But as what she'd said began to sink in, I suddenly foresaw, no, felt, down to my oldest soul, the devastations of Miriam's lovers-to-be (would they be myriad?) parading through my life with her: what would I do, how would I react, what miserable god-awful light would burn up and off in me, every time I found out?

When the smoke began to clear, and it did, gradually, slowly, over long hot days and nights of silence and bitterness and weeping and soothing, the bottom line, for the time being, was that I really could get over Miriam's first groupie—especially since, if the truth be known (and it be), she and I were really Richard's groupies. In fact, some chunk of my resentment seemed to fall to just one side of feeling slighted. . . .

And, a heady draught of the clearing smoke: in the aftermath Richard told Miriam that he didn't feel as though they could have an affair (way to go, Richard), principally because of me, and secondarily because of their working together, and, Miriam later surmised, fundamentally because sex with her had been something Richard had been curious about, and having satisfied that portion of his curiosity, he declined to invest his energies further.

So Richard stopped coming over to the house.

Adieu, adieu, young prince of Khartoum, I said to myself, you and your young god's eyes, you and your lips of the almond Buddha. . . but I missed him, and I missed our innocence, Miriam's and mine and Richard's.

(As a footnote, I feel obliged to mention that a mere five weeks following The Incident, Richard told Miriam at work that he'd begun seeing a young baritone in Barnes' opera company. Irony, I say, is infinite. Yes it is. And as a second footnote, I should also mention that Richard did eventually re-befriend us, and we him, about oh, six months later. We still see him and Robert every now and then. And of course we go to the opera.)

And What Happened After That

But Miriam was pretty damned schitzy for the remainder of that summer, after Richard. We all were, Syd included. One evening Mir came home and Syd, mostly as usual, was encamped before the television watching godknowswhat. I was out in the kitchen making a salad, and I could hear their voices rising. Syd was saying, "But I was watching that, mom."

And Miriam, her voice rising even more, saying: "It will make you blind, Sydney—blind, and piss-ignorant! Millions of your poor little peers are growing up before TV screens, learning only from screens, absorbing things from screens, their entire lives, nothing but *screens!* blind babies, brainless babies, manic-depressives at CRTs, air-traffickers, Apple twos and threes, talking checkouts, drive-in banking, word processors, CB radio, radio! short-wave, radar, bombscreens—" as I came into the living room Syd looked up at me helplessly, a look of, is she cracking up or what? "—fluorescent lights, and, and—video games! VIDEO GAMES! Posterity growing up from this, trying to live, blinding themselves, killing themselves—"

I reached over to her arm and touched it lightly. She pulled it away from my touch with the force of ten, and turned sharply on me; for an instant I thought she was going to strike me.

"Miriam," I said quietly, "what is it. Just stop now, please, please just calm down."

"Ah goddammitohell," she said, and stormed off to the bedroom and slammed the door.

And then, there was this, this grim-enough precursor, itself.

Sydney had, in order to make a financial killing—an entire ten dollars, megabucks—undertaken the task of mowing the lawn.

She was out back, and had evidently just pushed the mower under a clump of four o'clocks, when from inside the house Miriam and I heard her screams—and the two of us swift as arrows ran out the back door. There was Syd, scurrying crazily around the yard, screaming still, waving her arms over her head at a cloud of wasps. Mir, ahead of me, grabbed her up under one arm and began waving at the cloud herself and running back into the house with Sydney, and as I opened the back screen door three or four of the wasps, still on target, got inside, into the kitchen, and all three of us ran into the bathroom and slammed the door in there.

Syd was crying, her shoulders heaving up and down, and then she screamed again, and we realized there were a couple of wasps stuck in her hair, stinging her scalp. We got them.

Then I darted out to the kitchen and grabbed up the Raid and an old *Texas Monthly* and made short work of the four venomous invaders. I yelled, "It's O.K., I got 'em." And Mir and Syd came out of the bathroom, Mir babbling, breathing hard still, "She'll have to go to hospital, Bobs."

"Right," I said, "I'll get the keys, you can sit with her in the back." So we took her to the minor emergency clinic, and discovered that she'd gotten stung some fifteen or so times, and they gave her a shot of Benadryl and a prescription for some Benadryl pills. Within a very short time we were back out in the car again, on the way home, and Syd began to fall asleep.

The next day, a Sunday, was spent tending Syd and trying to get her to not scratch and feeding her stuff like chilled cucumber soup, and chocolate custard—sweet, smooth, and cold.

September 9, 1982 _____

—was the Thursday before Labor Day weekend, for which we'd decided we'd, what the heck, brave the crowds and tool on down to Padre Island, stay over at a friend's condo in Port Aransas. We would leave just after five o'clock, Friday.

Everybody made such a big goddam to-do about it, afterward: I was in the papers, and everything. But then, freakish things do have this tendency to make the news. And God knows it was a bona fide freak and a fluke and a miracle and all that, but I'm about as sure as I can possibly be that most anybody else in my shoes could've done precisely the same thing, if they'd had to. The fact is, you just never know what you're really capable of until the right moment.

And I guess I'd never realized just how much I really do love Sydney.

Mir had been home for a couple of hours already, that evening; we'd sat out on the front porch for some time, sipping iced tea and talking over the day. She was tired, I was tired, but we were both looking forward to the beach. And Syd—Sydney was ecstatic; she'd never been down there before. By that afternoon, that Thursday, even, Her Grace was all packed and rarin' to go. After a while Miriam sauntered off to take a shower, and I went out back to pull some weeds, pick a few tomatoes (though most of them had burned off already), and give the soil a little water. I was standing out back there in the garden, when from the front of the house I heard it: a thick clang of metal, a great thud, a sickening scream—Sydney's. I flung the hose, ran, darted through the chain-link fence gate, down the driveway. And there, there was Syd, lying with her back flat to the ground, underneath the Volks. . .and the Volks was—aw godchee it's on top of her! A tire, a jack, she's pinned under there! Look at her face, white, dead-white, her eyes squinting glassy, black, at me, her lips working, what? But within seconds I can hear her, she's groaning this *whoah* of agony—both her legs, those spindly little legs, under the weight of the car. . .Sydney—aw Syd! And I'm bending down close to her face; Syd, she's shaking. Miriam: I bound back into the house, slamming the screen door open, jump in three giant steps across the living room, down the hall, into the bathroom, Mir showering, pull back the curtain. . . .

Miriam told me later that I shrieked, "C'mon hurry, Syd's pinned under the car." But I don't remember what I said.

I bolt back out to the driveway. Syd's burbling, her voice tiny, so tiny it sounds like she's dying, *Bobbie, Bobbie I'm cold,* and I squat down and with my hands reach under the car, and I try to lift, and I heave, and nothing...except my biceps bursting, my lower back pulling hard, as hard as it can. And then Syd moans again and I think I say, *hold on, hold on baby*—oh God how do we get this off her? And then I swivel around, my back against the car, and squat again, and lift behind me and strain, my feet planted hard, straining, and my shoulders feel as though they will break through the skin at front, and I am gritting my teeth and sweating and heaving, and Miriam in her bathrobe is just bounding out the front door and I can feel the car begin to move—lift! behind me, I have it, I have it! and Mir's right there, the horror full on her face, and I gasp, *move her,* as I hold the car up, and she reaches down and pulls Syd out from under the car—

September 10, 1982 _____

Through a haze of Darvon I sit and watch as the clouds roll on by, beyond the window.

I am in a semiprivate room at St. Ann's Hospital; the other bed is unoccupied.

By lifting up the Volkswagen to unpinion Sydney, I have succeeded in dislocating both of my shoulders. Both of them are wrapped, taped, my arms in close to me, in velcro slings (one velcro, two velcri?). I am lying perforce flat on my back, because my lower back muscles are blown out the kazoo.

See, what they never tell you about people who do these fantastic one-shot feats of strength, is: when the adrenalin and the endorphins wear off, all the real damage you've done to yourself is plainly evident, and plainly, plainly painful. Fakirs and yogis put their heads in some other place to be able to lie on beds of nails or walk on beds of coals without puncturing or burning themselves, but with Sydney's life and legs on the line, it simply never occurred to me to put myself in a trance, first.

See, there's just no way for a one-hundred-thirty-five pound woman to lift a 1900-pound car without some material muscular damage. Besides the sockets getting unsocked, the rotary cuff muscles around them got all torn up too. And the latissimus muscles in back, and my deltoids. Guess I won't be working any weights any time real soon.

Excuse me, reader *mia,* someone's tapping at the door. The door's opening, a throat is clearing, "A-hem"; it's Miriam. She's saying: "You conscious in there?"

"Stupefied and blasé, but conscious, yes. Enter, friend."

And in she comes, smiling sheepish and wry, or rather, affecting sheepitude and wryness, and I notice that she's moving rather stiffly, rigid, and, yes, she's sitting down on the side of my bed and she's keeping her spine perfectly vertical, perfectly right-angled to her shoulders; she winces as she sits and then smiles again. For some reason I think of Cary Grant and the fact that in forty years of film, his spine has never seemed to bend—a sign of the aristocrat perhaps, or has he just always had a bad back?

"What's wrong with you," I say.

"Woke up this morning with me neck all fucked up—incipient wryneck or something."

"Sympathy pains?"

"I s'ppose I felt left out, yeah."

"Welcome to the club."

She's smiling, looking at me and smiling, and then the tears just well up in her eyes. "Oh God," she breathes low.

"Oh now, Judy/Judy/Judy," I say, like Grant. Because of course I can't move my spine either. "Give me your hand." And she reaches out and takes my hand in hers. And I say, tapping a finger on her hand, "If you stick around here long enough, beloved, you just might get a loada the day nurse they've got on this morning—Jessica Lange's baby sister. I swear. And nice? Jesus! I'm gonna ask her over for cocktails."

Miriam harrumphs, perks up a bit, smiles again. With her free hand she reaches for a Kleenex and blows her nose. "Slut," she sniffs.

Not the Last Letter

Cara Alma,

Como estás chica, y Gloria. Well, over here we're all over the immediate-vicinity trauma and all: I'm out of the slings, though the brace lingers on for a few more weeks, at night (makes sleeping an adventure, which of course is just what I've always wanted, adventuresome sleep). Sydney, however, is not as well off. One of the breaks was what they call a greenstick fracture, and it will have to heal entirely, and then be broken again and reset. So she's gonna be hobbling around for quite a while, I'm afraid. She's taking it pretty well though: being a star and all helps—all that crap in the papers, plus the status of having *two* casts on. Her friends have been flocking over in the afternoons after school to visit and leave their graffiti behind, on her.

One of her new friends this year is a little boy named Raymond. He's been over three times this week already. Syd is highly irritated by my teasing her about him, says they're "just friends." They do sit and chat together very nicely and all, but there really does seem to be some perceptible electricity of sorts between them, and I suspect she's more like her mum than I'd imagined.

Last week I was razzing her about not doing the homework her tutor left with her, told her I didn't think she was self-actualizing, and she hit me right in the stomach, knocked the wind right outta me. Fortunately, I was sitting down on her bed at the time. Had I been standing, I might've had to bend, suddenly, and I could've blown the back out. Syd was instantly contrite: I didn't mean for it to be that hard, she *said.* I figure she's probably more than a little testy these days, so I was more or less promptly forgiving.

Wednesday night Eileen and Clabber came over and we did boiled shrimp. Jan Springer showed up later on, dead drunk (do you remember her, Mita? the one with the Mustang and the grandmother?). We got her to drink some coffee and later discovered that her dog had been run over that afternoon. She ended up sleeping over.

Heef—something died inside one of our hallway walls. We are talking terminal smell here. Took it four days to stop stinking, whatever it was.

Hold up. I'm gonna put on some music—Schubert's C-Major String Quintet, the one Mir calls the "Arthur-Rubenstein-Goes-to-Heaven Music" because she saw him once on "60 Minutes" and he played a recording of a movement from this quintet for Safer or one of 'em, and he said that when he died he hoped the angels would play it for him when he came through those pearly gates.

Chee, Mir and I had another row last night—this time about our friends. She thinks we've been seeing too much of them lately. And I just think it's because they've all been so concerned about me and Syd and that she's jealous or something weird like that. She said, and I seek to quote: "It takes a fluid kind of person to run alone. To do without friends, to wing it, improvise end on end. People like me don't truck with packs." And I blew a raspberry at her, because it just isn't so, she's the biggest damn party girl ever, but it had been such odd phrasing, *truck with packs,* it kind of rang in my ears, and somehow its obverse, *pack with trucks,* came to mind, then "Mack trucks," and then, "macked out," a new fave phrase of Syd's. And Miriam caught me, she said, "You're not even listening, are you."

Well, I wasn't right then, dammit, but I do try, mostly, and so does she, to give her credit. We try to concentrate, pay attention to each other, "communicate" (yuck pitooey, pop-psych poopoo), though sometimes I just have to filter her out—when she gets so bitchy, when I get bitchy. So I keep trying to hit that balance of concentrating and filtering out, and mostly, it works.

Such a fascinating old baggage, she is. And I suppose that's why she stays with me too. I'm funny. She's funny. I guess we just both wanna see how the movie ends. And to think, if Aliens On a Far-Off Planet were looking at us in their little alien telescopes, they might not even see Mir and me at the hotel in Los Angeles for another hundred years yet! (Sorry, Mita, I just smoked a little pot.)

If you and Gloria come to Texas at Christmas, is there any

chance you could come before the nineteenth? Mir's all steamed up to go see her mum in Britain over the holidays, and I'm going along too, this time (Ullo mum!). Miriam says she's real keen on seeing the statue of Eros at Piccadilly Circus before it crumbles to shit. She read that the New Year's Eve revelers keep swinging from him, and now he has a fractured ankle and a dislocated thigh (as one recently dislocated myself, my heart goes out to him). Let us know, o-my-love. Hey, did all your classes make? I miss you very much—take good care,

Love,
Bobbie

Georgia Cotrell is a writer who lives in Austin, Texas.

Other titles from Firebrand Books include:

Dykes To Watch Out For, Cartoons by Alison Bechdel/$6.95

Getting Home Alive by Aurora Levins Morales and Rosario Morales/$8.95

Good Enough To Eat, A Novel by Lesléa Newman/$8.95

Jonestown & Other Madness, Poetry by Pat Parker/5.95

The Land Of Look Behind, Prose and Poetry by Michelle Cliff/$6.95

Living As A Lesbian, Poetry by Cheryl Clarke/$6.95

Mohawk Trail by Beth Brant *(Degonwadonti)*/$6.95

Moll Cutpurse, A Novel by Ellen Galford/$7.95

My Mama's Dead Squirrel, Lesbian Essays On Southern Culture by Mab Segrest/$8.95

Sanctuary, A Journey by Judith McDaniel/$7.95

The Sun Is Not Merciful, Short Stories by Anna Lee Walters/$6.95

Tender Warriors, A Novel by Rachel Guido deVries/$7.95

This Is About Incest by Margaret Randall/$7.95

The Threshing Floor, Short Stories by Barbara Burford/$7.95

The Women Who Hate Me, Poetry by Dorothy Allison/$5.95

Words To The Wise, A Writer's Guide to Feminist and Lesbian Periodicals & Publishers by Andrea Fleck Clardy/$3.95

Yours in Struggle, Three Feminist Perspectives on Anti-Semitism and Racism by Elly Bulkin, Minnie Bruce Pratt, and Barbara Smith/$7.95

You can buy Firebrand titles at your bookstore, or order them directly from the publisher (141 The Commons, Ithaca, New York 14850, 607-272-0000).

Please include $1.50 shipping for the first book and $.50 for each additional book.

A free catalog is available on request.